THE FALLEN STAR

THE
FALLEN STAR

BILLY SMITH AND THE GOBLINS

Book 2

ROBERT HEWITT WOLFE

TURNER

Turner Publishing Company
Nashville, Tennessee
New York, New York
www.turnerpublishing.com

The Fallen Star: Billy Smith and the Goblins, Book 2

Cover artwork: Tom Fowler
Cover design: Maddie Cothren
Book design: Glen Edelstein

Library of Congress Cataloging-in-Publication Data

Names: Wolfe, Robert Hewitt, author.
Title: The Fallen Star / Robert Hewitt Wolfe.
Description: Nashville, Tennessee : Turner Publishing Company, [2018] |
   Series: Billy Smith and the goblins ; book 2 | Summary: Billy, Lexi, Hop,
   and Kurt draw on their deepest strengths and hone their skills, hoping a
   mysterious Fallen Star will allow them to defeat the powerful Hanorian
   Army—but at what price? |
Identifiers: LCCN 2018004214 (print) | LCCN 2018009377 (ebook) | ISBN
   9781681626178 (e-book) | ISBN 9781681626154 (pbk. : alk. paper)
Subjects: | CYAC: Fantasy. | Goblins--Fiction. | Fate and fatalism—Fiction.
   | War—Fiction.
Classification: LCC PZ7.1.W627 (ebook) | LCC PZ7.1.W627 Fal 2018 (print) |
   DDC [Fic]—dc23
LC record available at https://lccn.loc.gov/2018004214

Printed in the United States of America
18 19 20 21 22   10 9 8 7 6 5 4 3 2 1

For my nephews Cody and Zack

*One reason I wrote these books
is so you could have a hero who looks like you.*

CONTENTS

CONTENTS

THE FALLEN STAR

CONTENTS

THE FALLEN STAR

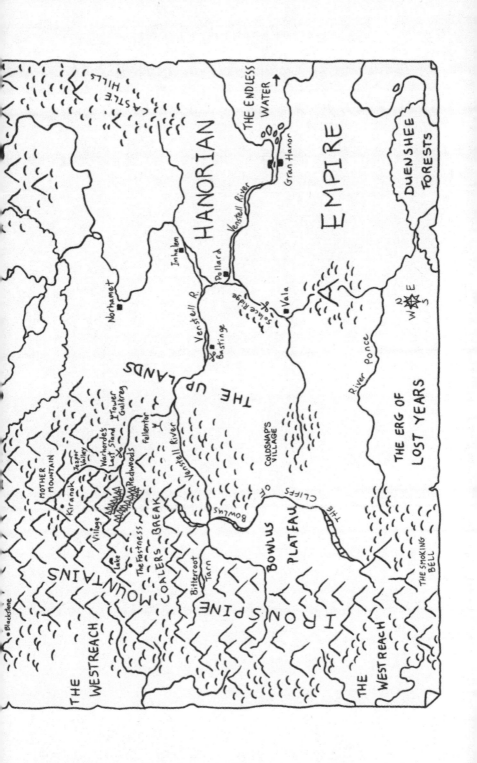

ROBERT HEWITT WOLFE

PROLOGUE
Countless Miles from Home

Pausing from his labor, Cyreth Gant adjusted his cloak, futilely trying to shield himself from the bitter wind. Then he lifted his pick and resumed his task, trying to dislodge a huge rock and free the Hanorian soldier trapped underneath.

Cyreth knew it was most likely a useless effort. A few minutes earlier, he'd uncovered the soldier's booted foot, giving him a moment of hope. The foot hadn't so much as twitched since then. The soldier was probably dead. Still, Cyreth had to keep digging. He had to know for certain.

All around him, Cyreth's fellow Lion Guards dug away at the massive pile of rock, ice, and earth that had come crashing down on the Hanorian encampment from the slopes of Monster Mountain. Cyreth knew the goblins called the towering peak "Mother Mountain" in their own tongue, and sometimes he felt as if the mountain itself was at war with the human soldiers entrenched on its slopes. This wasn't the first landslide the mountain had flung down at the Army of Light, but it was the deadliest yet. The avalanche had smashed into a row of tents just before dawn, trapping over three dozen human soldiers as they slept. Cyreth and his soldiers had been camped only forty or so paces to the west of the avalanche. If not for a trick of fate, they'd have been the ones buried. Instead, they'd been the first to come to the aid of those struck by the landslide. They'd been digging for over two hours now. In the first few minutes, they'd pulled a handful of victims from the rubble. The soldiers had been badly injured, some even beyond the ability of a light-worker to fix, but at least they'd been alive. Then, as time went on, the Lion Guards stopped finding injured men and women and began unearthing the dead.

Cyreth finally dislodged the boulder covering the fallen soldier. It rolled downhill, nearly crushing Cyreth's right foot. He dodged it just in time, saving himself from becoming yet another wounded soldier crying for a wizard's help.

Cyreth looked down at the soldier he'd unearthed. As he feared, the man was dead. He'd been crushed in the avalanche, probably killed instantly. Bits of his torn tent were wrapped around his body. The thin tents issued to the Army of Light provided little protection against the wind and none whatsoever against arrows or catapult shot or landslides. On the other hand, they made passable funeral shrouds.

Dirt stung Cyreth's eyes. He tried to wipe his face clear, but the dirt clung to creases and worry lines much too deep for a man of twenty years. Two years as an officer in the Lion Guards had lined his light-brown face with care. A jagged scar ran from his cropped sandy hair to just above one hazel eye. His once handsome nose had been broken and rebroken three or four times. Maybe more. He'd lost count.

As he started digging at a new section of the rubble, Cyreth found himself wondering, not for the first time, what in Light's name he was doing camped at the foot of a hostile mountain countless miles from home. He supposed it had all started with the parades. When he was a boy, not all that many years ago, he'd loved parades. Every Mustering Day, he'd made his parents take him to the Riverway to watch the Imperial Army march by. To the accompaniment of signal horns and drums, the soldiers of the Empire would parade through the Gate of the Sun and across the Bridge of Heads to Founders' Square, where they'd pledge their allegiance to the Hanorian Emperor. Young Cyreth had loved the uniforms and the music, the thousands of men and women moving in unison. He'd thought nothing could be so wonderful and brave. He particularly loved the look of the Lion Guards in their gold-washed chain mail, flowing white cloaks, and leonine helmets. Oh, how they'd sparkled in the sun.

For his eighteenth birthday, Cyreth's parents bought him a lieutenant's commission in the Lion Guards. The Hanorian Army hadn't fought a real battle in Cyreth's lifetime, and his parents had thought he'd never have to do much except look dashing in his chain mail. A few months later, the goblins had attacked the Hanorian settlements in the Uplands, and the Lion Guards had marched off to war.

In the field, Lieutenant Cyreth Gant discovered just how impractical the Lion Guards' signature armor could be. His golden chain mail got boiling hot in the summer and freezing cold in the winter. His lion-head helmet restricted his vision and made it hard to hear. The flowing white cloaks were woefully thin, providing little protection from the elements. And after over a year at war, his armor didn't look so brave anymore. His lion helm was battered and scraped, and his gold chain mail and white cloak bore dark, rust-colored stains that Cyreth could never wash completely away.

So much blood, shed by him, by his friends, and by the goblins they fought. To what end? Defending the Uplands was one thing, but the goblins were no threat to the human settlements anymore. Now Lord Marshal Jiyal, the commander of the so-called Army of Light, had declared that the war would continue until they'd killed every last goblin in existence.

Cyreth had had his fill of goblin killing.

He'd first faced the goblins in combat when the Lion Guards fought to defend the town of Bastinge from their Warhorde. That had been Cyreth's first actual battle, and he'd hated every moment of it. Hours of soul-shaking dread while his unit maneuvered into position, then a few minutes of sheer terror when they and the goblins finally clashed. As heavy infantry, the Lion Guards had battled the goblins face-to-face. Cyreth had done his part, shouting for his unit to form the line, ordering the advance, holding his shield steady, and thrusting with his sword. He knew he'd struck home more than once. He'd felt the thunk, heard the inhuman screams of the goblins he'd wounded. He'd probably killed a goblin or three, but he wasn't sure. After the battle, he'd been too shaken to remember the specifics. He couldn't bring himself to look in the faces of the dead to see if he recognized any specific opponents.

Solace Ridge had been more of the same. Cyreth knew he'd killed at least one goblin that day, a quick little kobold barely three feet tall that had come spinning under the

Lions' shield wall, slicing at the ankles of Cyreth's fellow guardsmen. Cyreth had somehow managed to smash the goblin across the face with his shield, and then, once it was down, he'd stabbed it a dozen times with his sword. After Cyreth had killed the thing, all he could think about was how much it looked like an odd, misshapen child.

The Lion Guards had spent most of the battle chopping at the goblins' front lines, trying to climb Solace Ridge itself, where the goblin leaders stood. They'd paid in blood for every foot they climbed. Captain Lecyl, Cyreth's mentor and superior officer, had died at the hands of a giant female goblin, twelve feet tall and a thousand pounds, who'd killed a dozen Lion Guards with her enormous hammer before they finally chopped her down. Old Sergeant Bashel had died on the ridge. So had Cyreth's childhood friend Verella, a lightworker who'd been impaled by an arrow while she was trying to treat the wounded. Happy-go-lucky Ralin; dour Grimsy; clever Zigno, who cheated at cards—they'd all fallen on the bloody slopes of Solace Ridge.

But the Hanorian Army had won. Despite all the death and horror, the Lion Guards had reached the crest of Solace Ridge, paving the way for a cadre of Hanorian wizards led by a charismatic young miracle worker named Mig. The wizards slew the goblins' mad elf prophetess, the Dark Lady, with a volley of spells. Once she was dead, the Lion Guards had stuck her head on a pike. The war was over.

That wasn't enough for Lord Marshal Jiyal, though. That very evening, before Cyreth and his remaining Lions had even had a chance to bury their dead, Lord Jiyal stood on the hill where the Dark Lady had died and announced his grand crusade. The Hanorian Army would not return home after its great victory. Instead, its ranks would be refilled by new recruits from the heartland and renamed the Army of Light. Once they'd been reinforced and resupplied, the Army of Light would march toward Monster Mountain, torching every goblin village they found along the way. The Hanorians would smash their way into Goblin City and kill every last greenskin, ending the goblin menace forever.

The soldiers had cheered at the end of Lord Jiyal's speech, though Cyreth suspected many of them felt the same way he did. In truth, he had no more heart for war. The Lord Marshal promoted Cyreth to captain that same day. The next morning, as the Hanorians marched west, he'd daydreamed about slinking back home to Gran Hanor, to his parents' home off Brine Street, where he'd bury his golden chain mail and lion helm in his mother's garden, stash his sword in the gardener's shed, and never think about marching or uniforms or combat again.

Except he was an officer; he was supposed to lead the soldiers under him, to help them win battles, and most importantly to keep them alive. No matter how much he wanted to run, he couldn't abandon the Lion Guards. His honor wouldn't allow it.

"Slide!" Cyreth heard someone yell.

He dropped his pick and ran as another huge wall of dirt and ice came roaring down the mountain. He barely got clear before the avalanche hit. Gravel and ice pelted his back, knocking him to the ground. Cyreth felt a stone about the size of a man's fist smash into the back of his lion helm, making his ears ring. For once, he was grateful for the overly ornate helmet. It had probably saved his life.

Cyreth got unsteadily to his feet. Another ten feet of rock and ice had slammed down on the rubble from the previous landslide. There was no hope of uncovering more survivors now. The lost soldiers had been entombed for all time. They would never go home now. Not even their bodies.

Cyreth looked up accusingly at Monster Mountain. She'd won this battle. The humans would have to retreat a little from her slopes to protect themselves from further landslides. Still, this was only a minor setback for Lord Jiyal's Army of Light. They'd regroup, and eventually, when the time was right, they'd attack.

The wind picked up, blowing even colder, and small white flakes danced through the air. There was snow higher up on Monster Mountain, but this was the first time flurries had reached the Hanorian camp. It was only mid-autumn. Back home in Gran Hanor, the snows would still be months away. Some years they never came at all. Here though, beneath Monster Mountain, winter was coming early.

Cyreth wrapped his cloak a little tighter and straightened his helmet. Let Monster Mountain have her day. Eventually, inevitably, the Hanorians would break into the mountain and destroy Goblin City. Light willing, Cyreth would be there with them. He'd realized long ago that there was only one way he and his fellow Lion Guards would get to go home, and that was to give Lord Jiyal what he wanted.

For Cyreth and his friends to live, every last goblin had to die.

CHAPTER ONE
This Skerbo King

Hop's feet hurt. The former goblin soldier had been climbing stairs, scrambling up ladders, and walking up ramps for almost an hour, traveling from his spacious new quarters near the Hall of Kings all the way to the Moonbridge, the highest of the hundreds of bridges that spanned the huge chasm in the center of Kiranok, the goblins' vast underground city. Up this high, the chasm narrowed to almost a crack, which also made the Moonbridge the shortest bridge in Kiranok, barely ten paces long. Folks liked to argue about how the Moonbridge got its name. Was it because it was shaped like an inverted crescent moon? Or maybe because it was carved from white marble and set so high up in the chasm that, from below, it sometimes looked like a pale moon? Or was it because, from time to time, the moon itself could be seen from the bridge? The Moonbridge stood under a small hole in the roof of the huge cavern that formed the center of Kiranok. On clear nights when the moon was full and when the hole wasn't choked by snow, the moon's path would take it directly over the bridge, and it would light up the Moonbridge's smooth stone walkway and intricately carved handrails.

In me opinion, Hop thought, *it're called the Moonbridge acause a gob have to climb halfway to the bleedy moon to get to it. Should've called it "Footache Bridge" if they were being honest about it.*

Hop was very particular about his feet. He'd been a soldier or a city guard for most of his life. As a result, he'd learned that nothing was more important than having healthy feet. When your feet were in good shape, you could stand watch for hours without pain, you could march for miles and still have enough energy to set up your tent before you went to sleep, and most crucially, you could run away. Well-timed running away was the reason Hop was a live veteran instead of a dead hero. So when his feet hurt, it always put him on edge. It meant he couldn't get away from trouble.

Though to be truthful, I do nai *see much running away in me future.* Hop's aching feet weren't the only things keeping him in Kiranok. The city was besieged by a hostile human army, the snows were beginning to fall, and all of goblinkind was depending on him and his friends. Specifically, they were depending on the person he'd climbed all this way to see.

The person in question was sitting in the middle of the Moonbridge, dangling his feet off the edge. The feet were small compared to a normal goblin's, but what made them stand out was the shoes: bright red canvas with white lacing and white rubber soles. They definitely weren't goblin made. They weren't Hanorian either. They were shoes from someplace else entirely. The shoes, and the feet inside them, belonged to a human boy named William Tyler Smith Junior. Billy to his friends. A human boy Hop had recently helped become the Goblin King.

Rounding the final turn leading to the bridge, Hop nodded to his friend Frost, a diminutive wizard who was keeping watch on one side of the bridge. Frost's giant brother, Leadpipe, stood on the other side, making sure no one approached Billy without permission.

"*Wazzer*, Your Majesty," Hop said as he stepped onto the bridge. "Enjoying the view?"

"I hate it when you call me 'Your Majesty,'" Billy said glumly, staring down into the city.

"You're our king. 'Your Majesty' are the proper way to address you," Hop responded.

The Goblin King was a fairly average-looking human adolescent as far as Hop was concerned. Light-brown skin with speckles across his nose and cheeks; small, roundish ears that stuck out a bit from his head; curly reddish-brown hair. Despite his unassuming appearance, however, Billy was the prophesized savior of all of goblinkind, transported to Kiranok from another world by some sort of magical destiny. Hop, along with Frost and Leadpipe, had gotten him crowned. Now they just had to help the boy fulfill his destiny—or everyone they knew would die.

Billy kept his eyes on the city below, but Hop could tell he was upset. "You're worried," Hop observed. "Feeling the burden of the crown?"

The Goblin Crown sat slightly askew on Billy's head. Though the iron circlet was a bit too big for him, the ruby at its center glowed red whenever Billy wore it, proof he was the rightful king.

Billy sighed. "Look down there," he said, nodding

toward the city below. "Kiranok is amazing. Your people have built something special here. But somehow it's up to me to save it?"

Hop sat down next to Billy, letting his own feet hang off the edge of the bridge. He looked down at Kiranok. The city was made up of hundreds of terraces built into both sides of a great central chasm. Countless stairways, bridges, and ladders connected the terraces to one another. Gondolas on cables clattered across the cavern and taxi-bats flitted through the air, all loaded with goblins rushing about the city. The Underway, the network of streets and balconies by the edge of the chasm, bustled with activity. Hop could see goblins packing Deepmarket, desperately buying up food to last them through the siege. The various temples and shrines to the Night Goddess were equally busy as goblins flocked to the holy places to pray. Hop thought the food shoppers had made the better decision. *You can* nai *eat faith. Plenty of time for praying once the food run out.*

Hop scratched his mangled left ear. It was a nervous habit; he wanted to blame the dizzying view, but Hop knew it was more than that.

"It're *nai* just up to you to save us," he said, trying to reassure his young friend. "It're on all of us." He gestured to Leadpipe and Frost. "All what maked you king."

"What if we can't do it?" Billy asked, eyeing the teeming city below. "What if we fail and all those goblins end up dead?"

Hop had asked himself that same question a hundred times, so he had a ready answer. "Most likely we do *nai* have to worry about that. If the Hanorians take the city, we're the first ones they'll kill."

Billy looked over at Hop. "Thanks for coming all this way to cheer me up," he said sarcastically. "You're doing great."

Hop flashed Billy a lopsided grin. "It are cheery in a way. Right now you're spending all your time worrying about the future. But there are only two ways it'll go. And either way, worrying will do *nai* good. If we lose, we die pretty quick. So we'll *nai* have to live with the consequences. If we win, then we get to celebrate for a long, long time. Nothing to lose. All to gain."

"Nothing to lose but our lives."

"*Ahka*. We were all sentenced to death *nai* that long ago," Frost chimed in from his position at the end of the bridge. All goblins have good hearing, but Frost's hearing was even keener than Hop's. The little wizard continued, "One way to taste it, every day we've lived since then are a day we stealed from destiny. We've already getted more time than we expected, time we're using to give other folk more days too. To us *goben*, a clever theft are a beautiful thing. So I say we steal all the days that we can."

"I've never stolen anything in my life," Billy objected.

"Other than a crown," Leadpipe rumbled, grinning.

"Leadpipe are right, Your Majesty," Hop said. "You stealed the Goblin Crown, and now you have to wear it. I know that are *nai* cheery, but truth are I *nai* climbed all this way to put a smile on your face. I comed to find you acause Shadow have a scouting report on the enemy she want to show us. So that're enough staring into the deeps. You have kinging to do."

Billy nodded and then slowly stood up. He took one last long look at the city below, then turned to go.

"Lead on then, General Hop," Billy said, feigning royal airs.

"I are *nai* general. I were a sergeant, a bat-captain, and just a guard. But *nai* ever so lofty as a general."

"I was never a king before either. If I have to have a

big important title, you do too. So I say you're a general. It's only fair."

Hop could see Billy wasn't joking. For most of his life, Hop had hidden from responsibility, fled from danger, done everything he could to remain unnoticed and unimportant. Now he was a general? It didn't seem right. Plus . . . a general couldn't run. A general had to lead until the end. Still, Billy was the Goblin King. And he'd promised Billy at his coronation that he'd help him every step of the way.

"I suppose if you say I are a general, that're what I are," Hop said, resigned. "Come on then. Shadow are waiting."

Bracketed by Frost and Leadpipe, General Hop led King Billy down the winding path from the Moonbridge to the Hall of Kings, his feet aching every step of the way.

Bakalikam Coldsnap watched King Billy and his companions descend from the Moonbridge, her heart full of anger.

Coldsnap hated humans. It was as simple as that. Humans had killed Snap's father and mother in a border raid when she was still too young to have a calling-name. Snap had been raised by her older brothers, Grub and Pockets. It had been a difficult life, growing up parentless in a hardscrabble village in the Uplands. Snap's two brothers had blamed every misfortune that came their way on the human marauders who'd murdered their parents, and Snap had been raised on their bitterness and hatred.

Still, they'd survived. Grub and Pockets kept their parents' forge running, against all odds, and Snap had taught herself engraving and jewelry making. By the time she reached adulthood, they'd built a comfortable life for themselves.

Then two events changed everything.

The first had come one chilly spring day when Hulogrosh Boomingshout, their town's hulking old *kijakgob* butcher, had burst into the forge, angry about a gate latch Snap's brothers had sold him. Boom claimed the latch had failed, allowing several valuable *kijakhofen* to escape the pen behind his shop before he could turn them into spiced sausage. Grub and Pockets defended their work, insisting the aging giant had just forgotten to close the latch. Snap hadn't paid much attention to the argument at first. She'd been in the middle of a delicate bit of engraving, and Boom was always yelling about something or other. So she kept scratching carefully on her engraving plate as accusations flew back and forth. Suddenly Snap heard a loud thud and then a crash. She looked up and saw Pockets lying on the floor, groaning, blood pouring from his nose, and Boom standing over him with a clenched fist.

Snap remembered feeling a chill rush through her body. She remembered speaking to Boom in a cold whisper and stepping toward him. After that though, everything was a white blur. The next thing she remembered was Grub shaking her. She opened her eyes as the feeling of cold faded away.

And she saw Boom standing perfectly still, covered in a thin sheet of ice.

"Break the ice," she sputtered. "Before he suffocates."

Grub grabbed his smith's hammer and gave the ice a sharp rap, shattering it. Boomingshout gasped for breath and then fell to the floor, shivering. Snap realized she'd encased Boom in ice. She'd never worked magic before. No one in her family had the gift as far as she knew. On that day, though, Snap realized she was a wizard. She got her new calling-name and a new destiny. A few weeks later, she moved to Kiranok to study under the Blue Ones, the ancient wizards who taught spellcasting to young goblins with the gift.

Then came the second event fated to change Snap's life: Sawtooth's War.

General Sawtooth, inspired by the mad elven prophetess known as the Dark Lady, invaded the Hanorian Empire, determined to reclaim the lands the goblins had lost to their human neighbors over the generations. Both Grub and Pockets joined Sawtooth's Warhorde, vowing to avenge their parents' deaths.

Grub never returned from the Battle of Solace Ridge. Later, one of Grub's fellow soldiers told Snap he'd seen her brother get crushed by a huge boulder flung by a human catapult. And Grub was just one of the many goblins who'd died in Sawtooth's War. The general had convinced the Blue Ones to join his cause. The goblin wizards had marched out of Kiranok along with many of their older students. The Blue Ones had declared Coldsnap too young to go to war. They'd promised she'd be able to resume her studies once they returned.

That day never came. At the battle that would become known as the Warhorde's Last Stand, the Blue Ones had come under attack from the Hanorians' newest weapons—flying ships powered by magical, light-focusing mirrors. The lightships had blasted the Blue Ones into ash, along with their students and countless other helpless goblins.

The only goblin who Snap cared about who'd survived the war was her brother Pockets. Though sometimes she wished he hadn't. Pockets had lost his legs at Solace Ridge. For a long time, Snap had thought he'd died there too. Then Snap ran into him one day in Deepmarket. He'd been begging for change. She tried to talk to him, tried to help him, but he wouldn't talk to her. Or anyone. As far as Snap could tell, Pockets spent every morning begging at the market. Then he'd crawl to the nearest bar, where he'd spend every *jegen* he'd earned on mushroom wine and drink himself unconscious. Snap had tried several times to break through his silence. It never worked. With every passing week, he'd looked a little thinner, a little more bleary-eyed. During her fifth or sixth run-in with her brother, Snap realized Pockets was dead too. It was just taking his body a long time to stop moving. After that, Snap avoided Deepmarket altogether. She didn't want to see her brother slowly fade to nothing.

So Coldsnap had lost everyone she cared about to the human invaders. Small wonder that, when the last surviving goblins had crowned a human boy as their king, it had triggered a cold fury in Snap. After all she'd lost, she could never bow to a human. That day, she'd vowed no goblin would ever serve this *skerbo* king.

Now it was time for Snap to put her vow into action.

"One hundred thousand soldiers. More or less."

Ishkinogi Slipshadows, the goblin Templar better known as "Shadow," presented Billy and his friends with her latest scouting report on the Army of Light. The vengeful Hanorians were camped at the base of Mother Mountain, only a few miles from Kiranok's main gate. Goblin scouts, observing the humans from high up the mountain, had done their best to get an accurate count of the enemy forces, and their report was even worse than Billy expected. He passed the report to Hop, who scratched the stump of his mangled left ear as he read it, his worry obvious.

Once Hop had processed the report's grim details, he offered it to Starcaller, the High Priestess of the Night

Goddess. She'd been sitting quietly in a corner in her black robes, a silent but powerful presence. Starcaller shook her head, which was nearly entirely covered by a black hood. She was the goblins' spiritual leader, and officially, Shadow and her Templars were under her command, but so far she hadn't weighed in on the practical matters of defending Kiranok.

Once it was clear that Starcaller didn't need to see the report herself, Frost took it from Hop. The little wizard glanced at the document, keeping admirably cool, as usual. Leadpipe read over his diminutive brother's shoulder, reacting with a deep bass grunt. Lead was sitting on the floor, but his eyes were level with Billy's, who was seated on his high throne. Kurt Novac, formerly the quarterback of Drake Prep's football team, took the report next. He flipped through it quickly, his expression grim, and then handed it to Lexi Aquino, Billy's short but fierce classmate. Lexi looked at the pages, which started to smoke and curl.

"Lexi," Billy said, a gentle reminder.

"Sorry," Lexi replied sheepishly. Somehow, when she'd come to the goblins' world, she'd gotten the ability to work fire magic. Unfortunately, she couldn't control it very well; things around her tended to burst into flames when she got upset. Lexi blinked, and the pages stopped smoldering. "So we're outnumbered ten to one?" she asked Shadow.

"That're generous," Shadow answered, her brows furrowing gravely. "We have ten thousand trained fighters, but a *maja* lot of 'em are old or wounded or both."

Billy knew the goblins' situation was dire. Their Warhorde had been battered in a series of failed battles against the Hanorians. Only a tiny fraction of their original army remained, holed up in Kiranok with the rest of the surviving goblins. The goblins were hurt, desperate, and hopelessly outnumbered. And they all expected Billy to tell them what to do.

Billy wasn't used to people depending on him. He wasn't used to *mattering*. For his entire life, he'd been the weird kid who didn't fit in. Half black, half white, with a family that constantly moved from city to city because of his father's job, Billy had never been very good at making friends. His life had been a parade of new places and new people, none of them all that welcoming. Now, due to some bizarre twist of fate, he'd finally found a place where he belonged and people he could call friends. It should have felt good. Except his new friends were all depending on him for their very survival.

Not for the first time, Billy tried to make sense of his current situation. It had started with a series of panic attacks on his first day of high school. The final attack, triggered by fleeing with his first-day-of-school crush, Lexi, from bullying quarterback Kurt, had somehow transported Billy, Lexi, and Kurt to the goblins' world. They'd been found by Hop, Frost, and a small band of goblins hoping to overthrow the goblins' military dictator, Sawtooth. Hop had believed that their arrival in the caves beneath Kiranok fulfilled a goblin prophecy. Whenever the goblins were in danger, a human Goblin King was supposed to appear and save them.

Billy still couldn't quite believe that he was the prophesized Goblin King. The previous kings had all been descendants of a Polish boy named Piast who'd lived over a thousand years ago. Kurt was part Polish. Plus, he was a quarterback and was used to being the center of attention. Then there was Lexi. Even though she was a girl and her family was originally from the Philippines, she seemed infinitely more regal than Billy or Kurt. Not to mention she was a wizard. The ruby in the Goblin Crown hadn't glowed for them though. Instead, it had glowed for Billy. Somehow the blood of Piast the Wheelwright ran in his veins. Which was how a half African-American, half Irish-American misfit had become the Goblin King.

That also meant that whatever happened to the goblins from now on would be his responsibility—or his fault. To him, there didn't seem much of a difference.

Frost spoke up, as if reading Billy's mind. "It're *nai* on you alone, Your Majesty. We all wanted you on the throne. So it're our jobs to give you any help you need to rule and rule well."

Trying to reassure Billy, Starcaller finally joined the conversation. "When you asked me to make you King, young one, I *nai* hesitated. Acause I knowed you were the one. I knowed the Goddess sended you to us. Which mean you have the answers. You only have to let yourself find them."

Following Starcaller's advice, Billy tried to relax his mind. *Think of this as a game*, he told himself. *If this were a computer game, what would you do?*

Billy was really, really good at video games. He particularly liked real-time strategy games and massive multi-player online games, games that demanded the players make quick, strategic decisions on the fly. So thinking of his dilemma as a game actually helped. *The enemy has a hundred thousand attackers,* he reasoned. *But they have to fight their way uphill. You may have only ten thousand defenders, but you have a fortified position. It's like one of those game where you have just a few units to fight an entire swarm of enemies. Make it work for you.*

"We need to create lines of defense," Billy finally said. "Choke points where they can't use their numbers against us. Can I see a map of Kiranok?"

Shadow signaled to a twitchy little *jintagob* dressed in muted colors who stood in the shadows at the back of the Hall of Kings. The small goblin rushed forward with a roll of papers.

"This're Scurry, my best scout," Shadow said.

Scurry did a quick little bow, handed the papers to Shadow, and then stepped back into the shadows, as if afraid of the light.

"He do *nai* talk much," Shadow explained.

As the inky-skinned female goblin unrolled the papers, Billy caught a glimpse of Hop staring at Shadow. With his mangled ear, short-cropped hair, sharp fangs, and yellow eyes, Hop could look pretty frightening, but whenever Billy caught him sneaking a glance at her, the scrappy goblin seemed more like an adoring puppy dog. Billy hoped he didn't seem so derpy when he looked at Lexi.

The roll turned out to be several dozen maps, each attempting to illustrate a different section of the goblins' underground capital. One map diagramed the city in profile, showing how all the sections interconnected. The huge chasm of the Underway divided Kiranok roughly in two. All the various caverns, caves, tunnels, mines, and other excavations that made up the city eventually connected it, but Billy still had a hard time picturing how all the pieces fit together.

"Maps of Kiranok are *maja* complicated things, acause of all the levels," Shadow explained, seeing Billy's confusion.

"I mostly need to see the entrances," Billy said.

Shadow moved a few of the maps to the top. "This are the main entrance. The Great Gate."

Billy looked at the map. Both times he'd entered Kiranok, he'd come in through the caverns beneath the city. He'd never actually walked in through the front door. From the maps, Billy could see that the Great Gate was a natural cavern entrance set high up on Mother Mountain. A huge wall had been built across the cavern mouth. A thick tower protruded from the mountain almost directly atop the Great Gate, providing a view of all the paths leading up the mountain to Kiranok.

"So it's protected by this wall . . . and this tower," Billy said.

"That're Sunderwall across the entrance," Hop volunteered. "The Overwatch up above it."

"Do we have any soldiers outside?"

Shadow nodded. "The Road Towers," she said, pointing to several outlying towers that guarded the road leading to the Great Gate. "There're a few dozen soldiers at each tower."

"We need to evacuate those towers," Billy said. "Then destroy them."

Shadow and Hop both looked at him in surprise. Billy explained, "The Road Towers won't even slow down the human army. Any goblin inside is going to die for nothing. Plus, once our soldiers are dead, the humans will be able to use the towers against us. We need to concentrate our forces where they have the best chance to hold off the humans."

"You want to play prevent defense," Kurt said.

That got blank looks. And not just from the goblins. Billy and Lexi weren't exactly experts on football.

"It's when you don't try to rush at the enemy, because you know it won't work.," Kurt said. "So you move your defense back. Make them come to you."

Billy nodded. "There's this game I play, and the enemy always outnumbers you. They come at you in a rush. So what you have to have is layers of defense. Like rings. If they get through one line of defense, you fall back to another. Eventually, they run out of attackers."

Billy could see the goblins understood what he was getting at. Shadow pulled out another map.

"This are Seventurns," she said, pointing to a long, winding passageway that led from the Great Gate to the Underway at the heart of Kiranok. "We can build more walls through here, close off the side passages. Make 'em fight for every inch."

That seemed to meet with everyone's approval. Everyone except . . .

"So that's our plan? We lock ourselves in and hope the big bad wolves don't blow our houses down?" Lexi said glumly. "I know how that story ends. Two out of three times, the house falls down and the pigs get eaten."

"Yeah, but in your analogy, we're the pigs in the *brick* house," Kurt said to her. "The wolf couldn't blow that one down."

"I've got a better story then. A true one. The story of Moro Crater." Lexi didn't wait for the blank looks; she knew no one, not even Billy or Kurt, would have heard of Moro Crater. "This happened in the Philippines, where my family comes from. There was a war. The Americans . . ." She looked at the goblins, explaining, "America. That's the country where Billy, Kurt, and I were born. Anyway, like a hundred years ago, the Americans conquered the Philippines. Some Filipinos, including a tribe called the Moros, rebelled. The Moros had this hideout, the crater of an extinct volcano, deep in the jungle. They thought no one could find them there. So they brought their families to the crater and fortified it and used it as a base to raid the pro-American towns. The Americans found the crater, though, and surrounded it. The Moros thought the crater was such a great fort that they could hold out forever. Except the Americans had more soldiers and better weapons. They used their weapons to blow up the crater. They killed everyone inside."

"So in this story, we're the Moros and the Hanorians are the Americans?" Billy asked.

"We're trapping ourselves," Lexi answered. "That's all I'm saying."

"Do we really have any other choice?" Billy asked.

Lexi didn't answer right away. The truth was, she hadn't really thought about alternatives to Billy's plan. She just couldn't stand the idea of hiding inside a mountain, waiting for the Hanorians to attack. She'd never liked being cooped up indoors; she had too much energy. Having walls around her made her feel trapped. She needed to get outside. To do something. To drive the human army away or find an escape route for the goblins.

Still . . . she knew it wasn't that simple. It wasn't just Lexi and her friends stuck inside Mother Mountain. There were over a hundred thousand goblins in the city, mostly old people and children, widows and orphans. They didn't have enough healthy soldiers left to fight their way out. So Billy was probably right. They were going to have to stay here and defend the city, even if Lexi hated it.

"I don't like being cornered," Lexi admitted. "But I don't have any better ideas."

Then Kurt, who'd been studying Shadow's scouting report and the maps while Lexi and Billy had their debate, spoke up. "Maybe that's because we don't have enough information."

Kurt turned to Shadow. "I don't mean any disrespect. Only back in our world, I read scouting reports on the teams we play against all the time. The reports I'm used to are usually a lot more detailed than this. They tell us how the other team likes to defend, who their best players are, all that kind of stuff. There's none of that here. Just . . . guesses." Kurt read from the report, "'Thousands of tents, with each tent holding at least two men.' 'Large numbers of horses.' 'Some evidence of siege machines.' It's not much to go on."

Typical Kurt, Lexi thought. *His whole life he's been the popular guy, the king jock. It must kill him that Billy ended up being the Goblin King and I'm a freaking wizard and he's just . . . nothing special.*

Her next thought was more sympathetic. *Except . . . he's not wrong.*

Shadow seemed to think so too. "It're the best we can do," she said. "Scurry and his scouts could only get so close. The Hanorians have scouts of their own and fire wizards what can see for miles. Scurry and them could count better if they could use daysight instead of redsight, but that'd mean getting near the human camp when the sun are up. Do that, and they'd get spotted for certain. So they goed at night and counted with redsight. That mean all they seed were blobs of heat. It're *nai* easy to count blobs."

Kurt took that in. He wasn't done yet, though. "So what you're saying is, we need to get inside the camp to really know what we're up against."

"May as well wish for ripe *hika* berries in midwinter," Hop said, coming to Shadow's defense. "It sound tasty, but it're impossible."

"Getting into the Hanorian camp might be impossible for a goblin," Kurt replied, sounding more confident than he had in a long time. "But not for me." Then he turned and looked at Lexi. "Not for *us*."

Lexi realized what Kurt meant. She and Kurt were human, just like the Hanorians. They could even speak the language, thanks to one of Lexi's spells. Kurt was volunteering to infiltrate the Hanorian camp, a mission that seemed crazy dangerous at best.

"You want to sneak into an armed camp so we can count how many people are down there trying to kill us?" Lexi asked. Then she grinned. "Sounds fun. I'm in."

Because even though Kurt's idea might be crazy, as far as Lexi was concerned, it was still better than hiding under a mountain waiting to die.

Snap arrived at the Blue Chambers and then descended through the abandoned hallways to an old dining hall, where her two coconspirators awaited her.

Not long after the *skerbo* king's coronation, Coldsnap had recruited a pair of the Blue Ones' surviving students to her cause. Icewall was a rotund *kijakgob* with tremendous raw talent and very little control. Snap knew he was hopelessly smitten with her, so it hadn't been hard to manipulate him into agreeing with everything she said. She'd told him that humans were evil. That they were determined to kill every goblin in existence. That the *skerbo* "Goblin King" was probably a spy sent to lead the goblins to their doom. Icewall had believed every word. He'd pledged to do whatever Snap asked to protect their people, ultimately hoping, she was certain, to earn her love.

Snap's second recruit didn't care about love. Grinner didn't share her hatred of humans either. As far as she could tell, Grinner didn't care about anything except magic. An intense, unnaturally pale young goblin, he loved spells—shaping them, casting them, seeing their effect on the world. Most especially, Grinner loved spells that broke things . . . or killed them. Snap had once caught him collecting the mice that infested the food storage areas of the Blue Chambers. He'd spot a mouse with redsight and then cast a spell to slowly lower its body temperature until it drifted into sleep, like a goblin succumbing to hypothermia. Then he'd put the unconscious mouse in a cage and warm it back to consciousness. Snap had thought Grinner was being merciful by just caging the mice. She soon learned otherwise.

In a tiny forgotten cave deep in the Blue Chambers, Grinner had collected dozens of mice. He kept them in cages, feeding them, getting them used to his presence, treating them like pets. Then, once every few days, he'd select a mouse, take it from its cage, and invent some new and horrible way to kill it. With great pride and attention to detail, he'd described to snap all the ways he'd killed mice. He'd frozen them, slowly and quickly. He'd turned different internal organs to ice one by one. He impaled several with sharpened icicles. He'd frozen one's mouth shut to see how long it would take to die of thirst. He'd inflicted a slow death on another via frostbite, freezing off little bits of it over the course of several days until it had finally expired.

It had been easy for Snap to recruit Grinner to her cause. She just had to promise him that he'd get to use his spells on humans instead of mice.

When Snap arrived at the dining hall, she'd found Grinner whiling away the time by playing with a captured bug. The pale goblin had trapped a tiny insect in a small clear dome of ice. As Snap entered, Grinner used his magic to make the ice dome smaller and smaller. The insect, panicked, battered against the dome, making a rapid tapping sound. Icewall was lying on the floor, studiously ignoring Grinner, singing quietly to himself. Though Icewall could be graceless and lumbering, his voice was clean and clear and surprisingly high for a *kijakgob*. He was singing an old folk song from down south, by the Smoking Bell, where he'd been born:

Oh I seed her at the fair, the fair, the fair
With rings on her arms and beads in her hair
And I sayed, "Walk with me 'neath the night sky
And if you agree, then happy I'll die."
But she sayed nai *one word, onward she goed*
And the crowd parted and gived her the road

Oh I seed her at the fair, the fair, the fair
With rings on her arms and beads in her hair

I runned ahead and falled down to my knees
I sayed to my queen, "Oh how I may please
One so flawless as if carved from black stone
What can I give you to make you me own?
I'll bring fine perfume, sweet honey, pure gold"
I begged and pleaded, but onward she strolled . . .

"I know that one," Snap interrupted. "'I Seed Her at the Fair.'"

Icewall stood when he noticed her, straightening his tunic and trying to look his best. He was twice her size, but somehow he always looked small and vulnerable around her. Grinner barely looked up at Snap. His attention was focused on his captured bug and its rapidly shrinking ice dome. The taps were coming much faster now. Tap-tap-tap.

"It're a pretty tune," Icewall said. "*Nai* as pretty as you though."

Snap didn't acknowledge the compliment. She tried not to lead Icewall on any more than was absolutely necessary. Just like the *svagob* in the song.

"I like her response to his question," she said. She sang a verse from later in the song:

I nai *want your perfume, honey, or gold*
I want a partner, a love when I're old
Calm hand to hold me, Va *for me brood*
Nai *empty gifts will warm me when I're cold*

Grinner snorted in amusement. "The truth are, at the end, when the cold come, *nai* anything will help."

The bubble of ice around his trapped bug was tiny now, smaller than Snap's palm. The tapping became erratic, slowed, and then stopped entirely.

Grinner finally looked up. "You *nai* look like you came here just to listen to Icewall sing." Grinner was right. He could be surprisingly observant. *He read folk so he can get an edge on 'em*, Snap thought. *Still, best to get to it.*

"I seed him," Coldsnap announced. "The so-called king. He were up at Moonbridge. With that one-eared Copperplate. Guarded by Atarikit Bluefrost and his brother, Leadpipe."

"That *skerbo* are a fool," Icewall said, using the goblins' most insulting term for humans. "He walk around the city like he own it. Like he have *nai* fear in the world."

Grinner grinned. "He will *nai* be a fool for long. Not once we're done."

"So we're all agreed then?" Snap asked. "We all know what we need to do?"

Icewall thought about it for a moment, clearly taking

her question seriously. Then he answered in his slow, plodding way. "Whatever you think are best, Snap."

Grinner didn't hesitate. "*Yob'rikit*," he said with his characteristic grin. "I're game."

"Then it're settled," Snap said decisively. "We're to kill us a king."

CHAPTER TWO

Wrong Place. Wrong People.

Kurt loved the rush of the game.

When the ball was snapped and in his hands, when the other players were flying around the field, when his every move could bring victory or defeat, that's when he felt most alive. For Kurt, there was nothing better than being at the center of the action, carrying his fate and the fate of his teammates on his shoulders.

Which meant it'd been rough when the ruby at the center of the Goblin Crown had failed to glow for him. He'd always been the hero in his own story, the star athlete, the quarterback. Only he wasn't the Goblin King. In the eyes of the goblins, geeky, awkward Billy was their savior. Even Lexi was a wizard. In this world, Kurt was nobody special.

So maybe volunteering himself and Lexi for a suicide mission was a bit desperate. An attempt to be relevant, to matter. But it was a way for Kurt to be in the middle of things again. To be the star.

Of course, the point of this mission was to go unnoticed. He and Lexi were supposed to sneak into the human camp, get an idea of what the goblins were up against, and then slip back into Kiranok without getting spotted. Still, at least Kurt was off the bench. At least he was in the game.

He and Lexi approached the huge Hanorian encampment. They were wearing human armor captured by the goblins during Sawtooth's War. Unfortunately, even with the armor, Lexi and Kurt didn't look much like Hanorians. Kurt's blond hair and blue eyes would help him fit in, but his fair skin and the shape of his nose and eyes were all wrong. Lexi's skin color and eye shape were a better match, but her nose was too small and her hair and eyes were too dark. So in addition to the armor, Lexi had cast an illusion on herself and Kurt to make them look like Alyseer and Azam, two Hanorian refugees. The humans were Celestials, part of a religious sect that worshiped both Father Day and Mother Night, in defiance of the mainstream Day-worshiping Hanorian church. The Hanorian Empire had declared them heretics and traitors and sentenced to death any Celestial who wouldn't repent. Rather than convert or face martyrdom, Alyseer's and Azam's families—and many like them—had fled the Empire. High Priestess Starcaller had given them sanctuary at the Fastness, the goblin fortress-town she ruled, where Kurt, Billy, and Lexi had met them and become honorary members of their community.

Lexi had learned her disguise spell from Sarlia, Alyseer's mother, an accomplished lightworker. She'd modeled her and Kurt's disguises after Alyseer and Azam because they were the two Hanorians she knew best, and she felt confident she could get all the details right. As far as Kurt could tell, the spell was working great. Unfortunately, Lexi had told him that keeping it up required all of her energy, meaning she couldn't cast any other spells.

Still, Kurt figured Lexi's disguise spell should get them into the camp. Hopefully. He and Lexi had snuck down the mountain and were finally approaching the wooden stockade surrounding the Hanorian camp. There were only a few entrances into the stockade, and all of them were guarded.

"Maybe this was a bad idea," Lexi said, looking at the camp nervously. "How do we get in?"

Kurt looked around and then spotted something on the side of the camp facing Mother Mountain.

"The stockade is broken up there," he pointed out. "Looks like there was some kind of landslide. Let's try that."

Kurt and Lexi circled the camp to the broken stockade. Unfortunately, Kurt could see a line of sentries guarding the gap.

"We can't get in," Lexi said.

"You're the wizard. Can't you magic us past?"

"I could fly us over the fence, but I'd have to drop our disguise spell. They'd see us. I don't know how to make us invisible."

Kurt thought about it for a second before he came to a decision. "Then we'll just have to deal with it. Let me do the talking."

With that, he strode toward the gap, exuding confidence. Before the sentries could challenge him, Kurt called out to them. "Scouting party returning," he said in Hanorian. Kurt was glad Lexi's spell that allowed them to speak and understand Hanorian still worked.

Kurt glanced back to make sure Lexi was still following

him. She was. Not breaking stride, Kurt walked boldly through the gap in the stockade.

Unfortunately, a sentry intercepted him.

"What's the password?" the Hanorian asked. From the way he said it, Kurt could tell the man was just going through the motions. He looked sleepy and unconcerned.

"Light?" Kurt guessed. The Hanorians worshiped a god of light, and their wizards cast spells that manipulated light and heat. It was as good a guess as any.

"That was the password over a week ago," the sentry replied, still not overly concerned.

Kurt tried to maintain his confidence. His father was extremely strict, so Kurt had gotten pretty good at lying to him. The trick, he'd found, was to be fearless, to make yourself believe you'd never get caught. Nothing made a lie more obvious than fear.

"I gotta be honest," Kurt said with well-practiced nonchalance, "I have no idea what it is. They change it all the time, and I always forget." He gestured toward Lexi, "And Alyseer here got hit in the head back at Solace Ridge and has a hard time remembering anything."

The sentry studied them, finally growing mildly suspicious. "I don't think you're scouts," he said. "I think you and your girlfriend snuck out of camp for a little private time." The man winked.

Kurt gave the sentry his best disarming grin. "You're right. You caught us." He held out his hand and Lexi, figuring out what he was up to, took it and moved closer to him.

"They don't give us the passwords," Lexi said. "We work in the kitchens."

Kurt was surprised she'd lied so smoothly. He'd always thought of her as being annoyingly blunt and honest. Then again, he figured she had parents too.

"Extra meat in your dinner tomorrow if you let us through," Kurt said.

"Every night this week," the sentry countered.

"Deal," Lexi said. She headed into the camp, leading Kurt by the hand.

They were in.

Coldsnap stood in a tunnel mouth with a view of the Hall of Kings, trying to look inconspicuous. She, Grinner, and Icewall had been lurking in the tunnel, watching the entrance to the throne room for a few hours, waiting for the so-called Goblin King to emerge. Snap didn't think they'd get an opportunity to attack, but maybe they'd get lucky. Even if they didn't, the more they could observe the *skerbo* boy, the easier it would be to kill him.

Unfortunately, Grinner and Icewall didn't share Snap's focus. Grinner lived in his own cruel little world. Icewall spent most of his time mooning over Snap, asking her stupid questions, trying to get her attention. At some point, both of them had wandered off, leaving Snap to watch the throne room alone.

She was about to go looking for her missing companions when Icewall lumbered up, carrying something in one massive hand. He held it out to her and opened it, revealing a pretty bracelet.

"For you, Snap," he said. "I bought it from that jeweler's cart over there."

Snap glanced at the nearby cart, which was one of the nicer ones on the Underway. The vendor smiled at her, happy with the sale. Snap looked at the bracelet, a series of gold links and polished pieces of blue topaz. It was skillfully crafted from the highest-quality materials. Snap had to admit, it was better than her own finest work, back when she'd made jewelry at her brothers' forge. She knew it represented several days of labor by a master jeweler and, as such, would command a hefty price.

"You can *nai* afford this, Ice," she said.

"*Nai* reason to save me *duen*," Ice replied. "Probably we die when we attack the *skerbo* king. So spend it while I can, I figure. Aside, I want you to have this."

Snap couldn't argue. She knew there was a good chance none of them would survive an attack on the human boy. King Billy was well protected, with Atarikit Bluefrost and his giant brother watching over him, plus dozens of Copperplates and Templars. Not to mention the *skerbo* girl who was usually at his side was rumored to be a powerful fire witch.

We can probably kill King Billy if we choose our moment well, Snap thought to herself. *Odds are, though, one or all of us will die right along with him.*

Snap knew that if Icewall were forced to choose, he'd gladly sacrifice himself to save her. She couldn't say she'd do the same for him. *I're* nai *going to give him what he want. And I're* nai *going to protect him. So why* nai *give him a smile while he're still breathing?* She accepted the bracelet and put it on.

"*Ganzi*, Ice," she said. "It're beautiful."

Icewall grinned widely. Snap shifted uncomfortably. She didn't want to get his hopes up, so she changed the subject.

"Where're Chillinggrin?" she asked.

"Last I seed him, he were headed farther down the tunnel," Ice answered.

The passageway they were hiding in led to the old royal banqueting halls, which had long been abandoned. Refugees had set up a squatters' camp in the unused chambers. Since Snap, Ice, and Grinner had begun their surveillance of the Hall of Kings, a handful of bedraggled goblins had entered or exited the tunnel. Why would Grinner have bothered going deeper inside?

"Wait here," Snap said, then she moved down the tunnel.

After a dozen paces or so, she noticed the tunnel was strangely cold and getting chillier the farther she went. Kiranok was always a little warm, heated by the breath of Mother Mountain, which rose from the caverns deep below the underground city. So the creeping cold emanating from the passageway felt out of place. Though to Snap, it was unsettlingly familiar. It was the same sort of cold that had frozen Boomingshout in a skin of ice. The same cold that filled Grinner's secret cave in the Blue Chambers. The cold of wizardry.

Dreading what she might find, Snap tracked the cold to its source. She went down a side passage, then down a smaller tunnel, and finally arrived at an archway barely four hands high. The cold was coming from inside.

Snap bent down to slide through the archway. A hand fell on her shoulder, huge but gentle.

"I can *nai* go through there with you," Icewall rumbled, clearly worried. Snap had been so intent on her pursuit, she hadn't noticed that the giant goblin had disobeyed her orders and followed her. "It're too small. If you get into trouble—"

Snap cut him off. "I'll handle this."

She went through, finding exactly what she feared.

In the small chamber on the other side of the archway, Grinner stood over a wizened old refugee, who was slowly turning blue at his feet. Ice coated the floor below the helpless goblin.

"Grinner! Stop!" she shouted, shoving him in the back.

Grinner stumbled, then recovered. The cold began to diminish.

"What're wrong, Snap?" Grinner said, turning to face her. "He're just some old *gob* with *nai* family and *nai* future, dying by the days. And I're *nai* ever frozen anything this big afore. I need the practice. Aside, he're *nai* even fighting it. You ask me, he want the cold sleep."

Snap recognized Grinner's victim. He was an old beggar who worked the Underway outside the Hall of Kings, blind, stooped, and usually muttering incoherently. Grinner wasn't wrong. The old *gob* was close to death, and likely no one would mourn him. Still, Snap couldn't help but picture Pockets lying on the cold floor, mutely letting Grinner freeze him to death.

"We *nai* kill *goben*," Snap said decisively. "Only *skerboen*."

Grinner wasn't impressed. "What about the *skerbo* king's bodyguards? What about the Copperplates and the Templars? We come for the human, they're going to fight us. What then?"

"Then we do what we must and *nai* one nibble more," Snap answered. She knew that if Grinner tried to continue his "practice," she'd have to fight him. Kill him if she must. She could see in his face that he knew it too. "Go," she said. "Save your games for the king."

Grinner bowed and left the small chamber.

Snap concentrated then inhaled, pulling the cold from the room into her lungs. The old goblin stirred, no longer suffering from Grinner's icy spell. Snap left the small chamber without looking back. She could have tried to warm the old *gob* further, but she needed to save her magic. She had an assassination to carry out.

Billy was worried. That seemed to be his normal state of mind lately. Imagining Lexi and Kurt sneaking around the human camp was making him extra paranoid. Under the watchful eyes of Frost and Leadpipe, Billy went over Shadow's scouting report and the various maps of Kiranok for the umpteenth time. Reviewing the reports wouldn't help Lexi or Kurt, and Shadow and Hop already had crews working on the fortifications Billy had ordered, but double-checking the documents kept Billy's mind occupied. Plus, he wanted to be sure he wasn't missing anything.

Billy shivered. A cold breeze wafted through the Hall of Kings. Frost looked around, suspicious. Leadpipe checked the main entrance to the throne room, then shrugged.

"All clear," he said.

"*Nai* to worry about," Frost assured Billy, not all that convincingly.

Which was when Hop returned to the Hall of Kings. The one-eared goblin looked every bit as tired as Billy felt. But he had a small smile on his face. That made Billy take notice. Hop hadn't smiled much since the coronation.

"I have a surprise for you," Hop said.

"Hope it's a good one," Billy replied. "Most of my surprises lately have been pretty scary."

"I think you'll like this one," Hop said. "There're an old friend of yours come a long way to see you."

"Torrent!" Billy threw his arms around the neck of the shaggy black *vargar*, happier than Hop had seen him in days.

Hop knew Billy and Torrent had a special connection. The giant wolflike beast, with its rhino-like horn and leonine mane, had been Billy's mount in the Sunchase. Winning the race had earned Billy the support of High Priestess Starcaller in his pursuit of the Goblin Crown. So it was no surprise that Billy had regretted leaving Torrent behind when he'd returned to Kiranok. Which was why, after a group of refugees from the Fastness had slipped into Kiranok, Hop had been pleased to learn that they'd brought Billy's *vargar* with them. He knew the boy king needed a little joy in his life. If Hop believed in divine intervention, he would've thought Torrent was the answer to a prayer he'd never whispered. He'd brought the *vargar* to a large animal pen, one of many inside a huge cavern not far from Seventurns, usually reserved for newly arrived *bokrumen* and *kijakhofen* waiting to be brought to market.

The beast licked Billy's cheek. Billy scratched the spot where Torrent's horn met his muzzle. The black *vargar* let out a low, happy *rrrrr*. A purr . . . or near enough.

Then Billy noticed the other new arrivals, a dozen or so Hanorian teenagers. Hop had had them wait at the pens as well. He wasn't sure they'd be safe on the streets of Kiranok.

"Alyseer, Azam!" Billy greeted the new arrivals. "I never expected to see you here."

Indeed, the small group of humans looked extremely out of place in the goblin city. Hop had to admire the Celestials' courage, to come all this way to a potentially hostile city under siege by their fellow Hanorians. The teens and their families had fled their homeland to escape a death sentence for heresy. So while misinformed goblins might kill the Celestials by mistake, Hanorian soldiers would execute them on sight.

"We go where Night and Day take us," Alyseer replied. Hop remembered that she was a skilled young lightworker and that her parents were the leaders of the Celestials.

"Alyseer had a vision," Azam said, looking at her with admiration.

Azam was an athletic young Celestial who'd become friends with Kurt while they were all at the Fastness. Hop understood he was something of a leader among the young Celestials. Azam certainly looked capable enough, in that straight-spined, broad-shouldered human way.

"The Balance is threatened," Alyseer said gravely. She turned to Hop. "If the Army of Light burns away your people, the world will be lessened. The Gods of Balance chose us to help save you."

Hop had gotten to know the Celestials during his short stay at the Fastness. He respected how much they valued balance and peace. He admired how they practiced their religions through games, parables, dance, and song. So while he might never fully understand the human heretics, he'd grown to like them. Still, it surprised him that they'd come all this way to risk their lives for his people. Goblins and humans had been at war for thousands of years. To Hop, the Celestials' willingness to help the goblins was a sign that maybe someday the war might end and humans and goblins might finally live in peace.

Billy looked similarly impressed. "I'm glad you came," he said. "We can sure use your help." Billy went around to greet each of the Celestials in turn. In addition to Alyseer and Azam, there were about a dozen other young humans. Hop could see that Alyseer seemed especially happy to see Billy. The boy hadn't noticed though. Hop had realized a while ago that his new king wasn't very perceptive when it came to girls.

Finally, Billy reached Azam. Azam greeted Billy, but clearly he was hoping to see someone else.

"Where is Kurt?" Azam asked.

"He's not here," Billy said with obvious discomfort.

"What you mean?" Azam asked, surprised.

Billy looked toward Hop, clearly wondering what he should tell the Celestials.

"You can tell them," Hop said after a moment's thought. "These are friends, *zaj*."

Billy explained how Kurt and Lexi had gone to infiltrate the Hanorian camp, wearing stolen Hanorian armor and disguised by Lexi's magic.

Alyseer reacted in horror.

"You shouldn't have let them do that," she said, alarmed.

"Lexi's spell was perfect," Billy said, sounding a little defensive. "She made herself and Kurt look just like you and Azam. No one's going to know they're not Hanorians."

Hop could tell that Billy was trying to reassure himself as well as Alyseer.

"You don't understand," Alyseer said. "Lexi is as powerful a spark as I've ever met, but she's still no expert. And the Army of Light has wizards too."

Lexi's brain itched.

Sarlia, the Celestial lightworker who'd trained her in spellcasting, had warned her that keeping a spell going for a long time would tax her energy and make it hard to concentrate on anything else. She hadn't mentioned the itch, though. To Lexi it felt like she had ants crawling around her brain. Scratching her head didn't help. The itch was on the inside.

So Lexi didn't absorb much of what she saw inside the Hanorian camp. The itch made it impossible for Lexi to keep track of the various soldiers and war machines and horses they saw in the sprawling Hanorian camp.

Luckily, she had Kurt for that. For a few hours, he led her through the camp, poking around, seeing what there was to see. Finally, as the sun was going down, he announced, "Shadow was right. She said this camp held around a hundred thousand people. The football stadium back home holds sixty-eight thousand people. I've been to a lot of games, and there are way more people here."

"A lot of them are kids though," Lexi said.

Despite the itch, Lexi had noticed that most of the soldiers weren't much older than her. There were girls working all over the camp too. Most seemed to be handling menial tasks like keeping the camp clean, gathering firewood, distributing water, and preparing and serving food, but there were a few women and girls wearing armor and standing guard along with the men and boys.

"They must've lost a lot of their experienced soldiers in the war," Kurt said. "Just like the goblins."

Lexi and Kurt rounded a large tent and came upon a startling sight. Several dozen human bodies had been stacked behind the tent, and exhausted soldiers were bringing even more corpses.

"Wow," Kurt said, stopped in his tracks by the sight of the dead. "What happened to them?"

The bodies were crushed and mangled, covered in dirt. Lexi had seen bodies like that in the news, after a bad earthquake in the Philippines. The earthquake had triggered a landslide, burying an entire town not far from where some of Lexi's relatives lived. Luckily, Lexi's cousins and aunts and uncles had all escaped harm, but she never forgot those horrible images.

Lexi knew that Mother Mountain was a dormant volcano prone to earthquakes. There'd been several tremors since she, Billy, and Kurt had arrived at Kiranok, including a fairly strong one a day or so ago. Lexi guessed the quake had set off a landslide like the one in the Philippines, with equally devastating results.

"We shouldn't be here," Lexi said, the itching in her brain forgotten for a moment.

A young Hanorian officer, his once-gold chain mail covered in dirt and grime, spotted Lexi and Kurt as they stared at the corpses.

"What are you two looking at?" he snapped. "Either help or move along."

As far as Lexi could tell, the Hanorian soldier was only in his twenties, but based on his broken nose and the prominent scar across his forehead, he'd been through several battles. Lexi suspected he might have friends among the dead. He certainly didn't like people gawking at their bodies. Not that she could blame him.

"Sorry," Kurt said. "We'll leave."

As Kurt and Lexi turned to go, they heard a voice calling to them, "You should stay. See what the greenskins did to your fellow humans."

Lexi spotted two people who'd just emerged from the large tent. One was a tall, hawk-faced man in his fifties. Like most Hanorians, he had brownish skin, which contrasted sharply with his short-cropped silvery white hair and neatly trimmed white beard. He wore a gold-plated breastplate over a sky-blue uniform, all topped by a yellow-and-blue sash decorated with medals and insignia. He carried a gold-plated helmet with a tall horsehair crest tucked under one arm. *Definitely some kind of bigwig*, Lexi thought.

Only the bigwig wasn't the one who'd called out to them. It was the girl at his side. She seemed out of place in the military camp. She was about the same age as

Lexi, though she was a bit taller and sturdier, with broad shoulders and strong arms. Her skin was on the light side for a Hanorian, and her hair was bright red. She wore a silk dress made of several layers of fabric: white, red, yellow, and orange. She stood oddly, as if she were balancing on roller skates, swaying slightly from side to side.

"Young Mig has a point," the silver-haired man said. "We should all spend time contemplating the crimes of our enemies. Better to fuel the righteous wrath that we'll bring down upon them."

"Goblins didn't do this," Lexi blurted out before she could stop herself. She regretted it immediately. She should have stayed silent, but it was too late for that. "They died in an avalanche," she finished quietly, hoping the truth would protect her.

"Address Lord Marshal Jiyal with proper respect, recruit," the scarred young soldier barked. "And I deserve a 'sir,' too, while you're at it." Lexi thought he looked a little less sure about the last part, but she knew better than to argue.

"Sorry, sir," she said to the young officer, then she turned to the silver-haired man and tried to look properly respectful. "My apologies, Lord Marshal Jiyal."

The older man's expression softened. He looked sympathetic. "I understand, recruit. You didn't go through much training before you got here, did you?"

"No, Lord Marshal."

"I apologize for that. I know it can be confusing, to come from some farmstead, to be given a uniform and weapons, to be sent so far from home. However, your Empire needs you. Your people need you. You're willing to do your part, aren't you?"

"Yes, Lord Marshal," Lexi answered, hoping the conversation wouldn't go on much longer. She didn't know a whole lot about the Hanorian Empire, and the longer she talked to this Lord Marshal person, the more likely she'd be to trip up and give herself and Kurt away.

"Good," Lord Marshal Jiyal said with a friendly smile. "And don't be mistaken. The goblins killed these soldiers. They began this war. They killed the garrison at Fellentor. They slaughtered helpless villagers in the Uplands. They sacked Bastinge. They tried to do the same to Pollard. They're a warped, evil race, and they'll settle for nothing less than our annihilation. Any soldier who dies here, dies because of what the goblins set in motion. Brave young Hanorians like you will deliver the Light's justice for these soldiers' deaths . . . for all the deaths the goblins have caused."

Lexi wanted to tell Lord Marshal Jiyal that he was twisting the truth. Maybe the goblins had attacked the humans, but only after centuries of losing their land to the Hanorian Empire. Even then, they'd only attacked after they'd been whipped into a frenzy by some crazy elf wizardess called the Dark Lady. Now the Dark Lady and her bloodthirsty warlord, General Sawtooth, were both dead, along with most of the goblins' best warriors. The goblins knew the war had been a terrible mistake. They were no threat to anyone anymore. They just wanted to be left alone to live in peace.

She wanted to shout that at the Lord Marshal. Shout it until he listened.

Or better yet . . . what if she breathed fire on the smug old man? He seemed like a pretty big deal. He might even be the leader of the Hanorian Army. If he died, would the Hanorians give up, the same way the goblins had given up once Sawtooth and the Dark Lady were dead? Lexi knew that she'd probably be killed if she attacked Jiyal. Maybe it'd be worth it.

Suddenly, as if sensing what she was thinking, Kurt stepped between Lexi and the Hanorian commander.

"Thank you, Lord Marshal," he said, bowing deeply, like a character in some BBC television show about old dead British people. "You honor us with your words."

Lexi was afraid Kurt had laid it on too thick, but Jiyal seemed to accept Kurt's serf act as if it were his due.

"You honor me with yours, soldier," the Lord Marshal replied. "We are but servants to our great cause."

That appeared to conclude the conversation as far as Jiyal was concerned. He turned to go. Relieved, Lexi suppressed her urge to set the Hanorian commander on fire and likewise turned to walk away.

Before she could take more than a few steps though, the girl by Jiyal's side spoke again. "Wait."

Kurt and Lexi both stopped immediately.

"You two are wrong," the girl said. "Wrong place. Wrong people. Wrong faces."

Lexi's brain itch got ten times worse. There was something about the girl that put her on edge. Mig . . . that was what the general had called her. When Mig spoke, she sounded like she was speaking to insects, bugs she could crush without a second thought. Lexi could tell Kurt sensed it too. He'd been nervous interacting with the Lord Marshal, but when Mig talked his body visibly tensed.

Then Lexi noticed something else alarming about Mig. Her layered silk dress was rustling, as if it were being blown by a breeze. Only there was no wind behind the tent, yet the layers were wafting upward, as if Mig were standing on top of a fan. Lexi looked down at the girl's feet and saw that they weren't touching the ground. Mig was floating three inches in the air.

"Your faces are shimmery," Mig said, staring intently at Lexi. "Your faces are made of light."

Mig made a small gesture, opened her mouth, and inhaled sharply. Lexi's illusion shredded as the woven light that had covered her and Kurt's faces streaked into Mig's open mouth.

Lexi looked over at Kurt. He now looked like . . . well, Kurt, with his round eyes and pale skin. In other words, nothing at all like a Hanorian. Lexi was certain she looked equally out of place, with her dark hair and dark eyes. Without the illusion, she and Kurt looked like what they really were. Outsiders. Spies.

"Who are you?" Lord Marshal Jiyal gasped, looking at Kurt and Lexi in horror. "What are you?"

Lexi flung her hands up and a wall of fire roared to life in front of her, momentarily shielding her and Kurt from Mig and Jiyal.

"Run!" Lexi shouted.

Kurt didn't need to be told twice. They ran.

CHAPTER THREE

An Outwardly Unremarkable Girl

Cyreth wasn't usually caught off guard. He prided himself on being alert and prepared, always ready for a fight. The problem, he supposed, was that he'd never been so close to Lord Marshal Jiyal before. More importantly, he'd never been so close to Mig.

Everyone in the Army of Light knew Mig's story. How she'd been raised in an orphanage in Pollard, so baseborn and common that she didn't even merit a last name. How, when she was old enough to work, the housemaster for the High Lord of Pollard had bought her from the orphanage to work as a scullery maid. How she'd lived in obscurity, scouring pots and scrubbing kitchen floors, no one ever suspecting the power hidden inside such an outwardly unremarkable girl. That is, until the goblins came down from the mountains.

When the goblins attacked the Uplands, Mig had been working at the High Lord's country house, a large unfortified villa several leagues from the city. Hearing rumors of a goblin incursion, the High Lord had ridden forth with his scouts to ascertain the nature of the threat. He never came back.

A few nights after the High Lord left on his fatal scouting mission, a goblin war party stormed the isolated villa. They killed every human they could find and carried off all the food and valuables they could get their grasping claws on.

The way Cyreth heard it, when the goblins attacked the villa, just before dawn, Mig had been tending the bread oven. Her lord liked fresh-baked bread with his breakfast, and the staff always made sure to have several loaves hot and ready, even when he wasn't expected at the house. One never knew when he might arrive after a brisk morning ride, hungry and craving fresh bread. Since the cooks didn't like to wake up early, it was Mig's job to arrive at the kitchen hours before the sunrise, start a fire under the big cast iron bread oven, and pop the raw loaves in to cook. According to the story, she'd just placed the final loaf inside the piping-hot oven when a mob of howling goblins burst into the kitchen. Panicked, Mig hid the only place she could think of.

She crawled into the oven and closed the door behind her.

Mig should have baked to death along with the bread. Instead, she fell into a peaceful sleep.

When Mig awoke, she discovered the goblins had killed everyone she cared about. And she could work magic.

Cyreth had his doubts about the story. There were several different versions, and many included details

Cyreth found highly improbable. The business about the oven for example. When he was a boy, his family's cook had been like a second mother to him, so he'd spent countless hours in his family's huge kitchen. He'd found dozens of good places to hide—in the ice room, inside empty soup kettles, under the chopping counter—all of which made him doubt that Mig had really hidden in an oven. Then again, Mig was the most powerful spark anyone had come across in hundreds of years. If anyone could survive being baked alive, it was Mig.

Cyreth himself had seen Mig chase away clouds and stop the rain. He'd seen her call down fire on the goblin Warhorde. He'd seen her battle the Dark Lady at Solace Ridge. Other wizards had certainly helped drive back the goblin invasion, but if not for Mig, Cyreth was certain the goblins would have triumphed in the end.

So seeing Mig a dozen feet away, confronting two seemingly innocent soldiers, had thrown Cyreth. He'd forgotten everything to gawk at the powerful young wizardess. When Mig stripped away the illusion to reveal the young soldiers were actually odd-looking outlanders, he'd been caught completely by surprise. And when the female intruder created a wall of fire and then ran away with her tall companion, Cyreth had been slow to react. The intruders had disappeared behind a tent before Cyreth could even move.

Cyreth recovered, gathered a handful of Lion Guards, and began searching for the intruders. As the sun set, they found the entire camp abuzz. Soldiers were running everywhere, checking every possible hiding place. Suspecting the intruders would try to get away from the camp as quickly as possible, Cyreth led his Lion Guards toward Monster Mountain, where the recent landslide had broken the stockade.

The fire told him he was right.

Flames burst from a cluster of tents not far from the break, bright against the darkening sky. Some soldiers fled the fire, while others desperately tried to extinguish it. The female intruder was a lightworker. Cyreth knew she must be close.

"This way," Cyreth barked, weaving between the burning tents. His Lion Guards followed.

Suddenly a blast of hot wind slammed into Cyreth, stopping him in his tracks. He spotted the two intruders, a dozen yards away, not far from the break in the stockade.

"Don't come any closer," the female intruder shouted, in perfect Hanorian.

Cyreth signaled his men to stand by. He didn't want them to rush the lightworker and force her to respond with something more damaging than wind.

"Who are you?" Cyreth asked. "Why are you helping the gobblers?"

"We're strangers here," the girl answered. "We were in trouble, and some goblins rescued us. They're not the monsters you think they are. They know the war was a mistake. They just want to be left alone."

Cyreth felt a pang of guilt at that. Continuing the war after Solace Ridge and trying to wipe out the goblins had never felt right to him. Still . . . "I'm just a soldier. I just do what I'm told."

"Where we come from, 'I'm only following orders' is no excuse for doing something wrong," the male intruder said.

Cyreth didn't know how to react to that. Soldiers followed orders, right or wrong. That's what they did.

"Surrender," he said, placing his hand on his sword hilt, hoping the intruders would listen. "Surrender, or we'll show you no mercy."

The female intruder stepped forward. She was tiny, much smaller than Mig, but Cyreth didn't like the wild look in her eyes.

"The person who should be hoping for mercy right now . . . is you," she said. Fire danced around her fingers.

Cyreth and his Lion Guards froze in their tracks. They'd all seen what a fire wizard could do.

"Lexi, come on," the male intruder said. "We don't have time for this."

Despite her companion's concerns, the girl didn't move. She kept her eyes fixed on Cyreth.

"Go home," she said. "Leave the goblins in peace. Last warning."

Cyreth broke out in a sweat. He felt weak and feverish. He realized the air around him was getting hotter, as if he were suddenly trapped in Mig's bread oven. Behind him, a Lion Guard collapsed to his knees. Pyke had suffered a chest wound at Solace Ridge. He'd been short of breath ever since.

"You're killing him," Cyreth gasped.

The girl seemed to hesitate at that. Cyreth felt the air around him cool. It became easier to breathe.

"Just leave us alone," she said. Then she and her male companion turned to go—

And the ground around them exploded with fire.

Mig had found them.

"They might leave you be, but the fire will find you," Mig said, floating over a burning tent a dozen yards away. "The fire always finds you."

Mig sent another wave of flames toward the intruders. Lexi deflected it and responded with a blast of fire of her own.

"Fall back!" Cyreth ordered.

His Lion Guards quickly complied. They all knew that in a battle of wizards, no one was safe.

Hop knew something was wrong the moment Snails rushed into Beastpens Cave. Snails had been the spotter on Hop's warbat crew. Since Billy's coronation, Hop had found himself relying on Snails and his other former crew members. He trusted them with his life . . . and Billy's life, for that matter. He'd assigned the keen-eyed Snails to the sentry tower overlooking the main entrance to Kiranok. He trusted Snails's eyes to see any approaching danger and his legs to carry the message as quickly as possible. From Snails's expression, the news he was bringing wasn't good. Had the Hanorians begun their assault?

"Say it quick, Snails," Hop said to the young spotter.

"Fire spells," Snails sputtered. "*Maja* fire spells. In the human camp."

Hop knew what that meant. So did Billy.

"Lexi and Kurt," Billy said. "We have to help them."

"We may *nai* be able to," Hop said, trying to dissuade Billy from doing anything rash. "If they were spotted—"

Billy had no interest in Hop's plea for caution. "It's not a discussion. We're going to help them. Right now."

Hop reflected that the problem with making someone a king is that, afterward, you have to do what they say. *Arguing now are a waste of time*, Hop thought. *Best to come up with a way to do it right.*

"*Zaj*, Your Majesty. Only *zajnai* there're a way to save them where *nai* one end up dead."

Finally, Snap thought she might have found her opportunity. She, Icewall, and Grinner had followed the *skerbo* king to Beastpens Cave. The livestock holding area had only one major entrance, and they'd found a mix of

Templars and Copperplates standing guard outside. From what they could tell, the cave had been cleared of its usual occupants, the butchers and beast-sellers who did their business inside. It seemed that whatever he was doing in the cave, the human boy didn't want any witnesses. Which meant if she, Icewall, and Grinner could get inside, King Billy would be vulnerable. Getting in, though? That was the tricky part. Snap and her coconspirators were discussing ways to get past the guards, when a goblin messenger came running down Seventurns and dashed into the cave. The guards let him past. They obviously knew him.

"What if we follow him in?" Icewall asked. "Say we're with him. He seemed important."

"What're his name, you giant *drakbonch*?" Grinner shot back. "What're we to him? If we can *nai* answer, they'll do more than stop us. They'll attack. Then, even if we get away, the *skerbo* king and his turncoats will be on guard for us. And we'll *nai* catch him unawares ever again."

"It were just a suggestion," Icewall muttered.

"It're *spog*," Grinner replied, using an especially insulting goblin word for stupidity. "*Naizaj* try to come up with a plan that make more sense than a *kijakhof* in a flying contest. That're about as elegant as you dancing the *prejba*."

Snap blinked at Grinner's vicious insults. Icewall could be a bit unrealistic, but he was loyal and well-meaning. Comparing him to a giant rabbit trying to fly, or saying his suggestion was as clumsy as the big goblin attempting the leaping, twirling dance of goblin brides? That was just Grinner being nasty for nastiness's sake.

"Leave him alone," Snap said.

"*Ahka*, for someone what need me help, you spend a *maja* lot of time salting me soup," Grinner snarled.

"If I let you do as you like, you'll end up with your head lopped off for being a *graznak*," Snap shot back.

"If I were a *graznak*, could *nai* anyone stop me," Grinner replied, his face expressionless.

"We could," Icewall said, stepping closer to Grinner. "Together."

Snap hoped Icewall was right that they could stop Grinner if his murderous impulses spun out of control. She hoped she would never have to find out. Not just because she wasn't sure she and Icewall could contain Grinner. The truth was, she needed him if she wanted any chance of getting to King Billy.

"There're no cause for that," Snap said, trying to calm the *kijakgob* wizard. "So long as Grinner keep himself on track and use his magic for the greater good."

"Meaning that instead of killing whoever I want, I are supposed to kill only them what you want dead," Grinner said.

Snap wanted to say that she was trying to help Grinner focus his abilities and turn him away from his worst instincts. Only that would've been a lie. What Snap really wanted was for Grinner to kill her enemies instead of whatever random target stumbled across his path. Not that she wanted to admit that. So she struggled for a response. Before she could formulate an answer to Grinner's all-too-accurate accusation, Icewall jostled her shoulder.

"He're here," he said quietly.

Snap turned and saw King Billy emerging from Beastpens Cave. The guards at the entrance fell in around him as he rushed up Seventurns toward the Great Gate, apparently on some urgent business. Frost, the tiny but powerful wizard, led the way, and his towering brother, Leadpipe, guarded Billy's back. The traitorous

Copperplate Hop trotted at the *skerbo* boy's side.

Snap pulled Icewall and Grinner back into a shadowy alcove, hoping they wouldn't be seen. She muttered an incantation, interposing a field of cold between them and the king's guards, so that no one could redsight them.

"We can get him," Icewall whispered. "Right now. If we attack."

Snap was tempted. They might be able to kill King Billy if they attacked immediately. The *skerbo* boy and his guards were in a hurry. Even Leadpipe looked distracted in their dash up Seventurns.

It're nai *certain though*, Snap thought. *I* nai *have a clear shot at the boy. Take the chance now and miss, and we'll be finished.*

"*Nai*," she said. "We wait. Till it're sure. Till it're easy. We only need one moment to fall our way. Sure as day, sure as night, we'll get our chance."

Snap glanced at Grinner, who seemed annoyed to have let the opportunity pass. King Billy and his guards disappeared around a bend in the passageway. Snap understood that the *skerbo* king wouldn't die this moment. Eventually though—whether Billy was frozen to death, impaled by ice, or suffocated in snow—Snap was confident he would die at their hands.

So long as Grinner nai *kill me and Icewall first*, she thought.

Lexi didn't like running. For one thing, her legs were too short. She had to run five steps to cover the ground most people could manage in four. Plus she'd been born several weeks premature, before her lungs had fully developed. So she'd end up exhausted after even a brief run. Running didn't suit her, physically.

Then there was the emotional factor. Lexi's mom loved running. She got up early every morning and ran at least five miles. When Lexi was a little girl, she'd always wanted to go running with her mom, but her mother wouldn't let her. She didn't want her daughter to slow her down. It wasn't until Lexi turned twelve that her mother declared that she was old enough to join her morning runs and invited her to come along. By then, it was too late. Lexi and her mother had already begun their long, occasionally explosive feud. So anything Mom wanted, Lexi reflexively opposed. If her mother liked running, running had to suck. It was only logical. She'd turned down the invitation, and her mother had never asked her again.

So Lexi didn't like running. And she really hated running *away*.

She had always been smaller than her classmates, so she'd been bullied a lot. She'd found that the best way to respond to a bully was to get right back in the bully's face. The way she figured it, running just made her look weak.

Now she and Kurt were running away from an entire army with a dangerous wizard leading the pursuit. For once, running seemed like the best option. Still, that didn't mean Lexi had to like it. Or that she'd gotten any better at it.

Lexi tripped and fell as she and Kurt scrambled up a scree of loose rocks. As Lexi struggled back to her feet, a volley of arrows plunged into the slope just behind them. She instinctively summoned another wall of flames between them and their pursuers, but that only drained her even more. She stumbled up the hill, half blind from exhaustion.

Then, suddenly, she was lifted into the air.

"I got you," Kurt said as he threw her over his shoulder and charged up the hill.

"Put me down," Lexi said. She'd been carried quite enough recently.

"I said, I got you," Kurt said stubbornly. "You can barely walk, let alone run."

"You're not getting far carrying me," Lexi pointed out.

"Farther than you would," Kurt said, still powering up the hill.

She had to admit he was right. He was stronger and faster than Lexi could ever hope to be. She hated that about him. Despite having to carry her, he was moving them steadily away from the camp. Hopefully they could lose the Hanorians in the deepening darkness.

Lexi couldn't help by running herself, but maybe there was something she *could* do. Trying to ignore the jostling she was taking from being carried by Kurt, she focused on the fires she'd left burning behind her. The fires had burned hot and quick, discouraging their pursuers momentarily, but now they were smoldering uselessly. Lexi sent out energy toward the fires. Not to make them burn hot again, but to make them smolder even more.

Dark black smoke poured from the fires, choking the area around the slope.

"Was that you?" Kurt asked. He was huffing and puffing, finally tiring himself. "Now they can't see us," Lexi said.

"Yeah, but I can't see anything either," Kurt coughed.

"Put me down," Lexi said. "We don't have to be fast anymore. We just have to be smart."

"Smart how?" Kurt asked as he set Lexi down.

"Like this."

Lexi faced up the mountain, then blew out air, like she was blowing out birthday candles. Her breath became a

gentle gust of wind, clearing a path through the smoke.
Kurt and Lexi moved up the path, out of the cloud. Lexi
looked around. No one had followed them. She could
hear the Hanorians below them, lost in the smoke,
shouting and searching frantically without success.

"We made it," Lexi said, happily surprised. For once
in her life, running had actually worked.

Then fire fell from the sky, just ahead of them. And
Mig stepped out of the flames.

Lexi's optimism turned to smoke just like her fires had.
Mig glowed with power. Lexi felt completely drained. If
this came down to a wizard battle between Lexi and the
Hanorian girl, Lexi and Kurt were doomed.

"You know a lot of tricks," Mig said to Lexi. "But
so do I."

"We don't want to hurt anyone," Lexi said. "We just
want to go back to our friends."

"So you can tell the greenskins everything you've
learned about *my* friends," Mig replied coldly. "So they
can kill everyone I know."

To Lexi's surprise, Kurt stepped between her and Mig,
holding his arms wide and trying to look nonthreatening.

"Scary, right?" Kurt asked the Hanorian girl. "I know
I'm scared, being in the middle of all of this."

"The Light fills me," Mig answered. "The Light burns
away all fear."

Kurt didn't look discouraged. Lexi could tell he was
just trying to keep her talking. As long as she was talking,
she wasn't blasting them with fire.

"You're lucky then," Kurt answered. "I don't have
any magical light in me. I'm just a regular guy. I'm not
a king or a lightworker or anything special. I mean, not
here. Back home . . ." Kurt trailed off. It was like he'd read
Lexi's mind. This Hanorian girl wasn't going to care what

a star Kurt had been back home. "Back home doesn't matter," he continued. "What matters is that me, Lexi, and our friend Billy are from another world. Somehow, we ended up here, in the middle of a war none of us really understand."

"Billy?" Mig reacted to Billy's name, startled. "That's the name of the Goblin King."

"How do you know that?" Lexi blurted, taken off guard by Mig's recognition.

"We caught one of the greenskins trying to reach Monster Mountain. He told us all about the human traitor who'd become their king."

"Before or after you set him on fire?" Lexi asked. She regretted it as soon as she'd said it. She knew challenging Mig was a bad idea, but sometimes her mouth moved faster than her brain.

"During, mostly," Mig answered emotionlessly.

To Lexi's relief, Kurt pressed ahead, getting Mig's focus back on him.

"The point is, Billy is playing at being king," Kurt insisted. "He doesn't really care about the goblins. None of us do. We only cooperated with them so they wouldn't hurt us. Believe me, the second we find a way back to our own world, we're out of here, and you'll never have to worry about us again."

This time Lexi was able to restrain herself and not call out Kurt's lie. She knew that she and Billy, at least, cared deeply about the goblins and their fate. She suspected Kurt cared too, though she sometimes had her doubts.

"Look, we don't have to be enemies," Kurt continued. "What can we do to convince you we're no threat?"

Kurt continued in that fashion for a while, talking slowly and calmly. Mig seemed willing to listen. Kurt was one of the most handsome boys Lexi had ever met. She might've fallen for him herself if he hadn't been such a jerk to her and Billy. So it didn't surprise her that Mig, for the moment, appeared to be taken in by his charms.

Kurt went on and on, reassuring, persuasive, charming. Lexi lost track of what he was saying, distracted by her own internal struggles. Lexi figured that sooner or later, no matter how charming Kurt was, the fire inside of Mig would force its way out. She'd lived with the fire magic coursing through her own body long enough to know that it was like a living thing—an animal in a box, always scratching to get out. The magic wanted to be used.

Lexi could feel her own magic clawing at her brain. She'd been still too long. She was in danger. It was time to set the fire loose—before Mig decided to do the same.

Something caught Lexi's eye. A streak in the sky. A shooting star was passing overhead. In another circumstance, she might have thought it beautiful. But cornered, exhausted, and fighting a losing battle against the magic burning in her veins, Lexi saw it completely differently.

To her, at that moment, the shooting star looked like a weapon.

Lexi let the magic flow out of her. Out and up. She pictured her spell as a giant, invisible hand, reaching into the sky. Then the hand grabbed. And pulled.

The shooting star resisted for a moment. In the sky, it slowed . . .

Then it came plunging straight at Lexi, Kurt, and Mig.

The meteor was above and behind Mig. Lexi was sure it would hit her target. It was traveling faster than anything she'd ever seen, growing bigger and brighter by the second.

It was probably the light that alerted Mig. The incoming meteor turned their surroundings from dark and smoky to eerily bright in the blink of an eye. She looked over her shoulder and saw the shooting star roaring toward them.

"You lunatic!" the Hanorian girl said, stunned. "You'll kill us all!"

Kurt looked at the meteor, his eyes wide. "Lexi, what did you do?"

Lexi had thought the shooting star would hit Mig without hurting her and Kurt. But as the meteor zoomed their way, it expanded into a giant ball of fire. Too late, Lexi realized she'd basically just aimed a bomb at Mig . . . and she and Kurt were going to be caught in the blast.

She tried to reach out again, to stop the incoming missile, but her magic was exhausted. She had nothing left. She pushed harder, desperately trying to find one last drop of magical energy to undo her fatal error. She screamed out with the intense effort, clenching her fists so tightly that her nails dug into her palms.

Nothing happened. The white-hot shooting star was still barreling their way. Lexi's world felt like it was spinning. Her vision blurred, and then everything went black.

"Lexi!" Kurt cried out as Lexi staggered, then collapsed to the ground.

He stumbled to Lexi and picked her up once again. This time she didn't protest. She was unconscious.

"Lexi," he whispered. "You have to wake up. You have to stop this thing." There was no answer. He shook her gently. "Lexi, please."

Lexi didn't move. She'd cast too many spells too fast, with no time to recover. She was out cold. She couldn't save them. Kurt was about to run for his life when a column of fire rose to meet the shooting star.

Mig was an inferno. She held both hands high, shaping a fiery tornado that surged skyward. It rose higher and higher and higher, until it finally hit the oncoming meteor, deflecting it away from them with a thunderous . . .

Boom!

"Down there!" Billy shouted, pointing to the column of fire blasting skyward from a cloud of smoke on the side of Mother Mountain.

Convincing Hop to let him go on the rescue mission had been no small feat. Still, Billy had refused to back down. He made it clear he wasn't going to wait around while his friends were in danger. Eventually, Hop relented. Bit by bit, the goblin was learning that Billy could handle himself in a crisis.

Bit by bit, Billy was realizing the same thing.

Which is how Billy ended up on the back of a warbat named Daffodil, along with Hop, Frost, and Hop's bat-rider crew, soaring through the night sky and scouring the mountainside for any sign of Lexi and Kurt.

Goblin sentries had seen magical flames rising from the human camp on and off for almost an hour. The Hanorians must've realized Lexi and Kurt were spies. Billy knew if anyone tried to mess with Lexi, they were in for a fight. He just hoped that Lexi could hold her own long enough for Hop and his crew to swoop in and rescue her and Kurt.

At least the blast of fire gave them a likely place to look.

Daffodil turned toward the column of fire just as it struck a speeding fireball screaming down from the sky.

There was a bright flash of light as the blast deflected the fireball up and away from them. A second later, a fiery shock wave hit the warbat and her riders like a hammer.

Billy lost all sense of up and down. Daffodil spun and tumbled through the air, and he spun and tumbled right along with her. Somehow he grabbed a bit of harness and found himself dangling in the air. He was hanging by one hand from the warbat's chest straps, looking at her enormous face just out of arm's reach.

Daffodil was unconscious. The ground was coming fast.

"Wake up!" Billy shouted, as loud as he could.

The warbat didn't blink. She was out cold. Billy couldn't see Hop or Frost or any of the other bat-riders. For all he knew, they'd fallen to their deaths. If he couldn't rouse Daffodil, he and the warbat would be dead soon too.

Desperate, Billy kicked his legs forward, like he was on a swing. He swung forward, then back. He kicked again, frantic. He swung back and forth from Daffodil's harness, the muscles in his arm straining, his shoulder wrenching. Swing, kick, swing, kick.

Then, on a forward swing, Billy let go of the harness. He flew through the air, clawing blindly . . .

And somehow he snagged another piece of harness, this one on Daffodil's neck.

"Wake up, Daffodil!" Billy shouted again, shaking the harness.

The warbat startled awake, struggling to get her bearings.

"FLY!" Billy shouted.

Daffodil spread her wings.

The effect was pretty much what Billy imagined it'd be like to use a parachute. There was a tremendous jerk, and then Daffodil went straight up. Billy nearly lost his grip on her neck straps, but a strong, knobby hand grabbed his arm.

"Getted you!" Hop barked. The goblin pulled him

up onto Daffodil's back. Billy was glad to see that Frost, Hop, and Daffodil's crew were safe.

"You saved us, Billy," Frost said, still shaken. "If you haved *nai* waked the bat, we all would've splatted ourselves to death."

"We wouldn't be here at all if not for me," Billy said. He couldn't take credit for rescuing anyone when he'd been the one to put them in danger. And it wasn't just Hop, Frost, and the bat-riders he'd put at risk.

"Lexi," Billy said. "Where is she?"

In quick, out quick, Hop thought to himself. *If a gob have to do anything heroic, that're the best way.*

Daffodil swooped down toward the rocky slope, her powerful wings blowing clear the smoke around the three prone bodies. Daffodil hovered a few feet off the ground. Billy, Snails, and a pair of Hop's archers leapt from her back and ran to Kurt and Lexi. As they carried the unconscious humans back toward the bat, Hop looked at the third human, a teenage Hanorian girl. She was out cold. Her once fine clothing was scorched. Her formerly elaborate hairdo was a sooty tangle.

"What about her?" Hop asked Frost, nodding toward the Hanorian girl. "She're a wizard most like."

The scouts had said Lexi was engaged in a wizard's duel with a female Hanorian lightworker. The unconscious girl met the description.

"You saying I should kill her?" Frost asked. "*Zajnai* freeze her while she're lying there helpless?"

Hop could hear Frost's distaste. He wasn't very happy with the idea himself.

"Something about her feel dangerous . . . and

familiar," Hop said. Then he realized, "I think she're the one what slew the Dark Lady."

"*Chom-chom* to her then. The Dark Lady were a monster."

Hop couldn't argue with that. Billy, Snails, and the others climbed onto Daffodil's back, hauling Lexi and Kurt up behind them.

"Hold tight!" Hop shouted, then whistled for Daffodil to rise. The warbat beat her wings harder and began to climb.

"Look out!" Snails shouted, pointing back at the ground.

The Hanorian girl had struggled to her feet. Her hands were on fire.

With a sharp whistle and a poke from his prod, Hop urged Daffodil to climb faster, but he knew it wouldn't help. The warbat was too big; she could climb at only one rate, and it wasn't quick.

"Eat snow!" Frost yelled, leaning over the side of the warbat. He kept on yelling, "Snoooooooooooooow!" and a miniature blizzard blew out of his mouth, gusting toward the human wizard. Frost's snow met her blossoming fire, extinguishing it and creating a cloud of fog.

That seemed to be exactly what Frost wanted. He gestured, and the fog swirled around the warbat, making it impossible to see more than a few feet.

"She can *nai* see us *nai* more," Frost said. "Fly high. Fly fast. Fly home."

Hop didn't need to be told twice. He guided Daffodil higher and higher, eager to get out of range of the Hanorian girl's spells as soon as possible.

As Daffodil climbed, Hop looked over at Billy and his friends. "Are Lexi and Kurt . . . ?"

"They're breathing," Billy answered. "I think they'll be okay."

"Glad to hear that," Kurt said with a moan, sitting up slowly.

"Kurt!" Billy hugged his fellow human. Hop knew that Billy hadn't always been fond of Kurt, but apparently his relief outweighed any lingering animosity. Then Billy seemed to remember his history with Kurt and let him go.

"Sorry," Billy said sheepishly. "I never should have let you try to sneak into the Hanorian camp."

"I'm the one who's sorry," Kurt said. "We blew it. We got spotted."

At Hop's urging, Daffodil continued to climb, hidden by Frost's magical fog.

"You're all still alive," Hop said. "So even if today *nai* go our way, at least we all have tomorrow."

"Barely," Kurt said. "When that shooting star came down at us, I didn't think we'd make it."

Frost perked up at that. "A shooting star?" the little wizard asked. "Were that what that fireball were?"

"Lexi pulled it from the sky," Kurt said. "She was trying to stop Mig—that's the name of that Hanorian wizard girl—but Lexi nearly killed us all."

Hop saw that Frost was thinking something over in his head. Something important.

"What're you chewing, Frost?" he asked.

"*Naizaj* Lexi and Kurt maked a mess of things down there," Frost explained. "But on second taste, *zajnai* Lexi just saved us all."

CHAPTER FOUR

A Thing of Power

The pain woke her. She hurt everywhere. Her eyes ached. Her skin stung and itched. Her head felt like it was about to split wide open.

Then the whispers started. Three words, echoing in her mind: *Burn it all, burn it all, burn it all.*

It was as if the magic was speaking to her, urging her to let it out.

Burn it all, burn it all, burn it all.

"Tell me your name," she heard. To her relief, it wasn't a whisper inside her head this time. There was someone nearby, talking to her. The voice was familiar.

She slowly opened her eyes, trying to focus on her surroundings. She was lying in a huge bed in a luxurious bedroom. Vivid tapestries covered the stone walls. The room looked familiar. It was her room. Not her original room, back home. The room they'd given her. The goblins.

She turned and saw a tiny goblin perched on a chair to one side of her bed. The chair was several sizes too big for him. If not for his wispy beard, it'd be easy to mistake him for a child . . . a green-skinned, fanged, pointed-eared child.

"Tell me your name," he repeated insistently. He nervously fingered his thick gold necklace with one hand. He kept the other low, moving his fingers in a slow, deliberate pattern. She realized he was preparing a spell. The whispers intensified.

Burn him, burn him, burn him, burn him.

But she didn't want to burn the little goblin. She knew he was a friend. Her friend.

"You're Frost," she said, the world around her slowly coming into focus.

"I are indeed," Frost said. The little goblin's fingers kept moving, and his expression remained alert and more than a little concerned. "Right now, though, the *maja* important question are . . . who are you?"

She realized he was worried she'd become a *graznak*, an empty shell animated by magic. She remembered him warning her that could happen if she cast too many spells. They'd been on a ship of some kind. He'd called her . . .

"Lexi," she said, relief flooding her body. "My name is Lexi Aquino. I'm from Pacifica, California. My father is named Jay, and my mother's name is Liza."

Frost finally relaxed, even smiled a little. "Good to hear that, Lexi."

"You thought I'd become an empty jar?" Lexi said, as much an accusation as a question.

Frost's smile faded, and his expression turned somber again. "That're a *maja* armful of magic you throwed around. I warned you about that. More than once."

Burn him, burn him, burn him.

"I'm still me," Lexi said, hoping it was true. "And if I hadn't used so much magic, Kurt and I would be dead."

Burn it all.

Frost sighed, sounding a lot like her dad when he realized his latest paternal lecture wasn't making an impression. "I know you keep finding yourself in a corner where magic seem the only way out. And *naizaj* I sound like an echo, giving you the same warning over and over. But I have to say it."

Though Lexi would never admit it, the truth was she liked her father's lectures. Even if his advice was pretty lame, she knew his talks were his way of showing he cared. She felt the same way about Frost. He was wrong. She could handle the magic. Still, it was nice to know he cared about her.

Burn it all, burn it all, burn it all.

At least, she hoped he was wrong.

"I just hope it was all worth it," Lexi said. "I hope Kurt was able to get a good idea of what we're up against."

"*Ahka*, that're *nai* the only thing you doed. Truth are, your mission accomplished something *maja* more important than you know. *Naizaj* you finded the key to saving every *gob* in Kiranok."

Lexi was confused. She couldn't think of anything that she and Kurt had done that would save the goblin city. Maybe if they had killed the Hanorians' big boss . . . but they hadn't. They hadn't done much aside from running away.

"What do you mean?" she asked. "What did we do?"

Frost's smile returned. "*Nai* much. Aside from pulling a star from the sky."

"All this over some rock," Billy said as he watched Hop's warbat crew scramble to prepare for their journey.

"*Nai* just any rock," Frost reminded Billy. "A Fallen Star."

A few hours earlier, in the Hall of Kings, Frost had explained to Billy, Lexi, and Kurt that Lexi's shooting star could be the salvation of goblinkind . . . or its doom.

"Most shooting stars are just light," Frost had explained. "They streak across the sky and then disappear. Sometimes, though, there're a solid bit in the middle. It hit the ground like a hammer, blow up entire hillsides. I think the one Lexi pulled down were like that. Our sentries in Overwatch Tower seed it streak over Mother Mountain and strike ground in the far north. They say it sended up a big column of dirt and fire when it hit. Could be there're nothing left. Or *naizaj* there're a starstone sitting in a crater somewhere north of here. If that're so—if this're a true Fallen Star—it're magic.

"Fallen Stars are things of power," Frost had continued. "They come down from the heavens. They're as old as the universe. They're magic through and through. Coaler drawed on the power of a Fallen Star to cut his break through the Ironspine Mountains. He used it to blast a pass through mountains three thousand span high. The great spells what protected the pass were casted the same way. They say the Underway were shaped by wizards using a Fallen Star. And once, when the Smoking Bell were shaking and about to erupt, a local wizard called Pepperstew used a Fallen Star to put the mountain back to sleep. She saved every village near the Bell."

Frost believed that if they could retrieve the Fallen Star from its landing place in the north, he could use it to save Kiranok from the attacking human army. With the Fallen Star, he could summon a blizzard, or build walls of ice, or dig a canyon between the humans and the goblin city. Frost had proposed a half dozen spells that might keep the humans away or drive them back home. But they all depended on getting the Star.

Unfortunately, the sentries who'd seen it crash to the ground estimated that the Fallen Star was at least fifty *loktepen* away. A *loktep* was as far as an average-sized goblin could walk in an hour. It would take days to walk that far, get the meteorite, and walk all the way back to Kiranok.

Which was why Hop and his crew were readying a flight of bats. He and Kurt had volunteered to lead the expedition. Billy had wanted to go himself, but Hop and Frost had argued that he needed to stay in the city. The goblins were depending on him to lead them. If he were to suddenly disappear, they might lose hope. Billy had seen their point. So as much as he hated it, he was going to have to let his friends go off and risk their lives while he remained behind. Again.

Hop had insisted that Frost and Leadpipe stay by Billy's side and protect him. Lexi had wanted to go on the expedition, but eventually she admitted that after everything she'd been through in the human camp, she needed time to rest and recover.

So it had fallen to Hop and Kurt. Hop had originally planned to fly north on his warbat, Daffodil, but after conferring with Frost, he'd commandeered four of the city's taxi-bats for the mission instead, enough to carry sixteen volunteers. The taxi-bats couldn't fight, but they were much faster than a warbat. Hopefully, fast enough. Because Frost believed trying to get the Star wouldn't just be a mission—it would be a race.

"You're sure the Hanorians will go after the Star too?" Billy asked Frost as they watched Kurt, Hop, and Hop's crew load the last of their supplies onto a taxi-bat.

Billy heard a low rumble behind him. "'The Shepherd

and the Flood.'"

It was Leadpipe. He was standing guard by the main entrance to the Bat Cavern, a huge cave where the taxi-bats and warbats slept. On the other side of the chamber, a long, wide passageway ran to an exit from Mother Mountain via a gaping cave mouth set high in a cliff face. Though it was nearly impossible for anyone to get into the city that way, there were several Copperplates stationed there, just in case.

"What's 'The Shepherd and the Flood'?" Billy asked.

"I like to read. Not important books like my brother do. I like stories. I readed all the goblin ones afore I were even twelve years old. 'The Littlest Giant,' 'Cloak the Bandit King,' 'The Big Book of Tales,' 'Adventure of the Nineteen Templars.' Then I runned out. Remember, brother?"

"He were upset," Frost said. "He keeped asking me why there were no more stories. He'd readed every one we haved, and I could *nai* find *nai* more in the market. So I searched the Library of the Blue Chambers and finded Lead all the stories I could."

"Including human ones," Leadpipe said. "He finded me a book of Hanorian tales, translated into *Gobayabber* by some old wizard. One of them was 'The Shepherd and the Flood.' In the story, there were a big storm in the Ironspines. It triggered a *majamaja* rush of water down the Venstell River. A wave a hundred span high come thundering down the Venstell, bursting its banks, wiping out everything in its path. When the water comed, there were this shepherd downstream trying to rescue a lamb what were sticked in the mud by the riverbank. He seed the water coming when it were *loktepen* away, but he *nai* wanted to leave his little lamb behind. So he tried to dig the baby sheep out, and as he digged, he finded a stone buried in the mud. The shepherd pulled the stone out, then seed the water were nearly on him. He clutched the stone and wished the water would stop. Suddenly, the ground rised up and maked a wall ten thousand span long and a thousand span thick. Turn out the boy were a spark, and the stone were a Fallen Star. Without even meaning to, the boy had used the stone to make the biggest dam in the world. It backed up the waters 'til they formed the Long Tarn, a lake over sixty *loktepen* around. The flood were stopped, and the cities downstream were saved."

"So the Hanorians have stories about Fallen Stars too," Billy said.

"More than one, but that're the most famous," Leadpipe said. "They seed Lexi's star crash to the ground, just like us. They'll try to get it, just like us. Except if they get it, the Hanorians will use it to kill us all."

Cyreth coughed. He knew he probably shouldn't, given the circumstances, but he couldn't help it. He'd inhaled a lungful of smoke during the battle between Mig and the outlander wizardess, and his throat was scratchy and raw.

"Would you like me to stop talking, Captain?" Lord Marshal Jiyal snarled.

"No, milord," Cyreth answered. "Sorry, milord."

"So you'd like me to continue to review your numerous failings?" Jiyal asked.

Jiyal had ordered Cyreth to report to his tent for an after-action review of the failed attempt to capture the intruders. It hadn't been a very pleasant conversation so far. Jiyal had peppered it with phrases like "traitorously incompetent," "borderline insubordination," and "obvious cowardice." On the bright side, he hadn't threated to strip Cyreth of his command . . . or execute him. Yet.

"As the General prefers," Cyreth answered, trying to keep his composure. He knew that Jiyal wanted him to grovel or admit fault, but he had no intention of doing either. In Cyreth's experience, when dealing with people like the Lord Marshal, begging or pleading never helped.

"Tell me, Captain," Jiyal asked. "Do your soldiers share your heretical beliefs?"

Cyreth could feel his stone-faced expression slip. He hadn't been expecting that.

"I . . . I don't know what you mean, sir," he stammered.

"I understand your mother was a Celestial, when she was young," Jiyal said, gesturing to a written report on his desk.

"She was," Cyreth admitted. There was no point in denying it. "But only until the movement was declared heretical. She left the Celestials after the Decree of Vala."

"Just in time to marry your father, Lord Gant. Rich family, yours. Shipping, I believe. Your grandfather bought his title." Lord Marshal Jiyal didn't bother to hide his contempt. He was descended from one of the original first families of the Empire. People like him often looked down on Cyreth's family, as if buying a title were somehow morally inferior to inheriting it.

"My mother's side of the family has titles dating back to the Founding. To the First Ships."

"But no money. Small wonder they married her off to a rich upstart."

"I've been told it was a love match, milord," Cyreth said. "I don't see what that has to do with—"

"I had your tent searched," Jiyal interrupted. "They found this."

Lord Marshal Jiyal pulled a kerchief out of his pocket and laid it on his desk. "I assume your mother gave this to you? A parting gift for a son off to war."

"That's right," Cyreth said, trying to keep his face expressionless. "I wear it under my helmet. Helps the fit. Absorbs sweat."

Jiyal unfolded the kerchief to reveal the hand stitching Cyreth's mother had added to the cloth. "Suns and moons both," the Lord Marshal pointed out.

The design was composed of intricate interlocking suns, moons, and stars, along with symbols of health and protection. Cyreth's mother wasn't a particularly skilled or enthusiastic embroiderer, but the pattern was incredibly precise. He knew it had taken her weeks to complete, every careful stitch a prayer for his safety. The inclusion of both suns and moons in the design might be a harmless artistic choice on his mother's part . . . but it could also be a Celestial invocation of the powers of Day and Night to guard her eldest son in combat.

"It's just embroidery, milord," Cyreth said, not really believing it himself.

"Did you know there are Celestials helping the goblins? Traitors to their own kind."

"I've heard the rumors, sir," Cyreth said carefully.

"Here's what I think," Jiyal said. "I think your mother is still a Celestial . . . and you're one too, raised on heresy from birth, sucking down false doctrine with your mother's milk. I think your family embodies everything that's wrong with the Empire these days. You're rot and corruption in the very heart of the Army of Light. That's why you failed to capture the intruders. You're on their side."

The truth was, though Cyreth wasn't very religious, he would certainly qualify as a Celestial. It was the secret faith of both his mother and father. He'd played the Celestials' ritual games growing up. He'd learned to juggle and spin fire. Before dinner, his mother would send the servants out of the dining hall so the Gant family could say prayers to both Day and Night. So he supposed he really was a heretic, even if he'd never admit it. Lord Marshal Jiyal could have Cyreth burned at the stake for being a Celestial, so he wasn't about to confess. Besides, regardless of his beliefs, he was no traitor.

"I'm a loyal soldier of the Empire, milord," Cyreth said, meaning every word.

"And your subordinates?" the Lord Marshal asked. "How many of them pollute the Day's Faith with their heresy?"

That question was even more troubling. Though they never talked about it, Cyreth had seen other Lion Guards engaging in Celestial rituals that only a fellow heretic would recognize. He'd spotted Speryco juggling behind his tent at night when the moon was up. Ysalion wore a veil over the lower half of her face in the fashion of the most conservative Sun worshippers. But whenever she was on guard duty on the ramparts, she'd balance on the very edge of the parapet walk like it was a tightrope. Harfin had a lucky coin he liked to make dance across his fingers. It had a moon on one side, a sun on the other. All told, Cyreth guessed there were at least a few dozen secret Celestials in the Lion Guards, all of whom risked execution if discovered.

"The Lion Guards are good soldiers, milord," Cyreth said, hiding his fears. "We've never refused an order. We've lost many good troopers to win your battles, and we're ready and willing to risk our lives for the Empire again. Test us, and you will not find us wanting."

Lord Marshal Jiyal studied Cyreth for a long moment. Cyreth maintained his parade-rest stance, doing everything in his power to hide his worries. Would the general order his execution and a purge of the Lion Guards? Or would he give them another chance?

Finally, Jiyal spoke, "The Light smiles on you, Captain. I've the perfect test in mind."

Kurt worried that volunteering for suicide missions was becoming a habit. He'd barely survived the scouting trip into the Hanorian camp, and now here he was getting ready to fly on the back of a giant bat into the wilderness in a life-or-death race against enemy soldiers and wizards. All to get ahold of some magical rock. Still, it felt good, doing something that mattered. The goblins' entire civilization was at risk. Kurt definitely didn't want to stand on the sidelines if he had a chance to help.

He moved through the crowd of goblins loading the bats, carrying a crate of rations for the trip. The goblins didn't seem nearly as worried as Kurt. Several of them sang as they worked. Hop's former warbat crew started the song, but after a few bars, the rest of the goblins loading the bats joined in, at least with the chorus.

Oh off we go again
Into the blue again
Ahka, what can go wrong?
Zajnai we fall headlong
From the sky to the ground
And end up nice and round
Just a greasy stain, me friends
But off we go again

Oh off we go again
Into the blue again
We belong to the sky
To the blue, live or die

We do nai *count the odds*
Like them poor earthbound slobs
With the wind in our ears
We forget all our fears
We throw them to the wind
So we can fly again

We belong to the sky
To the blue, live or die
Oh off we go again
Into the blue again

Flying? Nothing better
Falling? Nothing deader
That are the price we pay
To fly into the day
To soar high, far above
Up in the sky we love
Oh off we go again

After "Off We Go Again," the bat-riders launched into a few more ditties. "The Ballad of Flyrat" seemed to be a favorite. There was an old song about the first bat-rider and how she tamed the first riding bat and used it to fly a thousand *loktepen* home to her children. There was another about the equipment the bat-riders used and how, if anything failed, it could result in an unexpected fall and a sudden death. All the songs were bright and cheerful and inevitably mentioned how easy it was to die when you were a bat-rider. It seemed like the goblins particularly enjoyed those passages, as if singing about their possible gruesome deaths made them less likely to happen. Kurt didn't feel reassured. The morbid lyrics made him all too aware he might not survive this mission. On the bright side, the songs made the work go by quickly. Kurt realized he'd loaded several more crates without even thinking about it. The bats were almost ready to go. As Kurt struggled to load one final crate into a taxi-bat's giant saddlebags, he heard someone calling his name.

"Kurt, my friend," he heard in Hanorian, "may Night and Day bless you."

Kurt turned and saw Azam moving through the crowd. He and Azam had met at the Fastness, the goblin fortress-city where the Celestials had been living in exile and where Kurt had been waiting out a death sentence. The athletic Celestial had taught him fire-spinning, juggling, tightrope walking, and the other games his people used in their worship. Kurt had never been much for church, but he'd enjoyed the Celestials' rituals, with their emphasis on movement and fun. He and Azam had become fast friends.

"Azam," Kurt replied. "Day and Night's blessings to you too."

Azam laughed. "You almost sound as if you believe."

Kurt shook his head. "There are worse things to believe in."

"It's good to see you." Azam embraced Kurt, as the Celestials typically did when they greeted their friends. Kurt wasn't much of a hugger, but he'd gotten used to it.

After their quick hug, Kurt felt a pang of guilt. "Sorry. I'd heard you'd come to Kiranok, but I didn't have time to track you down."

"I understand you have pressing matters to attend to," Azam said, not looking the least bit hurt. "In fact, that's why we're here."

Azam gestured toward several other young Celestials who'd just arrived in the Bat Cavern. Kurt recognized most of them from his time in the Fastness, including

Alyseer, the daughter of the Celestials' leaders. "We want to come with you. We think we can help."

Kurt could see the goblins in the cave looking at Azam and his friends with suspicion. The goblins were understandably reluctant to trust any human, even ones outlawed by their own kind. Azam and his friends, however, seemed to be genuinely good people. Apparently, such good people that they were willing to volunteer for what might turn out to be a suicide mission.

"You know this is going to be dangerous, right?" Kurt asked.

"No more dangerous than staying here," Azam answered. "We're no warriors. But Alyseer is a light-worker. As for the rest of us . . . we can ride, we'll work hard, and if we can help you, that frees up more goblins to defend the city."

That made sense. Plus, Kurt had to admit, it would be good to have Azam along for the journey.

"Have you asked Billy about this?" Kurt asked. "Or Hop? It's his mission."

"Hop looks a little busy," Azam said.

Kurt looked over at Hop and saw that the one-eared goblin was in the middle of an intense conversation with Shadow. Her skin was so dark it was difficult to make out her expression, but he could read Hop. The goblin's face showed a mixture of surprise and panic.

"Something's wrong," Kurt guessed. "Shadow's brought bad news."

"That's not the way a man, or even a goblin, reacts to bad news," Azam said with a smile. "That's something else entirely."

"I do *nai* understand," Hop stammered.

"It're *nai* complicated," Shadow said, looking amused. "Do *nai* die. If you die, I'll *nai* ever forgive you. Come back in one piece. For me. You understand now?"

Hop understood. He just couldn't completely believe it. He'd fallen for Shadow the moment he first saw her, despite the fact that she was Sawtooth's daughter and, at the time, he'd been trying to overthrow the goblin dictator. In the end, she'd helped Hop and his friends depose her father. After which, Sawtooth had been torn to bits by an angry mob. Hop knew that had hurt Shadow, no matter how much her father might've deserved his fate. Plus Shadow was brave, while Hop was a coward at heart. Shadow was beautiful, and Hop, with his mangled ear, looked like something the world had chewed up and spat out. Shadow was honest and insightful and honorable . . . and Hop didn't think of himself as any of those things. So he never imagined she might feel the same way about him as he did about her.

"I're *nai* worthy of you," Hop said quietly. "I're just scraps and leftovers. You deserve a banquet."

Shadow smiled at that. "I like leftovers. Sometime *nai* thing taste better." Then her expression became more serious. "I know you think you're a coward. But I're *nai* ever seed you run from anything. You finded the Goblin King. You saved your warbat and her crew. You defeated the lightships. You ended me father's madness and getted Billy his crown. You're *maja* more a hero than you want to admit."

"I're still ugly," Hop said. "Covered in scars. Sewed together from patches."

"I're a Templar. A warrior," Shadow said. "I have scars too. *Zajnai* you come back alive, and you ask nice, I'll show them to you."

That flustered Hop completely. As he stammered for

a response . . .

The room turned to ice.

They'd walked right into the Bat Cavern. It'd been much easier than Snap imagined. There were so many goblins coming and going that the guards weren't even bothering to question them. They'd even let a group of humans inside. The *skerboen* had walked past the guards without so much as an "*ahka*" or a "*wazzer.*" Grinner had lost his patience when he saw that.

"If they can go in, then why *nai* us?" he'd snarled and then walked, bold as can be, right past the guards and into the Bat Cavern.

Grinner disappeared through the entrance. Seeing he hadn't been stopped, Snap walked past the guards herself, almost without thinking. Icewall followed dutifully at her heels, like a pet *bokrum*, docile and loyal.

Inside, the Bat Cavern was bustling with activity. Dozens of goblins loaded supplies onto taxi-bats. In addition to the newly arrived *skerboen*, the big yellow-haired human—the one they called Kurt—was also there, carrying impressively large loads of food and water to the taxi-bats. King Billy was there too, standing by Frost, talking quietly and intently. Frost was fully focused on Billy, so he hadn't noticed Grinner, Icewall, or Snap, despite the time they'd spent together in the Blue Chambers. Hop, the one-eared Copperplate, and Shadow, Sawtooth's turncoat daughter, were standing together at the far side of the cave, engaged in an intense conversation of their own. Courting, if Snap had to guess.

It looked like the perfect time to attack. With a little luck, they could kill Billy, his too-tall friend, his traitorous goblin advisors, and the *skerboen* Celestials in a single strike.

And then they'd die.

Snap could see that. The cavern was too big and too crowded. Even three wizards working together couldn't kill everyone fast enough to stop the various goblins and humans from fighting back.

Snap didn't want to die. The problem was, she wasn't sure her two companions felt the same way. She looked over at Grinner, afraid he was about to lash out without thinking . . .

But Grinner stood stock-still, his eyes darting around the cavern, clearly measuring his odds and not liking what he saw. Snap moved to his side, trying not to draw attention to herself.

"*Zajnai* this're *nai* the right time," she said quietly.

Grinner didn't answer right away. Snap figured he was thinking things through. Finally he replied, equally quiet and measured, "Are *nai* much point to it if we do *nai* walk out of here to enjoy it."

Snap felt relieved. As much as she wanted to kill the *skerbo* king, she didn't want to die in the process.

"Another time, then," she said. Which is when she heard—

"This're for you, Snap!" It was Icewall, shouting with pride.

Then he unleashed a blast of snow, ice, and wind toward King Billy.

ROBERT HEWITT WOLFE

CHAPTER FIVE
The Telltale Scars of Battle

No one had tried to kill Billy in days. He hadn't really appreciated how nice that felt until someone tried to do it again.

He wasn't sure how he noticed the bulky *kijakgob* in time. Maybe it was the way he was staring at Billy. Billy had gotten a lot of awe since he'd been crowned. Undeserved in his opinion. There'd been fear, mistrust, and even some hate, but Billy hadn't taken any of it personally. Plus, with his mixed-race heritage and the way his family had constantly moved around when he was growing up, he'd gotten used to being looked at as a weird, possibly untrustworthy stranger. So being a human among goblins didn't feel all that different. But the big goblin with the double chin and the droopy ears looked at Billy with no emotion at all. It was as if, to him, Billy was just a thing . . . or an obstacle in his way.

So when the flabby *kijakgob* flung a blast of ice and wind his way, Billy was only half surprised. He dove behind a crate of supplies, which shattered in a flurry of snow. He was pelted by ice and wood and frozen bits of whatever was inside the crate. Realizing the crate wasn't protecting him anymore, Billy looked for more shelter. The Bat Cavern was a whirl of snow and ice and wind, punctuated by sporadic bursts of light from where Alyseer had been standing. A huge dark shape moved above him, and wind blasted down at him in pulses. It was one of the warbats, flying through the cave, attacking someone or something Billy couldn't see. The warbat's wings beat down again; the wind roared and the snow flurries cleared . . .

And Billy saw there were at least three hostile goblin wizards trying to kill him. All three wore dark-blue robes. One was the chubby *kijakgob*. He was conjuring enormous blocks of ice and flinging them through the air. One block nearly hit Hop, but the resourceful Copperplate deflected it with a barrel lid. The second attacker was female. Her dark hair was curled high in the middle and braided tight to her skull on the sides. Her ears were long and animated, flicking around as she spat out clouds of snow at the goblins coming to Billy's defense. The third enemy wizard, a sharp-eared *drogob*, had pale green skin and bright blue eyes. He summoned small, sharp icicles and flung them at Billy and his defenders with cold, methodical precision. Despite Frost and Alyseer's efforts to defend him with spells of their own, Billy found himself dodging nonstop, desperately trying to avoid being impaled by an icicle, bashed over the head with a block of ice, or frozen solid by a blast of subzero wind.

Between the thick fog, the swirling snow, and his own frantic dodging, Billy found it nearly impossible to keep track of what was happening around him in the chaos. He caught a glimpse of a taxi-bat crushed under a block of ice. He saw a Celestial get hit in the chest with a flying icicle. He spotted a roaring Leadpipe charging the pale green wizard, only to get swallowed up by a flurry of foggy snow.

Somehow Billy found his way to the fallen Celestial. He'd never learned the boy's name. He was one of Azam's friends, quiet, with long blond hair and bright eyes that were almost gold in color. By the time Billy reached him, his eyes were dull and glazed, and his hair was stained with blood. The flying icicle had pierced his heart. He was dead.

Suddenly the pudgy *kijakgob* wizard came charging at Billy out of the snow, wielding a giant ice-club in both hands.

"Die, *skerbo*!" he shouted, swinging the club at Billy's head.

Billy ducked, but the club clipped the top of his head. He felt a shock of pain, and then . . . nothing. The next few moments were blank. The next thing he knew, Billy was standing over the *kijakgob* wizard with a dagger-shaped icicle in his hand. There was blood on its tip . . . and blood seeping from several wounds on the big wizard's prone body.

Billy tried to reconstruct what had happened in the moments he'd lost. He knew he'd gotten grazed by the club. After that, though, it was all a little fuzzy. Had he really grabbed one of the icicles lying by the Celestial's dead body? Had he really leapt on the *kijakgob* and somehow knocked him to the floor? Had he really stabbed him, over and over? That would explain why Billy was standing over a dead goblin wizard with a bloody icicle in his hand. But Billy couldn't remember any of it.

Part of Billy was glad that a piece of his memory was blank. Part of him, though, was ashamed. *You should remember killing someone*, Billy thought. *It's the last moment of their life. They're not there to remember what happened, so someone should. I should.*

Billy shuddered uncontrollably. He started to sweat. His legs felt weak. Then he fell to his knees and threw up.

The instant he'd stabbed the *kijakgob* might've been lost to Billy, but the moments thereafter seemed to stretch into eternity. Billy emptied his stomach again and again as the ice wind swirled around him. The bile burned his throat. Tears ran down his face. He'd killed someone. It may've been self-defense, but telling himself that wouldn't bring the *kijakgob* back to life. Billy wished he could take it all back, but he couldn't.

Billy curled up into a ball. He knew he should be fighting or running, anything to survive the battle, but he couldn't move. His head ached, his muscles were shaking, and his gut was churning. Plus, there was a part of him that wasn't sure he deserved to survive. He'd taken a life. Maybe it was only fair that he should die too.

Consumed by his own regret, Billy barely noticed as the wind died down, the snow stopped blowing, and the fog began to lift.

He barely noticed anything until Hop gently shook his shoulder.

"You alive?" Hop asked.

"Yeah," Billy answered. "I think so."

"*Yob'rikit*," Hop said. "I were worried there for a thump."

Billy sat up and looked around. The Bat Cavern was a mess. Most of the supply crates had been shattered, and there were frozen chunks of food and camping supplies everywhere. Several goblins had been injured, and their moans of pain echoed through the confined space. Then there were the bodies. There were three corpses on the ground. The dead Celestial boy had been blasted by more snow and ice since his death. A thin coating of frost covered his body, mostly white but with speckles of red. The big *kijakgob* wizard lay in the middle of a pool of frozen blood. Not far from him, a taxi-bat lay sprawled in the middle of the chamber, its head smashed in by ice. For some reason, it was the taxi-bat that made Billy want to puke again. It couldn't have possibly understood what was happening in the cavern. It was just an innocent creature that had died for nothing.

Billy fought back his nausea and got to his feet. Kings shouldn't vomit. It wasn't kingly.

"We won?" Billy asked.

"Suppose you can say so," Hop said. "Them other two wizards runned for it once their friend died. That were brave work. Fighting the big wizard by yourself. I were afeared you would *nai* survive. But you killed him with your bare hands and stopped the attack. More would have died if you *nai* doed what you doed. You know that, *zaj*?"

Billy swallowed. He didn't know if Hop believed what he said or if he was just trying to make Billy feel better, but it didn't matter. Billy would never feel good about what he'd done. Still, he knew he needed to look strong, if only for the sake of the goblins. They'd put all their hope in him. If he looked like a weak, scared little boy, their hope would melt away, just like the ice and snow that had filled the Bat Cavern only minutes ago and was now quickly turning to water.

"We need to clean all this up and get the bats loaded," Billy said in what he hoped was a commanding voice. "Try to figure out where this wizard's two friends went."

"*Zaj*, Your Majesty," Hop said, throwing a goblin salute and rushing to organize his bat-riders into clean-up and supply teams. Kurt joined in, and soon the Bat Cavern was bustling with activity as the loading of the expedition's bats began again in earnest.

Not everyone was working, though. Azam, Alyseer, and the other Celestials had gathered around their dead friend. There were tears in their eyes, and they were singing, softly, some kind of Hanorian hymn:

> *Now at last his pain has left him*
> *Like chaff from grain, it drops away*
> *And Father Sun shines upon him*
> *As Mother Night welcomes him home*
> *And when his soul is weighed and judged*
> *His loved ones know it will balance*
> *For balanced was the path he danced*
> *And good deeds are the gift he left the world*

Billy joined them. "I'm sorry," Billy said quietly. "He died because of me. I . . . I didn't even know his name."

But before the Celestials could tell Billy the name of their lost friend, a female Copperplate ran into the Bat Cavern. "*Skerboen*! There are *skerboen* here."

Billy winced at the goblin's use of the derogatory name for humans. Especially now. Hop objected even before he could.

"Do *nai* call them that," Hop snapped. "Them are our friends."

The Copperplate's eyes darted to Billy and the Celestials. "I *nai* meaned them," she said, looking panicked. "It're the Hanorian Army. They're in the city!"

This is a suicide mission, all right, Cyreth thought as his Lion Guards formed ranks in the face of growing goblin opposition.

Cyreth knew he and the Lion Guards were in for it from the moment Lord Marshal Jiyal laid out his plan. Hanorian scouts had identified a vulnerable watchtower with a tunnel beneath it leading into Monster Mountain. Jiyal ordered Cyreth and his soldiers to take the tower, slip into the goblin city, and open its main gate for the Army of Light. The Lord Marshal had personally assigned twenty Lion Guards to the mission along with Cyreth. The chosen guards included Ysalion, Harfin, and Speryco, plus several others Cyreth thought might be Celestials. Jiyal's intentions were obvious. Either Cyreth and his fellow Celestials would succeed and open the way for victory, or the Army of Light would be free of twenty or so heretics. Or both.

The first part of the plan had gone well. Cyreth and his companions had approached the tower under the cover of a cloaking spell woven by Hanorian war wizards. Another wizard, traveling with the group, blasted a hole in the tower wall. The Lion Guards poured in, cutting down the tower's goblin defenders before they even knew what was happening.

Then the wizard left. He'd done his part. Sneaking down tunnels into a hostile goblin city wasn't for him.

The journey down the tunnel was long and nerve-wracking. The passageway twisted and turned, its well-worn stone floor was slick and slippery underfoot, and the only light came from the feeble glow of bioluminescent mushrooms. Cyreth feared they'd be discovered at any moment.

Somehow, though, they'd reached the end of the tunnel, where it joined a major thoroughfare. According to human merchants who'd done business inside Kiranok before the war, the goblins called the passageway Seventurns. Luckily, as best anyone could tell, the tower tunnel entered Seventurns much closer to the main gate than the center of the city. Cyreth led his Lion Guards to the right, uphill toward the gate, which was theoretically only two turns away.

The Lion Guards made it only a few dozen yards up Seventurns when things went wrong.

Someone had built a wall across the passageway. It was brand new, with fresh-cut stones and mortar that didn't look completely dry. It was about seven feet high, though it looked like it was still under construction and might end up much higher, maybe even all the way to the roof of the passageway. There was a small gate in the wall, and ramparts and ladders behind it for use by the construction workers. Several dozen goblin soldiers guarded the new construction.

Luckily for Cyreth and his Lion Guards, the goblin sentries were facing away from them, up Seventurns, toward the main gate. They weren't the most polished soldiers Cyreth had ever seen, either. Most of them were extremely young, with the characteristic high-pointed ears of goblins still in their adolescence. They didn't look particularly alert. Some were playing dice; several others were eating. None of them saw the Hanorians.

Cyreth had learned the hard way how keen goblin hearing was, so he didn't say a word to his troops. Instead, he raised his hand and brought it down sharply. It was the signal to charge.

The Lion Guards ran full bore at the unprepared goblins. Keeping their spacing tight and their pace quick but even, they hit the goblins like a thunderbolt. Cyreth didn't want them to get bogged down in a real fight, though. Following his orders, the Lion Guards cut down the handful of young goblins who dared to try to stop them, then swarmed up the ladders and over the wall.

When he landed on the other side, Cyreth noticed his sword was wet with goblin blood. He wasn't even sure how it had gotten that way. He took quick stock of his troop.

They were missing someone.

"Harfin?" Cyreth asked.

Bytha, a burly female guard, shook her head grimly. Harfin's lucky coin hadn't done him any good. He hadn't made it over the wall.

They'd have to mourn Harfin later, though. The Lion Guards still weren't at the main gate. Cyreth could hear the goblin soldiers on the other side of the wall gathering themselves. A sergeant was barking at them, rallying his troops. They would counterattack soon.

On a signal from Cyreth, the Lion Guards charged up the passageway, even as the surviving goblin sentries began climbing the wall themselves, ready to fight.

As they sprinted up Seventurns, the Lion Guards soon found themselves charging another wall, just a hundred yards or so short of the main gate. This one was much higher and much better guarded. Warned by the howling mob of goblins pursuing the Lion Guards, the goblins at the wall ahead prepared to meet their charge. The goblins behind them were closing fast. Cyreth barked a sharp command, and the Lion Guards closed ranks, preparing for a real fight.

"Shields high, blades free," Cyreth said, keeping his voice calm and confident. "Alert, alive, together. Make them work for it."

Shouting their inhuman war cries, the goblins closed in on the Lion Guards from all sides, like a noose tightening around a neck.

Kurt gripped the passenger platform of the taxi-bat as it sped through the tight tunnel. It twisted and turned violently as it navigated the passageway, reminding him uncomfortably of a roller coaster ride.

Kurt hated roller coasters. It wasn't that he didn't like to go fast. He loved speeding in his car, or sprinting up the field with the ball in his hands and nothing but green grass and the goal line ahead. Except in those cases, he was in control. Being on a roller coaster meant someone else was in control, an absentminded high school dropout operating the controls of a machine that might fail at any moment. If Kurt messed up and hurt himself, that was one thing, but if he trusted his fate to someone else and they messed up? That was unthinkable.

So Kurt really didn't like clinging to the back of a taxi-bat as it flew far too fast through a tunnel barely wide enough to fit its wings. The hooting and hollering of the goblins riding alongside him didn't make him feel any better.

This is worse than a roller coaster, Kurt thought. *A roller coaster would be over by now.*

Kurt felt his gorge rising as the bat whipped through another seemingly impossible high-speed turn.

Don't throw up, he thought desperately. Not only would throwing up be gross and embarrassing, Kurt was afraid if he lost control of his gut, he might also lose his grip. And then he'd be worse than embarrassed. He'd be dead. *Don't throw up. Don't throw up.*

Kurt found himself thinking of Billy, who'd lost his own breakfast just minutes earlier. Billy hadn't hurled because he was scared or motion sick. He'd done it because he'd killed a goblin. Kurt couldn't imagine how that must feel.

A life is . . . everything, he thought. *Take away a life, and there's no way to make up for it. Nothing you can do to fix it. Killing someone must be the worst feeling ever. Way worse than being on the back of this stupid bat.*

Remembering Billy's plight put things in perspective. It reminded Kurt why he was riding the bat in the first place. Humans were coming to kill every goblin in Kiranok. They had to stop them. Because if killing one goblin, even in self-defense, was a crippling, gut-wrenching nightmare, then imagine letting the humans kill all the goblins. Forever.

Finally, the taxi-bat reached Seventurns. The main thoroughfare leading into Kiranok was wide and tall. The bat no longer had to constantly twist and turn to avoid a collision. Kurt could breathe again. Behind him, he saw a half dozen more bats emerge onto Seventurns, all loaded down with goblins and Celestials. Billy was on the bat right behind him, along with Hop. After everything the scrawny, mixed-up kid had been through, he was still trying to live up to his role as the goblin's chosen savior. If he could manage that, then Kurt could be at least as brave. Right?

The taxi-bat flew over a wall then abruptly flared its wings and landed. Kurt lost his grip and spilled to the hard stone floor of Seventurns. It hurt, but he was used to taking hits and playing through pain. He scrambled to his feet as quickly as he could, drew the sword that Hop had given him, and tried to get his bearings.

That's when he noticed that his clothing was stained red from where he'd hit the ground.

The stone floor of Seventurns was covered in blood.

"Move, you *nokbonch*!"

Hop pushed past Kurt. The human teen might be

strong and athletic, but he didn't have much experience in combat. He'd frozen at the sight of the wounded and the dead scattered about Seventurns. Hop had experienced more than his fair share of battles, so the sight of blood didn't overwhelm him anymore.

Still, Hop preferred to look at battles over his shoulder while running for his life. The problem was, he was a general now. Generals couldn't run. So despite his every instinct, he charged into the fight.

The human invaders had fought their way past two of Billy's new walls and reached the Great Gate, where they were battling the last stubborn goblin defenders. They'd left a trail of dead and wounded goblins in their wake. Only a handful of the humans had fallen, despite being outnumbered ten to one. Hop knew the goblins didn't have many experienced soldiers left. Most of their best had died during Sawtooth's disastrous war. The Hanorians, on the other hand, were obviously elite soldiers, well-trained, well-equipped, and expertly led. They wore lion-shaped helmets and gold-washed chain mail, but despite their ostentatious armor, they fought with discipline and courage.

As Hop closed the gap between him and the invaders, he watched in dismay as they cut down the last of the guards at Great Gate and stormed the gatehouse. It wasn't hard to guess their goal. They were going to open Kiranok's massive twin iron gates. The unimaginably heavy slabs of iron could be moved only by special levers and chains built into the gatehouse. As Hop reached the gatehouse door, the gates began to creak open. He knew that meant that somewhere inside, the humans were already turning the wheels and pulling the lines. It would take time, but slowly, inexorably, the gates were opening.

Through the crack between the gates, Hop spotted a

sea of waiting human soldiers. There were thousands of them, just waiting for the gates to swing wide enough to charge in all at once. He knew if that happened, Kiranok was doomed.

Hop had to stop the gates from opening or, better yet, crank them back shut. To do that he'd have to get inside the gatehouse and take out the humans operating the controls. Unfortunately, there was a human standing in the gatehouse doorway ready to defend it with his life. The human was a bit taller than average with light-brown skin and eyes almost amber in color. Like Hop, he bore the telltale scars of battle, including a long, crooked scar above one eye and a bent nose that looked like it had been broken more than once. Hop knew the gold sash across the man's chest marked him as a captain, a midlevel officer. He looked like a formidable opponent. Beating him was the only way to stop the gates from opening, though.

Nai *helping it*, Hop thought.

He pointed his spear at the human captain. "He surrender and we let he and men walk away," Hop said in what he hoped was intelligible *Hanoryabber*.

The human looked surprised. Humans always looked surprised when Hop spoke their language. He'd picked it up as a caravan guard in his youth. It came in handy from time to time. Maybe this would be one of those times.

"Thank you for the offer, but I'm afraid I can't accept," the Hanorian captain replied, sounding perfectly calm and reasonable, as if they were discussing a simple business transaction. "If I surrender to you, my own leaders would execute me. And my soldiers."

Hop imagined he and the human captain weren't all that different. They were just two soldiers doing their best to serve their leaders and protect their comrades.

Hop imagined he and the human might get along well under different circumstances. Unfortunately, he could hear the gears moving in the gatehouse as the Great Gate slowly creaked open. Right now, the human was a threat to every goblin in Kiranok. If he wouldn't surrender, Hop had only one other course of action open to him.

"Then I kill all," Hop said, knowing the *Hanoryabber* wasn't quite right but confident the human would get the gist of it.

"So be it," the human captain replied, spinning to one side and cutting at Hop with his sword. Hop narrowly avoided the sword, then pulled back his spear, using the blades at the base of his spearhead to slash the man's side. The human's chain mail blocked most of Hop's unexpected attack, but it still made the Hanorian wince in pain.

Hop felt bad about that, but he quickly suppressed the feeling. For his people to live, this human had to die. Besides, it was just as likely that when this was over Hop would be dead, and the human would be the one feeling bad. Either way, their fates were tangled now. And the only way to untangle those threads was for one of them to die.

To Hop's surprise, the human spun and smashed his shield into Hop's face. Pain shot through his entire body. For a moment, Hop thought he might fall to the ground.

Fall and you're dead, he told himself.

Hop recovered, then reversed his spear with a spin of his own and smashed the butt end into the side of the human's lion helmet.

All in all, if it're a choice between death and regrets, I prefer regrets.

Cyreth could tell the one-eared goblin with the spear knew his business. He wasn't one of the raw recruits the

Lion Guards had faced until now. This goblin was a savvy fighter, skilled and tricky, and determined to stop Cyreth and his men from opening the gate. Cyreth couldn't blame him. In the event the Lion Guards actually succeeded in their mission, the Hanorians would sweep into Monster Mountain and kill every living thing inside.

Cyreth was certain he'd fight every bit as hard as the one-eared goblin if their positions were reversed. In a way, the goblin probably had the more righteous cause. At that moment, though, Cyreth didn't care about right and wrong. All he wanted was to live, and to make sure the remaining Lion Guards lived right along with him. They'd already lost at least five members of their band. Several more were injured, including Ysalion, the female Lion Guard who loved to balance atop the camp palisades. She'd suffered a nasty thigh wound during the battle at the gatehouse. She'd made it inside, but only because two other guards had carried her. Her leg was soaked with blood. Cyreth knew she'd only survive if he got her to a lightworker soon. And to do that he'd have to open the gates and unleash the Army of Light on the goblin city.

The one-eared goblin nearly gutted him with a tricky combination attack. Cyreth barely got his shield in the way in time.

"You tire," the goblin said in his thickly accented Hanorian. "You already fight long. I fresh."

The goblin was right. Cyreth was getting short of breath. The jerkin under his chain mail was soaked with sweat. His arms ached from swinging his sword and raising his shield. He fell back a few steps, farther into the gatehouse. The one-eared goblin followed, pressing his attack, lunging again. This time, Cyreth's parry came too late. The tip of the goblin's spear skittered off the edge of

Cyreth's shield and jabbed into his lion helm, hitting him less than two fingers' widths from his left eye. The power of the blow tore his helmet off, and the spear's edge cut a painful, bloody furrow down the side of Cyreth's head.

But the goblin wasn't done. He turned the stab into a backswing, trying to cut Cyreth's throat with the jagged edge of his spear blade. Cyreth ducked just in time, and the spear whooshed over his head. The Lion Guard saw an opening in the goblin's defense, just for an instant, but he was too tired and slow. The goblin easily avoided his belated thrust, then reset his stance, pointing his spear at Cyreth's now-unprotected head.

Cyreth knew he was overmatched. The next time he missed a parry, the goblin's spear would catch him in the head or the neck and it would be all over. Cyreth was going to lose.

Then he heard a roar. A thousand human voices shouting in triumph. The one-eared goblin heard it too. He retreated back, out of the gatehouse, a look of dread on his dark, pointed face. Cyreth used the opening to counterattack, driving the goblin even farther back, far enough that he himself could emerge from the gatehouse door and see what had happened.

The gates were open.

The Army of Light was charging into Mother Mountain. Cyreth and the remaining Lion Guards were saved.

And the goblins had lost. The slaughter was about to begin.

CHAPTER SIX
The Dirty Work

Hop had told Billy to hang back, and then he'd shoved past Kurt, sprinted to the gatehouse, and begun his duel with the human in the lion helmet. Still reeling from killing the *kijakgob* wizard in the Bat Cavern, Billy had done as he'd been told, for once. Guarded by Leadpipe, he stayed back by the final wall he'd ordered built. Unfortunately, the walls had done no good at all. The small band of Hanorian attackers had somehow gotten behind them, overwhelmed their inexperienced defenders, and reached the gatehouse. Now they were trying to open Kiranok's main gates. Billy had no doubt countless more human soldiers were waiting just outside, enough to kill every goblin in Kiranok.

Despite everything that had gone wrong, though, Billy knew his walls might still be the key to saving the goblins and their city. If he could get enough goblins to defend them, they might be able to hold off the humans.

"Kurt!" Billy called out.

The quarterback turned toward him and Leadpipe. "What do you need?"

Billy was surprised Kurt sounded so cooperative. Usually he gave Billy a ton of attitude. At the moment, though, he seemed like he really wanted to help.

"I need you and Leadpipe to organize the defenses. Get the surviving goblins back on the walls. Send runners for reinforcements. Quick."

Kurt ran off immediately and started shouting orders at the goblins. He was good at shouting. Billy supposed that quarterbacks got lots of practice telling people what to do.

Leadpipe didn't move. "I're gonna stay here and watch over you," the big goblin said in his slow, deep voice.

Billy didn't have time to argue. Instead he spotted Frost, farther down the wall, building it up with ice.

"Frost, don't worry about the wall," Billy shouted. "Can you freeze the gates shut?"

Frost looked over at Kiranok's towering main gates. They'd already cracked open. Billy could see a huge milling crowd of human soldiers on the other side. They'd be in soon.

"Too late," Frost said grimly. "I'll try to slow them down."

Frost began conjuring a field of icicles in front of the final wall, like daggers planted in the stone floor of Seventurns, blades up. It looked impressive and deadly, but Billy didn't think it would be enough.

"I can stop them from getting in," Billy heard a familiar voice say.

Billy turned and found Lexi standing behind him. She

was wearing a *svagob* nightdress, as if she'd just gotten out of bed. There were dark circles under her eyes, her hair was a mess, and her skin was slick with sweat. She looked exhausted.

"How'd you get here?" Billy asked. "They just sounded the alarm a minute ago."

"I flew," Lexi said, as if it were the most normal thing in the world.

"You used all that energy to get here, and now you want to use even more to stop the humans?"

Lexi stood a little straighter, looking determined. "Isn't that why we came here? To save the goblins? You as their king, me as a wizard, and Kurt as . . . I don't know what."

"You can't kill them all," Billy said, trying to come up with a plan that didn't involve Lexi charging the enemy and burning herself out entirely.

"Watch me," Lexi replied, fighting past her fatigue with her usual determination.

Billy thought about the *kijakgob* wizard, bleeding to death after he had stabbed him. Lexi was volunteering to kill countless humans, to take responsibility for more deaths than Billy could imagine.

"It's too much," Billy said quietly. "Too much power, too much responsibility. I can't let you do it."

"You can't stop me," Lexi said, stronger than before. "No one can stop me."

"That're true," Frost said, joining them. "*Nai* one can stop a wizard as powerful as you from doing whatever she want. So it're *maja* important that you stop yourself."

"It won't work anyway," Billy said. "It'd take a lot more wizards than just the two of you to hold off an entire army."

Billy racked his brain. There had to be a better way.

And then it came to him. "I think I have a plan."

Before Billy could explain himself though, a hot wind blasted down Seventurns and the Great Gate swung open wide. A wave of Hanorian soldiers dashed inside Kiranok and assembled into a battle line. Billy saw Hop running for all he was worth from the gatehouse as a swarm of human javelins clattered to the stones just behind him. Billy looked back to the wall, where Kurt was rallying a few dozen goblin soldiers, not nearly enough to defend the walls against the Army of Light.

"Frost," Billy shouted. "I need you to freeze the ceiling of Seventurns. Right there!" He pointed to a spot a little in front of them and high above their heads.

"Freezing will *nai* do anything to all that stone," Frost said glumly.

"Just do it. Now!" The humans were advancing, a wall of shields and swords. "Before it's too late."

To Billy's relief, Frost focused, and ice began to build on the tunnel ceiling.

Billy turned to Lexi. "Lexi, as soon as the rock is frozen solid, I want to you heat it back up. As fast as you can."

Billy was thinking of a mistake he'd made in the kitchen once, when he and his family were living in Georgia. His mother had bought a pizza stone, a large stone disk for making fresh pizza in the oven. One cold winter day after school, when his father and mother were both working late, Billy had decided to make pizza for himself. He'd preheated the oven while he readied the ingredients, assembled the pizza, then put the pizza stone in the hot oven . . . and it snapped in half. His father later explained that the stone had suffered something called "thermal shock." Take a cold stone and heat it quickly, and it would crack from the shock of the rapid heating.

The humans were almost upon them. Billy hoped this worked. If it didn't, the consequences would be infinitely worse than the mild scolding he'd gotten from his parents for breaking the pizza stone.

"Now!" he shouted.

Lexi roared, sounding like a thousand lions giving it their all. A huge blast of fire shot from her mouth and torched the roof of Seventurns. The Hanorian soldiers froze in fear at the fiery roar. There was a huge cracking sound . . .

And it started to rain rocks.

In Cyreth's experience, there was a point in every battle when he could tell which way it would break. Would he and his men win the day or be forced to retreat? He thought he'd seen that point. He'd held off the one-eared goblin. The gates had swung open and the Army of Light had poured into Monster Mountain. At that moment, as far as Cyreth could tell, not only had the battle turned the Hanorians' way, so had the entire war. The humans had won. The goblins would never march into the Uplands again. They'd be gone. Forever.

Then the roof fell in on the Army of Light.

It was just pebbles at first, raining down from the high ceiling of the massive tunnel leading into the goblin city. They pelted Cyreth's unprotected head, stinging like bees. As Cyreth retrieved his lion helm from the gatehouse, the first fist-sized rocks began to fall, bringing down Hanorian soldiers with cracked skulls and broken bones, halting the advance of the Army of Light.

"Stay inside!" Cyreth shouted to his Lion Guards as they clambered down the gatehouse stairs after success-fully opening the main gates.

Suddenly, a huge boom shook the gatehouse as a massive boulder smashed through the roof, crushing the stairway and killing the last Lion Guard in line. Cyreth wasn't even sure who it was. All he'd seen before the boulder came down were the man's legs. Now he couldn't see him at all. The gatehouse shook from successive boulder hits, groaning and shuddering like a dying animal. Cyreth could tell it was on the verge of complete collapse.

"Night and Day!" Cyreth swore. "Get out!"

Cyreth stepped aside and shoved one Lion Guard after another out of the gatehouse. Once the last Lion Guard was out, Cyreth followed them into Seventurns. Huge stones were coming down now. A massive sheet of rock fell just in front of Cyreth, smashing a group of Hanorian soldiers like ants.

In the distance, Cyreth heard an officer yelling, "Charge!"

Darkness take him, Cyreth thought. *Light burn his suicidal orders.*

"Run!" Cyreth shouted to anyone who could hear him. "Get out of the mountain while you still can!"

Dirt and rocks fell down all around him. Blinded by the dirt and battered by the stones, Cyreth staggered toward what he hoped were the main gates of the goblin city. Night and Day willing, he'd find his way outside to safety and live another day. *Unless Night and Day are on the goblins' side. Then there will be no tomorrow.*

Cyreth flailed forward, praying that at least this once, the Divine Balance would smile upon him.

Lexi closed her eyes, slid into the warm water, and tried to forget the worst parts of the past few days and focus on what had gone right.

She'd made it in and out of the Hanorian camp alive.

She'd survived a magical duel with the Hanorians' most powerful wizard. She'd pulled a shooting star from the sky that might actually save Kiranok. Then to top it all off, she and Frost had stopped a full-scale assault on the city. She'd even managed to do it all without going mad. She was a hero. A superhero, even.

She had every reason to be proud of herself. Mostly, though, she was just tired. And she kept wondering how many people she'd killed.

"Lexi, I think the water is hot enough," she heard Billy say.

Lexi opened her eyes and looked over at Billy on the other side of the pool. After the battle, Frost had suggested they come to Nokala's Pools, a series of caves containing natural hot springs that served as public baths for Kiranok. The little wizard worried that the battle at Seventurns had strained Lexi to the breaking point. Plus, Frost was exhausted himself. "We need a good soak," he'd said. For Lexi and Billy, it'd sounded like a welcome break. Leadpipe had insisted on coming along, to watch over Billy. Hop and Kurt had been invited too, but they'd begged off. They needed to return to the Bat Cavern to finish preparations for their expedition. Lexi, Billy, Frost, and Leadpipe soon found themselves wearing the goblin equivalents of swimsuits and sitting in a pool of warm, volcanic water, trying to soak away their various aches and pains.

But the water wasn't just warm anymore. It was getting hot. Lexi could see beads of sweat on Billy's forehead, and the water between them was steaming.

"That're you making the water steam, *derijinta*," Leadpipe rumbled. He was sitting cross-legged in the middle of the pool, at the deepest part, but the water still barely reached his waist.

Lexi realized the water around her was boiling. *It's*

because I was thinking about all those Hanorian soldiers, she realized. *All those faces.*

"Sorry," she said, trying to calm herself and cool the water.

"It're *nai* surprising after all you've been through," Leadpipe said, comforting. He turned to his brother. "Frost, fix it."

Frost was standing in the shallows. He was neck deep. "It're . . ."

"Do *nai* say it're a misuse of magic," Leadpipe cut him off. "I can *nai* relax if the water are too hot. So cool it down."

Frost relented. "I're *maja* too tired to fight with you."

Frost concentrated, and a cool breeze shot through the chamber. Snow fell on the hot pool. In a few seconds, the water was comfortable again. Not only that, as the breeze swirled around Lexi's head, she felt herself relax. She wasn't sure if Frost was intentionally casting some kind of spell to calm her down or if it was just the relief of the cold air. Either way, she felt better. She blinked away snow from her eyelashes, then dunked under the water. She stayed under for a long moment, enjoying the splashy silence. Finally, she bobbed back up.

"That's perfect, Frost. Thank you," she said.

"It're *nai* burden," Frost said. Still, his expression was troubled. Lexi could tell there was something on his mind.

"But?" Lexi asked. When Frost didn't answer right away, Lexi pressed. "I know you want to lecture me about magic again. So go ahead. Tell me how I'm being reckless. That I should be more careful. I mean, I get it. Next time Kiranok needs saving, I'll let someone else do it."

Lexi didn't intend to sound so angry, but as usual, her mouth ran away from her.

"I didn't mean that," she corrected herself. "It was

sarcasm. All of it. That's a bad habit of mine. I say the opposite of what I mean. The truth is . . . I appreciate how much you worry about me. I do. But I'm not going to let you and your people die. When I have to, I'm going to do everything I can to save innocent lives. No matter what it does to me."

The words hung there a moment, like steam, until Frost finally replied.

"*Zajnai* I were going to caution you again," Frost admitted, "but that're cause if I worked half the magic you doed over the past moon, I *nai* think I could have stayed sane. Only you have. You're a better wizard than me, to tell it plain. You may *nai* have the training or the discipline, but you have the will, and you resist the madness *maja* better than I could . . . better than any wizard I ever knowed. So I're scared for you sometimes. *Naizaj* I're even a little scared *of* you. Truth are, though, if *nai* for you, we'd all be dead. So *zajnai* it're time I admit that you're a better judge of what you can and can *nai* do than I will ever be."

Lexi took in what Frost was saying. She couldn't remember the last time an adult had trusted her. It sure didn't feel like her parents ever had.

"Thank you, Frost," Lexi said. "That means a lot."

"What Frost said goes for me too," Billy said. "The goblins may call me their king, but without you, I never would've gotten crowned. I definitely wouldn't be able to save Kiranok."

Lexi couldn't help but smile. Billy could be a bit awkward sometimes, but his heart was always in the right place. His trust meant more to her than she wanted to admit.

"It's going to take all of us working together," Lexi said. "But I know we can do it."

"*Chom-chom*," Leadpipe rumbled in agreement.

"Now that that're settled, how about everybody shut your chewers and let me soak."

No one wanted to argue with that. Billy closed his eyes and leaned back into the water. Frost stretched out and floated on his back. Leadpipe lay flat in the pool, slipping his considerable mass under the water until only his long nose stuck out. For a moment, Lexi was actually able to enjoy the warmth and the quiet. She felt calm, safe, and capable, basking in her friends' trust as much as the hot spring.

Then the steam dissipated and the water went still for a moment, and she caught a glimpse of her own reflection in the pool.

Her reflection was mocking, snarling. It was Lexi at her worst. Like when she got so mad at her mom in particular and the world in general that she wanted to break every mirror in the house, smash her furniture, and set it all on fire.

Burn it all, her reflection seemed to say. *Burn it all*.

Snap woke to Grinner's smiling face. She shuddered, despite herself. His eyes were cold and emotionless, his smile as humorless as any she'd ever seen.

"What're you grinning at?" she said, sitting up and scooting back from him, trying to put some space between herself and his horrible smile.

She and Grinner had returned to the Blue Chambers after their failed attack. They'd moved through the abandoned school, down into the subbasements, then through a small hole in the wall of a storage room, through a claustrophobic tunnel, and into Grinner's secret room. The small cages lining the walls were mostly empty, but a few half-forgotten mice and rats remained trapped inside. They scurried and chittered when Snap backed up into the cages with a clatter.

"That're what I're asking myself," Grinner said, his expression unchanging. "Are I looking at a wizard what're going to free her fellow goblins? Or a broken thing with no strength left? Acause if you still have fight in you, I can help with that. And if you do *nai*, well, I can end your pain, make you sleep, long and cold and forever. What kind of help do you want, Coldsnap? What can Grinner do for you now?"

Snap realized why Grinner's expression was so disturbing. He was looking at her the same way he looked at his mice. He was thinking about *experimenting* on her.

"I're *nai* broken," she said, rising to her feet.

"Are you *nai*?" Grinner asked. "You look all bits and pieces to me."

"I were exhausted from all the magic I worked," Snap replied, trying to keep the fear from her expression. "I needed rest, to put myself back together."

"Are you? Together?"

At that moment, out of the corner of her eye, Snap caught a glimpse of the bracelet Icewall had bought for her, dangling from her wrist. She felt drained, half asleep . . . but that didn't mean she was ready to join Icewall in the grave.

"I are *nai* ready to sleep forever, if that're what you're asking," Snap said, trying to convince herself and Grinner both. "Icewall died acause he believed in our mission. We give up now, we betray him, make his sacrifice into *drak*. I're *nai* going to do that. I're going to see things through."

"Icewall were fat and weak and looking at you maked him stupid," Grinner said, not a hint of sympathy in his voice.

"And you love death more than you love life," Snap said with a strength she didn't know she had. "But when a *gob* are making breakfast, she can only cook with the ingredients what're in her kitchen. You're foul, but you're all I have."

Snap stepped toward Grinner, meeting him eye to eye. "Now, are you with me?" she said. "Or should I make you sleep? Long and cold and forever?"

"With an invitation like that, how could I say *nai*?" Grinner said. "I're with you."

Then he grinned again.

Snap finally realized what was so unnerving about Grinner's smile. Grinner didn't smile like a living thing. The muscles of his mouth didn't curl up. The upper part of his face didn't move at all. Instead, he just pulled back his lips and bared his teeth. He smiled like a skull.

"I wish I could go with you," Billy said to Kurt.

"I wish you could go *instead* of me," Kurt said. He'd meant that to sound like a joke, but when it came out, it was a little more honest than he'd intended.

The bats were finally ready. Billy, Lexi, Frost, and Leadpipe had come to the Bat Cavern to see Hop and Kurt off. The expedition was set to depart at any moment. And though Kurt didn't want to admit it, the thought of flying on bat-back into an unknown wilderness with only goblins and a few human heretics for company had him on edge.

"I'm sorry I got you into this," Billy said.

Kurt hated it when people apologized to him. An apology implied someone had hurt Kurt in some way. Kurt liked to believe no one could hurt him worse than he could hurt them back. Which meant apologies were a stupid waste of time. Billy's apology just served to remind him of a time, not too long ago, when Billy had been utterly terrified of him. He kind of missed that.

Still, he'd sort of grown to like Billy. Not that he'd ever admit it out loud. More importantly, he felt sorry for the kid. After all, Billy had been saddled with a huge burden when he'd been crowned Goblin King. Back when Kurt had thought the crown belonged to him, he hadn't felt much responsibility to save the goblins. He just figured it'd be fun to be a king. Billy took the job seriously, though. He was willing to do whatever it took to protect his "royal subjects," even if it ended up killing him. Kurt had never felt that way about anything in his life. All he'd ever wanted was to be a star, to have everyone cheer for him. He'd never really thought about the people doing the cheering and what he might owe them.

"You don't have to apologize," Kurt said. "You're a king."

"If everyone keeps saying that, maybe someday I'll actually believe it," Billy said.

Kurt could tell Billy was struggling. Not that he blamed him. Being the focus of everyone's attention could be hard. Even for someone with all the self-confidence in the world. Even for Kurt.

"It's okay to doubt yourself," he said. "The trick is not to show it. No one wants a quarterback who freaks out under pressure. So never let them see you worry. Even when a two-hundred-and-fifty-pound linebacker is trying to kill you, you gotta look like you don't have a care in the world."

Kurt could see Billy try to stand a little straighter, to keep the panic off his face.

"That's better," Kurt said. "As for me and Hop, don't feel guilty. In this game, you're the quarterback. You stay in the pocket and control the game. Me and Hop are like wide receivers. We're the ones who have to run downfield and catch the ball. We all have to play our parts if we want to win."

"I guess that makes sense," Billy said. "Just try not to get injured."

"I'll do my best."

Kurt slapped Billy on the shoulder and climbed aboard a taxi-bat, joining Azam and the goblin bat-handler.

Another Celestial, a younger boy named Lanath, joined them. Kurt looked around the cavern. He could see Hop on the lead bat with Alyseer and two other goblins. The last few stragglers climbed aboard the other bats. All four bats were now fully loaded with a mix of goblins and Celestials. They were ready to go.

"We doing this?" he shouted over to Hop.

"We can only die once," the goblin answered. Then he stood up on the back of his taxi-bat and called out to the other riders, "*Ahka*, you heroes. Time to fly!"

Hop's bat-handler whistled a command. In response, his taxi-bat began flapping its wings. It lifted off the cavern floor and flew into the long tunnel that led out of the cavern and into the wilderness beyond. More whistles filled the cavern, and the other bats took off, one by one, until Kurt's bat—the last in line—flitted forward toward the exit.

No turning back now, he thought. *It's game time.*

Billy watched the bats fly single file into the tunnel that led out of Mother Mountain. He, Lexi, Frost, and Leadpipe followed them up the tunnel. He wanted to watch them as long as he could. Everything was riding on Kurt and Hop's expedition. And getting the Fallen Star wouldn't be easy. Their enemies were almost certainly after it, too, with their huge army and their countless wizards. For the goblins to have a chance, everything had to go just right . . .

Instead, everything went very, very wrong.

The explosions started seconds after the last bat flew out of the tunnel. Flames and screams filled the air. Billy realized, too late, that there must've been human wizards lying in wait outside the tunnel. He watched in shock as a taxi-bat caught fire and fell out of the sky. Hop and Kurt's mission had failed before it had even begun.

CHAPTER SEVEN
The Only Hero They Had

The fire came from nowhere. One second, Hop, Snails, Alyseer, and Rounder, their bat-handler, were flying out of the tunnel on the back of Rounder's bat. The next, there were flames everywhere and Hop was falling.

The tunnel from the Bat Cavern opened up onto a sheer cliff face thousands of feet above the ground. So it was a very long fall indeed.

This're it, Hop thought as the trees and rocks rushed up to meet him. *This're how I die.*

Then he felt a hot wind blowing from beneath him. He was slowing down. He looked around. Alyseer, the young human lightworker, was hovering nearby. Snails was a dozen yards away, likewise floating in the air, looking confused and a little panicky. Still, it looked like Alyseer had saved them all.

Hop flicked his vision to redsight, searching for the source of the attack. With his night vision, he spotted the glowing outlines of three humans on the slopes of Mother Mountain. A moment later, one of the human-shaped glows flared bigger and brighter. Almost too late, Hop realized what he was seeing. The glow was a human wizard . . . and he or she was conjuring fire.

"Look out!" Hop shouted to Alyseer. "They're magicking at us again!"

Alyseer looked back at the mountain, toward the growing fire.

The bottom dropped out of Hop's world. He was falling again, plummeting toward the ground, faster and faster. Below, in the moonlight, he could see the trees getting closer. There was a scattering of snow on the ground below but not enough to cushion his fall.

Hop wondered if he should try to land head first, which would probably kill him instantly, or feet first, which would break every bone in his body but might leave him alive for a few agonizing extra minutes.

Feet first, he thought to himself. *Those minutes will probably be horrible, but they'll be mine.*

Hop did his best to get his feet pointed down, then tried to forget about the ground rushing at him. With the wind whipping all around him, if Hop closed his eyes, he could almost believe he was flying.

We're all flying toward death every heartbeat, Hop thought. *Might as well enjoy the breeze.*

Suddenly a gust of wind blasted him sideways. Tree branches whipped him across the face. Hop opened his eyes and saw that he was still flying, but now he was parallel to the ground, smashing through the pine trees that covered the lower slopes of Mother Mountain.

So much for a quick death, Hop thought.

Another wind gust slammed him in the face, blunting his forward momentum and slowing him just as—

Hop hit the ground.

Kurt and Azam's bat had been hit by a blast of fire just seconds after it flew out of the tunnel from the Bat Cavern. Their goblin pilot and the other Celestial boy had been blasted right off the bat, falling in flames down the cliffs of Mother Mountain. Somehow, though, Kurt and Azam had managed to hold on to the burning taxi-bat. Kurt clung for his life to the leather webbing that attached the bat's saddlebags to its passenger platform. On the other side of the bat, he could see Azam gripping the platform itself. As best Kurt could tell, the blast had knocked the bat unconscious. Against all odds, though, its wings had locked in an outspread position. So even though the bat was unconscious and on fire, it was going down in a long, fiery glide. For a moment, Kurt thought that he and Azam would survive unscathed.

Then the bat reached the trees. At first it just clipped the treetops, jostling Kurt and Azam. Somehow, both of them managed to keep their grips on the bat's harness. At first. As the bat descended farther, thick tree branches began pummeling them. Kurt could feel his grip weakening. Then the taxi-bat hit a tree trunk.

Kurt flew loose, smashing though brush and skidding along the ground. Fortunately for him, almost a decade of playing football had taught him how to take a hit. He relaxed his body and rolled with it. When he came to rest, he was battered and bruised, but, as far as he could tell, nothing was broken. He struggled to his feet . . . and heard a groan.

Kurt ran to Azam, hoping he was just a little banged up.

There was a tree branch sticking out of the Celestial's chest. He'd been skewered completely through. Azam was dying.

"I'll find help," Kurt blurted.

"No," Azam replied weakly, in obvious pain. "No helping this. Stay. Don't want to . . ."

He trailed off, gasping for breath. But Kurt knew what he was going to say. Azam didn't want to die alone.

"You're going to be okay," he said. He sat down next to Azam and took his hand.

"I walked in balance. I have no regrets," Azam said quietly. "No. That's . . . lie. I have one."

Kurt could see how much trying to speak was hurting Azam. The words came out slowly, each laden with pain. There was blood on his lips.

"Don't try to talk," Kurt said.

"Just . . . always wanted to say . . . glad I met you," Azam managed.

Kurt was surprised by that. When he'd met Azam, Kurt had been feeling pretty low. He'd just failed to prove his claim to the goblin throne. He, Billy, Lexi, and their goblin friends had been captured and sentenced to death. They'd been shipped to a goblin fort in the middle of nowhere. He hadn't been sure he'd ever get home. But Azam had gone out of his way to make him feel welcome in the Celestials' community. Kurt figured Azam had taken pity on him because he and his people were exiles too. Whatever the reason, he and Azam had become fast friends. The Celestial had taught him how to rope walk, how to juggle, how to spin fire. Azam's friendship had saved him from a dark time. Still, he hadn't realized he'd meant that much to Azam. The Celestial had a lot of friends. Kurt just counted himself lucky he'd had room for one more.

"I'm nothing special," Kurt said.

"Special to me . . ." Azam said, his voice getting softer and raspier. He coughed violently, and more blood came out of his mouth. The Celestial fell back and closed his eyes. "Live well, Kurt," he whispered. "I . . ." Azam trailed off, and then his eyes opened as if he'd been startled.

"Light," he said. Then he went still.

Kurt sat with Azam for a long time, until the Celestial's hand grew cold. He knew his friend was gone, but it didn't feel right, just leaving him behind. He couldn't believe the Celestial had come all the way from the Fastness to help, only to die minutes into their expedition. It didn't seem fair.

Kurt vowed that he wasn't going to let Azam die in vain. As far as he could tell, Hop, Snails, Alyseer, and everyone else on their expedition was dead. So Kurt would have to go north alone, find the Star, and bring it back to Kiranok. Hop had said the Star was fifty *loktepen* away. That was a fifty-hour walk by an average goblin. But Kurt figured he walked a lot faster than an average goblin. Hopefully he could make it to the Star before the Hanorians.

Before Kurt headed north, though, there was one last thing he had to do. The quarterback wasn't much of a singer, and he couldn't remember all the words to the song the Celestials had sung over their dead friend only a few hours earlier, but someone had to sing it for Azam. There was no one else around. That meant it was up to him. Kurt sang softly, his voice cracking:

> *Now at last his pain has left him*
> *And Father Sun shines upon him*
> *And Mother Night welcomes him home*
> *For balanced was the path he walked*
> *And good deeds are the gift he left the world*

Kurt knew he'd messed up the lyrics. Plus, the song had seemed longer, so he'd probably skipped a few lines. But it was the best he could do.

Snow was falling. A light dusting of flakes already clung to Azam's body. If the snow kept up, he'd be covered soon. It was as much of a burial as Kurt could manage. He had to go. The Fallen Star wouldn't wait. He gently closed Azam's eyes and then headed downhill in a direction he hoped was north.

"Sun's Name," Cyreth swore. "How can you say there are no lightworkers available?"

Cyreth was dumbfounded. He'd been waiting almost a whole day to get a wizard to tend to his wounded, ever since he and his remaining Lion Guards had staggered down Monster Mountain. Of the twenty Lion Guards on his ill-fated mission, seven were dead, and almost all the rest had suffered some level of injury. Cyreth himself had a deep cut on the side of his head and another on his flank. Others were hurt far worse, most notably Ysalion. She'd nearly bled to death from her thigh wound by the time Cyreth and the other surviving Lion Guards had dragged her out of the collapsing goblin tunnels. Somehow, Bytha had managed to stanch Ysalion's bleeding, then the muscular female Lion Guard personally carried the young archer down the mountain to the Army of Light's camp. Cyreth had tried to get her to share her burden, but Bytha was one of the few uninjured Lion Guards, and she and Ysalion were close friends. Bytha refused to entrust her to anyone else. Now Ysalion was lying in the Lion Guards' command tent, unconscious and pale as her white cloak. Bytha had removed the wounded archer's blood-spattered half-veil so she could breathe freely, but her breathing was

ragged and shallow. Only a lightworker could help her. So
Cyreth and Bytha had gone to the red tents that housed the
Army of Light's wizards and healers, only to get intercepted
by a harried-looking sentry who'd tried to turn them back.

"They're all spent," the sentry replied. "After the assault,
the wizards that still had juice left used it to take down some
enemy bats. The rest left camp with the little spark."

"Mig isn't here?" Bytha asked. "Where did she go?"

"Do I look like they tell me anything important?" the
sentry asked. "Believe me, I'm sorry about your archer,
but you're not the first soldiers I've had to break the news
to. Now turn back and let the wizards sleep," he said
decisively. "Lord Marshal's orders."

"She's going to die," Cyreth said, his voice hollow.

"We're all going to die, brother," the sentry said, looking
every bit as beaten down as Cyreth felt. "Probably soon."

Cyreth couldn't argue with that. But he wasn't going
to let it stop him, either.

"Fix her." Cyreth shoved a frightened lightworker into
the Lion Guards' oversized command tent, where Ysalion
lay, waiting for a miracle.

The lightworker's name was Dumen. He was Cyreth's
height, though much thinner, with an equally thin beard
carefully trimmed to emphasize his handsome features.
He was graying slightly, so he must have been older than
Cyreth, though his face was unlined, with not a single scar
or blemish. Until a few minutes ago, he'd been sleeping
in his own well-appointed tent, on an actual bed with
a feather mattress. The bed had no doubt been carried
hundreds of leagues by soldiers who slept on the ground
under rough wool blankets. So Cyreth hadn't felt particularly bad when he and Bytha kidnapped the pampered

wizard. After confronting the sentry, they'd pretended to leave the wizards' quarters. Then they'd doubled back almost immediately and come in from another angle. Avoiding the sentries, they'd snuck into Dumen's tent. Surprising the sleeping wizard, they'd shoved a rag in his mouth and tied his hands to prevent him from casting any spells, and then they stuffed him into a large sack. Just before dawn, as a few stray snowflakes had begun to fall, they'd slipped out of his tent and carried him to their dying comrade.

Dumen looked at Ysalion and went pale. He obviously wasn't used to seeing wounds, and hers was particularly nasty.

"I'm on caster's rest," he protested. "I'm not supposed to work any magic for two full days."

"Nap time is over," Bytha growled, glaring at the wizard with obvious contempt.

"You clearly don't understand," Dumen said. He continued slowly, as if explaining something particularly complex to small children, "I helped blast open the gates of Kiranok. Then I had to fly directly to a cave mouth on the other side of the mountain and burn down some gobblers on bat-back. I've already pushed myself too far."

"Well, now you're going to push yourself again," Cyreth replied. "You're going to fix our friend. Then you can sleep as long as you want."

"If I work more magic without enough rest, I could go insane," Dumen said with a sneer. "If that happens, there's no telling how many of your fellow soldiers I might kill in my madness. Or I could die myself," he added, "which would be a crippling blow to the war effort."

"Clearly, you don't understand your situation," Cyreth said, trying to sound as reasonable as possible. "Either you fix our friend, or you're definitely going to die."

Bytha poked Dumen's ribs with the tip of a dagger.

Dumen's expression darkened. "I'm a wizard, fools. I could turn you all to ash."

"Before my friend shoves her knife through your heart?" Cyreth asked. "I don't think so. If you want to live, you're going to heal our friend. No other options. And afterward, you're going to keep your mouth shut about it. Because there are still a few hundred Lion Guards left. If you talk, every one of them is pledged to cut you down. We're no wizards, but you'd be amazed at how good we are at making people disappear."

The last part was a bluff. None of the Lion Guards except Bytha were in on Cyreth's plan to kidnap a light-worker and force him to mend Ysalion's wound. But Cyreth figured the smug wizard would help only if refusal meant certain death.

"What if I go mad?" Dumen asked.

"Then you get the knife," Bytha answered.

"Cut his face," Cyreth said, "to show him we mean what we say."

Bytha raised her knife toward Dumen's face, but the wizard quickly relented. "Wait. No! I'll mend the woman's wounds," Dumen said.

"You'll tell no one?" Cyreth asked.

"Tell people that I was captured by common soldiers and forced to do their will?" Dumen asked in response. "That would make me look the fool. Why under the Sun would I do that?"

Dumen placed his hands on Ysalion's wounded thigh. "Touch my shoulders, then hold each other's hands. I'll need all your energy for this."

Cyreth put one hand on Dumen's shoulder and then held out his other to Bytha.

The female Lion Guard hesitated. "What if he's just trying to get me to put away my knife?"

"We have to trust him," Cyreth said. "A little. And if he betrays us . . . I've never seen anyone who can draw a knife faster than you."

"He's right about that," Bytha said to Dumen, sheathing her knife. She put her hand on the wizard's shoulder. "Not to mention my hand is inches from your throat."

She took Cyreth's free hand in hers.

"Charming," Dumen snarled. "Now think about healing. Think about your friend getting better. And pray I don't change my mind."

Cyreth did as he was told. He thought about healing Ysalion. Wished for it with all his heart. Despite the cold wind and whipping snow outside the tent, Cyreth started to feel warm. Dumen's hands pulsed red. Cyreth couldn't tell whether he was casting a healing spell or preparing to attack. He supposed they'd find out soon enough.

Hop always expected the worst, so he was rarely disappointed.

But though he'd pictured a thousand ways his quest to retrieve the Fallen Star could go wrong, none of them had involved getting shot down only seconds after leaving Kiranok.

He had to admit—that one hurt a bit. Actually, it hurt a lot. His body ached all over. There was a gash on his head that wouldn't stop bleeding, despite the torn cloth he'd wrapped around it. He was pretty sure the little finger on his left hand was broken, along with at least one of his ribs. To top it off, his left leg had been burned by wizard fire. Still, he'd gotten off relatively lightly. He'd landed in a small snowdrift, slid a few dozen yards, then bumped gently into a tree trunk.

After shaking off his rough landing, Hop had struggled to his feet, determined to find any other survivors. It hadn't taken long to find the first. As he stood up, Alyseer drifted gently down next to him without a scratch on her. He rushed to her side, shouting her name, trying to get her attention. She didn't say a word, didn't seem to notice him at all. She just sat down in the snow, eyes open but unreactive. Hop feared the young human had broken something inside herself by working so much magic. After several minutes trying to rouse her unsuccessfully, he realized there was nothing he could do for her. He went looking for the others.

He found Snails a few dozen yards away. Snails had broken his left arm in the final fall. Hop bound it up, brought him to Alyseer, and then continued his search. He soon found four more survivors, all of them with at least one broken bone, many with more than one. He brought each one back to his landing spot, then went back for more. Eventually he realized he'd found all the survivors he was going to find. Six members of the expedition were missing entirely, including Kurt and his Hanorian friend, Azam, and Hop's trusted signal goblin, Flutter.

At least the missing might still be alive. That wasn't true for the bodies. Hop found three.

Littletwig was a spotter who'd served on one of the warbats that Hop had saved from Sawtooth's Last Stand. She'd burned to death.

Brassclaw was an archer on Daffodil, Hop's warbat. He had a nasty temper. No one else on the crew had liked him much. Still, he'd been part of Hop's team, and he was the very first bat-rider to volunteer for Hop's mission. Hop found his corpse in a tree.

Rounder wasn't a trained warbat flier at all. He'd been a taxi-bat pilot. When Hop had commandeered his bat for the expedition, Rounder had insisted on piloting her himself. Now both he and his beloved bat were dead. Hop had found them together, lying atop a sharp boulder, their bodies still smoking. He wasn't sure if they'd been killed by the Hanorian wizards' fire blasts or their ensuing crash to the ground. He hoped it was the fire blasts. That would've been quicker.

Not for the first time, Hop wished the stories he'd heard as a child had been more accurate. The traveling puppeteers and story-singers that visited his remote home village had always made battles and quests sound like great adventures. If someone died, it was usually for dramatic purposes. It was never anyone important, unless they died at the very end. The puppeteers never told the stories of the various guards, bandits, and mercenaries who fell along the way, either battling the noble hero or trying to defend him.

Hop often wondered if the person who should have been the hero of his particular story had died earlier, unnoticed. He thought of all the people he'd lost who would have made better heroes than him.

Cotton, his first love, had been plucky and smart. She was just the sort of person who'd have found the magic spear in a puppet show. Cotton could've given the spear to her handsome hero, or maybe she would've even killed the dragon herself.

Then there were his fellow soldiers who'd died at Solace Ridge, and the bat-riders who'd been shot out of the sky by the Hanorian lightships after Sawtooth's Last Stand. So many dead soldiers and fliers, foremost among them Sergeant Flyrat, who'd taught him how to be a bat pilot. Flyrat had been a battle-tested, wily old *gob* who would've probably come up with a plan to stop the Hanorians long before now.

Mallet and Peashoot had been Templars, bodyguards of the High Priestess of the Night Goddess. They'd also been *kijakgoben* twice Hop's size, trained to fight since they could walk. Hop had barely gotten to know them, but they'd seemed brave and strong and practically indestructible. They would've made great heroes. "The Twin Templars" they'd have called them. Hop could practically see their puppets, towering over the other characters in the show, leading the *goben* to victory.

Except they'd died getting Billy his crown.

Sun and Fire, Hop thought. *Rounder would've maked a better hero than me. Unexpected like. A cabby and his trusty taxi-bat flying north in a race against time. The songs would've writed themselves.*

There'd be no songs though, not about any of them. They were all dead now. So it all came down to Hop. Which, as far as Hop was concerned, wasn't the least bit fair. He'd much rather sit and watch a puppet story than play the hero in real life. One good thing about expecting the worst, though—it meant Hop didn't spend much time sitting around in shock and horror when things went wrong. He'd gotten pretty good at dusting himself off and muddling forward. He'd had an awful lot of practice. Now it was time to do it again.

"Snails, I need you to get all them what're injured back into Kiranok," he said to his young spotter. "Can you do that?"

Snails looked around at the other wounded goblins. Despite his broken arm, he could still walk. That wasn't true of some of the others. Plus, Hop had always found Snails extremely capable. He didn't just have keen eyes, he had a keen mind and a can-do attitude. He seemed like the right *gob* for the job.

"Thinking we can look for them missing folk too, afore we head in," Snails said after a moment's thought. "Not too long, but give it a nibble at least."

"Sound good," Hop said. Then he turned and looked at Alyseer. She still hadn't said a word, hadn't moved, hadn't even blinked. "Treat this one gentle. She saved us both."

"She saved us, too," one of the injured goblins said. It was Bead, another of Hop's former warbat crew, an archer of few words. Hop had learned that whenever Bead spoke, it was important. "*Nai* ever thought I'd owe me life to a *sk*—" Bead corrected himself, "to a human. But she sended a wind to lift me. Warm-like. Seed it lift others too. All of us what're alive are alive acause of her."

"What're wrong with her, Cap?" Snails asked, using the calling-name Hop got during the war.

"*Maja* magic, *maja* fast, that're my guess," Hop answered. "Are *nai* thing free. *Zajnai* this are the price."

Hop squatted next to Alyseer, meeting her blank gaze.

"If you're in there, know you have me gratitude," Hop said. "You saved me and mine. *Nurganzit.* I will balance this. Do *nai* know how, but I will."

"Get them home alive," Hop said to Snails, then he picked up his spear and a supply pack he'd salvaged from Rounder's dead bat and started walking north, at a right angle to the rising sun.

"Will do, Cap," Snails called after him. "You come home alive too. With the Star. We're depending on you."

Hop grunted his acknowledgment. He knew they were depending on him. All of Kiranok was depending on him. At the moment, he wasn't the hero his people needed, but he supposed he was the only hero they had.

As a gentle snow began to fall, Hop trudged north, traveling ever deeper into a story he couldn't seem to escape.

CHAPTER EIGHT
The Best Night

Two days had passed since Hop and Kurt's expedition had been blasted out of the air. There hadn't been any sign of them since. Billy had sent several scouts to look for them, but so far, there was no evidence that anyone had survived the wizard ambush. Billy tried to keep his hopes up. He knew how resourceful and hard to kill Hop was. And Kurt seemed like a survivor. For that matter, so did bat-riders and Celestials who'd gone with them. But one thing was clear, Billy couldn't count on anyone bringing back the Fallen Star to save Kiranok.

And Kiranok was going to need saving. Soon. So far, there hadn't been any more Hanorian attacks, but Billy knew it was only a matter of time. Goblin sentries had reported that the Hanorians were slowly moving their fortifications up the mountain, a few hundred feet a day. So Billy had called a meeting of his inner circle to try to figure out their next move. Lexi, Frost, Leadpipe, Shadow, and Starcaller had joined him around a huge dining table in Billy's private quarters. Shadow had spread a large map of Mother Mountain out on the table. On the map, she'd placed small, carved blue figures to represent the Hanorian Army and small black ones for the surviving units of the Warhorde. There were a lot more blue pieces than black ones. After a moment of study, Shadow inched the blue pieces closer to the part of the map showing the Great Gate.

The dining table was huge, made from a giant slab of jet-black stone. It was the centerpiece of Billy's so-called "royal quarters." Billy's new home once belonged to a rich merchant who'd supported the goblins' former dictator, Sawtooth. When the merchant and his family fled Kiranok after Sawtooth's death, Hop and Shadow had insisted Billy move in. The sprawling dwelling was carved out of a natural cave. Located on its own private rock shelf overlooking Kiranok's central chasm, the home was impressive enough for a king and easily defensible. Billy's new quarters could be reached only by a long, winding staircase. The handful of Copperplates stationed on the stairs could hold off a small army of attackers. More guards stood watch on the home's front ledge, and there was also a private bat landing so that Billy could come or go by bat in an emergency. Still, while Billy understood why his goblin allies wanted him to live here, the size and luxuriousness of his new home made him uncomfortable. The dining room alone was bigger than the entire apartment where he and his parents lived in San Francisco. Sometimes he worried he'd get lost in the maze of bedrooms in the back of the cave dwelling and never find his way out. Still, he had to admit, it made a good place for private meetings.

"*Ahka*. Them are their current positions, far as we can tell," Shadow said. "I think they're awaiting their wizards. They used them heavy in their last attack, so they need to rest them. Another day, *zajnai* two. Then they'll come at us again, mark me."

Since Hop and Kurt had been shot down, Billy had done everything he could to make Kiranok ready for another attack. He'd had the secondary entrances sealed, only leaving open the handful needed for Shadow's sentries to come and go. Even those were harder to get through now. Billy had ordered the passageways narrowed every few dozen yards to make them impassible except to one person at a time. He'd also deployed guards at all the choke points.

Unfortunately, Billy knew it wouldn't be enough. Because of the wizards. The Hanorians had over a hundred of them, while the goblins had just nine: Frost, Lexi, Starcaller, and her six sub-priests. That wasn't counting the two surviving wizards from the trio who'd tried to kill him, wherever they were hiding. But they were working against Billy and his friends, not for them.

"The Hanorians will blast their way in," Billy said. "No matter how much we reinforce the entrances, once their wizards are rested, we won't be able to stop them."

Shadow tipped her head from side to side. It was a goblin gesture Billy had only recently figured out. Goblins called it a *vajk*. It was something like a nod and something like a sigh. As far as Billy could tell, it meant "I wish that were *nai* true, but it is."

High Priestess Starcaller was more philosophical. "Wishing things were different will *nai* change them. *Nai* even praying will do that. Only hard work and quick minds."

Frost looked at the map, wiggling his long, bat-like

ears as he thought. "*Naizaj* Lexi and I can stop them. Drop another ceiling on them."

Billy shook his head. "That worked once because they weren't ready for it. But I bet you could think of a way to stop it, if you try."

Frost didn't have to think long. "If it were me, channeling cold, I'd create an ice arch to hold the ceiling up. Or I'd freeze the stones tight together. For them . . . use heat to fuse the ceiling stones. Counter our cold spells with fire so they don't touch the ceiling at all. Or just blast fire at our wizards until we're all dead."

Shadow tilted her head again. Another *vajk*. She'd been doing that a lot lately. "Once they get through to the Underway, we can *nai* drop anything on them. Crack the roof in there, you'll destroy the entire city. Along with all the *goben* in it."

"Fine," Lexi said. "If we can't stop them inside, I say we stop them outside. You said their wizards are all resting? How about we sneak into their camp again, and Frost drops a blizzard on them. Or I blast them to pieces. Or both."

"Violence are *nai* always the answer, *derijinta*," Starcaller said, shifting in her black robes, clearly uncomfortable with Lexi's proposal.

Billy didn't like the sound of it either. He looked at Lexi, worried she might be slipping toward madness.

Lexi seemed to sense what he was thinking. "I'm not a *graznak* yet," Lexi said with a small smile. "But it might be the only way."

Billy thought that over. There had to be a better way. "Two of you against an entire army, not to mention all those wizards? Even if they are resting, I bet they could cast a spell or two in an emergency. I've seen you work magic when Frost said you shouldn't plenty of times."

Leadpipe, who'd been sitting to one side of the table so as not to crowd the others, echoed Billy's worries in his deep bass voice. "You and Frost would die. Would *nai* kill half of them, and you'd die. That're useless. *Drakik*. I do *nai* want me brother to die. *Nai* you either, Lexi. You're family now. Family do *nai* let family toss their lives away."

To Billy's relief, Lexi didn't argue. Instead she looked downcast. "Then I don't know what to do," she admitted. "I have all this power, but there doesn't seem to be any good way to use it."

"We'll come up with something," Leadpipe said, reassuring. "Or at least Billy, Frost, and Shadow will. They're smart that way. With plans and such."

"None of my plans have worked so far," Billy said. "I wish we could just make everyone in Kiranok vanish so there'd be no one for the Hanorians to kill." Then Billy realized . . . "Maybe that's the answer. Maybe we can make everyone disappear."

"How?" Shadow asked. "With magic? Are *nai* spell big enough to do that, *nai* enough wizards in the world to cast it."

"Not with your kind of magic. With the kind of magic we have in our world."

"*Ahka*, you have magic in your own world?" Frost reacted in surprise. "Afore you sayed you only have *teck-noll-o-gee* and *sigh-ins*," Frost sounded out the unfamiliar words, "whatever that are." Billy had once tried to explain to Frost how airplanes and computers and cell phones worked. And how science and technology weren't magic. Frost had had a hard time understanding the difference. "Are you going to use *sigh-ins* on them?"

"No. Like I said, we'll use magic," Billy said. "Except the magic we have in our world is just tricks. Ways to fool people into seeing things that aren't real or not seeing things that are."

Billy explained his plan to Lexi, Shadow, Frost, Leadpipe, and Starcaller.

"That could actually work," Lexi said.

"It could," Starcaller agreed. "Only it will *nai* happen tonight."

"Why not tonight?" Billy asked.

"It're near sunset. The Night Song will start soon," Starcaller said. "And then . . . it're *Pikoghul*."

"What's *Pikoghul*?" Lexi asked.

"Step outside and see," Starcaller answered.

They emerged onto Billy's private terrace as the Night Song was ending. Lexi loved the goblins' ritual nightly hymn, especially the way the last few notes would echo through Kiranok's huge central chamber, creating their own eerie harmonies:

> *Come the darkness*
> *Come the night*
> *End the day*
> *Douse the light*

As soon as the last note faded, the goblins struck up a new tune. It was jaunty and fun, fast and loud. Down in the Underway, Lexi could see goblins dancing as they sung. Many of them were wearing masks and elaborate costumes. To Lexi's surprise, there were children everywhere. She hadn't seen many children in Kiranok. The city had been at war ever since she, Billy, and Kurt arrived. Lexi realized the children must've been hidden away, kept safe. Now they were

out on the streets, dancing and singing with the rest
of the city.

One day I'll be all grown
And all I'll do are moan
About how life are hard and full of responsibilities
But me life are just beginned
My story are still nai *singed*
And all I see are an endless land of possibilities

Ahka *I could wear a Copperplate or fix them as a*
tinker
Ahka *I could wear a blue robe and be quite the*
thinker
Zaj *I could be a farmer and grow mushrooms for*
your cupboard
Or I could ride a bat or play soldier in the Warhorde

But now I are a squeaker
Pikogob, *little seeker*
I are only just starting life's tangled dance
Crow all day like a rooster
Acause all me life are future

Do nai *you wish you were back at the start?*
Nai cares, nai *pain, full of promise and heart*
And your life were an endless land of possibilities?
Well tonight your wish are granted
A night the Goddess enchanted
When we can all act like children once again
So grab the mask and rattle
Forget the work and battle
And embrace the games and songs and we'll pretend
That your life are just beginned

Your story still not singed
And your future are an endless land of possibilities
Tonight forget your troubles and responsibilities
And life can be an endless land of possibilities

"Tonight are *Pikoghul*," Leadpipe explained happily.
"Child's Night. When every young *gob* get to play like
there are *nai* tomorrow, and every old *gob* get to act like
a child again. It're the best night of the year."

Leadpipe might've sounded happy about the celebration, but Shadow was her usual grim self.

"Sorry, Your Majesty," Shadow said. "Your plan
are a good one. It're just *nai* timed well. *Nai* goblin will
agree to do what you want tonight. To tell them to *nai*
celebrate *Pikoghul* . . . that're like ordering them to stop
being *goben*."

Lexi looked down at the goblin festival with a little
envy. Despite the terrible circumstances, despite the
Hanorian Army at their doorstep—or maybe because of
it—the goblins, young and old alike, were celebrating with
abandon. The festival-goers wore elaborate costumes and
carved wooden masks. Bands performed on a hundred
improvised stages. Puppet troops put on shows. Vendors
sold all manner of treats. The many balconies, terraces,
bridges, and layered streets of Kiranok overflowed with
revelers. There were goblin children dressed as *vargaren*
and *bokrumen* and bats; little ones playing at being Templars and bat-riders and priestesses of the Night Goddess.
Lexi even noticed a few human caricatures with round,
pale faces and tiny ears. Most of the human masks looked
mean and scary, but a few were happy and smiling. Some
even looked vaguely familiar.

"Hey, is that supposed to be . . . me?" Lexi asked,
pointing out a goblin child wearing a bright red tunic and

a feminine human mask with dark hair and a halo of fire. The little goblin was running down the street, throwing red balls painted with flames at anyone else in a human mask. The balls would bounce off, and then the goblin child would chase them down and throw them at the next human she saw.

"You're a hero," Billy said with a smile. "You saved the entire city. I bet there're going to be a lot of goblins dressed as you tonight."

Lexi smiled back. She knew Billy had had a rough time since they'd arrived in the goblins' world. Becoming the Goblin King had made him only more serious and worried. It was good to see him smiling.

"You as well, Your Majesty," Starcaller said, pointing to a goblin infant, barely big enough to walk, toddling down the Underway wearing a wooden Billy mask and a tiny copy of the Goblin Crown.

"That one is Kurt," Billy said while pointing out another, his smile fading.

Lexi spotted a larger goblin child, either a teenager or a young *kijakgob*, wearing a replica of Kurt's Drake Prep Wildcats shirt and a bright-pink mask topped with gold-washed hair and carved with a pretty good facsimile of Kurt's cocky grin.

"There's a Hop," Leadpipe rumbled sadly, pointing at a goblin child in a Copperplate costume wearing a fake mangled ear made from papier-mâché. "I hope that're *nai* the only thing we'll see of him and Kurt . . . costumes on *Pikoghul* . . . as if they're folk from history. Like Pepperstew the Mountain-Talker or Piast the Boy-King."

"He're coming back," Shadow said with forced confidence. "Hop are a survivor. He'll be back here afore we know it. He'll be back, his friends at his side, the Fallen Star in hand, and all our worrying will be for *nai*."

"Kurt too," Billy said. "All of them. We don't know what happened after the ambush. The scouts didn't find any bodies. Everyone could be fine."

Lexi could tell Billy didn't entirely believe that. There was a way he carried himself when he was pretending to be strong but wasn't feeling it. He'd pull his shoulders back and stick out his chest and speak a little louder. But his eyes would stay slightly downcast, and there'd be a hint of a slouch in his neck. Just like now. He was trying to stay positive, but he was worried.

"So where do we get *our* costumes?" Lexi asked, making her own effort to sound upbeat.

Shadow looked at her, surprised. "Costumes?"

Lexi didn't want Billy to dwell on what might or might not have happened to their friends. He needed a distraction. They all did. "What did the song say? 'Grab your mask and rattle, forget the work and battle.' Worrying about Hop and Kurt won't help them. We can't start Billy's plan until morning. I don't know about the rest of you, but I could use a night of pretending I have no problems and acting like a kid again."

"You are still a kid to us," Leadpipe rumbled. "That do *nai* mean you're wrong, though. *Zajnai* you should be down there in a mask and celebrating *Pikoghul*. *Naizaj* we all should."

"It's settled then," Billy said. "Let's be kids, costumes and all. Happy *Pikoghul*, everyone. That's an order."

Lexi grinned. "Your wish is our command, Your Majesty."

Kurt was cold and wet and hurt. All he wanted to do was lie down and rest. Except he knew if he stopped moving, he'd freeze to death. He had to keep walking.

Kurt was glad he played football. It would've been easy to feel sorry for himself, battered and bruised, alone in the snowy woods, trying to find the Fallen Star all on his own. Luckily, football had taught him to deal with pain and bad weather and misery. Playing football, he'd broken his wrist, he'd twisted his knee, and he'd gotten hit so hard in the gut he'd ended up puking on the sidelines. He'd played in the snow in Mammoth and Reno. He'd played in San Francisco's rain and fog and wind. He'd played after arguments with his father and in the middle of breaking up with his girlfriend. He'd always played on.

Though the truth was, he'd never played through someone dying before. Thinking about Azam was hard. That's what really made him want to lie down in the snow and give up. But he couldn't let his team down like that. Billy and Lexi and Frost and Leadpipe were counting on him. He would play until the clock ran out.

Kurt forced himself to take another step, then another, then a dozen, then a hundred. Soon he stopped thinking about anything but the next step and the next.

So he wasn't sure how much time had passed when he heard the voices.

At first, the distant voices were barely audible over the blowing wind and the crunch of his feet in the snow. As he continued to walk, though, they got louder and more distinct. He couldn't make out the words right away, just the tone. It sounded like a lot of people struggling to keep moving through the dark and the cold. Giving each other encouragement. Singing an occasional bit of music. Could it be Hop and the other goblins? Maybe he wouldn't have to find the Fallen Star on his own after all.

Kurt reached a small hill. He could hear the muffled voices ahead, just on the other side of the ridge. Kurt trudged up the hill, struggling to keep his footing in the slushy mud and patchy ice. Still, his legs were strong from spending countless hours in the gym, lifting weights and doing squats. He'd trained himself to shrug off tackles from three-hundred-pound linemen. He wasn't going to let a snowy hill stop him.

He'd almost reached the top when he finally understood what the voices were saying . . . and more importantly, what language they were speaking.

It wasn't *Gobayabber* he was hearing. It was Hanorian.

Deciding he'd better see what he was up against, Kurt dropped to the snow and crawled to the crest of the hill. He saw two dozen Hanorian soldiers moving through the woods below him. They had several mules to carry their supplies. They were dressed in warm winter clothing and heavy boots. They had swords and bows . . .

Plus, they had Mig.

The Hanorian girl was at the front of the Hanorian column, gliding inches above the ground, leaving a path of melted snow below her feet. She was dressed in the same white, yellow, red, and orange silk dress she'd been wearing in the human camp. Her arms and head were bare, but she didn't look the least bit cold.

"Faster," she snapped at the Hanorian soldiers in her wake. Mig floated farther forward, and her followers struggled to keep up.

"Is she serious?" Kurt heard one soldier grumble. "We're moving as fast as we can."

"Close your mouth, fool," another replied. "If she thinks you're slowing us down, she'll set you on fire to warm the rest of us."

Another soldier sung a little ditty:

Oh the Army of Light
We're not very bright
We follow our orders
March far from our borders
Just like good soldiers
We'll never get older
We'll die for Gran Hanor

"You too, Yven," the first soldier snapped.

"Aye, sergeant," the singer answered. "Mouths closed, minds closed, do as we're told."

"Pick up the pace," the sergeant replied. "Left-right, left-right, left-right."

The Hanorians fell in with their sergeant's cadence, moving a little faster and keeping their mouths shut. Kurt waited until the last soldier had passed his position, then he slid back down the hill, away from the enemy troops. Once he was on level ground, he turned north, paralleling the Hanorians' path, taking pains to stay out of sight. The Hanorians were the enemy. They outnumbered him twenty to one. They had a half-mad fire wizard on their side. Still, Kurt figured at least they were moving in the right direction.

Billy adjusted his goblin mask so the eyeholes lined up a little better with his eyes and took in the show. In preparation for braving the Underway, Frost and Leadpipe had taken him and Lexi to a high-end costume shop in the nicest part of Kiranok. There'd been a crowd of revelers trying to get last-minute costumes, but Leadpipe had grumbled, "Make way for the King," and they'd all scattered. A kindly *svagob* had helped them choose their costumes, fussing to get every little detail just right.

Billy had asked if he could dress as Hop, just like the young goblin he'd seen earlier in the evening. He'd wanted to dress as their missing friend as a way of including him in the celebration, and Leadpipe strongly approved of any costume that included actual armor for Billy's protection. The shopkeeper had provided him with a reproduction of Copperplate armor, made with real metal. Then she'd taken a wooden goblin mask and quickly modified it to match Hop's mangled left ear.

Frost and Leadpipe had been less enthusiastic about Lexi's costume choice. She had chosen to dress as a *duenshee*, a pale, sharp-featured humanoid that reminded Billy of an elf. Not cute and fun like Christmas elves, though. The *duensheen* were more like the dangerous, magical elves Billy had seen in movies or read about in the book of Irish folklore his mom had inherited from her grandfather. The Dark Lady, the magical prophetess who'd inspired the goblins' ill-fated war against the Hanorians, had been a *duenshee,* and from what Billy had heard, she'd been very dangerous indeed. Lexi's mask was pretty, made of bone and silver, with elegant features and long, pointed ears. She wore it with a hooded black silk dress decorated with silver thread and long black gloves that hid her human hands. Her costume may have reminded Frost and Leadpipe uncomfortably of the Dark Lady, but it concealed her identity perfectly. There was no way to tell she was human under the eerie mask and swirling silks.

Frost wore a bat mask and a brown leather jerkin with large leather bat wings sewn to the back. With his mask hiding his grown-up face and wispy beard, it was hard to tell that Frost wasn't a child. Leadpipe had kidded him about that when he'd first put on the costume, but Frost had seemed pleased.

"Looking like a child on *Pikoghul* are *nai* such a bad thing," he'd said. "Tonight we're all young again, *zaj*?"

Leadpipe had responded with a chuckle. "*Nai* one will mistake me for *nai piko*," he'd said. "So if I can *nai* pretend to be a child, *zajnai* I can make the real *pikoen* laugh."

With that, Leadpipe picked out a huge *kijakhof* costume composed of an oversized rabbit mask with long floppy ears, gray furry overalls, and a big fluffy tail. Once in costume, he assumed a bent-over posture that made him look even more like a giant rabbit. From time to time, he would hop as high as he could and bellow an exaggerated "*Doik! Doik! Doik!*" True to his word, he made goblin children laugh all along the Underway as their small group moved through the festivities.

So far, the costumes had worked perfectly. No one had recognized them. Billy, Lexi, Frost, and Leadpipe had been able to enjoy *Pikoghul* without being swarmed by goblin admirers or having to worry about being attacked. The four of them had wandered the Underway for an hour or so, taking in the sights and sounds, the costumed goblins, the endless stalls selling sweets and toys and musical instruments, and the various bands, acting troupes, and acrobats. Finally, they'd paused in front of a puppet show that had caught Lexi's eye. The hero of the show was a goblin wizard, but the little puppet flung red balls at his enemies instead of blue ones. He was using fire, not ice.

"I didn't know goblin wizards could use fire," Billy whispered to Frost as they watched the show.

"That're Coaler the Fire Wizard," Frost explained. "*Zajnai* the greatest wizard in all of *goben* history. He're one of the few *goben* what could work light magic. He're the wizard what cut Coaler's Break across the Ironspine

Mountains and chained up the Dragon of Blackstone and turned back the Marching *Duensheen*."

On the puppet booth's little stage, a new puppet appeared, a tall human wearing a crown made of skeletal hands and carrying a skull. The audience growled enthusiastically, the goblin equivalent of booing.

"*Ahka*, that're the Emperor of Bones," Frost said, clearly delighted.

"There'll be no moving Frost now," Leadpipe chuckled. "Watching Coaler and the Emperor of Bones are his favorite thing to do on *Pikoghul*. It're that way ever since he were tiny. Tinier than now, I mean."

"If it's a good story, we should all watch it," Lexi said.

"It're terrible," Leadpipe said. "There're all kinda killing and death and scary stuff. I never understood why they tell this one to children."

"Leadpipe have the worst taste in puppet shows," Frost said in return. "He only like the ones about cute animals and flower fairies. Or the ones when everyone sing."

On the puppet booth's stage, the Emperor of Bones pointed his skull at another puppet. The puppet shrieked and shook, then the puppeteer pulled it down below the stage and quickly replaced it with a skeleton version of the same character. The skeleton bowed to the Emperor.

"He're building his skeleton army now," Frost said, obviously excited to see the rest of the story.

"You three watch the show," Leadpipe said. "I're gonna buy us some candymoss. It're *nai Pikoghul* without candymoss."

Leadpipe hopped away with a booming "*Doik! Doik! Doik!*" setting off peals of laughter from the nearby goblins, children, and adults alike.

Lexi and Frost found places to sit in front of the puppet booth, settling in for the show. Billy followed their example, sitting next to Lexi. To his surprise, she scooted closer to him and leaned against him as the show continued. On the puppet show stage, the Emperor of Bones used his magical skull to turn dozens of his fellow humans into skeletons, creating an undead army, then leading them into goblin territory. The story had uncomfortable echoes of their current situation, but the puppeteers kept it light by making the invading skeletons comically incompetent. They were constantly losing their skull heads, tripping over each other's bony legs, and falling apart into piles of bones, all to the increasing consternation of the Emperor.

Billy found himself laughing along with the rest of the crowd and rooting for Coaler the Fire Wizard to defeat the Emperor of Bones and his hapless minions. He couldn't remember the last time he'd been so happy. He didn't know if it was the festival, the puppet show, or Lexi's shoulder gently resting on his arm. Probably all three. All he knew was he didn't want the show to end any time soon.

Coldsnap and Grinner moved through the *Pikoghul* crowd undetected. Grinner was dressed as the Emperor of Bones, with a snarling human mask, red robes, and a crown made of finger bones. He carried a wooden skull and took pleasure in terrifying the little children they passed, pointing it at them and snarling, "Join me army of the dead."

Coldsnap wore a Button the Mushroom Girl costume. The plucky heroine of "The Goblin King and the Mushroom Girl" had been her favorite as a child, and the costume was easy to make. All Coldsnap needed was a green country girl dirndl, a bucketful of mushrooms, and a red handprint painted on the right side of her face where Button had been touched by the Red Stranger. As simple as it was, though, she regretted the costume as soon as she reached the Underway. Not only did her Button outfit do a poor job of hiding her identity, wearing it brought back bittersweet memories from before her parents' deaths, when she, Grub, and Pockets would go out for *Pikoghul* in their little Uplands town. Coldsnap would always dress as Button, Grub would be the Red Stranger, and Pockets would play the Goblin King. They'd take turns chasing each other through town, reenacting the old stories. Now—like at the end of the stories, after the Red Stranger had died and the Goblin King had vanished—Coldsnap was alone, just like the Mushroom Girl.

"Dance for your Emperor, Captain Bones!" Grinner growled at a passing *pikogob* dressed as a Copperplate.

"You do *nai* scare me!" the goblin child replied, turning to Grinner and shaking his toy spear. "I're Hop, the bravest *gob* what ever were! I killed Sawtooth. I'll kill you too, *zaj*!"

Snap saw that the little goblin had a fake chopped-off ear. He wasn't the first Hop impersonator she'd seen in the crowd. The King's trusted goblin advisor was one of the most popular costumes at this year's *Pikoghul*.

"I'll show you fear," Grinner said in the same calm, quiet voice he'd used when explaining his "experiments" on the rats in the Blue Chambers.

"*Nai!*" Coldsnap shouted, realizing that Grinner intended to hurt the small child, maybe even kill him. Unfortunately, her very real protest drew attention from nearby revelers, who eyed her and especially Grinner with suspicion. Trying to deflect their concern, Coldsnap went into her old Button act, still familiar from her childhood.

"Do *nai* be so mean, Emperor of Bones," she said cheerfully, stepping between Grinner and the child dressed as Hop. "Have a plate of mushrooms and *naizaj* some tea, and we can all be friends." She locked eyes with Grinner, behind his human mask, and then shook her head slightly, hoping her message was clear: *Do* nai *hurt him.*

Grinner's eyes remained cold and still. Then, after a tense moment, he shrugged. "Whatever you say, Mushroom Girl."

He walked away from the child. Snap followed. "What were you thinking? You were going to kill him?" she asked quietly.

Grinner shrugged again. "He'll die soon enough, when the humans come. We all will."

"That're *nai* true," Coldsnap said. "We can stop it."

"By killing the one person what can save us?"

"You mean the *skerbo* king?" Coldsnap responded, incredulous. "He're *nai* saving anyone," she insisted. "He're a trick, sended by the Hanorians to fool us and lead us to our slaughter."

"You really believe that?" Grinner asked.

Coldsnap answered quickly, without hesitation, "'Course I do."

But the truth was, she knew it was at least possible the human boy wearing the Goblin Crown was their only real hope to drive the Hanorians away. Perhaps there was a chance, if she just trusted him . . .

Except Coldsnap could never do that.

"It're a lie," she said. "The prophecy, the Crown, all of it. *Nai skerbo* are gonna save us from his own kind. *Skerboen* kill *goben*. That're the way it're always been. That're the way it'll always be."

"Button the Mushroom Girl *nai* thinked so," Grinner said. "She worked with the Goblin King of her time."

"Button were a lie too," Coldsnap said. "Her, Coaler the Fire Wizard, Good Witch Pepperstew, Copperplate the First—them're all but stories. We have *nai* time for such childishness. We have a *skerbo* to kill."

"Only we can *nai* find the *skerbo* king in all this maskery, hard as we look," Grinner pointed out. "If he're even fool enough to have joined the crowd."

That was when Coldsnap spotted a huge *kijakgob* hopping around the Underway in a ridiculous bunny suit. Despite the distance and the costume, she recognized the giant goblin instantly.

"Look," she said to Grinner. "Are that *nai* Frost's brother, Leadpipe? The *skerbo* boy's bodyguard?"

Grinner slipped off his human mask to get a better look. "That're him."

"We keep failing to kill King Billy acause he're too well protected, *zaj*?" Snap asked. "So *zajnai* we can make it easier on ourselves the next time."

By the candymoss cart, Leadpipe bounced again, booming a *"Doik-Doik-Doik"* they could hear even above the din of the festival.

"He're like a package of *Pikoghul* candy," Grinner said. "Just waiting to be torn open." With that, he pulled his human mask back on and strode through the crowd, waving his skull at the *Pikoghul* celebrants to clear the way. "Move aside," Grinner snarled. "Or I'll turn you to bones."

Children giggled and moved out of his way, thinking it was all some game. Snap knew Grinner wasn't joking, though. He'd kill them all if he could.

Snap followed in Grinner's wake. She wasn't going to let him kill any *pikogoben*. Only one *gob* was going to die tonight. And despite his idiotic, floppy-eared *kijakhof* costume, their target was far too big for anyone to mistake for a child.

On the puppet booth's tiny stage, Coaler had just incin-erated the Emperor's skeleton army when the screaming started. A blast of cold air rippled through the audience, making Lexi's black silks flail wildly for a moment, then go still. Lexi saw panicked festival-goers fleeing from the direction of the cold wind. She grabbed one, a young adult *svagob* who'd lost her mask in the stampede.

"What happened?" Lexi demanded.

"Wizards," the frightened goblin replied. "They attacked a big *kijakgob* by the food stands. Froze him solid."

Frost asked the next logical question before Lexi had a chance to react. "This *kijakgob*. What were he wearing?"

"A rabbit suit," the *svagob* answered. "With big floppy ears."

Lexi didn't wait for any more questions. The crowd was still rushing toward them, making it hard to move toward the site of the attack, but she wasn't going to let that slow her down. She conjured a warm wind to lift and stabilize her, then concentrated and poured energy out of her feet. Lexi rose into the air. In the distance, she could see Leadpipe, standing motionless by a food cart, covered in frost.

If she was going to save him, she couldn't wait.

Lexi flew.

CHAPTER NINE
No Grave for Me

Billy pushed through the fleeing goblins toward the food carts, Frost at his side. A phalanx of Copperplates quickly fell in with them. Billy realized the city guards must've been waiting at the edge of the crowd in case of an emergency.

As they broke free of the throng, they saw Lexi, in her Dark Lady costume, flying toward Leadpipe. The *kijakgob* was frozen in place by a food cart, surrounded by a small cluster of curious goblins.

"Everyone back!" Lexi shouted as she landed next to Leadpipe.

The sight of Lexi flying at them while dressed as the Dark Lady was too much for the gawkers. They fled screaming. "The Dark Lady! She're back! She're back!"

Billy and Frost joined Lexi. The Copperplates spread out around the food carts, cordoning off the area.

"Maybe you should take off your mask," Billy said. "I think you scared those poor goblins half to death."

Lexi flung off her mask, then reached out and touched Leadpipe's arm.

"He's so cold," she said.

"He're freezed solid," Frost said, despondent. "Like those Templars when we getted Billy his crown."

"It was those two wizards who did this," Billy realized. "The ones who attacked us in the Bat Cavern. It must've been."

Billy felt a sudden flash of heat coming from Lexi. Her black silk costume fluttered and smoked.

"I'm going to find them," Lexi said. "Then I'm going to kill them."

"Lexi, no!" Billy said. He didn't want his friend killing anyone if he could help it. Besides, there was something more important he needed Lexi to do. "You can't go looking for trouble," Billy explained. "Not when you can still help Leadpipe."

"Help Leadpipe?" Lexi asked. "How?"

"I do *nai* know if he can be helped now," Frost said, his voice choked with grief.

"I think he can," Billy insisted. "My mom is an ER nurse, remember? She told me once about this thing they do when someone is hurt bad. The doctors chill the patient's body down. It helps keep down the swelling or something. I don't know. But once the patient is better, the doctors warm them back up. The trick is to do it slowly, so it doesn't make the cells break down or whatever. Maybe you can do the same thing to Leadpipe. Warm him up, nice and slow."

"Warm him slowly?" Lexi asked, not sounding as confident as usual.

"It're a good idea," Frost said with a trace of hope.

"Just a dollop of heat. You want to make him warm bit by bit so he *nai* boil, *zaj*."

"I'll try," Lexi said.

She put her hands on Leadpipe. Billy felt a gentle warmth radiating from her.

"Give her your energy," Frost said to Billy. "The same way we doed it when we helped her heal her leg."

Billy placed his right hand on Lexi's left shoulder and then held his left hand out for Frost. The little wizard joined hands with Billy, then reached as high as he could and put his other hand on Lexi's right side, forming a circle around Leadpipe.

"Slow and easy," Frost said quietly. "Like cooking a roast. Keep the heat low so you *nai* dry it out."

"You can do this, Lexi," Billy said. "We believe in you."

The gentle heat continued to radiate from Lexi, like the first warm breeze in springtime. Not summer-blast furnace hot . . . just a hint of the sunny days to come.

"It's not working," Lexi said after more than a minute. "He's still cold."

"Have patience, *derijinta*," Frost replied. "That mean you're doing it right."

Billy kept concentrating. Minutes went by. He could see how much effort it was taking for Lexi to maintain the heat at just the right level. Her brow was furrowed, her jaw clenched. At one point, Billy felt her shoulder growing warmer, as if she'd turned up the heat a little.

"Don't push it," Billy said. "Nice and easy."

Lexi's shoulder went back to a gentle warmth. More time went by. It seemed like hours, but Billy knew it had only been maybe ten minutes total. Still, he'd been hoping to see some kind of reaction from Leadpipe by now.

"Look at his feet," Frost said.

Billy looked down and saw a pool of water slowly spreading around Leadpipe's feet. Tiny droplets ran down the giant goblin's skin as the ice covering him melted away.

Suddenly Leadpipe gasped for air, then collapsed in a heap.

"Lead!" Frost cried out, letting go of Billy's hand and bending down over his brother.

"*Ahka*! Look at me, Lead!" Leadpipe didn't react. His eyes were closed. He wasn't moving.

"Is he . . . ?" Billy started. He was going to ask if Leadpipe was dead, but he couldn't bring himself to say the words.

"He're breathing," Frost said. "*Nai* telling if he'll make it yet. But he have a chance."

Billy looked over at Lexi. "You did it."

Lexi looked exhausted. She hadn't put out her usual huge amount of energy all at once, but the slow, steady effort seemed to have drained her just the same.

"You should rest," Billy said. "Sit down, catch your breath."

Lexi didn't look interested in resting. "I'm going to find them," she said. "I'm going to burn them alive."

Lexi stalked off toward the nearest exit from the Underway. Billy ran up and caught her arm.

"Wait," he said.

"I'm tired of waiting," she snapped back, pulling her arm away. "I'm tired of being a target. I'm tired of losing my friends."

"I am too," Billy answered. "But think. The festival is almost over. In a few hours it will be morning. And we have a lot of work to do."

"Your plan," Lexi said. Billy could tell she'd momentarily forgotten what they'd planned to do the next day.

"We can worry about the bad guys later," Billy said. He looked back to where a half dozen Copperplates were gently lifting Leadpipe, ready to carry him to safety. "There are too many good ones we still have to save."

That seemed to sink in. Lexi slumped, finally letting her exhaustion get the better of her.

"It's hard being the good guys," Lexi said. "It's a lot easier blowing things up than protecting things . . . or building them."

"Yeah. Only who would you rather be in the end?" Billy said. "Coaler or the Emperor of Bones?"

Lexi smiled at that. "The Emperor had a better outfit. But Coaler was pretty cool."

"You'll be the star of the puppet shows next *Pik-oghul*. 'Lexi the Fire Wizard and Her Way-Less-Amazing Friends,'" Billy said with a smile. "All we have to do is save the world."

"Wake up, snoozyhead," Cotton said.

Hop opened his eyes. He loved seeing Cotton first thing when he woke. He'd always thought she was the prettiest *svagob* he'd ever laid eyes on, from the day he first saw her hanging up wet clothing outside Tower Gulkreg's little laundry. Now that she was his wife, he found her more beautiful than ever. Her cheerful smile, with her expressive green eyes and shining white fangs, made him excited for the day. He was with family, and all would be well.

"The *derijintaen* are still asleep," Cotton said. "They overdoed it last night at *Pikoghul*. Just like their father."

Hop was glad their children had enjoyed the festival. Still, something about what Cotton was saying struck him as wrong.

"I do *nai* remember *nai* thing about *Pikoghul*," Hop said.

"That're *nai* surprise," Cotton said. "Someone haved too many cups of *zobjepa*."

"Hope I were *nai* too foolish," Hop said sheepishly.

"*Nai* more than usual. Come eat something warm afore you go inspect your troops."

Hop nodded. He had to inspect the *goben* keeping watch over Tower Gulkreg every morning, even though the Hanorians hadn't attacked the watch post in several decades. It was easy for his soldiers to get complacent, so he insisted on everything being just so, from their patrol rotations to their daily passwords to the condition of their arms and armor.

Once again, Hop got the feeling something was off. He must've drunk an awful lot of mushroom wine last night. He was sore and tired. And strangely cold.

"Are a window open? Did the fire go out?" Hop asked, looking around the cozy little home he shared with Cotton and their children. How many children did they have? What were their names? Hop couldn't remember.

"*Nai*, all are well," Cotton answered. "Snug and warm."

Only Hop knew everything wasn't well. Cotton's voice sounded distant, as if she were far, far away. The cold was more intense now. Hop could feel it in his bones. He was afraid if he couldn't get warm, he'd freeze to death. He stepped up to the fire in the main room and tried to warm his cold hands. The flames felt like ice.

Suddenly they were ice, frozen and bright blue. Hop looked around. His entire home had turned into ice. All but Cotton, who still stood there, smiling.

"You look tired, Hop," Cotton said. "*Zajnai* you should go back to sleep. Your duty can wait. Stay with me."

Hop wanted that more than anything, even though he knew it was a lie. He stepped up to Cotton and kissed her gently. Her lips were cold.

"I wish I could," Hop said. "But too much depend on me right now. I need to go."

"The snow will feel warm if you lie in it long enough," Cotton said. "It'll feel warm until you do *nai* feel *nai* thing. And then you can join me."

"In the grave?" Hop said sadly.

"There are no grave for me," Cotton replied. "The Hanorians burned me up. They burned us all. Better to die freezing."

Hop startled awake. At first he couldn't see anything. It felt like a heavy wet blanket was laying over his face. Then he realized he was covered with snow.

Hop sat up, shaking the snow loose. It was still dark, and he was chilled to the bone. He didn't remember lying down or deciding to sleep. He must have dropped in his tracks.

"Move, you *drakbonch*," Hop said to himself. He grabbed his spear with his left hand, and pain shot through his arm. The little finger of his left hand was definitely broken. Shifting the spear to his right hand, Hop used it to prop himself to his feet. He looked around for his pack.

Nai, *it're still strapped to me back. Must've fallen asleep still wearing it. You have everything you need,* Hop told himself. *Time to get moving.*

Moving would warm him up. Moving would get him closer to the Fallen Star. Moving would help him forget Cotton and the life they might've had together if not for Sawtooth's War.

Hop took a tentative step, then another. It had snowed at least a hand's width while he slept, and moving through the thick powder wasn't easy. Still, he soon built up a little momentum. As he walked, his body warmed up, bit by bit. After a hundred yards or so, he could feel his fingers again, though his feet were still cold and damp. Once it was light, he'd build a little fire to warm his feet and dry out his boots. But for now, the best thing he could do was to keep walking.

That're life, Hop thought. *When things're bad, best thing to do are just to get going. Even when all you want are to lie down and dream of better times. Get up, get moving. Can* nai *fix things when you're flat on your back.*

It had been nice, dreaming of Cotton. But he had a mission, folks depending on him, Shadow to get home to, and a long way still to go.

Time enough to dream of what might have been once you're old and gray and your responsibilities are over and done. Today are nai *for dreaming. Today are for doing.*

So on Hop went through the snow, knowing nothing would be handed to him, not even his next step.

The sky was glowing faintly in the east. The sun would rise soon. Kurt knew it was now or never.

He had followed Mig and her Hanorian bodyguards all through the night. A few hours ago, they'd finally made camp in a clearing that was sheltered from the wind by a ring of small hills. Kurt had been able to spy on the camp from one of the hills. Mig had cleared the snow with a gesture and then started a fire by igniting a fallen tree. Her men had set up a tent for her, then pulled out sleeping rolls from their packs for themselves. Before Mig retired to her tent, she'd spent some time sitting by the fire, studying what looked like a map. From his hiding place Kurt hadn't been able to see much detail, but he could guess what the map showed—the area to the north of Mother Mountain and the Hanorians' best guess for the location of the Fallen Star.

As she'd studied the map, Mig had muttered to herself, as if voicing some internal argument. Kurt hadn't been able to make out the words, but from time to time, Mig would hit her own thigh, hard. Like her argument with herself was growing violent.

Kurt was terrified of Mig, but watching her punch her own leg had made Kurt feel sorry for the young Hanorian wizard. He wondered if she was suffering from some kind of magic-induced madness.

Ultimately, though, it didn't matter if Mig was crazy or not. If she saw Kurt, she would kill him. If she made it to the Fallen Star before he did, she would use it to destroy Kiranok. He might not be able to beat her in a face-to-face confrontation, but right now they were in a race. Him versus her, winner gets the Fallen Star. Unfortunately, the sides weren't exactly even. She was a wizard. She was better supplied, had better information to work from, and had a cadre of bodyguards at her side.

Kurt had to level the playing field. Luckily, he knew exactly how to do that.

Kurt was going to steal her playbook.

In football, playbooks are big documents that cover all the plays a football team might want to execute on the field. The map was Mig's playbook. If Kurt could get it, he'd have an advantage over the Hanorians. He wouldn't need to follow them anymore. He could rush ahead to the Fallen Star. One person could travel a lot faster than a small army. He would be able to retrieve the Star before the Hanorians could even get close.

Assuming he could pull off the theft.

After she was done studying it, Mig had placed the map in a leather tube and hung the tube off a small tree next to her tent. She'd gone to sleep, as had most of her men. Five of Mig's bodyguards were keeping watch, but they looked half-awake after an entire night of marching. Kurt thought he had a chance.

Now or never.

Kurt got slowly to his feet, making as little noise as possible. Then he broke into a run, dashing down the hill at full speed, praying he wouldn't trip on any rocks or roots hidden in the snow. Kurt had trained for years to run around flailing linemen and charging linebackers. He was fast. He was sure-footed. He could do this.

He was at the map before any of the Hanorians even noticed him. He grabbed the leather tube just as one of the guards finally spotted him and shouted out a warning. Kurt never missed a stride. In football, when a quarterback decides to run, the defense can hit him as hard as they want. Kurt wasn't going to let himself get hit.

A Hanorian guard managed to draw his sword and charge at Kurt. He swung low, intending to cut Kurt's legs out from under him.

Fortunately, Kurt had spent years practicing what to do when someone tried to tackle him low. He jumped over the sweeping sword, landed smoothly, and dashed into the woods. Behind him, he could hear the Hanorians shouting to wake their fellow guards and Mig. From the sound of crashing brush, at least a few of the Hanorians were following him into the woods.

Kurt knew they were too late. He had the ball. He'd gotten past the defenders. Now he just had to beat them to the end zone.

High Priestess Starcaller removed her hands from Lead-pipe's forehead. "That're all I can do for now."

Lexi couldn't see her face. Starcaller had her black hood and veil on. But there was a sadness in her voice that made Lexi imagine her frowning. She felt the same way.

After Billy's Copperplate bodyguards carried the unconscious *kijakgob* back to Billy's quarters, Lexi and Frost had done everything they could to wake him. Nothing had worked, so they'd sent for Starcaller, hoping that the High Priestess of the Night Goddess would succeed where they'd failed. Unfortunately, it didn't look like she'd had any more success than they had. Leadpipe was still out cold.

"What's wrong with him?" Lexi asked.

"You sayed he were attacked by two of our own wizards?" Starcaller asked.

"*Zaj*," Frost said. "I think it were Coldsnap and Grinner. They were behind me in their training at the Blue Chambers, so they were *nai* called to war like me. Coldsnap were a promising student, though I *nai* knowed her all that well. Grinner were always a bit . . . wrong. The type what were *maja* excited to learn spells what could hurt people and haved *nai* interest in the ones what could help folks or fix things. They were the ones what attacked Billy in the Bat Cavern. We stopped them back then. *Zajnai* they decided to make sure the next time they attack, Leadpipe would *nai* be there to protect Billy."

Starcaller thought this over for a moment and then gave a *vajk*, tilting her hooded head from side to side, signaling her reluctant acceptance to the reality at hand.

"Too *maja* many *goben* haved losed too *maja* much in this war," she said. "That much loss break folks. And breaked folks break even more folks. They're like pebbles what roll into rocks what roll into boulders what start a landslide."

"We have to stop them," Lexi said, knowing even as she said it that the High Priestess wouldn't agree.

"For now, your only concern should be Leadpipe," Starcaller said.

"I already tried to help," Lexi said, angrier than she'd intended. "I can't do anything for him. No one can."

"That're where you're wrong," Starcaller said, looking at Lexi sadly. "If *nai* for you, Leadpipe would be dead. The warmth you gived him saved his life. Still, there're more work to do. I casted a spell that'll help him heal. It're *nai* a sure thing, and it're slow, but it're the best I can manage. Now he need watching over. You need to keep him warm, drip water in his mouth from time to time, little by little, so he will *nai* choke. Give him your healing magic when you feel strong enough, but do *nai* force it. If the Goddess are kind, bit by bit, he should heal up. When he're healed enough, he'll open his eyes."

"What if the Goddess are *nai* kind?" Frost asked.

"Tomorrow are *nai* promised, *derijinta*," Starcaller answered gently. "The Goddess can take us whenever she like. Be with Leadpipe now, in his time of need. That're all you can do."

For once, Lexi didn't feel like arguing with an adult who was telling her what to do. As much as she wanted to hunt down Grinner and Coldsnap, she wanted Leadpipe to live even more.

"We're going to have to move him," Lexi said. "It's morning. Time to put Billy's plan into action. He's already in the city giving orders. So we can't leave Leadpipe here."

Starcaller nodded. "King Billy are a clever lad. We're lucky to have him. But his scheme mean there're a thing I need to do now too. Something I were putting off that can wait *nai* longer. So I can *nai* stay with you. I'll send Templars to help, and Mendbreak, the healer what helped Billy after the fight against Sawtooth. He'll give Leadpipe whatever healing magic he can, keep him stable for the move. So I are entrusting him to you. I know you will *nai* let your friend down."

Then she turned to Frost. "Holy Night bless your brother, Frost."

"*Ganzi*," Frost replied. "Holy Night bless us all."

Starcaller turned to go. Lexi could tell the High Priestess wasn't telling them everything about her personal mission.

"Is there anything we can do to help you?" Lexi called after her. "With whatever it is you have to do?"

"What I must do, I must do on my own," Starcaller answered. "Where the Goddess lead, I follow."

With that, she exited the room, leaving Lexi and Frost alone with Leadpipe. Lexi silently wished Starcaller luck. She got a feeling that the goblin priestess was going to need it.

"It's okay, boy," Billy said, petting Torrent's thick chest. "We'll see each other again."

Torrent snuffled. To Billy, the black *vargar* seemed skeptical. Billy didn't blame him. Billy was pretty skeptical himself.

Billy's plan meant that all of Kiranok's livestock and large animals had to be released into the wild. He'd sent Shadow to supervise the release of the remaining war- and taxi-bats. They were supposed to fly with their crews from three different cave mouths, all of which had been reopened for their departure and would be resealed once they were gone. Billy hoped that by exiting from multiple locations at random times, the bats would avoid getting shot down, unlike Hop's expedition. The bats and their riders had orders to scatter to various outlying goblin communities, like the Fastness, Blackstone, and the Smoking Bell. He'd heard many of the bat-riders were planning on taking their families, despite the risk of getting ambushed by the Hanorian wizards. Billy couldn't blame them. If they got past the Hanorians, the riders and their families would be safe, at least for a while. He wished there were enough bats to evacuate the entire city, but they'd need a hundred times as many bats as they had. Plus, there was no guarantee they'd escape unharmed.

He was a lot less worried about Torrent and the rest of the *vargaren*. From Billy's experience, the giant wolflike beasts were more than capable of taking care of themselves. He was certain they'd be able to slink out of tiny out-of-the-way exits from the mountain and disappear into the wilderness.

Still, he would miss Torrent. The black *vargar* might have a nasty temper, but he was brave, determined, and fiercely loyal to Billy. Billy had never had a dog before. In fact, he'd never had a pet of any kind. His family moved too much, and his father was a neat freak who wouldn't put up with the mess and chaos of having an animal in the house. He and Torrent hadn't known each other long, but Billy loved the big shaggy beast, from his bushy tail to his maned, horned head.

"I wish I could take you home," Billy said. "You could live in our backyard. Dad wouldn't like it at first, but we'd win him over."

Torrent's tongue lolled, as if he approved of the idea. Sometimes Billy was certain the *vargar* could understand every word he said, though Frost assured him that wasn't true. The goblin wizard insisted *vargaren* were animals, no smarter than riding bats or *kijakhofen*. Billy didn't buy it. Torrent seemed a lot more intelligent than some dumb riding bat or giant pet rabbit.

"You'd like San Francisco," Billy said. "There are lots of dogs everywhere, and the weather never gets too hot."

Billy pictured himself riding Torrent to school. He imagined the reactions of the students and teachers at prestigious Drake Academy when he trotted up on *vargar*-back. Heck, if he really wanted to make an impression, he could put on the Goblin Crown and the light chain mail shirt Leadpipe insisted he wear all the time. No one would mess with him then.

Billy knew he was procrastinating, delaying and daydreaming so he wouldn't have to say goodbye to Torrent. It was time. At the entrance to the Beastpens, goblin riders and animal handlers were already moving out the last of the *vargaren*, *kijakhofen*, *bokrumen*, and other beasts that had populated the cavern's many stables.

"This is it, boy," Billy said to Torrent, hugging his thick, maned neck. "Get as far away from here as you can. Once it's safe, I'll find you again."

Or maybe I won't, Billy thought. *But he'll be free and safe, and that's better than letting him die.*

Billy pushed Torrent's huge muzzle toward the entrance. "Go."

But Torrent didn't move. He looked back at Billy, sadness in his giant dark eyes.

"I said go! Get out of here!" Billy tried to shove Torrent toward the cave exit, but there was no way he could force the black *vargar* to move when he didn't want to.

"Torrent, please," he pleaded.

As if he understood every word, Torrent nuzzled Billy, then turned and leapt toward the exit from the Beastpens. In a few powerful bounds, the *vargar* was gone. Billy had accomplished his goal.

So why did it feel like he'd lost a friend?

As he stood there, looking at the cave mouth, secretly hoping the *vargar* might come back, Shadow approached him with a small phalanx of Templars. They were in their black battle armor, ready for anything. Shadow bowed.

"Your Majesty," she said.

Billy blinked. His eyes felt a little wet. That wouldn't do. Kings didn't have watery eyes.

"General Shadow," he said, trying to sound royal. "How are we doing?"

"The bats are away. The animals will be loose soon," Shadow said. "Now it're time for the *goben*."

Billy nodded. It all came down to this. If he could convince every last goblin in Kiranok to cooperate with his plan, they might survive. If not . . . It was better not to think about what would happen then.

Setting aside his sadness over Torrent, Billy headed for Seventurns.

"You've been leading goblins your whole life, right, Shadow?" he asked the Templar commander as she fell in at his side.

"*Maja* much of it, at least," she answered.

"How do you do it?" Billy asked. "Is there a secret or something?"

"The trick are to make them think that whatever you want them to do, it're their idea."

"They're never going to think my plan was their idea," Billy said. "They're going to hate it."

"If kinging were easy, everyone would do it," Shadow

said as they reached Seventurns. "Just be yourself. You'll manage."

Shadow sounded confident, so Billy didn't correct her. But what he thought was, *I'm still a kid. I barely know anything about anything. How am I supposed to sell an entire city on a plan I'm not even sure of myself?*

CHAPTER TEN
By Jump, Pull, or Fall

For generations, we have lived in fear of goblin raids on our cities and towns," Lord Jiyal's voice boomed out across the Hanorian camp, magically amplified by the lightworkers standing behind him. "We have seen our livestock stolen, our villages burned, our children slaughtered. But today I say to you, no more!"

The Army of Light erupted in cheers. The entire expedition had been ordered to form up in the center of the camp. As fresh snow fell, the soldiers had assembled in neat rows, unit by unit, with the Lion Guards in their traditional place at the front.

First in line, first to charge, first to die, Cyreth thought. He had no doubt that the final assault on the goblin city was about to begin. He also had no doubt that the Lion Guards would be right in the fore, charging straight into the teeth of the goblins' defenses. All but Ysalion, who was still healing up in her tent, thanks to Dumen's light magic. The reluctant lightworker had stopped Ysalion's bleeding. She was recovering well, though her leg was still sore and weak. Just as importantly, Dumen had apparently kept his mouth shut, since there hadn't been any reprisals. So Ysalion would be okay, and she hadn't had to attend Lord Jiyal's pep talk. On the other hand, not only did Cyreth and the rest of the Lion Guards have to stand at attention through Jiyal's entire speech, they were almost certainly going to die soon, which neutralized whatever morale boost the Lord Marshal's rally might have provided. Cyreth had to admit, Jiyal was a stirring speaker. If only he cared more about his troops than his glorious victory.

"We never asked for this war," Lord Jiyal continued. "We were willing to live in peace, as we have always been."

Sure. We're willing to live in peace as long as the goblins never try to take back the lands our ancestors stole from them, Cyreth thought.

"But goblins don't understand peace," the Lord Marshal thundered. "They're a violent, primitive, murderous race. They live for war. They eat human flesh. They worship an evil goddess of darkness."

Cyreth had prayed to Mother Night plenty of times himself and didn't find her at all evil, but he certainly wasn't going to say that out loud.

Lord Jiyal continued, "The only thing goblins understand is violence. So that's what we'll give them. Do not hesitate. Do not falter. With Father Day's blessing, we will smash our way into their vile nest and exterminate every last one of them. Into their foul darkness, we will bring purifying fire. We will end their threat forever. We march into battle now for each other, for our families, for our people, and for our Empire. But most of all, we march for the Light."

"For the Light!" Lord Marshal Jiyal shouted, as loud as a hundred men. Snowflakes swirled toward the assembled soldiers along with his words, blown by the same spells that gave Jiyal's voice its unnatural power.

The soldiers took up the call, because that's what you were supposed to do during this sort of thing. "For the Light! For the Light! For the Light!"

Cyreth shouted right along with them, but what he was thinking was, *Light and Darkness save me. Light and Darkness save us all.*

From the center of Broadbridge, Billy looked out over the assembled population of Kiranok. Goblins filled the Underway, lining the streets and pathways on both sides of the city's great central chasm.

A cold, magical breeze blew at Billy's back. Frost had conjured it to blow his words to the assembled goblins so even the most distant could hear him clearly.

Billy didn't like public speaking, but he'd given a speech to his goblin subjects once before, at his coronation, so this time his mouth was less dry and he wasn't shaking from anxiety. He just wished he had a better message to deliver.

"Thank you all for coming to hear me," Billy began. "Especially right after *Pikoghul*. I know a lot of you celebrated all through the night."

That elicited a smattering of enthusiastic cheers and exhausted groans from the crowd, which in turn triggered a round of laughter. The party had gone extremely late. In fact, Billy suspected many of the goblins hadn't slept at all. But Billy's plan couldn't wait any longer. Nor could the unpleasant truth he had to share with the residents of Kiranok.

"I also know you're all hoping to hear my plan to save Kiranok from the Army of Light. To save you all," Billy said. "After all, that's why you crowned me King. To help you in your time of need."

A ripple of agreement spread through the crowd. Around the Underway, Billy heard several groups of goblins singing "Come the King." The various groups apparently couldn't all hear each other, since they'd started spontaneously, so no two groups were singing the same part at the same time. Still, Billy could make out bits and pieces of the tune.

Come the King, come the King
From the dark, through the gloom
Come the King, come the King
And make us live again

"Come the King" was Billy's least favorite goblin song. *It's hard not to feel the pressure when they keep singing about how great I am and how I'm supposed to fix all their problems. Especially now.*

"You made me your leader," Billy continued. "My dad taught me that leading is more about responsibility than power. That a good leader protects people and helps them and always puts everyone else first. But most of all, a good leader always tells the truth. And the truth is, I can't save Kiranok. This city is doomed."

The assembled goblins reacted with stunned silence. Then, after a moment, a ripple of discontented whispers turned to worried muttering and then to angry shouting.

Billy let them shout. He couldn't blame them for feeling betrayed and abandoned. He knew he was letting them down. But he couldn't see any other way. There was no way to protect Kiranok forever. Eventually, the Army of Light would break in and put the city to the sword. It was an ugly truth, but the sooner the goblins accepted it, the better. Because losing Kiranok wasn't the same as losing its people.

"Let me explain," Billy shouted, his words amplified by Frost's and Lexi's magic to carry over the noise of the crowd. "Let me explain," Billy said again as the goblins fell silent to listen.

"Let me explain exactly why that is," he said for a third time. "Then let me tell you what we're going to do about it."

Even deep inside the Blue Chambers, Snap could hear the sounds of King Billy's speech and the uneasy reaction of the crowd. She couldn't make out what the *skerbo* boy was saying, but she could tell that the assembled *goben* weren't happy.

Zajnai they'll kill him for me, Snap thought to herself. *Mother Night know I can* nai *seem to do it meself.*

Grinner had wanted to attack King Billy during his speech, but Snap knew that would've been suicide. Though he'd never lost his characteristic smile, Grinner was clearly angered by Snap's refusal to go along with his plan. He'd gone down to his secret chamber and sealed the door behind him. He was probably torturing his last few rats to get out his frustrations.

Better them than me, Snap thought.

Snap was starting to regret recruiting Grinner. He was far too dangerous to be a reliable ally. In fact, she was starting to regret her entire quest to kill the *skerbo* usurper.

It all maked sense at first taste, Snap thought, reviewing her logic. *Humans are bad. Humans are coming to kill us. A human maked himself our king. All humans must die. The King must die.*

But now Icewall was dead, Grinner seemed to be getting even more murderous, and Snap wasn't entirely convinced of her own sanity anymore. After all they'd been through, she and Grinner were back hiding in the Blue Chambers, with no idea what to do next. Snap wondered if she'd fallen into madness somewhere along the way. Had she become a *graznak*, an empty jar, addicted to using magic, relishing the power it gave her over others, hungering to destroy and kill?

If so, she had the solution in her hand.

Snap had sought it out after her most recent argument with Grinner. She'd waited until he'd disappeared, off to his secret room, then she'd gone to the alchemy lab, isolated in its own wing of the Blue Chambers.

The room had been sealed when the Blue Chambers' chief alchemist, Whiskglop, had marched off to Sawtooth's War, never to return. Snap had been the alchemist's favorite student, and Whisk had told her the secret to opening the door to his lab before he left. There were gears inside the door that could be manipulated with magic if you knew how. Turn this gear, lower that rod, rotate another gear the opposite direction, and *click*, the door would unlock.

Snap had gone to Whiskglop's lab to retrieve the alchemist's proudest creation, a potion called the Final Drop. Whiskglop had started working on the potion after a former student, Moonfall, had gone mad from using too much magic. Moonfall had become so powerful and erratic that every living goblin wizard had been forced to work together to kill her. Afterward, Whisk had decided there had to be a better way. After years of research and experimentation, he'd created the Final Drop. The alchemist had told Snap that if a wizard drank the potion, he or she would lose the ability to cast magic forever.

Unfortunately, Whisk had died at Solace Ridge, and his recipe had died with him. Snap knew the brilliant old wizard had managed to make only a single dose. But on the bright side, she also knew exactly where the alchemist had hidden it.

Inside the lab, Snap had lifted a floor stone to reveal a hidden compartment containing a single crystal vial. Inside the vial was a tiny amount of dark-green liquid. The Final Drop was exactly where Whiskglop had left it.

Snap brought the green potion to an old bunkroom deep in the Blue Chambers. She'd lived in the bunkroom for a few happy months when she'd first arrived at the Chambers. She'd always found the old group quarters comforting. It seemed like a good place to decide on her next move.

She had three choices: drink the Final Drop, somehow force Grinner to drink it, or put the potion back in its hiding place and continue her crusade to kill King Billy.

If she thought Grinner really was out of control, getting him to drink the Final Drop would render him powerless. Without his magic, Grinner wasn't a threat to anyone. Snap knew the mice would be grateful.

But Grinner wasn't her only worry. If she were losing her mind herself, becoming a *graznak*, drinking the Final Drop was the only thing that could save her.

Or zajnai *it're* nai *right for either of us to drink the Final Drop. There are still a chance I were right all along and the real danger are King Billy.*

Snap looked at the Final Drop, stirring the dark-green liquid in its crystal vial. She didn't feel insane. Confused and lost and a little afraid, but not crazy. She didn't want to kill everyone. She felt bad that they might have killed Frost's *kijakgob* brother. She wanted to kill only one person—the *skerbo* king.

Right or wrong, I have me reasons for that, Snap thought. *If me reasons are sane, then I can* nai *be a* graznak. *Can I?*

Which is when, to her surprise, Snap heard . . .

"You look troubled, *derijinta.*"

Snap turned toward the entrance to the bunkroom, closing her hand around the Final Drop. Someone had found her hiding place.

"*Zajnai* I can help?" the intruder continued.

As sincere as the offer sounded, Snap's first instinct was to cold-blast the intruder into oblivion. The problem was that she recognized the old *svagob* standing in the doorway, despite her hooded black robes and the veil covering her face. And she knew that not only would cold-blasting her probably fail, it went against everything Snap was trying to do. After all, she couldn't claim to be rescuing her people if she killed the leader of their religion.

"High Priestess Starcaller," Coldsnap said, trying to keep her voice calm. "I're honored you've come to visit me home. Such as it are."

"*Nai* of us get the lives we imagine," Starcaller answered. "Where and how we live are *nai* always up to us. It're only how we act that we can control. How we treat them around us."

There was no trace of accusation in the High Priestess's voice, and all Snap could really see of her face were her iron-colored eyes, but Snap could tell that Starcaller knew what Snap and Grinner had been doing. And Snap knew she didn't approve.

"I can explain—" Snap began.

Starcaller cut her off with a gesture.

"I are *nai* here for that," she said. "I're *nai* here about why you want King Billy dead. Or about them other folks you hurt. Or even them what you killed. I have deeper business."

"Deeper business?" Snap asked, confused.

"The Night Goddess's business," Starcaller replied. Then, to Snap's surprise, she removed her hood and veil. The priestess looked old and tired and a little sad. "The Night Goddess comed to me in a dream," she continued. "My time are near finished. When a High Priestess are nearing her end, the Night Goddess send her a vision of her successor. She sended me a dream of you."

"Me?" That confused Snap even more. "I're your enemy. You crowned the *skerbo* king. I're trying to kill him."

"I do *nai* claim to understand the ways of the Goddess," Starcaller said. "On first taste, *zajnai* she are telling me that you're right and I're wrong. But that're hard to chew, acause when I crowned King Billy, all my dreams telled me it were the right thing to do. So on second taste, *naizaj* even though you're wrong about the King, the Goddess see something in you . . . a promise, a wisp of a future. *Naizaj* the Night have a plan for you that're better than your own. Better than hiding in a hole, consorting with a lunatic, and plotting murder and destruction."

"What if I do *nai* agree with the Goddess's plan?" Snap asked. "What if I do *nai* want to wear the robes and hide from the sun and do her bidding for the rest of me life?"

"The Goddess do *nai* force *goben* to obey her words," Starcaller replied. "That're *nai* the way of the Night. The Night are for shelter and comfort, for peace and rest.

Her words are an invitation. Heed them or *nai*. That're your choice. But if you decide to follow in my path, when I're dead, you go to Chief Templar Shadow, and you say this . . ."

Starcaller leaned in and whispered a short poem to Snap.

"Can you remember that?" the High Priestess asked.

Snap nodded. She'd never been great at memorizing songs or poems, but it felt like the words that Starcaller whispered had burned themselves into her mind. Snap didn't think she could forget them even if she wanted to.

"Repeat it back to me," Starcaller said. "Just so we're certain."

But before Coldsnap could repeat the poem, a long blade of ice burst from Starcaller's chest. Blood sprayed out, then froze in the air, falling to the chamber floor like red hail. For half a heartbeat, Starcaller just stood there, looking surprised. Then the blade retracted and the High Priestess's body slumped to the ground, revealing Grinner, standing behind her, holding a spear made of ice.

"What're you doing?" Coldsnap shouted.

Grinner casually tossed aside the spear he'd conjured. It dropped to the stone floor and shattered into countless pieces.

"What we sayed we would do," Grinner said with his characteristic smirk. "Kill King Billy's allies. Make him vulnerable and weak. This old bug were the one what crowned the *skerbo*. The one what pledged the Templars to support him. She needed to go."

She wanted me to succeed her, Coldsnap thought. But she didn't say the words out loud. How much had Grinner heard? How long had he been in the room?

"I're surprised you *nai* killed her yourself," Grinner continued. "What were she jabbering about?"

So Grinner hadn't heard? Snap felt relieved . . . though she wasn't sure why. She wasn't going to take Starcaller up on her offer. So why did she care if Grinner heard it or not?

"Fate and such," Snap answered, some part of her not willing to divulge the full truth.

"The usual mystic *drak*," Grinner said dismissively. "I decide me fate. Other folks' fates too, if I can help it. I decided the fate of this old *svagob* when I stabbed her through the chest. The *skerbo* king are next."

I should open the vial and force the Final Drop down your throat, Snap thought.

But she couldn't bring herself to do it. And she knew why: *I decided me own fate, when I recruited Icewall and Grinner*, she thought. *Even though I knowed one were soft and the other were poison. I tied meself to them both regardless. And there are no undoing that now. It're like making an alloy. You blend the metals together, and they form something new. Me and Grinner and Icewall are* nai *the same people together as we were apart. Grinner are bolder. I're more ruthless. And Icewall . . . Icewall are dead.*

"*Zaj*," she said, seeing no other way. "Time to finish what we beginned. King Billy are next."

She headed out of the former bunkroom, the Final Drop still hidden in her hand. Grinner followed, leaving Starcaller's corpse behind them in a pool of her own half-frozen blood. Snap didn't look back at the body . . . or at the old bunkroom. She would never feel safe there again. It was a tomb now.

Hop was reasonably certain he was about to die.

Admittedly, it wasn't the first time he'd felt this way.

Hop was not, by nature, an optimist. And despite his best efforts to maintain a peaceful, boring existence, he'd lived a regrettably exciting life. So he'd anticipated his impending death many, many times. When he was a soldier, he'd gone into every battle certain he'd be slaughtered. When he was a Copperplate, he'd reported for duty each day wondering if he'd be killed by a criminal or swarmed over in a riot. As a warbat commander, he'd spent every waking moment afraid he'd fall to his death. As King Billy's advisor and confidant, he'd lived in constant fear of assassination by his fellow goblins or eventual execution at the hands of the Hanorians.

But I nai *ever imagined I'd get eaten alive,* Hop thought. *And right now, that are looking more and more likely.* Nai *seem like a good way to go though. Better do me best to avoid it. But how? That're the question.*

Hop had first suspected something was stalking him a few hours earlier. He'd slept for a few hours, right around dawn, then set out again, heading north, determined to find the Fallen Star. But not long after he resumed his journey, he'd noticed strange ripples in the packed snow behind him. He initially thought the movement was being caused by the wind, but he soon noticed that the ripples were moving steadily toward him, regardless of the wind direction. Something large was moving through the snow, following him.

Then, as Hop moved from an area of drifting powder into more packed snow, the ripples became a long, continuous ridge several hands wide and a dozen paces long. Seeing that, Hop knew what was after him.

It was an ice wyrm.

Hop had heard stories of the vicious predators, huge feathered snakelike beasts that stalked the lands north of Mother Mountain. They came out only in the winter, burrowing under the snow to stalk their prey, then attacking by ambush. According to the stories, they could swallow an entire *kijakhof* or *bokrum* in one bite. Hop had grown up on the Bowlus Plateau, near the southern end of the Iron-spine Mountains, where deep snow was rare. As a child, he'd loved hearing about ice wyrms and snow apes and greatdeer and the other exotic creatures of the far north. He'd told his father he would see a snow ape himself one day. That he would ride a greatdeer. That he would kill an ice wyrm and make a cape from its feathered hide.

His father, who'd traveled north in his youth, had told him he'd be better off staying home, marrying a local girl, settling down, and making a nice life for himself.

Not for the first time, Hop wished he'd listened.

Hop had retrieved his spear after his taxi-bat had died, and he was wearing chain mail . . . but that didn't make him feel any more confident that he could actually kill the wyrm and get his feathered cape. Avoiding a fight seemed like a far better option. So even after real-izing he was being stalked, Hop kept moving north. He tried to avoid the deep snow and keep to higher, rocky ground, following one ridgeline after another. He hoped the ice wyrm, unable to reach him on the ridges, would eventually give up. Unfortunately, the ice wyrm seemed determined to eat Hop, despite the inconvenient terrain. It pursued him doggedly. The tree-lined ridge Hop had been following seemed to be sloping down, with no new ridge in sight. He looked back. The ice wyrm was below him and to his left, paralleling the ridge, moving through the deep snow with ease. He glanced down the opposite side of the ridge. To his right, the ridge dropped sharply, more cliff than slope, plummeting to a deep ravine cut by a fast-moving river partially covered in ice. The only way to go was forward.

Hop rounded a tree, only to find a thicket of snow-covered brush blocking his path. He forced his way through the brush . . .

And stopped abruptly. There was a cliff just on the other side of the hedge, a sharp drop. Hop looked down. A dozen or so paces below him, the cliff ended in a pile of boulders. Beyond that, a long, uninterrupted snowfield stretched several *loktepen* to the north, sliced neatly in half by the river ravine. There was nowhere to go. Hop wondered if he should run back south. Hopefully the ice wyrm would lose interest, and he could find another way north. That's when he saw the glow.

Hop spotted an orange pulsing light coming from a depression in the snowfield, right by the ravine, a few hours, walk to the north. It looked like an ember from a smoldering fire. Hop could think of only one thing that could burn in all that snow.

It had to be the Fallen Star, sitting in a crater, still glowing with heavenly light.

All Hop had to do was jump down the cliff, dash across the snowfield fast enough to outrun the ice wyrm, grab the Star, double back, and get back to the cliff. A quick climb up to safety, and he'd have a clear path back to Kiranok.

The only problem with his plan was that it was impossible. It might cost him hours, but he'd have to head south again and find a safer route to the Star. At least he knew where it was now. Hop turned south . . .

Which was when he saw the Hanorians. A column of human soldiers was marching in his direction. They were on the other side of the ravine, maybe ten *loktepen* away, but their dark forms were clearly visible against the snow. From the rate they were moving, Hop guessed they'd be at the glowing crater by dusk. If Hop went south, the Hanorians would get to the Star before he did.

"*Nai* helping it," he muttered to himself.

Hop tightened the straps of his pack, gripped his spear as tightly as he could in his right hand, then looked down.

Sometime when you're at the top of a cliff, the void call at you, he reflected. *You get that feeling that, whether it're by push, jump, or fall, you're headed straight for the bottom. One way or the other.*

Hop jumped.

Hop didn't consider himself an expert at much, but he was a really, really good jumper. He'd gotten his calling-name, Hoprock, from how nimbly he used to leap and scramble across the rocky terrain of the Bowlus Plateau. So while jumping down the steep, stony incline might have been suicidal for most *goben*, for Hop it was just insanely dangerous.

He dropped over two body lengths before he hit a jagged rock protruding from the cliff face. Hop let his legs bend to absorb the impact, then kicked off for another leap. He landed on a narrow ledge several spans to the right and another body length down. He was moving too fast to stop now. He pushed off again, this time to the left, twisted in midair, and landed on a large, rounded boulder several body lengths above the ground. It should have been an easy landing, but Hop realized, too late, that the boulder was covered with a thin slick of ice.

Hop's feet slipped out from under him. He lost his footing and fell.

Luckily for Hop, he was something of an expert at falling off cliffs. He'd spent most of his childhood clambering around the Plateau's inclines and canyons. So he'd fallen off a cliff before, more than once.

The cliff face was sloped slightly instead of completely vertical. Hop hoped that would make all the difference. As he skidded along the cliff face, he used his dragging spear like a rudder to steer his body as best he could, trying to avoid the sharp rocks that studded the cliff. Unfortunately, he couldn't avoid them all. About halfway down the cliff, his head banged into one such rock. Hop lost his grip on his spear, which went clattering to the ground below. The blow made Hop dizzy and half blind, but he tried to keep his focus. He was falling fast. He saw a clump of brush protruding from the cliff wall, coming up fast. He figured if he could land on it, the bush might break his fall. He tried to control his skid and aim for the bush with his feet . . .

But he was moving too fast. His feet went wide of the bush by a few spans.

Somehow, though, as the brush rushed by his face, Hop managed to reach out and snag it with his injured left hand. He held on with all his might as his arm and the bush took his weight. The impact wrenched his shoulder and sent a lightning bolt of pain shooting from his broken little finger through his arm, but his grip held. He'd done it!

Then the bush tore out by the roots. Hop tumbled down the cliff. He had no control now, but he thought maybe, just maybe, he'd slowed himself enough that he wouldn't die when he hit the ground.

Hop smashed into the snowy ground, sending up a plume of white flakes. He'd missed the rocks. He was banged up, but he was alive.

Hop stood up in the waist-deep snow. He hurt all over, but he could still move. He brushed himself off, retrieved his spear, and began walking north, toward the Fallen Star.

Then he heard a horrible screeching roar as the ice wyrm burst from the snow a few paces away. It lunged at Hop, its slick white feathers shedding snow, its giant, toothy mouth gaping wide, trying to swallow him whole.

With a tremendous bang, the Hanorian wizards blasted away the rubble blocking Seventurns.

"Charge!" Cyreth yelled.

The Lion Guards roared into Monster Mountain at the fore of the Army of Light, ready to fight for their lives against dug-in goblin defenders.

Only there weren't any.

The Lion Guards breached the first wall without encountering any resistance. The next wall was no different. Nor was the next. The Lion Guards charged one wall after another, prepared to pay for every step in blood, only to find that the fortifications inside the mountain had been abandoned. There wasn't a goblin in sight.

Finally, after surmounting the final wall, Cyreth and his soldiers reached an open passage. They milled about, confused.

"Where are they?" Cyreth heard Bytha ask from her position in the front ranks.

"Could be a trap of some kind," Cyreth said. He was just as confused as the rest of the Lion Guards, but it was his job to be decisive, to give orders, to think for his soldiers so they wouldn't have to worry about anything except fighting.

"Form up," Cyreth ordered. *Better to be careful than dead*, he thought.

The Lion Guards fell into formation. Cyreth walked to the front.

"Lock shields!" he ordered.

The soldiers in the front line tightened their ranks until their shields overlapped. The following ranks raised their shields over their heads, creating a formation the Hanorians called the Steel Wall. The formation protected the Lion Guards from arrows or spears, turning them into a kind of moving fortress.

"Slow advance in cadence," he ordered. "Weapons ready."

Swords drawn, shields locked, the Lion Guards advanced, calling out a cadence to synchronize their steps:

We roar as one. Ur-rar!
Hear us. We come. Ur-rar!
You know you're done! Ur-rar!
It's time to run. Ur-rar!

With each "ur-rar," the formation took two measured steps forward, their boots making a loud bang, their armor rattling, and their shields clashing like thunder. The Lion Guards' Steel Wall moved down the corridor like a giant beast, its roar a thousand voices strong.

Still, the goblins didn't attack.

"Double time," Cyreth shouted. "Ur-rar! Ur-rar! Ur-rar! Ur-rar!"

The Lion Guards broke into a trot, taking up the double time "ur-rar." In moments, they'd reached the bottom of the corridor—a huge roaring, rattling monster come for blood.

The corridor opened into an enormous plaza overlooking a giant canyon. Cyreth scanned for danger. But all he saw were abandoned food carts and a few small stages scattered about the plaza, which was lined by homes and shops on two sides.

There were no goblins anywhere.

"Lion Guards, halt!" Cyreth shouted to his soldiers. The monster, with its two thousand legs and thousand scales and thousand sharp metal fangs, stopped on command and roared "Ur-rar!" as one, acknowledging the order.

"Deploy crescent," he ordered. "Three rows deep."

"Ur-rar!" The soldiers spread out, transforming their long, shielded column into a broad, sweeping crescent formation.

"Hold position," Cyreth said.

"Ur-rar!" the Lion Guards roared back.

Cyreth walked to the stone railing at the edge of the chasm, then looked down.

Below him was a world.

The chasm stretched into the mountain, as far as Cyreth could see in the dim light, which came from softly glowing mushrooms that grew along the cave wall. It was lined with streets and buildings, decorated with statues and fountains, and crisscrossed by bridges and gondola lines. It was an amazing sight, a magnificent city every bit as beautiful as Gran Hanor.

It was also completely empty. Not a living thing moved anywhere in the maze of streets, buildings, caverns, and chasms. There were no voices, no footfalls. All Cyreth could hear was the breathing and rattling of the Lion Guards behind him, the trickle of distant fountains, and the creaking of the gondolas swinging forgotten on their cables in the middle of the chasm.

"Captain, report," Cyreth heard behind him, amid a clatter of armor and hooves.

He turned and saw Lord Marshal Jiyal astride an armored warhorse, flanked by a trio of wizards and a dozen Black Hussars, the cavalrymen assigned to protect the Emperor and the imperial elite. Wearing their full-beaked helms and their black enameled armor and carrying their distinctive long lances decorated with black feathers, the Hussars reminded Cyreth of a murder of crows, flocking around the Lord Marshal. Only crows would be squawking and making noise. The Hussars were completely silent.

"Entrance secure, milord," Cyreth replied.

"I can see that, heretic," Lord Jiyal snarled. "Why aren't you advancing? Your orders were to put the city to the sword."

"Aye, milord," Cyreth said, wincing internally. It was one thing for the Lord Marshal to accuse him of heresy in private, but doing it here, in front of his Lion Guards, the wizards, and the Black Hussars could only lead to trouble. Still, Cyreth tried to stay calm and keep his voice respectful. "But there's no one to put the sword to. See for yourself."

Cyreth gestured toward the chasm. The Lord Marshal spurred his horse, riding up to the railing at the end of the plaza.

"They're gone?" Lord Jiyal said with disbelief. "An entire city gone?"

"It appears so, milord," Cyreth answered cautiously.

Cyreth had been perfectly polite and had observed the necessary decorum, but the Lord Marshal blew up at him anyway.

"It appears!" Jiyal repeated angrily. "It *appears*," he said again with even more venom. "But appearances can lie. As you well know, Captain."

The way Jiyal said "captain" made it sound like the vilest of insults. But the Lord Marshal wasn't done.

"Find them," he ordered. "Find the goblins, and kill them all."

CHAPTER ELEVEN
Time to Wake

When Billy proposed his plan, even his friends had doubted him. Moving the entire population of Kiranok into the caverns below the city had seemed impossible. But Billy had insisted evacuating the city was the only way to save the goblins. So he'd given the necessary orders and mobilized the Templars and Copperplates to coordinate the move. Then he'd given his speech . . .

And the goblins had taken it from there.

Billy knew goblins valued individualism. They didn't much care for getting ordered around. They liked to argue. So it could be difficult to get them motivated. But once they were convinced to do something, the goblins did it. Full tilt. Nonstop. Until he came to Kiranok, Billy's mother was the hardest-working person he'd ever met. As an ER nurse, she worked long hours at a stressful job, never complaining, always doing what needed to be done. But even Billy's mother, on her best day, couldn't work as hard as a motivated goblin. It sometimes felt like goblins had only two ways of doing a job: not at all or all at once.

After Billy's speech, the city swarmed with activity. Billy spent the day moving around Kiranok, trying to pitch in and keep things going. But he wasn't really needed. The goblins had embraced his plan with gusto. Billy saw goblin children running back and forth to the caverns, hauling sacks of flour and preserved mushrooms. He saw a *kijakgob* carrying three ancient goblins toward the caverns at once, one in each arm and one on her shoulders. He almost got run over by a hundred sloshing water barrels being rolled down a slope of the Underway by a half dozen howling *jintagoben*. Billy recognized one of the barrel-rollers. The vicious little goblin had tried to kill Billy, Lexi, and Kurt during their attempt to crown Kurt king. But this time he just shouted, "Out of the way, Your Majesty," as he herded the barrels downhill with a stick.

The entire evacuation became a chaotic blur. Billy moved some barrels himself, helped a panicked goblin track down his missing child, and directed traffic to clear a jammed intersection overfilled with carts and giant rams and heavily laden pedestrians.

Then it was over. Shadow came to him and reported that, incredibly, improbably, Kiranok had been almost entirely emptied. There were a few stragglers who'd refused to leave their homes, determined to fight to the death. But the vast majority of the population was now safely hidden in the caverns.

Billy ordered Shadow to seal all the entrances linking the city to the caves. A small army of masons went to work, aided by Frost, Lexi, and the handful of remaining goblin wizards. They didn't just seal the entrances, they hid them with stonework and dirt, making it look like the tunnels had never existed at all.

The goblins were safe . . . for now. But Billy knew the caverns weren't a permanent solution. He doubted the Hanorians would just leave in frustration after breaking into the empty city. He expected them to move into Kiranok and continue their quest to exterminate the goblins.

To make that as difficult as possible, Billy had had a few of the caverns' better-hidden exits to the surface left open. He'd ordered Shadow to plan raids out into the Ironspine Mountains to harass the Hanorians' supply lines and stop food and equipment from reaching their army. Still Billy feared that the goblins' hiding place would be discovered eventually. No secret could stay hidden forever.

Then there was the Fallen Star. It was looking more and more like Hop and Kurt and their entire expedition had been lost. It'd been days and, so far, no survivors of the Hanorian ambush had returned to Kiranok. Scouts who'd slipped out to search the mountain hadn't found any survivors either, only some scorched bodies of both expedition members and their taxi-bats. If the entire expedition really had been killed, not only had Billy lost his friends, it also meant Frost and Lexi would never be able to wield the Fallen Star against the Hanorians. Instead it was much more likely that the Hanorians would get it and use it against the goblins.

So there were still a lot of things that could go wrong and lead to the goblins' destruction. Billy knew he had to come up with a permanent solution to the goblins' plight, one that would protect them from the Hanorian threat forever.

And he needed to do it soon, before time ran out.

The ice wyrm struck.

Hop had ducked and dodged countless attacks from the beast as he ran north. So far, he'd successfully avoided getting swallowed. More importantly, he was getting closer to the Fallen Star. The glow was bright now. For the last few hundred heartbeats, he'd been running parallel to a long, deep gouge in the snow, a scar left by the Star as it skidded across the landscape. He was maybe a *loktep* south of the crater itself, heading up a slight slope, when the ice wyrm launched its latest attack, exploding out of the snow and roaring at Hop, its mouth agape.

This time he dodged a hair too late.

The ice wyrm's teeth raked down his left shoulder, tearing off his pack. If not for his chain mail shirt, the wyrm would've torn Hop's arm off. As it was, it knocked him to the ground and made him scream in agony.

Hop rolled to one side as the ice wyrm's maw came shooting at him for a second bite. It came up drooling snow. With a roar, it reared back, readying for another attack. Hop rolled again, raising his spear, but the ice wyrm smashed the spear out of his grip and sent it flying. But even though it had disarmed Hop, it didn't follow up with an immediate lunge. Instead, the monster held its head high in the air, weaving from side to side like a coiled snake, waiting for the perfect moment for a final, deadly strike.

The ice wyrm seemed determined not to miss Hop again.

Fighting to remain focused despite his pain and exhaustion, Hop noticed a large stone sticking out of the snow to his right. He inched closer to it. He figured if he dodged at just the right moment, he might be able to trick the wyrm into smashing its face into the rock. But he had to time it perfectly. Dodge too soon and the ice wyrm would be able to adjust and chomp right onto Hop's back. Dodge too late and the wyrm would rip open Hop's chest.

Hop thought he saw his moment. The monster's head reared back a little, preparing to strike. As its head came down, Hop rolled away from the stone.

But something snagged his chain mail. A branch buried in the snow? Hop wasn't sure, but he was stuck. The ice wyrm's mouth was coming straight at his face.

Then something hit the monster from behind and knocked its head wide.

The ice wyrm reared back up and roared in fury.

In response, Hop heard a familiar voice yell "Wildcats!" and saw a muscular figure in goblin armor swing a sword at its head.

It was Kurt. The quarterback had come to rescue him.

It was game time.

Kurt had been following the map he'd stolen from the Hanorians, pushing to get as far ahead of them as possible. He was exhausted, cold, and hungry, but he knew he was getting close to the Star. He'd first seen its glow over an hour ago, coming from a few miles farther north. He pushed even harder after that, slogging through the deep snow, drawing on the endurance and resolve that made him such a good athlete.

Fourth quarter, he told himself. *Your team needs a winning drive. Time to shine.*

Then he saw Hop.

When Kurt first spotted the former Copperplate, he

was maybe a half mile ahead, waist deep in snow, moving toward the Star. Even at that distance, he could tell it was Hop by his distinctive gait and his copper shield. Eager to catch up, Kurt tried to muster more speed. Despite his fatigue, Kurt was taller and stronger than Hop, so the snow didn't slow him down as much. Over the next few minutes, the quarterback steadily gained ground. He thought about calling out to the one-eared goblin, but he didn't want the Hanorians to hear him. He figured Hop would see him coming eventually. But as he got closer, he could tell the goblin was still oblivious to his approach. Hop kept glancing back behind him, anxiously, like something was chasing him.

Kurt was still several hundred yards away when he saw a giant, feathered white snake burst out of the snow at Hop. The goblin dodged, and the thing disappeared back into the snow. Hop began moving in a more irregular pattern, making it harder for the snake-monster to hit him. As Kurt rushed to catch up, the creature lunged at the goblin a few more times, trying to grab him with its huge jaws.

Finally, when Kurt was a dozen yards away, the thing raked Hop across the shoulder with its teeth, knocking him to the ground with a scream of pain.

Kurt drew his sword and charged.

Kurt had been training with swords ever since his time at the Fastness. He'd figured swordsmanship might be a good skill to have, given the circumstances. Luckily, it turned out being a good swordsman required a lot of the same skills as being a good quarterback. In both cases, the secret was the footwork. So he'd picked up the basics of sword fighting pretty quickly, but he'd never had to put his new skills into practice . . .

Until now.

He swung at the snake-thing's neck with all his might. His sword hit home, a perfect strike . . .

But the sword bounced right off. It felt like he'd chopped into a brick wall. All he'd done was scrape away a section of white feathers, revealing the monster's thick scaly hide underneath.

On the bright side, he'd made the thing forget about Hop. With a hideous screech, it twisted its entire body around and lashed at Kurt.

Don't get sacked! Kurt thought to himself as he pivoted away from the monster's giant mouth.

He raised his sword in a two-handed grip, parrying the way Azam had taught him back at the Fastness.

Which, in retrospect, was a mistake. The feathered snake's head smashed into his sword like a car moving fifty miles an hour. The blow sent Kurt's sword flying out of his hands and sent a shock through his body that nearly knocked him flat.

Faster than a blitzing cornerback, the thing reared back, ready for another blow.

Which is when Hop stabbed it in the back with his spear.

"Die, you *pizkret*!" Hop yelled as he struck.

Hop's lunging attack managed to penetrate the monster's thick hide, at least a little. It screeched in pain, jerking itself free from the tip of Hop's spear.

Kurt used its momentary distraction to frantically dig through the snow and retrieve his sword. He'd realized that slashing with the weapon wouldn't do much good. The only way to bring the monster down was with a well-placed stab. He knew just the spot. Unfortunately, as he was positioning himself for his attack, the feathered snake twisted its head toward Hop and slashed at the goblin with its fangs. Hop tried to dodge, but the thing tore at his chest, shredding his chain mail shirt and sending him flying.

"Hey, ugly!" Kurt shouted, trying to distract it before it could finish Hop.

The monster twisted toward Kurt, hissing.

Kurt jumped at the monster, reaching as high as he could and plunging his sword, tip first, into the thing's mouth. It hit with a meaty thunk and stuck deep. The monster thrashed and screeched, whipping Kurt through the air. He tried desperately to hang on to his sword, but the monster's violent thrashes were too much for him. Kurt lost his grip and flew through the air.

For a moment, time seemed to slow, like it did when he stepped back to throw a pass and a huge defensive end was charging him, trying to crush him before he could get the ball away. He could see the sky, a dusting of snowflakes swirling through the air. He could feel the cold wind on his face, hear the anguished screeches of the feathered snake-thing.

Then he hit the ground.

"I can *nai* tell if he're getting better or worse," Frost admitted to Lexi as they knelt over Leadpipe. "But if his life are rolling down the hill, I figure we need to stop it. Or if he're climbing up, *zajnai* he could use a little help."

Frost had found a place for his brother off in a corner of one of the larger caverns under Kiranok, behind a small cluster of stalagmites. Leadpipe was shaking and muttering to himself in his sleep. Lexi felt the giant goblin's forehead. He was feverish. She touched his hand. It was ice cold.

"It's shock, I think," Lexi said, trying to remember the first aid basics she'd learned as a Girl Scout.

Unfortunately, she'd got bored with Scouts and quit after only a year, so her memories were a bit fuzzy. "Or it could be an infection. I don't know. But I think he's sick."

She looked around. "Have you sent for Mendbreak?"

Mendbreak was the goblin healer who'd helped Billy after the battle against Sawtooth, when he'd won his crown. Billy had told her how gentle and skilled Mendbreak had been. If anyone could help Leadpipe, it'd be him.

But Frost frowned. "Mendbreak are in a deep cavern with all the patients from the Hall of Mercy. He're tending to dozens of the sick and dying, poor old *goben* what could *nai* hold up to the stress of the evacuation, soldiers and Copperplates injured during the battle at Seventurns, little *pikoen* what catched the growl-cough from the refugees. He can *nai* leave a hundred patients for just one."

"Then it has to be us," Lexi said, determined.

But the truth was, the last thing she wanted to do at that moment was work magic. Frost had sent for her as she'd been finishing up hiding one of the cave entrances, using her fire magic to fuse together a wall of rubble into a solid sheet of stone. She'd come running to help her friend, of course, but Lexi had never felt so tired.

The one good thing about being so hyper was that Lexi usually had boundless energy. She could work on a paper until super late at night and still spend a few hours watching music videos on the Internet while simultaneously chatting on her phone with any of her friends who might still be awake. And no matter how late she stayed up, how little sleep she might get, she was always ready to go the next day. When she was little, her father had called her "Tigger," after the *Winnie the Pooh* character who bounced on his tail everywhere he went. Lexi always had bounce.

Until she started doing magic. Channeling the hot energy swirling inside of her and focusing it into spells was the most exhausting thing Lexi had ever done. Just casting a single spell left her winded and tired. Casting several in a row, or keeping one up for hours, left her bone-tired. She'd never really understood that expression until now. Her father used to say it sometimes when he got home from work. He maintained boats for a living. He'd spend hours working at his dry dock near the Half Moon Bay Marina, sanding and patching and painting boats, then come home, plop on the couch with a beer, and stare at the TV. When Lexi was little, she'd always try to get him to play or look at her latest art project or read her a book, and he'd never have the energy.

"I can't right now, Tigger," he'd say. "I'm bone-tired."

She used to think that was a stupid expression. Bones were solid things. How could they get tired? Muscles got tired. But bones were just . . . bones.

Now, though, she knew what he meant. Working magic tired her to the bone. Lately, she'd been going nonstop. All she wanted to do was rest. Or even better, go back to Nokala's Pools and soak her weary bones. But Leadpipe was family, and he needed her help. She could rest later.

"I'll warm up his body. You cool down his head," Lexi said.

Without waiting for an answer, she placed her hands on Leadpipe's chest. His skin felt cool and slightly damp, like the cavern floor. She focused on warming Leadpipe back up, healing whatever in him was broken . . .

And then she was standing by the entrance to a giant cavern, facing the hastily installed wall that separated it from Kiranok. All around her, goblins were panicking as the wall came apart, piece by piece.

A massive golden lion smashed through the weakened wall. It was fifty feet tall and made of metal. Behind it came an army of dead men, rotting corpses in armor, staggering toward the cavern. Lexi's hand burst into flames. She looked at it, surprised, as it melted like wax.

Then Lexi's perspective shifted, and she was in a puppet booth holding the strings on a puppet that looked just like her. The puppet was covered in cloth flames of red and gold that she could make flicker and wave by operating a bellows with her foot. The golden lion was a puppet too, operated by a tall, faceless puppeteer dressed from head to toe in white robes.

But there were strings on the faceless puppeteer as well. Strings on Lexi too. When she looked up, she could see yet another puppeteer, a giant as tall as the sky. The giant was pulling both their strings and holding hundreds more strings from a thousand arms. The giant laughed and snow came out of its mouth and then it burst into flames, and everything around Lexi, the cavern walls, the goblins, the golden lion, caught fire—

"Lexi, wake up," Lexi heard. Whoever was speaking had a deep, bass voice. A voice that sounded familiar.

"Leadpipe?" Lexi muttered, opening her eyes.

Indeed, it was Leadpipe. But somehow, after Lexi had placed her hands on Leadpipe's chest, their positions had become reversed. Now she was the one lying on the cavern floor, and Leadpipe and Frost were kneeling over her.

"You waked me up," Leadpipe rumbled. "I were cold, and the world seemed *maja* far away, and then I felt your hands on my chest, and it all getted warm, and the next thing I knowed I were awake . . . and you were the one with your eyes closed."

Lexi could see that Leadpipe was still weak. His broad shoulders were slouched, and his sharply pointed ears, which he usually held high, hung low, their tips draping across the back of his neck like pigtails. But he was conscious. He was alive. Lexi felt a rush of joy at that realization. She hadn't felt so happy in a long time.

Lexi threw her arms around Leadpipe and hugged him for all he was worth.

"I'm glad you made it," Lexi said. "We were worried about you."

"Now me and Lead are worried about you," Frost said, looking at Lexi with concern.

"It was just a tough spell," Lexi said. "I'm tired."

"You were *nai* just resting," Frost countered. "You were . . . in another place. You were saying things in your sleep. Fearful things."

Leadpipe nodded his agreement. "'Burn it all,' you sayed. 'Let the world burn. I will become the fire,' you sayed. 'Make them all dance.' And you were laughing. You were laughing when you sayed all that."

Lexi didn't know what to say to that. She wanted to insist what Frost and Leadpipe were saying was wrong, but she knew it was probably true. She could half remember it all from her dream.

No. It was more than a dream, Lexi thought. *It felt like . . . a vision. Like the magic inside of me was talking. Like it was showing me the truth about myself and the world.*

It occurred to Lexi that if her own magic was trying so hard to communicate with her, maybe she'd been going about things all wrong. She'd been trying to resist the magic, ignore its voice, but that hadn't worked. The whispers and visions had only been getting stronger. So maybe it was time to stop ignoring what it was saying. Maybe it was time to listen.

"I'm fine," Lexi insisted.

She'd said it before, or words to that effect, but this

was the first time she really believed it. From Leadpipe's reaction, he believed it too. His ears raised a little as his concern decreased.

Frost looked more skeptical though. "Are you sure about that, *derijinta*?"

Lexi stood up. She wasn't very tall, but she towered over Frost.

"I'm not your little one," Lexi replied, her voice calm. "I'm not all that much younger than you. I'm bigger than you. And I'm probably more powerful than you. So if we're going to save your people, you have to trust me. I think I'm finally ready to."

Frost reacted in surprise, but he said nothing. The little wizard was at a loss for words, for once.

Just then, Billy ran up to them. He seemed like he had something urgent to tell them, but stopped short when he saw Leadpipe.

"Lead! You're okay!" Billy said with a grin.

"I're getting there, bite by bite," Leadpipe responded, his fatigue still evident in his voice.

"What did you have to tell us?" Lexi asked, impatient to hear whatever Billy had come charging up to say.

"Hop's expedition!" Billy said. "They're here! They're in the caverns."

Snap had never been so cold.

She was standing on a glacier atop Mother Mountain. The merest sliver of a crescent moon had just risen over the horizon, casting a feeble light in the night sky, and wind-blown snow whipped all around her.

She was alone, without even Grinner's uneasy presence. But she could hear a voice on the wind, words forming from its snowy howl.

"Why-why-why-why-why?" the wind seemed to say.

"Why what?" Snap answered, shouting to be heard.

"Listen-listen-listen-listen," the wind roared.

"I're trying," Snap replied. *"But it're* maja *hard to hear you."*

"Choosed you," the wind said. *"Choosed you."*

That's when Snap realized. It wasn't the wind speaking. It was the Night herself.

"That make nai *sense,"* Snap called back. *"I're* nai *your servant. I're my own* gob! *One what're pledged to kill your king."*

"Choose me, choose you, choose me, choose you," the Night whispered. *"Live-live-live-live-live."*

"Are you alive?" Grinner said quietly, shaking her.

Snap opened her eyes. She wasn't on a glacier after all. She was in Grinner's secret room. She and Grinner had been on their way out of the Blue Chambers when they'd heard a platoon of human soldiers tromp into the main entrance, a few rooms away. They'd retreated to Grinner's secret room while the humans searched the Chambers. Snap must've fallen asleep. Seeing her eyes open, Grinner stopped shaking her.

"I sayed, are you alive?" Grinner repeated.

"I think I are," Snap replied tentatively. "Hard to tell sometime."

To her surprise, Grinner sang a little song in response. He wasn't a very good singer:

Oh, sleeping taste a bit like death
Just a little, just a nibble
It shut your eyes and slow your breath
Just a little, just a dribble

It end your troubles for a while
For a breather, worries sinking
Nai more frowning and drop your smile
Just a breather, just a winking

But now it are time to wake
Now it are your time to shake
Up and grab the time you make
Crack the eggs and time to bake

Open your eyes, get to stirring
Draw your first breath, sharp as a knife
Jump to your feet, life are whirring
In waking you return to life

Move your body, no more stopping
You'll be smiling until you weep
Keep on going 'til you're dropping
Time for living until you sleep

Up and grab the time you make
Crack the eggs and time to wake

"My mother used to sing that to me," Snap said once Grinner had finished. "Afore . . ."

She trailed off. "The Waking Song" was one of the few things Snap remembered about her mother. She didn't like thinking about her.

"I growed up alone, in Rockbottom," Grinner said, referring to the worst neighborhood in Kiranok. "*Nai* one ever singed to me. But I heared that song sometime when I were outside a window, begging for scraps."

Snap was startled. That was the most Grinner had ever said about his history.

"That must've been hard," Snap said.

Grinner grinned. "Life are always hard. That're why I prefer death. Folk say death are hard, but I seed more death than most and I can tell you, death are easy. In life you struggle every moment. In death you struggle only once."

With that, Grinner stood up, his grin never faltering.

"The *skerboen* searched the Chambers while you were dozing, but they *nai* finded us. Time for stirring. The King are in the caverns, with his army of fools. We should join him."

"Kill him, you mean," Snap said, getting to her feet. "But we *nai* been able to end him yet."

"*Zajnai* that're so," Grinner said. "But we only have to succeed once."

Grinner headed for the exit. Snap lingered behind. And not just because the whispers from her dream were still echoing in her head. She'd hidden the Final Drop in a crack in the wall when Grinner wasn't looking. She looked into the crack and saw the crystal vial and its irreplaceable green contents were still there and still intact.

It're nai *too late to drink it,* she thought. Nai *too late to give it to Grinner, neither.*

But she knew she wasn't going to do either. Nor was she going to heed her dreams and give up her quest to kill the King.

The Night sayed she choosed me, Snap thought, *but I already choosed something else.*

Snap followed Grinner out of the secret room, leaving the Final Drop in its new hiding place, probably forever.

Cyreth put the torch to the pile of bodies himself. It seemed only right. If anyone had to take one final look at the goblins he and his Lion Guards had slaughtered today, it should be him.

It turned out the goblin city wasn't entirely deserted. A few goblins remained, mostly those too old or too sick to travel. By order of the Lord Marshal, the Lion Guards had spent their day moving from house to house, cave dwelling to cave dwelling, killing every goblin they found. Only a handful had put up any resistance. Some older goblins had tried to fight back from their sickbeds, but they were too feeble to pose much of a threat. A few had relatives standing guard, and those goblins fought fiercely to defend their elders. But they were outnumbered, and none of them seemed to be experienced fighters. Killing them had taken little effort.

Only once had the Lion Guards faced a real challenge. A half dozen goblin warriors had set up an ambush in a side cave lined with cliff dwellings. As the Lion Guards entered, the goblins dropped a boulder across the entrance, cutting the Hanorian column in half. Then they'd opened fire with bows from the balconies of the highest cliff dwellings. Several Lion Guards were shot down before the survivors managed to form the Steel Wall. But once the Lions joined their shields above their heads, the arrows could no longer bite. Eventually the goblins must've realized their bow fire wasn't having any effect, and the patter of arrows trailed off. Cyreth ordered the Lions to move together toward a stairway that gave access to the upper levels. In single file, they charged up the stairs. The goblins met them on a landing halfway up. Only two or three Lion Guards could force their way onto the landing at a time, where they'd have to face all six goblins. Three Lion Guards died trying to take the landing, including Speryco, the juggling Celestial who'd survived the suicidal attempt to open the goblin city's main gate. Finally Cyreth had ordered the Lion Guards to part ranks so he could charge the goblins himself. By then, most of the goblins had already been wounded, and the ferocity of Cyreth's assault proved too much for them. He cut down two of the goblins and forced the others back, allowing the Lion Guards to swarm them. One goblin was shoved over the railing and fell to his death. The other holdouts fell under a flurry of bashing shields and slashing swords.

In the end, the Lion Guards killed all six goblins at the cost of five Lion Guards killed and fifteen injured. Cyreth never liked losing troopers, but the death of those five hit him especially hard.

Not even close to worth it, Cyreth thought. *The war is supposed to be over. So why are we still dying?*

After that one brief battle, the rest of the day consisted of nothing but murdering the old and the sick and their overwhelmed protectors.

As useless and bloody as it had been, Cyreth almost preferred the battle.

Finally, at the end of the longest and possibly worst day of Cyreth's life, he found himself looking at a pile of goblin corpses that had been heaped onto alcohol-soaked scrap wood, ready for burning. Bytha sparked a torch and walked up to the pile, but Cyreth intercepted her and held out his hand.

"It should be me," he said.

Bytha handed him the torch. He took it and walked up to the bodies, forcing himself to look long and hard at what he and his fellow Lion Guards had done.

Dozens of dead faces stared back at him.

Cyreth tried to remember when he'd first joined the Lion Guards, young and eager. He tried to picture himself when he first donned his golden lion helm, how proud he'd been. He'd been confident that if the Empire were ever attacked, he'd defend his homeland with all his might, prove himself the hero his people needed.

He'd done that. He'd helped save the Empire. That should have been the end of it. He should've gotten a medal or three and then returned to a life of training and parades, with the occasional ball at the Imperial Court.

Instead, the Lord Marshal had launched his campaign of vengeance, and somehow, along the way, Cyreth had lost himself.

When he was young, playing soldier, he'd imagined someday someone might write a story about his exploits. But if the young Cyreth were to read the story of what his adult self had done this day, he'd have despised him. Because today, Captain Cyreth Gant had played the villain. After all, what else could you call an officer who oversaw the slaughter of old people and civilians? Who cut down young people defending their home? Who'd killed more than one of them with his own blade?

So it was only fitting he should finish this horrific, shameful day by setting fire to the dead bodies of his victims.

Cyreth touched his torch to the pile. The alcohol-soaked wood beneath the corpses caught fire instantaneously, putting out a thick black smoke that stung Cyreth's eyes. Still, despite the smoke and the tears running down his face, Cyreth kept his eyes fixed on the fire.

Don't look away, he told himself. *Looking away would be telling myself, and my soldiers, that today was just another day. That I can somehow escape blame. But I can't. This was my work. My honor is burning along with my victims. Never to return.*

Eventually the last goblin face disappeared into the fire.

That's when Cyreth noticed something odd about the smoke.

He'd had his men pile the bodies near the entrance

to the side cavern where the Lion Guards had been ambushed. The tunnel that led to the cavern opened up onto the goblin city's big central chasm. Cyreth had thought that would allow the smoke from the burning bodies to rise up through the chasm and, hopefully, into the night sky. He knew goblins worshiped Mother Night. He'd hoped the rising smoke might, at least symbolically, bring the dead home to their goddess.

Since there wasn't much wind this deep in the chasm, the smoke should have risen more or less straight up. But instead, it was blowing out toward the chasm center, directly *away* from the tunnel entrance.

That didn't make any sense. There shouldn't be a breeze coming out of the tunnel. It dead-ended at the cavern and the various cliff dwellings. After the battle, Cyreth and his men had searched the cliff dwellings thoroughly, trying to find a way out that wouldn't force them to move the huge boulder blocking the tunnel where they'd entered. They hadn't found any other away out, so they'd had to clear the boulder, an hour of difficult, back-breaking work Cyreth had hoped to avoid.

So where was the breeze coming from?

Cyreth lit a new torch off the pyre and headed for the tunnel.

"First and Second File, follow me," he ordered. "Combat ready."

The Lion Guards were exhausted. Many of them had shrugged off their armor and were lying down. Only a small picket was standing watch. But on Cyreth's command, twenty soldiers, the members of the First and Second File, hastily gathered their gear and fell into ranks behind him.

Cyreth strode through the tunnel, watching the torch the entire time. The flame was being blown ever so slightly back toward the chasm. With his helmet off, Cyreth could just feel the subtle breeze now. He'd missed it on the way in, never feeling it in his full armor.

Cyreth and his soldiers soon reached the cave dwellings. Using his torch, Cyreth tracked the breeze to its source, a seemingly solid rock wall on the far side of the chamber. The breeze was coming from a small hole in the wall, just at eye level and about as big as a finger. Without a word, Cyreth handed the torch to a Lion Guard, drew his sword, and shoved it into the hole. He worked the blade back and forth. The hole cracked open a little wider, then the rock face began to chip and flake away. Cyreth realized the wall wasn't solid stone at all. It was held together by some sort of mortar.

The wall was fake.

Cyreth pulled away a chunk of mortar, opening the hole even wider. He put his ear to the hole and listened. In the distance, he could hear voices. Goblin voices. Laughing, whispering, singing. Countless voices.

Maybe a whole city's worth.

Cyreth had been ordered to kill every goblin inside Monster Mountain. He had hoped today's bloodshed had been the end of that. But it looked like he'd just found the goblins' hiding place. Which meant the slaughter had only begun.

CHAPTER TWELVE
Your Honor or Your Life

Billy's hopes soared when he heard members of Hop's expedition had made it to the caverns. He'd been struggling to come up with a plan for what to do if, or more likely when, the Hanorians discovered the goblins' hiding place. He had a few ideas, but they all seemed pretty desperate. Now, though, if Hop and Kurt and the rest had made it back with the Fallen Star, he wouldn't need any of his crazy plans. The goblins could be saved without them.

So Billy was feeling optimistic as he and Lexi rushed to the crystal-studded cavern deep inside Mother Mountain where the survivors of the expedition had been found. The cavern wasn't far from one of the hidden entrances to the cave network. In fact, Billy and Lexi had passed through it twice, once when they first arrived in the goblins' world, then again when Starcaller had brought them back to Kiranok to win Billy his crown. The cavern was beautiful when lit, encrusted with colorful red, purple, and blue crystals. As they entered, Lexi cast a spell that made the crystals dance with light, illuminating the small group of goblins and humans who'd managed to sneak into the cavern.

"Hop? Kurt?" Billy called out.

But he quickly realized . . . Hop and Kurt weren't there.

Instead he found the young Celestial lightworker, Alyseer, plus Snails and Flutter, two of the bat-riders from Hop's warbat, along with six other goblins and a pair of young Celestials. The survivors were covered in scrapes and bruises, and there were a lot of broken bones. Snails had a broken arm, and he was in better shape than most. Flutter had broken her collarbone, a wrist, some ribs, and maybe even her hip. Only Alyseer appeared unhurt, at least physically. But she seemed only half there, staring at the world with an empty gaze. When Billy greeted her, she didn't answer. She didn't even move.

"*Maja* too much magic," Snails explained. "But she saved us all."

Billy glanced at Lexi when he heard that. She looked troubled. Billy couldn't blame her.

Snails went on to tell them everything that had happened since the taxi-bats had left on their ill-fated expedition. How they'd been shot down. How Alyseer had saved them with her magic. How Hop had gathered the survivors, then headed north alone to retrieve the Fallen Star.

"What about Kurt?" Billy asked.

Snails shook his head. "We *nai* seed him."

"But that do *nai* mean he're dead," Flutter insisted. "He's a tough one, *zaj*. He could still be out there someplace."

"In the winter?" Billy asked, whatever optimism he'd been feeling now crushed. "In the wilderness? With Hanorian wizards hunting for him?"

Given that Kurt had chased Lexi and Billy into a sewer on the first day they met, and that Lexi had broken her leg because of him, Billy supposed he shouldn't care what happened to the jock. Except somewhere along the way, Kurt had stopped being a bully and started being a friend.

"We should send out more scouts to search for him," Billy said.

"We already spent days searching the mountainside," Snails said. "That're how we finded Flutter, Skynna, and Beru." Snails nodded to the two Celestial survivors, a teenage girl and boy.

"Tell him about the tracks . . . and the body," Flutter blurted out.

"We finded a dead Celestial. Azam," Snails said sadly. "Almost missed him at first. The snow were piled atop him. But somebody haved closed his eyes. And there were faint tracks heading away from the burial. Headed north."

"Kurt and Azam were friends," Skynna, the Celestial girl, added. "They were on the same bat."

"If it were him, he were already a long way off," Snails said. "Add to that, we needed to get our wounded inside, so we could *nai* follow the tracks. But it're like I sayed—he're a tough one."

"I can look for him myself," Lexi said. "Fly north as long as my magic lasts. Hopefully Hop and Kurt are together."

Billy thought about that. As much as he wanted to find Kurt and Hop, he didn't like the idea of Lexi going on a search expedition on her own. He especially didn't like the idea of her using magic the whole time. She'd used too much as it was. He didn't want her to end up like Alyseer. Plus . . .

"We need you here," Billy said. "You're one of the only wizards we've got."

"The goblins are safe," Lexi said. "Your plan worked."

"For now," Billy frowned. "Only it's not a permanent solution. We have to get them out of here. Move them someplace where the Hanorians will never find them."

"Someplace like where?" Lexi asked.

"I don't know," Billy admitted.

"Okay. Well, while you figure it out, I'll find Kurt and Hop."

Why do you have to be so stubborn? Billy thought. He didn't say it out loud, because he knew that would only make Lexi dig in harder. Still, there had to be some way to convince her not to burn herself out looking for Kurt and Hop or get herself shot down by Hanorian wizards. Or both. But before Billy could come up with something useful to say, he heard . . .

"Your destiny is here."

It was Alyseer. She'd finally talked.

"Alyseer?" Lexi looked at the Celestial in surprise. "What are you talking about?"

"I see you here, in the caverns," Alyseer said, looking forward into the cave, her face strangely still, her eyes unblinking. "Fire. I see fire. Fire everywhere. You belong in the fire."

With that, Alyseer fell silent again. And despite their best efforts, neither Billy nor Lexi nor anyone else could get her to speak again.

Kurt bent over and puked on the snow.

Since the hard fall he'd taken during his battle with

the ice wyrm, he'd been feeling dizzy and a little queasy. The snow had done only so much to cushion his landing. When his head slammed back, it must've hit a chunk of ice or a rock or something, because Kurt nearly blacked out from the impact. Despite that, he'd struggled back to his feet, checked to make sure the ice wyrm was dead, and helped Hop stand up. Then, together, they'd headed north. Now, after over an hour struggling through the snow, Kurt's stomach was roiling, his head was throbbing, and his vision was blurry at best. The bright light reflecting off the snow didn't help. When the glare hit his face, Kurt felt like he was getting stabbed in the eyes, and his nausea got even worse. He'd muscled through the pain and queasiness for as long as he could, but it had finally gotten the better of him.

"Need to rest?" Hop asked him.

"Can't," Kurt said, trying to gather himself. His knees felt weak and his head was spinning. "We're almost there."

It was true. The glow of the Fallen Star was clearly visible in the distance, maybe a half mile away.

"You have the *kleng*," Hop said, concern in his voice. "It happen a lot in combat. A *gob* get hit on the head with a hammer or a mace or a flying rock. The helmet take the blow, make a big *kleng*. Soon enough, the poor *gob* are staggering about, half blind, spewing breakfast on the dirt. Happened to me more than once. One time I getted the *kleng* so bad I could *nai* remember me calling-name. Kept saying me name were Mushy, which're what me *eme* and *va* called me when I were a *piko*."

"I know what a concussion is," Kurt replied. "I've had one before. More than one. I played through them, and I'll play through this." Kurt resumed walking, uneasily, toward the glow in the distance. "Anyway, the sun is going down," he pointed out correctly. "My eyes won't hurt so much once there's no glare."

"Do *nai* serve to ignore the *kleng*," Hop said, hurrying to keep up with Kurt. "It can get *maja* worse. I knowed this old warrior back home in me village what getted bashed in the head so many times, he could *nai* think straight for the rest of his life. Wandered about town, his face blank, muttering to himself. You need to sit a moment, eyes closed. Wait for the world to stop spinning."

Kurt had been through enough coaches' lectures about concussions to know Hop was right. He'd been told a million times to report any concussion symptoms to his coaches and trainers so they could pull him out of the game and make sure he didn't make things worse.

Not that he'd listened. The few times Kurt had gotten hit hard enough to feel nauseated or disoriented, he'd hidden the symptoms and kept playing. He hadn't wanted to let his team down. So he wasn't going to pull himself out of the game now either, no matter how horrible he felt. Not with the entire population of Kiranok at risk.

"What would you do, if you were me?" Kurt asked Hop. "Sit and rest? Or keep pushing?"

Kurt could see he'd hit home. Hop might act like he was afraid of his own shadow, but he was no quitter. Especially not when the stakes were this high.

"Keep moving then," Hop said, continuing his northward trudge through the snow. "Only do *nai* blame me if you end up muttering to yourself when you get old."

"I'm not worried," Kurt said, forcing himself to keep a steady pace toward the Fallen Star despite his headache and dizziness. "I mean, I doubt either one of us is going to get old. We probably won't survive the night. Look behind us."

Hop glanced back, seeing the same thing Kurt saw the last time he'd looked south.

"The Hanorians," Hop said grimly. "They're catching up to us."

Kurt looked back too. The Hanorian soldiers definitely seemed a lot closer now. They were moving with steady determination, probably at a jog. No doubt they'd see Kurt and Hop on the horizon, heading toward the glow of the Fallen Star.

"*Zeesnikken eger zapergritten,*" Hop muttered.

Kurt had heard him use the expression more than once. "Bee stings on top of mosquito bites," he translated. "Sometimes, no matter what you do, bad things keep happening."

"It're the way of things when you're a *gob*," Hop said grimly.

"It happens when you're human, too," Kurt said. "We say, 'Out of the frying pan and into the fire' or 'If it's not one thing, it's another.' We have some other sayings I like better though. Like 'When the going gets tough, the tough get going' or 'It's not over 'til the final whistle.' Or my favorite: 'Leave it all on the field.'"

"'Leave it all on the field'?" Hop asked. "What do that one mean?"

"It means play until you have nothing left," Kurt explained. "You can throw up, cramp up, get dizzy, but you don't stop playing until the game is over or they drag you off the field."

"Leave it all on the field," Hop said, thoughtfully. "I like that. Leave it all on the field," he repeated with considerably more confidence.

Kurt looked north. The light was dimming as the sun went down. His head felt a little better. The glow of the Fallen Star was getting stronger as the light faded. Like it was calling to them. They didn't have far to go.

"Race you," Kurt said, breaking into a jog, taking a lead on Hop.

"*Zaj,*" he heard Hop say. Out of the corner of his eye, he saw Hop toss his spear aside so he could run easier.

"Leaving that on the field to start," Hop said, catching up to Kurt with a burst of speed. "It're *nai* over 'til the whistle," he said, pulling ahead of Kurt.

"Heck yeah," Kurt said, pushing himself to run even faster, despite the cold, despite the snow, despite his pounding head and churning stomach. The game was almost over, the clock was running out, and Kurt and Hop were driving toward the end zone.

Time for one last desperate play.

Lexi stood guard as Billy moved through the long string of camps the goblins had set up in the caverns. He'd been touring the caverns to reassure his goblin subjects. Billy was wearing the Goblin Crown, and the ruby in its center was glowing red, as it always did when he had it on. In the dimly lit caverns, the red was even more pronounced. It certainly attracted a lot of attention. Billy was handling it okay, though. Lexi admired how calm and confident he seemed. She figured he was probably pretty worried, but he managed not to show it. She remembered how confused and unsure of himself he'd been when they'd first arrived in the goblins' world. How he'd blush and stammer whenever he got nervous. He wasn't stammering now. Billy had come a long way in just a short time. He'd turned out to be a pretty good king.

Unfortunately, Lexi suspected that reassuring the goblins wasn't going to be enough. She and Alyseer had had the same vision. Lexi, in the caverns, surrounded by fire. People burning.

Lexi didn't want to hurt anyone. She hoped her vision wouldn't come true, but if it did, a lot of innocent goblins could die. She had to make sure that didn't happen. To do that, she'd need Billy's help.

So the next time he finished with a group of goblins and excused himself to head to the yet another cavern, she intercepted him, slipping past the small phalanx of Copperplates guarding him.

"You were right. We have to get the goblins out of here," Lexi whispered, walking close by Billy's side. She knew the sharp-eared goblins would still hear them, but she'd learned that if she really concentrated, she could speak English instead of letting Frost's language spell automatically translate everything into *Gobayabber*.

"All of them," Lexi continued in English. "We have to move them someplace safe. Someplace far away."

"You thought they were safe here before," Billy reminded her, also speaking English. "What changed your mind? The vision Alyseer had?"

"I had it too," Lexi admitted. "The same one. Or near enough. That has to mean something."

Billy looked worried, though not all that surprised. "I knew something was bothering you," he said.

"I'm not very good at hiding my feelings," Lexi admitted.

"I like that about you," Billy said. "My parents are the opposite. They never show what they're feeling. My father especially. Even since he's been sick, I don't think I've seen him look sad or worried. Just . . . stoic. I think that's the word. He's like . . ."

Billy made an expression that was absolutely neutral and held it. Stone-faced. It was exaggerated and silly and Lexi couldn't help but laugh, despite their situation.

"You'd love my family," Lexi said. "It's all emotions, all the time. Extra loud."

"Hopefully I'll get to meet them some day," Billy said.

"Hopefully you will," Lexi said. She meant it. She'd like it if Billy got to meet her parents, even though they didn't seem to like anything or anyone Lexi liked. Then she imagined how the meeting might go and chuckled.

"What?" Billy asked.

"I was just picturing myself introducing you to my parents. Like, 'This is Billy. He and I and our friend Kurt were all transported to a magical land together where Billy became king of the goblins and I was a wizard.'"

"Yeah, when we get back, we probably shouldn't talk about this to anyone," Billy suggested. "People will just think we're crazy."

"If we get back," Lexi said.

"*When*," Billy insisted. "We're going to get home. Once the goblins are safe. The other Goblin Kings went back to our world once they'd done their duty. Or at least, most of them did. We'll make it home too. I know it."

Lexi wished she shared Billy's confidence, though she appreciated his reassurance.

"I don't know how you do it," Lexi said. "Stay so calm. Everyone is counting on you. Even though you can't do magic like me or fight like Kurt. Even though the only thing you have going for you is a glowing metal hat. Somehow you keep going. Keep looking brave. Keep telling everyone else not to worry."

"Oh, inside I'm freaking out," Billy said. "But like I said, we Smiths are stoic. It's a family trait. That's how we do." Billy put on his stone face again, but it didn't last long. His expression suddenly brightened, and he said, "Blackstone."

"What?" Lexi asked. "What's Blackstone?"

"It's the town that Coaler the Fire Wizard came from. In the puppet show," Billy explained. "Some of the bat-riders flew there. It's way up in the north, on the other side of the mountains. I don't think there's any way the humans could get there."

"Moving thousands of goblins all that way through the mountains in the middle of winter won't be easy," Lexi pointed out. "It took a whole day to move them down here, and we didn't have to go very far. Getting them all to another city entirely with an army of humans trying to stop us? That doesn't sound very safe."

"It's either that or wait here with them to die," Billy answered. He suddenly looked worried and a little overwhelmed.

"Now you don't look so stoic," Lexi pointed out. She regretted challenging his plan. She knew it couldn't be easy, being king. So she felt bad she'd made things harder on him. She tried to undo the damage.

"If you think that's our best option, we'll make it work," Lexi said, forcing herself to sound upbeat.

Billy smiled a little. "You don't have to protect my feelings. I don't think it's the best plan. But it's the only plan I've got." Then Billy seemed to come to a decision. "We should talk about it. You, Shadow, Starcaller, Frost, and me. Leadpipe, too, if he's feeling better. Can you get everyone together? I have a few more camps to visit."

"I'll try," Lexi said. "The Painted Cave? In an hour or so?"

The Painted Cave was a medium-sized chamber that lacked the crystalline formations that decorated the rest of the caverns. The goblins' distant ancestors had taken advantage of the bare walls and covered the entire chamber with paintings. There were stylized images of *bokrumen* and *vargaren*, hawkbears and greatdeer, plus dozens of goblin handprints, all rendered in black, brown, red, and orange dyes and highlighted with white chalk. The ceiling had a single, huge abstract image representing the Night Goddess, a pattern of black and gray swirls and lines speckled with hundreds of tiny white stars. If you squinted, the stars formed a pattern that looked almost like a female goblin's gently smiling face.

Since the Painted Cave was roughly in the middle of the goblin camps and had only two entrances, both easily secured by just a handful of guards, Shadow had chosen it for Billy's temporary throne room. It seemed to Lexi like the best place to have a meeting.

"Make it two hours," Billy said. "I should be able to make it through the rest of the camps by then."

Billy headed off, his phalanx of guards all around him. Even though it might be difficult to get all the goblins to Blackstone, Lexi was glad they had a plan. Because a plan meant that maybe her vision of fire and death wouldn't come true.

But as she went off to find Shadow, she thought she could hear a distant whisper echoing through the caverns.

Burn it all, it seemed to say. *Burn it all, burn it all, burn it all.*

"What in Light's name are you thinking, Captain?" Bytha asked.

"I was thinking I would get drunk," Cyreth said, looking down dubiously at a glass of goblin booze.

Bytha sat down across from him. "You know what I mean."

Cyreth had commandeered an abandoned goblin tavern to serve as the Lion Guard's temporary headquarters. A door behind the pub's kitchen led to a private apartment that probably belonged to the owner. Cyreth had taken over the apartment to use as his office and quarters. It was a tidy space, clean and well-kept. And it came with its own supply of goblin alcohol, which, at the moment, Cyreth saw as a significant benefit.

As soon as he'd gotten his fellow Lion Guards situated in the deserted homes near the tavern, Cyreth had poured himself a large glass of whatever was inside the first bottle he'd spotted. Now he was trying to work up the courage to drink it. The goblin concoction smelled like mushrooms. Cyreth was reasonably certain it wouldn't kill him or make him go blind. And if it did, well, it wouldn't be the worst thing he'd been through in the past few months. Or even today.

"Why haven't I reported what we found to Lord Jiyal?" Cyreth finally replied. "Is that what you're asking?"

"I know he has his eyes on the Lion Guards," Bytha said. "It'd be one thing if our swords were sharp and our shields were polished, only . . ."

Bytha trailed off. Cyreth knew she tried to avoid sounding overly critical, even when it was justified.

"Only our metaphorical gear is not in order," Cyreth finished for her. "Our ranks are full of heretics, and we're teetering on the edge of mutiny."

"I wouldn't say that," Bytha said. "Not out loud anyway. But given the situation, maybe now isn't the time to withhold important information from the Lord Marshal."

"So what am I supposed to do?" Cyreth said, staring at the drink. "If I tell him where the goblins are hiding, he'll kill them all."

"Them or us," Bytha said, her voice hollow.

"I don't want to make that choice," Cyreth said. "I just want to drink until I can't remember my own name."

"You won't, though," Bytha said confidently. "You'll stare at that cup. You'll want to forget yourself inside it. But you won't actually do it. Because you're the captain. That's why you haven't even taken a sip yet. Because you have to decide between telling Lord Jiyal what we found or keeping your silence."

"If I keep my silence, I risk him finding out about the hidden caverns on his own," Cyreth said. "If he realizes we kept the truth from him, he'll execute me and decimate the Lion Guards."

Cyreth knew people sometimes used the word "decimate" without knowing its exact meaning. They thought it just meant to destroy something. However, it originated as a military term that literally meant "to kill every tenth man." Decimation was a punishment the Hanorian Imperial Army reserved for a mutinous military unit. The unit would be ordered to line up in formation, at which point executioners would behead the unit's officers, then proceed down the formation and kill every tenth soldier in line. The Hanorian Army hadn't ordered a decimation in over a century. Cyreth wasn't eager to see the Lion Guards suffer that fate, especially not because of him.

"Still, say nothing, and there's at least a chance we can avoid more bloodshed," Cyreth added. "Tell him about the goblins' hiding place, and the blood on my hands will be a certainty. Innocents will die."

"Your honor or your life," Bytha said, clearly not envying him. "Our lives or theirs."

Cyreth wanted to drain his cup, pour another, and keep drinking until his mind was blank. Except he knew Bytha was right. He couldn't. Not while his fate and the fates of the Lion Guards was on his shoulders. Cyreth shoved the cup aside. If he lived through the next few weeks, he'd have an entire lifetime to drink himself into oblivion. For now, though, better to stay sober.

The moment he set the cup aside, Ysalion entered the bar's back room. She was recovering well from her wounds, thanks to the unwilling help of Dumen. She'd managed to find a clean uniform and a new half-veil to replace the blood stained ones she'd been wearing when she was wounded. Still, Cyreth hadn't cleared her for combat yet, so she'd been serving as the Lion Guards' messenger and camp guard.

"Message from Command," Ysalion said. "The Lord Marshal wants to see you immediately."

Cyreth's heart sank. *Maybe Lord Jiyal already knows about the goblins' hiding place,* he thought. *Maybe I've already waited too long to decide what to do.* Cyreth tried to calm himself. *Or maybe it's nothing and everything will be fine.*

Regardless, Cyreth knew it wouldn't do to keep the Lord Marshal waiting. He poured the goblin alcohol back into its bottle and corked it, then stood up and straightened his tunic.

"How do I look?" Cyreth asked Bytha and Ysalion.

"You look . . . battle-tested," Ysalion said reassuringly. "The Lord Marshal will be impressed."

"I doubt that," Cyreth said. Then he headed for the door.

"You look worried, Your Majesty."

Billy turned and saw an ancient *svagob* hobbling toward him, bent over from age and walking with a cane. She had to be the oldest goblin Billy had ever seen. Her ears hung to her shoulders, her face looked like a dried-up green apple, and her joints were knobby and swollen. There was something familiar about the gnarled old goblin, but Billy couldn't quite place it. He hadn't noticed her when he'd begun his visit to this particular goblin camp. It was made up of a collection of families from Rockbottom who'd taken shelter in a small, damp cavern divided by several clusters of columns and stalagmites. They looked miserable, so Billy had tried to raise their spirits. He'd assured them that he had a plan to get them all out of the caverns alive. Once they looked more or less convinced, he'd headed off for the next camp. Which was when the ancient goblin woman emerged from behind a column and intercepted him.

"I'm not worried at all," Billy lied. "We're going to get everyone to safety," he continued, trying to sound confident.

"I're too *maja* old for pretty lies," the *svagob* said with a chuckle. "Though it're nice you're trying to make me feel better. But it're you I're concerned with. A youngster, *gob* or human, should *nai* look like he're carrying the entire world on his back the way you do. I seed that look afore. Folk what have that look do *nai* end up well."

"It's just . . . I've got a lot of responsibility," Billy admitted. "I'll be okay."

"You sound *maja* like him too, *zaj*," the ancient goblin said.

"Like who?" Billy asked, confused.

"Ian Smith. The last Goblin King afore you," she answered.

That was the last thing Billy had expected to hear. Ian Smith was his great-great grandfather. He was a British soldier who'd disappeared during the First World War. Billy hadn't known anything about him until he saw his statue in the Hall of Kings, wearing his uniform with its distinctive brimmed helmet. Later, Billy had seen the soldier in a dream. He'd told Billy his own reign as Goblin King had been a failure. He'd wished Billy better luck.

"You knew him?" Billy stammered. "That was like a hundred years ago."

"*Zaj*. It were a long, long time ago, though I do *nai* think time move the same way in your world and ourn," the old *svagob* explained, looking mildly amused. "But

I remember him well. He were like you. Brave, kind, always thinking of others afore himself."

"I saw him once, in a dream," Billy admitted. "That can't be real, right? Dreams aren't real."

"*Zajnai* dreams are *nai* real in your world. But here? There are magic in all things. Dreams can connect us to that magic. It *nai* happen to me often, but now and then me husband come to me while I're sleeping with something important to say. And when he do, I listen."

"In my dream, my great-great grandfather said he failed. He never made it home."

"He were a humble man," the old *svagob* said. "But he were *nai* failure. He saved me children from the Swarming Death. He saved a *maja* lot of *goben*. Then he died trying to break the Swarm Lord's Blue Cauldron. That were *nai* the end of the story, though. His friends, *goben* and human both, they finished what he started. They defeated the Swarm Lord and melted down his cauldron. You'll succeed, too, in the end, one way or the other. I knowed that the moment I first seed you."

Billy finally realized why the old goblin looked so familiar. "You were with Hop when he and Frost and the others found us," Billy said. "You were one of the goblins who rescued Lexi, Kurt, and me from the caverns."

"*Nai* far from here," she said and nodded. "I could tell even then that you were the King. But I are too old to fight and scheme, so I leaved it to Hop and them others. Were a little worried when they tried to crown the big blond boy, but it all worked out in the end."

"That's still kinda up in the air," Billy said. He didn't want to give the ancient *svagob* false hope. He still had a lot of work to do before the goblins would be safe. Billy knew it was just as likely he'd fail. But if he failed, he was afraid that, unlike with his great-great grandfather, it would be the end of the story. And not just for him. For his friends, and for every goblin in the caverns.

"Everything are up in the air all the time," the old goblin said with a sad smile. "Take it from someone what have seed more years than I can count. Are *nai* thing in life certain. Are *nai* thing promised. But you're a good boy, and you're trying your best. That're all any of us can do."

The ancient *svagob* prodded Billy with her cane. "On with you," she said. "Go save me people. That're a good lad."

With that, she hobbled away, her faith in her king seemingly unshakable. Billy wished he shared her confidence. But, he supposed, confidence didn't matter much in the end. It didn't matter if you were afraid or uncertain about doing something . . . so long as you did it. Or died trying.

"I'll do my best," Billy said to the hunched *svagob* as she disappeared around a bend of the cavern.

Then he turned to go, heading for the next camp. If he was going to save the old goblin's people, he still had a lot of work to do.

After the Hanorians killed Snap's mother and father, most of her childhood had passed in a sort of blur. She didn't have many vivid memories from the night of her parents' funeral to the day in her brothers' forge when she'd frozen Hulogrosh Boomingshout in a shell of ice. She had images of frequently repeated activities like making jewelry in the forge or drawing water from the well. But she didn't remember many specific events.

She remembered the mad *bokrum* though.

She must've been ten or twelve when the beast

came charging through her hometown. It was an old male ram, five times heavier than Coldsnap and a span taller, measuring from its massive hooves to the top of its dark, curved horns. She'd been walking home from the forge when it slammed into old Crunchpear's fruit cart, smashing it to pieces and sending spiny pears and bitter plums and other assorted fruit flying through the air. A bitter plum splatted by Snap's feet, making her step back in alarm. When she looked up, she saw Crunchpear ducking into the Night Goddess's shrine and other locals scattering as fast as they could.

Then she saw the *bokrum* charging at her, a crazy look in its eyes, snorting blood from its nose, its mouth speckled with reddish foam.

Coldsnap had frozen in fear. The beast galloped closer and closer, lowering its head to ram her. She remembered thinking she was going to die.

Then her brother Grub had jumped in front of the charging *bokrum* and hit it in the head with his smith's hammer. There was a loud crack, and the *bokrum* slowed its charge, then stumbled and fell to the ground only a few paces from Snap. It snorted and shuddered, mortally wounded.

Snap cried and ran to the *bokrum*, wanting to comfort it, but her brother stopped her.

"Do *nai* touch it," Grub said sternly. "It're sick with the froth. It're goed mad, lashing out at all around it from the pain and the fever. Touch it, and you could catch the froth too. Then there'd be no saving you."

Snap never forgot how the *bokrum* had looked when it charged her, madness in its eyes. Her brother later told her that it probably had been bitten by an infected greenfly, high in the mountains. The greenfly had given it the froth, and the disease had driven the *bokrum* insane, making it charge down into the foothills, attacking everything it saw.

"I killed it," Snap sobbed later that night, home safe but guilt-ridden. "If it *nai* seed me, *nai* charged me, it'd still be alive."

"It were the greenfly bite what killed it," Grub insisted. "It were doomed to die long afore it charged you and I hammered it down. If anything, we saved it a few days of suffering and dying by bits. It were a mercy."

Ever since, Coldsnap had wondered how much of life was like that. How much of what a *gob* did or said was the result of some tiny event in their past? How often did something like a greenfly bite send a *gob* on some mad charge, thrashing and lashing out until a final hammer strike put an end to it?

In me case, Snap reflected, *the insect bite were learning Grub were dead. Now me mad charge have bringed me here. Where the hammer could fall any time.*

"He're alone," Grinner said, joining Snap behind a cluster of tall stalagmites. "The King have leaved that last group of goblins and are heading through this cavern to the next camp, just like we planned. He'll pass us any time."

Snap peeked around the stalagmites and saw King Billy heading toward them, the red glow of the Goblin Crown lighting his way. He was alone, just like Grinner said. Neither of his wizard bodyguards—the human girl or the traitor Frost—were with him. Frost's giant brother was still recovering from their last attack, and the Copperplates that usually flanked the *skerbo* had fallen well behind. Snap could see them at the far end of the cavern, moving slowly and deliberately. Snap and Grinner had picked this cavern because the entrance was almost completely blocked by a long, wide, seemingly bottomless chasm. Only a thin ledge on one side of the chasm allowed passage into the cavern where Snap and Grinner were hiding. They'd hoped the chasm might slow down King Billy's heavily armored bodyguards and maybe thin out the phalanx of goblins that usually surrounded him. Their plan had worked even better than expected. King Billy had gone across the ledge first, continuing ahead while his bodyguards carefully skirted the chasm.

Walking alone through the caves with the too-big Goblin Crown sitting slightly askew on his head, King Billy didn't look like a threat to all of goblinkind. He looked like a boy. Maybe not a goblin boy. No goblin boy would have skin that shade of brownish-pink, or so much reddish-brown hair, or such small ears. But still, undeniably, a boy.

Part of Snap wanted to tell Grinner to forget about their plan. To leave the boy alone. To walk away. Only Snap knew it was too late for that. She'd been bitten. The madness was in her veins. She'd started a charge that she wouldn't be able to stop until she took a hammer blow to the head. And King Billy didn't have a hammer. He didn't have any weapons at all. He was defenseless. Just like Snap had been all those years ago when the *bokrum* charged her. Except this time, Grub wasn't there to save Billy . . . or her.

"Get him," Snap said.

She leapt out from behind the stalagmites and threw wind and ice at the *skerbo* king, trying her best to kill him and wondering when the hammer would fall.

The ice blast came from nowhere. The old Billy, the Billy who had arrived in these caverns months ago, would have been caught flat-footed and died in that moment, frozen solid.

But Billy had changed since then. He'd grown. He'd ridden a *vargar* and been through battles and seen friends die. He'd become more capable, more confident . . . and also more aware and far more paranoid.

So when the new, improved, more capable, more experienced, more paranoid Billy caught a glimpse of aggressive movement out of the corner of his eye, he didn't hesitate or stand gaping at what was coming.

The new Billy ducked.

The angry female goblin's ice blast flew over Billy's head, nearly knocking off the Goblin Crown. Billy grabbed the Crown to secure it, then dodged behind a stalagmite.

He'd seen the second goblin wizard just in time. Razor sharp icicles clattered off the stalagmite.

Billy was pretty sure his ambushers were the two surviving goblins who'd attacked him in the Bat Cavern, the curly-haired *svagob* with long, animated ears and the blue-eyed *drogob* with the disturbing grin. He didn't try to get a better look at them to confirm his suspicions, though. He ran.

He dashed back toward his bodyguards, shouting for help. Billy knew kings weren't supposed to yell in panic, but he figured if he outlived his regal dignity, that was okay.

Unfortunately, only a few Copperplates had reached his side of the chasm at the cavern entrance. They wouldn't be much help against the two wizards.

Billy rounded a stone column, chased by another barrage of icicles. The goblin wizards were catching up. He glanced back and saw the female goblin literally flying toward him, propelled by a howling icy wind. There was no way he could outrun her.

Billy looked ahead. He'd almost reached the chasm,

only to find that the ledge pathway was jammed with Copperplates. If he tried to get through, the wizards would definitely catch him. He and a lot of the Copperplates would die. And jumping over the chasm wasn't an option. Even though he was running as fast as he could, Billy didn't think he could vault it. The chasm was at least twelve feet across.

So Billy took the only path open to him.

He ran to the chasm and jumped *in*.

"It're smaller than I imagined," Hop said, looking down at the Fallen Star.

The Star was resting in the bottom of a deep crater at the end of a long furrow. It had skidded to a halt not far from the river ravine that bisected the snowfield. If the Star had skidded a little farther, it might have ended up in the river, and then he and Kurt never would have found it.

But there it was, about twenty paces down, a lump of iron about the size of Hop's fist, glowing a fierce orange in the twilight. Hop flicked his vision to redsight, expecting the glow to flare in his heat-sensitive night sight. Instead, the glow faded to almost nothing. The Star wasn't putting off any heat. Hop switched back to daysight; the glow returned. Hop figured that meant the Star's glow must be magical, though that didn't make Hop feel any safer than if the little lump of metal had actually been on fire.

"I'll get it," Kurt said, determined.

"You can barely stand," Hop pointed out. Kurt had struggled through the *kleng* to reach the Star, but he was still pale, with a queasy, unsteady stance.

"Aside," Hop added, cutting off any possible objection, "what sort of Hoprock are I if I do *nai* hop rocks every chance I get?"

Hop could see the human boy was too tired to fight.

"Okay, you show off then," Kurt said. "I'll sit here and watch."

Kurt took a seat on the long mound of snow and rock that lined the edge of the crater.

If I were being honest, Hop thought, *I'd much rather have Kurt get the Star than fetch it meself. I do* nai *like the idea of touching it. Still, I're the best* gob *for the job.*

"*Wazzer,*" Hop muttered to himself. Usually goblins used *wazzer* to call attention to themselves. Sometimes it could be an expression of excitement. When said in the right way though, *wazzer* could also mean something more like "Here go *nai* thing" or "I'll do this, but I're *nai* feeling good about it." This was definitely one of those times.

Hop leapt into the crater.

A few bounds later, he was at the bottom by the Fallen Star. Bracing himself, he reached down and picked up the glowing lump of iron.

He was pleasantly surprised when he didn't instantly burst into flames or freeze into ice or otherwise cease to exist. The Fallen Star was cool to the touch. It was roughly spherical, with an uneven surface covered in holes and ripples that reminded Hop of the top of a honeycomb mushroom. Still, despite the ripples and pockmarks, the Star felt smooth in his hand, with no sharp edges or points. It was also surprisingly heavy, easily weighing twice as much as Hop's shield. He could barely hold it in one hand, at least not for long. Hauling the Star home was going to be a lot of work.

Time to get started.

Holding the Star in both hands, Hop hopped back up the crater to where Kurt was waiting.

"Wow," Kurt said, struggling to his feet. "We actually got it."

"Have to admit," the one-eared goblin said, "I're *maja* surprised meself—"

A blast of concentrated hot air hit Hop in the back, like the fist of an angry *kijakgob*. He fell face-first into the snow and dropped the Fallen Star, which rolled to Kurt's feet.

Hop gasped for breath. He couldn't feel his legs. His back felt like it was on fire, and he could smell smoke and burning cloth. He couldn't move, couldn't do anything as he watched Kurt bend over and retrieve the Star. Then he heard . . .

"Give the Fallen Star to me."

It was a female voice, speaking Hanorian. The speaker sounded young but confident. Hop lifted his head and saw a human girl hovering over the crater, tall and broad-shouldered with strong arms, a plain face, and bright red hair. The girl's multicolored silk dress whipped around her, like she was floating in her own private whirlwind.

"Hello, Mig," Hop heard Kurt say. "I figured you'd show up sooner or later."

"You were right," Mig said, still flying above the crater. "Now surrender the Fallen Star. Or burn."

CHAPTER THIRTEEN
By Ax, Lash, Rope, and Fire

Kurt held the Fallen Star tight as he faced down Mig. The meteorite was heavy, maybe twenty-five or thirty pounds. Feeling the weight reminded Kurt of how much effort had gone into reaching the Star. Azam had died to help him get his hands on it. So had a lot of goblins. Hop was groaning in pain on the ground nearby. He could be badly injured. He could die. There was no way Kurt was giving up the Star after all that. There was one hard and fast rule about how to win a football game: don't drop the ball. Kurt had no intention of fumbling now.

"I said, give it to me or burn," Mig repeated, floating closer. "Do you want to burn?"

She was close enough now that Kurt could feel the heat radiating off of her. Once again he was struck by how confused the red-headed girl seemed, despite her immense power and the confidence in her voice. Her expression changed constantly, flitting from anger to happiness to a pitiful sadness.

Kurt knew he couldn't fight Mig and win. So he tried a different tactic.

"You've been through a lot," Kurt said, trying to sound as sympathetic as possible. "The war must've been hard on you."

"The war is over," Mig said, looking surprised. She clearly wasn't expecting Kurt to start a conversation with her. "The goblin army is dead. The goblin city has fallen. Soon there won't be any more goblins anywhere."

"Because you're going to kill them all?" Kurt asked. "That's why you want the Fallen Star, right? To kill every goblin alive."

"They killed my friends!" Mig roared.

Her voice boomed across the snowfields. The force of her words made Kurt stagger backward a step. Somehow, though, he managed to hold on to the Star. Once the echo from Mig's words faded, he looked her in the eyes and spoke quietly to her.

"So in return, you're going to kill *their* friends," Kurt said. "Maybe you think that's fair. But you're also going to kill their children. Their mothers. Their grandparents. Old goblins too weak to walk. Babies who haven't even learned to crawl."

"They killed my friends," Mig said again, much quieter this time, without the force of magic behind her words.

"You—or some wizard just like you—killed *my* friend," Kurt said, his voice breaking a little. "His name was Azam. He was human. Hanorian. Then Hanorian wizards shot down our bat. It crashed into the trees. A branch went right through Azam's chest. Now he's dead."

"I killed a human?" Mig said.

Kurt nodded at the admission. "You did. I guess I should want to kill you and your friends for that. Only Azam wouldn't have approved. He would've told me to forgive you. To not meet violence with violence. You would have liked Azam," he said. "He was a really good juggler."

"That means he was a Celestial," Mig realized. "They all like to juggle. They're heretics. Traitors. He deserved to die."

"For juggling?" Kurt asked. "For being kind? For wanting to protect children and old people?"

Kurt could see Mig's confusion intensifying. She muttered something, then hit herself on the thigh repeatedly. Finally, her face stilled into a look of determination. She flew closer, and the snow and ice on the lip of the crater began to melt from the heat coming off her. Then she landed right in front of Kurt. The hot wind died down.

"Give me the Star," Mig said as flames flickered from her eyes.

Kurt gripped the meteorite a little harder and resisted the temptation to step back from Mig. *If you show fear, you'll just open yourself up to attack,* Kurt thought. *Keep her talking. As long as she's talking, she's not setting you on fire.*

"My friend Lexi has powers like you," Kurt said softly. "She says it's really hard, keeping them in control. Not letting them control you."

"No one controls me," Mig said. "Not anymore."

"Not since you realized you could do magic," Kurt clarified. "Since you realized you were a spark."

A "spark" was what the Hanorians called an untrained lightworker. Mig definitely seemed to qualify.

"That changed everything," Mig said thoughtfully.

"It made me a person that mattered, instead of just a kitchen girl no one ever noticed."

"I can tell you want to do good with your powers," Kurt said. "The goblins attacked your family. You want to punish them for that."

"They slaughtered everyone I knew!" Mig said, almost shouting. "They deserve to die for that."

"Guess what? They did. The goblins responsible are all dead," Kurt pointed out. "The goblins killed General Sawtooth themselves. The Dark Lady, the elf that inspired him? She's dead too. You killed her yourself, right? At Solace Ridge."

Mig nodded. "She scared me. I've never been that afraid before. I beat her, though."

"They're both gone. My friend Billy is the goblins' king now. Billy is human like us. All he wants is peace."

Kurt could see Mig hesitating. He was reaching her. The heat coming from her became a little less intense. Her face relaxed, and her fists unclenched.

Suddenly Mig whispered something to herself. Kurt couldn't make out the words. A second later, Mig whispered again, her tone slightly different. She went on like that, back and forth, for several seconds. It was like she was arguing with herself. Then she pounded her thigh again. She looked up at Kurt, her face unreadable.

"If I let you have the Fallen Star," she asked, "what would your wizards do with it?"

Kurt thought back on the things Frost had said he could do with the Star. Some of them seemed harmless enough. Make walls of ice around Kiranok, or dig a big canyon between Mother Mountain and the human camp. However, a lot of them sounded pretty nasty. Summon a blizzard and send it against the Hanorians. Crush the enemy army under a sheet of ice. Freeze their soldiers solid.

"They'd use it against us, wouldn't they?" Mig asked. "They'd kill more humans."

"Maybe not . . ." Kurt sputtered. "That's not the only way to stop you."

"Stop us. Kill us. Murder us. It's all the same," Mig said, her voice growing louder. "Nothing has changed. Nothing!"

Kurt felt a surge of heat. Mig's eyes began to glow again. Her dressed whipped around her as a hot wind lifted her back into the air.

"Give me the Star!" she shouted.

A ball of fire formed in one of her hands. She cocked her arm back to fling it at Kurt—

Which is when Hop leapt at Mig, tackling her around the waist and sending them both tumbling into the crater below.

Hop bounced down the crater wall, seeming to hit every rock along the way. After numerous jolts and bumps, he and the human girl came to rest in the snow at the bottom of the crater. The snow was freezing cold, but at least it made for a soft landing.

The human girl groaned in pain as Hop struggled to his feet. He looked down. She was stunned, though nothing looked broken. Hop was relieved. He hadn't meant to kill her, just to stop her from killing Kurt and taking the Star.

Still . . . Mig had just confessed to downing the bats carrying his expedition. She and wizards like her had killed Kurt's Hanorian friend Azam, warbat riders Littletwig and Brassclaw, and innocent bat-handler Rounder. For all Hop knew, she'd killed his loyal signal *gob*, Flutter, and all the other members of his expedition who'd gone missing after the bats crashed. All he had to do was pick up one of the big rocks that littered the crater floor and hit her with it a few times, and . . .

Hop stopped himself. He knew he couldn't bring himself to kill the semiconscious human girl, even if it meant sparing his fellow goblins from future magical attacks. She was helpless. She was still a child. From what he'd overheard of her conversation with Kurt, goblin soldiers had killed her friends and family. So in a way, as a goblin soldier himself, Hop had helped create her. Murdering her now would make him exactly the kind of monster she thought he was.

"Hop! They're coming!"

Hop looked up the crater and saw Kurt waving to him, still holding the Fallen Star.

"The Hanorians!" Kurt shouted. "They're almost here."

"Run!" Hop shouted back.

Kurt immediately broke into a run, heading vaguely northeast along the northern lip of the crater, moving as fast as his injuries would allow. Hop figured that meant the Hanorians were coming from the southwest. He ran toward the northeast crater wall and bounded up it in a series of powerful leaps.

Being a maja *good jumper are* nai *the sort of thing that come in handy all of the time,* Hop reflected. *But sometime it're the best skill a* gob *can have.*

Hop reached the snowfield and looked back. Sure enough, a phalanx of Hanorians was charging toward him and Kurt from the southwest, carrying torches and swords. They were only a few score paces from the crater.

Up ahead, Kurt plunged forward through the snow-field, waist deep in snow. Hop ran after him. The snow was deeper for him, reaching almost up to his chest. Still, he was able to gain ground on Kurt. Hop realized that the human boy must be even more hurt than he was letting on, which meant that he and Kurt wouldn't be able outrun the Hanorians for long.

And that wasn't their only problem. He and Kurt were headed straight for the ravine that bisected the snowfield.

Up ahead, Kurt stopped in his tracks. He'd reached the edge of the ravine. A few heartbeats later, Hop was at his side. He looked down at the raging, snowmelt-flooded river several dozen strides below them.

"I forgot about the ravine," Kurt said, his voice hollow.

Hop looked back. The Hanorians would be on him and Kurt in moments.

"*Nai* helping it," Hop said. "There're only one way to go."

Kurt swallowed hard and looked at the distant river. "We jump?"

"Can *nai* think about it," Hop said, taking a few steps back. "Can *nai* wait. Just . . . GO!"

With that, Hop ran as fast as he could toward the edge of the ravine, then jumped.

Out of the corner of his eye, he saw Kurt do the same.

The fall took longer than Hop expected. He saw the ravine wall rushing by, felt the wind whipping around him, and then . . .

Splash.

"What do you mean, he's gone?" Lexi asked, horrified.

She'd arrived at the Painted Cave expecting to meet with Billy, Shadow, Frost, Leadpipe, and High Priestess Starcaller. She'd left word with the Night Goddess's Templars to relay news about the meeting to Shadow and

Starcaller. Then she'd personally escorted Frost and a limping Leadpipe to Billy's temporary throne room.

Unfortunately, when they reached the cave, only Shadow was waiting for them. The Templar commander informed them that no one had seen Starcaller in hours. She was missing. Even worse, Billy was missing too. And unlike Starcaller, there was no mystery to Billy's disappearance. The two goblin wizards who'd attacked him in the Bat Cavern had tried again. Billy had jumped into a chasm to escape. Before his guards could react, the wizards had stunned them with blasts of cold and followed Billy down the hole.

"His guards tried to follow once they recovered, but it were too late," Shadow said. "It're a maze down there, and they *nai* knowed what way to go."

"I've been studying maps of the caverns," Frost said. "There are *maja* many cracks and tunnels that lead off from that chasm. Most are dead ends. Only one connect to deeper into the mountain. If Billy *nai* finded that one, odds are, he're dead. On second bite, though, if he chanced on the right tunnel, I know a quicker way to get to where he're going. But *nai* time to wait."

Frost headed toward the door.

"I'm coming with you," Lexi said, catching up to him.

"Me too," Leadpipe added, struggling to his feet.

"*Nai*," Frost said. "*Nai* either of you are coming with me. Lead, you're too slow and too big. You will *nai* fit through some of the tunnels I have to use. And Lexi, with Starcaller missing, you're the most powerful wizard we have. If the humans find us, we need you here."

Lexi didn't know what to say to that. She'd been ready for Frost to tell her that she was too weak or too unstable to come with him. She hadn't expected him to say she was too *important*.

"Billy is the Goblin King," Lexi pointed out. "If we lose him, we lose everything."

"Billy are our king, that're true," Frost said. "But you stopped the attack at Seventurns. You hided the entrances to the caverns after we moved all the *goben* here. You saved me brother. Prophecy are a funny thing. It promise much, but it're often a puzzle. We were promised a Goblin King and a human child what'd save us. We always thinked that them were the same person. Except *zajnai* that're *nai* true. *Naizaj* fate sended Billy to be our Goblin King—and you to save us."

As Lexi took that in, Shadow added, "If the humans find us, I do *nai* think I can defend the caverns without you. Stay. Please."

Lexi was torn. She wanted to help Billy more than anything, but she didn't want to abandon Shadow and the countless goblins hiding in the caverns. In the end, though, Lexi knew what Billy would do in her place. Billy would choose the greater good. As hard as it might be, he'd choose to protect thousands of lives over trying to save a single friend, even someone he cared about.

"I'll stay," she said, turning to Frost, "if you promise me you'll find Billy."

"*Wazzer*, you protect the entire *goben* race, and I save one human boy," Frost said with a smile. "That're a *maja* fair bargain."

Billy was pretty sure kings weren't supposed to run away. In the stories he'd read, they usually charged into battle with their armies at their backs. Or they rallied their kingdoms against impossible odds. Or, if all else failed, they went down fighting in their throne rooms. Billy couldn't see himself doing any of those things. It made him wonder. What if the Goblin Crown had made a mistake? What if its Eye should have glowed when Kurt put it on in the first place?

Except it hadn't. The Goblin Crown was on *his* head. Its Eye was glowing to light *his* way as he ran for his life.

Luckily, the chasm hadn't been as bottomless as it looked, so Billy hadn't gotten hurt too badly when he jumped in, aside from a few scrapes and bruises. At the bottom, it had opened into a passageway, and Billy had gotten up, dusted himself off, and fled down it. So far, he'd been able to keep ahead of the two goblin wizards who were trying to kill him. Unfortunately, though, he hadn't been able to lose them. Even though his ears weren't as sensitive as a goblin's, from time to time he could hear them moving behind him. On the bright side, he was leading them away from goblin camps, so no one else would get hurt by their attacks. The only life at risk was his own.

Billy reached an intersection. The tunnel he'd been following forked three ways. One tunnel seemed to slope up. The next, a narrow crack, ran straight back into the mountain. The third, which was almost perfectly round and smooth, went down. Billy could feel a warm breeze coming from the round tunnel. Since air was moving through it, that probably meant that the round tunnel wasn't a dead end. Billy ran down the round tunnel, his sneakers squeaking faintly on the smooth stone surface. He wished his shoes would shut up. He wasn't going to elude his pursuers if they kept squeaking. Plus, he was wearing a glowing crown, which didn't help much. But running blind and barefoot wasn't very appealing either.

"*Nai* helping it," Billy said, quoting one of Hop's favorite sayings.

No matter how terrible things got for Hop, he

somehow always managed to keep going and survive. Billy had to do the same.

He ran deeper into the mountain.

To his surprise, he started hearing voices coming from up ahead. They were faint at first, then grew louder as he ran. For a moment Billy thought he might've found his way back to the inhabited part of the caverns. If so, he might be able to get help against the wizards. But leading the wizards back to the goblin camps would put innocent lives at risk. He didn't want any more deaths on his conscience. Billy was considering turning around and trying a different path when he realized the voices he was hearing weren't speaking *Gobayabber*. They weren't even speaking Hanorian. They were speaking English.

Billy ran toward the voices. As he rounded a corner the voices grew louder, and Billy saw light ahead. He ran toward the light, quickly confirming that it and the voices both had the same source: a crack in the wall of the tunnel. He sprinted up to the crack and looked inside.

Through the crack, he saw home.

There was no mistaking it. The crack, which was about a dozen feet long and just wide enough to squeeze through, opened onto a city street. The voices he'd heard were from the patrons of a sidewalk café, enjoying lunch. Cars whooshed by; people chatted on cell phones. Billy could even hear a cable car ringing its bell somewhere in the distance. He was looking at San Francisco.

All Billy had to do was climb through the crack and he'd be home. He'd be able to see his mother again. He'd have a chance to see his father again . . . if his cancer hadn't taken him while Billy was missing. He imagined his dad, bald from his chemo, trying to find the strength to fight his illness despite the disappearance of his son. Billy had to see him again. This was his chance. Except . . .

Except if Billy climbed through the crack, he'd be abandoning Lexi and Kurt. They might never get home. If he climbed through the crack, he'd be abandoning Hop too. And Frost and Leadpipe and every other goblin hiding in the caverns. He'd be leaving them to fend for themselves in the face of the Army of Light. The goblins were in the caverns because of him. If he abandoned them now, what did that make him?

Useless, Billy thought. *It would make you useless.*

Billy had spent his whole life feeling like he didn't matter to anyone. Like the world, even his parents, would be better off without him. Now, though, he mattered to the goblins and to his friends. He belonged here, fighting at their side.

Billy heard movement from behind him in the tunnel. He dodged just in time. A blast of cold washed over the wall inches from his head, leaving a coating of frost behind.

"Might as well stop running, *skerbo*!" he heard the female goblin call out. "We're gonna catch you anyway."

Billy had to choose now. He could go through the crack, save himself from the goblin wizards, and finally get home to his parents. Or he could continue down the tunnel, wherever it led, on the slim hope he could escape the wizards and return to his friends and the goblins, who were depending on him.

Billy ran down the tunnel, leaving his home behind. Again.

Snap jogged past the strange hole in the wall, with its unnatural lights and odd-sounding human voices. The lights and voices didn't surprise her. Everyone knew that the caverns under Kiranok had passageways that led to other worlds and other times. That's where the Goblin Kings came from, after all. A portal like this was how Button the Mushroom Girl had traveled to the Screaming City, where she'd famously found both her wheeled boots and the cure to the Spotty Plague. The Masked *Skerbo* had also emerged from a world crack before starting his reign of terror over Kiranok. So too had his enemy, the fifth Goblin King. Religious goblins believed Mother Mountain gave birth to the world and entire universes could be found inside the tunnels that were her veins.

Still, Snap had more important things to worry about. She had a king to kill.

So it surprised her when Grinner stopped in front of the crack and peered inside.

"*Wazzer*! What're you doing?" Snap asked, looking back at her dangerous ally.

"Look at all them *skerboen*," Grinner said. "How about I climb inside and drop an ice storm on them?"

"There're only one *skerbo* we need to kill right now."

"Are *nai* having much luck with that one," Grinner said. "Aside, these will *nai* see me coming."

Snap thought Grinner might be joking. It was hard to tell, since he was almost always smiling. But while they stood and talked, King Billy was getting away.

"Time for that later," Snap said, annoyed. "You can come back and kill all the *skerboen* you want after the King are dead."

"You're *nai* fun," Grinner said. He turned from the portal and jogged after Snap. "*Zajnai* after the King are dead, I'll kill you too."

Then he giggled. Snap was sure he was joking this time.

Almost sure.

Together they ran after King Billy. Snap felt a hot breeze blowing in her face from farther down the tunnel. For a moment, she thought she could hear words on the wind, as if it were whispering in her ear.

"This way," it seemed to say. "This way to the end, this way, this way."

"Insubordination, thirty lashes," Lord Marshal Jiyal announced. "Dereliction of duty, thirty lashes. Attacking a superior officer, death by hanging. Attacking a wizard of the Imperial Army, death by fire."

Cyreth took in the charges and the sentences without betraying any emotion. It was no worse than he expected. Though Lord Jiyal's reasons weren't the ones he thought he'd hear.

Cyreth had been summoned to the Lord Marshal's temporary headquarters in the goblins' throne room. The vast stone hall was incongruously decorated with ten large statues of humans, all wearing the same simple crown. As a child, Cyreth had heard stories about human kings leading the goblins. Maybe they were true.

Unfortunately, the human statues weren't the only surprise waiting for Cyreth. As he entered, Cyreth had found Dumen—the vain wizard who'd been forced to heal Ysalion—standing at Lord Jiyal's side, looking pleased with himself. Dumen had obviously told the Lord Marshal everything.

"You see my problem," Lord Jiyal continued. "How can we hang you *and* burn you alive? Is there one you'd prefer?"

Cyreth knew Jiyal was only raising the question to prolong Cyreth's agony. To get him to beg for his life, to humiliate himself in a vain attempt to gain the Lord Marshal's forgiveness. Cyreth was determined not to give him the satisfaction. One benefit of facing death so frequently over the past few years was that Cyreth no longer panicked when he was threatened. In his mind, he was already living on borrowed time. So while the Lord Marshal might indeed have him executed today, the prospect of being hanged or burned alive wasn't any more terrifying that the several dozen other ways he'd recently expected to die. Remembering that made it easier for Cyreth to keep his voice calm and even as he replied to Jiyal's threats.

"Whichever milord believes to be just," Cyreth said.

"So you do not deny your crimes?" the Lord Marshal snapped, clearly annoyed at Cyreth's lack of fear. Cyreth knew that denying his crimes wouldn't do any good. Jiyal would doubtlessly believe a wizard over some junior officer, especially one he suspected of being a heretic. Not to mention, Dumen had the truth on his side; Cyreth really was guilty of every charge leveled against him. Still, he didn't see any harm in explaining himself.

"I did what I did to save the life of a Lion Guard," Cyreth said. "That's my duty as an officer—to preserve my unit, so as to better complete our assignments. And the Lion Guards have fulfilled our assignments, milord. Every last one."

"Are you trying to justify your actions?" Lord Jiyal snapped. He sounded annoyed.

"No, Lord Marshal," Cyreth said. "I submit myself to your justice."

Cyreth could tell Lord Jiyal wasn't going to listen. He knew he was doomed the moment the Lord Marshal accused him of a crime. As head of the Army of Light, Jiyal was sole arbiter of justice. There was no appeal.

There would be no mercy. His best course of action was to cooperate so that the Lord Marshal's wrath would be focused on him and him alone.

Sadly, even on that point, the Lord Marshal seemed determined to shatter Cyreth's hopes.

"And how many of your fellow Lion Guards were in on your little scheme, Captain?" Jiyal asked, glaring at Cyreth.

Cyreth swallowed hard. That was the question he'd been dreading. The truth was, only Bytha had accompanied him when he'd forced Dumen to heal Ysalion. Though, in a way, Ysalion was involved too. The last thing Cyreth wanted to do was give the Lord Marshal their names.

"There's no use hiding the truth," Jiyal said, seeing Cyreth's hesitation. "Lightworker Dumen told me there were at least two additional Lion Guards present. Both female. One slight, the other as tall and broad as any man."

"I'm their commanding officer," Cyreth said. "All guilt belongs to me."

"I can't agree," Lord Jiyal said, a dangerous smile on his face. "In fact, I find it hard to believe that your conspiracy was limited to just you and those two women. We already know the Lion Guards are prone to heresy. From there, treason and disloyalty are but a short journey."

"Milord—" Cyreth protested.

"Enough!" the Lord Marshal cut him off. "I've heard all I care to hear from you, Captain. I order you flayed sixty times, then hanged until you're unconscious, then burned alive. Before any of that occurs, however, you will witness the decimation of your Lion Guards, the execution of every tenth member, chosen at random. The Army of Light will be purified of your heresy and treachery. Purified by ax, lash, rope, and fire."

Lord Jiyal signaled to the Black Hussars keeping their silent watch by the entrance to the throne room.

"Take him away," he ordered.

A half dozen Black Hussars moved toward Cyreth. But while Cyreth had come to terms with his own death, he wasn't about to let a tenth of his Lion Guards be executed. Not while he had one more card to play.

"I know how to find them," Cyreth said as the Hussars grabbed his arms. "The goblins. I can show you where they're hiding!"

The Hussars dragged Cyreth toward the door.

"Wait," Jiyal said. The Hussars stopped. Apparently he'd gotten the Lord Marshal's attention. "Where are the greenskins?"

"I'll tell you everything," Cyreth said, "in exchange for a signed pardon. For me and all the Lion Guards. For all crimes, known and unknown, committed until today."

"I could torture it out of you," Jiyal snarled.

"You could," Cyreth said. "Except that would take time. You could lose your chance to wipe out the goblins forever. Or you can pardon us, and we'll lead the charge against the goblins. Most of us will probably die anyway, but at least we'll have a chance. That's all I ask."

Dumen leaned over and whispered something to Jiyal, but the Lord Marshal gestured dismissively.

"Your revenge doesn't outweigh our victory," he said. Then he looked back at Cyreth. "Tell me, and you'll have your pardon."

Cyreth nodded. Bytha said he might have to choose between his honor and his life. If that had been the two options, he'd have picked honor. But when forced to weigh the lives of the goblins against the lives of his fellow Lion Guards, Cyreth had to choose his soldiers. If it meant the death of his honor, and the deaths of countless goblins along with it, so be it.

At least I'm not dead, Kurt thought to himself. *So far.*

Somehow Kurt (and, he hoped, Hop) had hit the water at the bottom of the ravine. Initially he'd been relieved. Then he realized the water was moving fast, and he was being carried, out of control, downstream.

Plus the water was icy cold. Kurt didn't think he'd ever been so cold in his life. After only a few minutes in the river, Kurt's hands and feet were numb, and his entire body was shaking in a desperate attempt to get warm. But there was no way to warm up in the ice cold, rushing water. He needed to get out of the river. Only he couldn't fight the powerful current, couldn't swim in soaking-wet clothing while holding the Fallen Star in both hands, couldn't do anything but allow the water to take him wherever it wanted.

All Kurt could do was hold on to the Fallen Star and hope for the best.

Unfortunately, between his numbness and the swirling water yanking him around, holding on to the Star wasn't easy. It was taking all his years of football training experience to maintain his grip on the smooth, heavy ball of iron.

In football, players and coaches sometimes called the ball "the rock." So as he was swept along by the river, Kurt kept thinking to himself, *Don't drop the rock, don't drop the rock.*

Except he knew it was only a matter of time. If he didn't get warm soon, he was going to pass out from the cold, after which he'd probably drown. Then he'd definitely drop the Fallen Star.

Kurt slammed into a river rock. It hit him right in the ribs, knocking the air from his lungs with a whoosh. He managed to hang on to the Star, barely, but what little strength he had left was spent. He was exhausted. He was done.

Suddenly, he felt something pull him up, out of the water. He flew out of the river, water pouring off of him, then stopped in midair so that he was hovering above the surface of the river. It felt like countless little hands were holding him aloft, even though Kurt couldn't see anything supporting him.

He was flying.

Kurt heard another splash and saw Hop come soaring out of the river. The goblin looked badly beaten up, wet, and miserable. In the blink of an eye, some invisible force brought him sailing over to Kurt. Hop came to a halt a few feet from Kurt, looking bewildered.

Then they both rocketed into the sky.

The river dwindled below Kurt as he shot up at an alarming speed. The water clinging to his body went flying away. Instead of making him feel warmer, though, his skin became ice cold. His shivering got even worse. He was having trouble breathing. Kurt held the Fallen Star in an underarm tuck, just like a football, gripping it for all he was worth.

Don't drop the rock, don't drop the rock, don't drop the rock.

Whoosh! Now he was moving sideways, blindingly fast. The wind stung at his eyes, so he closed them. He could hear a long, anguished wail not far from him and realized it was Hop, screaming.

With his eyes closed, lost in the night sky, Kurt couldn't tell what direction he was moving anymore. It was all just cold and wind and pain.

Then he slammed to the ground.

The impact jarred the Fallen Star loose. Kurt had finally fumbled the ball. He opened his eyes and saw the iron sphere rolling away from him. He was too battered and exhausted to even try to get up and grab it.

Kurt took stock of his surroundings. He and Hop had landed in the middle of a sprawling ruin. Huge walls built from giant stones ten feet wide and ten feet tall loomed all around them. Impossible spires made of millions of tiny rocks towered into the air. Bridges arced from one side of the ruins to the other, made of stones both giant and tiny, leading from nowhere to nowhere. The structures were worn and crumbling, as if no one had lived in them for centuries. More stones lay strewn about, lying wherever they had fallen. The entire place gave off an eerie green light. So even if he was too tired to retrieve it, at least Kurt could see where the Fallen Star was going. It rolled to the center of the ruins and finally came to rest . . .

Against a woman's bare foot.

The woman picked up the Star and studied it for a moment. She was dressed in flowing robes that were somehow both black and silver. Her long dark hair cascaded past delicate pointed ears. Her brows were high and arched, her mouth thin and cruel. Something about the Star must've amused her, because she suddenly burst into laughter. Her laugh was indescribably beautiful, like the purest, most perfect music ever written. It terrified Kurt to the core.

Kurt looked to Hop, who was staring at the woman as if he'd seen a ghost.

"That's a *duenshee*, right?" Kurt asked quietly. "An elf. Like the Dark Lady? The prophetess who inspired General Sawtooth to go to war with the humans?"

Hop shook his head, clearly terrified.

"She are *nai* like the Dark Lady," Hop said, his voice barely audible. "She *are* the Dark Lady."

Kurt looked at the tall, inhuman woman, shocked. "You told us the Dark Lady was dead. Mig killed her. The Hanorians cut off her head."

Hop had no answer for that.

The *duenshee* did, though. Carrying the Fallen Star, she stepped closer to them.

"Off with her head, put it on a pike," she said in a beautiful, musical voice. "The view, the view. I could see the world from up there. The whole world."

As the *duenshee* moved toward them, Kurt could see a ragged scar at the base of her neck, like a necklace—the only flaw on her pale, shimmering skin.

"She are a thing of magic," Hop whispered. "Can be hard to kill a magical thing. Or keep them dead. Coaler killed the Emperor of Bones three times afore it sticked. *Nai* speak to her. *Nai* look in her eyes. She're mad. And powerful. That're a dangerous pairing."

"The world is tears and blood," the Dark Lady continued. "Every smile ends in mourning, every life ends in death. There is no peace, no happy breath."

She was inches from Kurt now, looking right at him. Despite Hop's warning, he caught a glimpse of her eyes. They were silver and wide, and her huge dark irises reminded him of pits.

"We can make it right," she continued. "We can wipe away the blood. We can end the tears. We can make a world at peace. Still and calm and free from fear."

"I don't know what you're talking about," Kurt sputtered, forgetting Hop's advice in his panic.

"You brought me a gift," the Dark Lady said, holding up the Fallen Star. "A gift that can end all suffering and all pain."

"You want to use the Fallen Star to end the war?" Kurt asked.

"Life is strife," the Dark Lady answered. "As long as there are beginnings, there will be endings. But with this"—the Dark Lady held up the Fallen Star—"I can end beginnings. With this I can create a peace that will never be broken again."

Kurt saw that behind the black pits of the Dark Lady's eyes there was only madness.

"She mean she're going to use it to kill everyone," Hop said, his eyes wide and his ears lowered back against his skull in fear. "Human, *goben*, every last one. She think the only way to have peace are to murder us all."

CHAPTER FOURTEEN

Swallowing the Bitter and the Sour

Cyreth walked along the ranks of the assembled Lion Guards, giving them a final inspection. Their cloaks were soiled. Their sashes were crooked. Their armor was stained with blood and dirt. Their helmets weren't properly polished, and half of their crests were missing. To him, though, they'd never looked better, braver, or more like soldiers.

Finally Cyreth reached the front of the formation. It was time for a stirring speech. Because he was their captain, and that's what captains did before battles. Only Cyreth couldn't find the words. He couldn't promise his Lion Guards victory. He couldn't tell them their cause was right. He couldn't say they'd go home covered in glory. He couldn't lie to them. Not today.

So he told them the truth.

"Today will not be a day to remember," Cyreth began.

"It will not be a day to tell your children about. Today will be ugly. Today we'll wage war on a desperate people, and, Light willing, we will slaughter them. The only thing I can promise you is this: our next battle will be our last. So think of those we've lost. Think of home. Think of your families. Then do what you have to do. And if it all becomes too much, if you find you'd rather die than carry on, blame me. Hate me. I am ordering you to fight, and to win, and to live. So all the guilt, all the shame, is mine and mine alone. The Lion Guards are eternal. Your honor is unbroken. Today is for victory and an end to war and the beginning of the long march home. Ur-rar!"

"Ur-rar!" the Lion Guards roared. "Ur-rar! Ur-rar! UR-RAR!"

There was no blame in their roar. No reluctance. He was ordering them into a horrific battle, yet they were cheering him like one of the heroes of old. Cyreth blinked away tears. He was no more worthy of their loyalty than Lord Jiyal was. He wondered if anyone could ever really deserve soldiers' cheers and still lead them into war. It seemed unlikely.

"Lion Guards!" he shouted. "Advance!"

With a final "UR-RAR!" the Lion Guards marched forward, one last time.

Hop had no idea what to do.

After her final grim pronouncement, the Dark Lady had stopped moving and talking entirely. She just stood stock-still in the center of the glowing green ruins, looking at the Fallen Star. She wasn't even blinking. Just . . . staring.

For a long while, he and Kurt waited for the Dark Lady's next move. It looked like that move may never come.

"I think it might be the ruins," Kurt whispered to Hop after several minutes of watching the Dark Lady stand still as a statue.

"The ruins?" Hop asked quietly.

"What if that's what brought her back," Kurt explained. "I feel better since we came here, don't you? My head's cleared up. My body doesn't hurt. And the closer I sit to these glowing rocks, the better I feel."

Hop flexed his broken finger. It didn't hurt. "You could be right. That're a problem for another day though. Today's problem are, what do we do now?"

Kurt seemed to think that over for a moment. "She's not doing anything. We could probably leave. Just walk away."

"Without the Star?" Hop asked, still keeping his voice low. "With *nai* Star, Kiranok will fall. Aside, if we leave it with her, *nai* good will come of it, you can be certain."

"So . . . what? We try to take it?"

Hop thought about Kurt's suggestion. He was feeling a lot better. Somehow, despite everything he'd been through, he still had his holdout knife tucked into his boot sheath. Hop figured he might be able to charge the Dark Lady, grab the Star, and make a run for it. Or better yet, stab her in the heart with his knife and end her threat forever.

On second bite, though, you seed her head on a pike, and now she're back, Hop thought. *If beheading the Dark Lady* nai *worked, why do you think a knife will end her?*

"How far do you think we'd go, grabbing it and running?" Hop asked Kurt.

Kurt looked at the Dark Lady, probably weighing the odds. "Not far," he said. Then another thought seemed to cross his face. "What if I tackle her and hold her? You take the Star and run."

"*Ahka*. She'd kill you."

Kurt shrugged. "Maybe. Maybe not. I'm willing to risk it."

"I're *nai*," Hop said. "Only one chance far as I can see. I're going to talk with her. If she kill me, run."

Before Kurt could object, Hop mustered his courage and walked up to the Dark Lady.

"We meeted afore, milady," Hop said, trying to sound respectful. "*Zajnai* you remember? It were at a Warhorde camp near the human town of Bastinge. It were night, and it were raining, and I were drunk. We talked about foxes and birds and such. Me name are Korgorog Hoprock. Folk call me Hop."

The Dark Lady looked up, and her eyes met Hop's. Just as he had been at Bastinge, he was instantly terrified to be the focus of her attention.

Then she spoke, "Are you fire, or are you stone? Are you spirit, or are you bone?"

Hop was more than a little confused by the question, but he did his best to answer. "I're *nai* fire unless someone burn me. *Nai* stone that I know about. I're bone a bit, on the insides. As to spirit, I're *nai* so certain of that one. What are you?"

"I am the Dance of the Uncrowned Flowers," the Dark Lady answered. "I am the Rot that Spreads Unseen. I am the Shadow that Measures the Hours. I am the Sudden and Relentless Dream."

Hop wasn't sure if the *duenshee* had answered his question or just told him her full name, but he plunged ahead.

"I were hoping to talk about what you sayed afore," Hop ventured, bracing himself for sudden annihilation. "About making peace by ending the beginnings and all that."

"Would you like peace, goblin?" the Dark Lady asked. "Would you like the gift after which there are no more gifts?"

Hop was struck by the irony of that. All he'd ever wanted was peace. He always imagined he'd done everything he could to avoid conflict, to live quietly and unnoticed. The truth was, though, he hadn't really chosen peace at all costs. Not for himself anyway. He'd chosen to fight to protect his people, to help his friends, to try to make the world better. He'd always wanted to run. Only, he rarely had.

So zajnai *peace are* nai *so* maja *important to you as you like to think*, he reflected. *Aside, the peace the Dark Lady are offering are the peace of the grave. As much as I hate fighting and struggling and suffering, I'd* maja *rather live a difficult, painful life than* nai *life at all.*

"*Ganzi* for the offer. But I can *nai* accept," Hop said. "Peace are a nice idea and all. But to speak true, I do *nai* think most folk want it as much as they say. What folk want are to live. And life are like a stew. It're all sorts of things, stirred together. The hurt, bumps, and tears are all mixed in with the happiness, friendship, and love. A *gob* can *nai* bite one without the other. Still, the good bits are so tasty that it're worth swallowing the bitter and the sour right along with them. I have *nai* had me fill yet, if you follow me meaning. So if it're a choice between peace and life you're offering, I choose life."

The Dark Lady blinked. "Are you singular? Are you alone? Are you the four-leafed clover among the trefoils?"

Hop wasn't sure what she meant by that. While he was still trying to puzzle it out, Kurt stepped forward.

"You're asking if he's the only one who thinks that way," Kurt said. "He's not. I . . . I watched a friend die a few days ago. He was in pain. But he fought to hold on, to have a few more minutes of life. That's what living things do. They fight for every last breath."

The Dark Lady blinked again. Suddenly, Hop couldn't

breathe. He tried to inhale, but no air reached his lungs. He flailed and gasped, but it was no use. He was going to die. Behind him he could hear Kurt struggling in the same way. Hop could think of only one explanation. The Dark Lady was suffocating them both with her magic.

Hop fell to his knees, still trying to somehow suck air in through his mouth and nose. Still desperately trying to breathe despite the magic that was slowly killing him.

He looked up and saw the Dark Lady studying him, as if he were a page in a book where the ink had run, and she could no longer make out the words.

Suddenly, air rushed into Hop's lungs. He gasped and wheezed, but he could breathe again. He inhaled deeply. He'd never appreciated fresh air more. The air in the ruins was slightly cold and smelled like pine trees and dirt with a trace of water. It was the best thing he'd ever smelled in his life.

Behind him, he heard Kurt gasping. He looked back. Kurt was on his knees too, panting as he pulled air into his lungs. They would both live. For now.

"A new thought is a rare thing," the Dark Lady said. "I wonder where it will lead me."

Then she looked back to the Fallen Star in her hands, as if she were thinking over what Hop had said. Still on his knees, Hop looked back at Kurt and swiped his fist across his mouth. It was a goblin gesture that meant "be quiet." He hoped Kurt would understand what he meant.

Keep your mouth shut, and let her think.

Kurt nodded. He understood.

As carefully and quietly as he could, Hop lowered himself so he was sitting instead of kneeling, then settled in to wait. He hoped he'd somehow reached the Dark Lady. Because if he hadn't, he didn't think he'd have the courage to speak to her again.

Well, Billy thought, *that explains the hot breeze.*

Billy had reached the bottom of the long, rounded tunnel, which ended at a huge chamber. Aside from a rocky shore a dozen yards wide, the entire chamber was filled by a large lake.

A lake made entirely of lava.

The lava glowed red and hot. As Billy watched, it churned slowly, like a thick stew sitting on a stove, set to simmer.

Billy had done a science fair presentation on volcanos once. He knew they were riddled with lava tubes. When enough pressure built up in the magma chamber, lava would shoot through the tubes toward the surface. But it hadn't occurred to Billy that the tunnel he'd been following was a lava tube until he reached the magma chamber itself. He realized he was in the heart of Mother Mountain now. The lava pool must be the source of its many caverns and tunnels, as well as the hot springs that fed Nokala's Pools.

So Billy was pretty sure there were plenty of other lava tubes leading out of the magma chamber. It was unbearably hot in the chamber, but hopefully he could make his way around the rim of the lava lake and find another tunnel leading back to the upper caverns. The trick would be finding the right lava tube. He knew that sometimes the tubes could get blocked. If he picked the wrong tunnel and the wizards followed him, it might mean a literal dead end for Billy.

Just pick a direction, he told himself.

Billy turned right. Before he could start along the rim, though, a blast of cold air slammed into him. Billy was knocked off his feet and tumbled toward the lava pool.

The lava stone near the lake was as slick as glass. For a moment, Billy thought he was going to slide straight into the fiery lava below.

Somehow, only a dozen or so feet from the magma, Billy found a handhold, a crack in the otherwise smooth lava stone. He snagged it with one hand, stopping himself but cutting his fingers badly. The edge of the crack was knife sharp. Still, Billy knew he had to hold on no matter how much it hurt. Let go and he'd burn.

Though he quickly realized he might burn up even if he didn't fall. This close, the heat from the magma was intense. Billy was having trouble breathing. The scorching air burned in his nose and throat every time he inhaled. Plus it tasted horrible and made Billy gag and choke. He knew he needed to get away from the lava, but he was so tired and weak, and the lava stone was so slick . . .

"In a bit of trouble, *skerbo*?" Billy heard a male goblin say.

Billy looked up. He saw the two goblin wizards who'd attacked him standing at the exit from the lava tube. The smiling male with the pale eyes looked pleased with himself. The female goblin with the curly hair seemed troubled, her expression grim.

"Do *nai* worry," the smiling male continued. "It'll be over in a wink." He turned to the female goblin. "Do you want to finish him, Snap? This're your quest."

"Could *nai* have getted this far without you, Grinner," Snap said. "You can do it."

"Much as I'd enjoy that, do *nai* feel right," Grinner said. "Together then?"

As the goblins coolly discussed which of them should kill him, Billy tried to figure out a way to escape. The lava stone around the lake wasn't entirely smooth. There were cracks and lumps. If he could get to his feet, he could try to run for it. One misstep and he'd fall right into the lava. It was better than just lying there though, waiting to be turned into an ice sculpture or something.

"He're trying to get up," Snap said as Billy attempted to stand.

"On a count then," Grinner said. "*Enik, menik, mynta, MOGH!*"

When Grinner reached the goblin word for "four," both wizards raised their hands to cast a spell . . . and nothing happened.

"Why're me magic *nai* working?" Grinner said, his smile vanishing for a moment.

"It must be the heat," Snap answered. "It're *maja* too hot in here for our spells."

"Too bad for you," Billy said.

Somehow, he'd managed to struggle to his feet. He clambered along the lava stone as fast as he could, moving up and to his left, trying to get away from the hostile wizards.

"Where do you think you're running to, *skerbo?*" Grinner said. "There are two of us and one of you. It will *nai* take much to push you into that lava."

With that, Grinner drew a small, sharp knife from his belt and circled around the rim of the chamber. Snap followed.

Things looked bad, but Billy knew what Hop would say.

"*Nai* helping it. Keep moving."

Billy kept moving, struggling to breathe, fighting the overwhelming heat, trying not to trip, trying not to slip, trying to survive.

I should be happy, Snap thought. *Why are I* nai *happy?*

Snap was moments away from achieving her goal.

True, the heat from the lava was preventing her and Grinner from casting any spells, but there was no way the human boy could escape the cavern. It was much easier for her and Grinner to move along the rim of the chamber than for him to navigate the treacherous shore of the lava lake. If he tripped, the lava would burn him up in an instant. If he tried to rush past Snap and Grinner . . .

Snap looked over at Grinner. He was smiling confidently, holding his knife. It didn't look like the *skerbo* would get past him alive.

So why are I nai *laughing? Why do I feel like crying instead?*

Below her, King Billy slipped, sliding toward the lava. He recovered and struggled back to his feet, but it was only a matter of time now.

It're the fumes from the lava, Snap told herself. *That're where the tears are coming from.*

But Snap knew that was a lie.

Ever since her encounter with High Priestess Starcaller, Snap had felt like she was on the wrong path. The fact that Grinner had murdered the High Priestess didn't help. The poem Starcaller had whispered in her ear kept repeating itself in her mind:

> *I are the comfort of the Night*
> *I are the gentle sunset breeze*
> *Mother's whisper, time to sleep tight*
> *Soft as snowfall among the trees*
> *Fear* nai *the day,* nai *fear the light,*
> *Let the Night set your mind at ease*

Snap was supposed to repeat the poem to the Night Goddess's Templars, who would then make her their High Priestess. But she suspected that there was more to the poem than just a signal that she'd been selected Starcaller's successor.

It was also a lesson.

The poem was a message about how the Night Goddess's magic should be used. To comfort and ease the mind; to persuade with gentle whispers. Not to kill or destroy. Starcaller had wanted Coldsnap to become a completely different goblin.

But instead she was here, in the heart of Mother Mountain, trying to drive the rightfully crowned Goblin King into a pool of lava. Despite the reddish light coming from the lava, Snap could still see the Goblin Crown on the boy's head was glowing. As if to say, "This're your King. Help him. Follow him. Listen to his words."

As she watched, King Billy tried to run up the lava stone toward a tunnel, but Grinner cut him off and swiped at him with his knife. The human boy was forced to retreat.

Grinner smiled, but Snap could tell he was losing patience.

"Enough of this," Grinner said. "Time for you to go for a swim."

Grinner moved down the slope toward Billy, his knife at the ready. But before he could reach the boy . . .

"*Ahka*. Get away from him."

The voice was familiar. Snap turned and saw a tiny goblin with a wispy beard emerging from a tunnel several paces away.

"Frost," Snap said.

"Bakalikam Coldsnap. Hakajaban Chillinggrin," Frost said, addressing Snap and Grinner by their full names, as if they were on trial. "I *nai* getted a chance to say '*Wazzer*' to you the last time I seed you. Sorry about Icewall. He were a decent sort. Easily swayed though, especially by a pretty *svagob*."

"Do *nai* test us, Atarikit Bluefrost," Snap said, "or we'll end you too."

"I have a few years on you two *pikogoben*," Frost said, moving closer. "You're the ones what better *nai* test me."

Frost had been one of the best senior students in the Blue Chambers when Snap first enrolled. A few years after she arrived, he'd graduated and been taken on as an apprentice by Hilldropper, the goblins' foremost war wizard. Hilldropper got his calling-name because he'd once sheered the top off an entire hill and dropped it on a swarm of rampaging axbeetles. Frost had no doubt learned a trick or twenty while studying under the dangerous old *gob*. He'd certainly been skilled and trusted enough, even as an apprentice, that he'd been at the center of the fight to put a stop to Moonfall and her madness. According to rumors, Frost had been the one to deflect Moon's killing spells long enough for the other wizards to bring her down. There were also rumors he and Moonfall had been in love before she went mad. So growing up, Snap had always looked at Frost as a kind of tragic hero.

Now she was going to have to kill him.

"*Ahka*," Grinner said impatiently. "If you are so *maja* certain you can stop me, why *nai* give it a try?"

Grinner dove at King Billy, slashing with his knife, driving him even closer to the lava.

"I *nai* wanted to do this," Frost said.

Then he gestured . . .

And nothing happened.

"Ice magic doesn't work here," Billy shouted to Frost.

"That're right," Grinner said, smiling even broader than usual. "It do *nai*. Which mean your friend can *nai* help you. It're time for you to die."

With that, Grinner took another step toward Billy.

And another.

Snap felt sorry for Frost. All he could do was watch, helpless. To her surprise, she felt sorry for King Billy too. The Goblin Crown had glowed for him. Now that she'd met him, he seemed like an innocent boy who was just trying to do what was best for the goblins. Snap wished she could go back in time and convince herself not to undertake her quest to kill the *skerbo* king. Not to recruit Grinner and Icewall to her cause.

I should have been the next High Priestess, she thought. *Billy should have been me king. But that will* nai *happen now. Acause of me.*

Frost charged toward her, shouting, "*Nai nai nai,*" helpless to save Billy. Down below Grinner's dagger connected with Billy's arm. Blood spilled on the lava stones. Some of it even spattered into the lava itself, where it burned off with a sizzle.

In a few heartbeats, it'll be over, Snap thought. *Nai one can stop what I setted in motion.* Nai *even me.*

The wall Lexi had helped build shook from impact. The cement the goblin masons had laid between the massive stones chipped and cracked.

The Hanorians must have set up a battering ram on the other side, Lexi thought. *Or they have a bunch of wizards blasting at the wall. Or both.*

One thing was certain. The wall between the caverns and the occupied city was going to fall. Soon.

Lexi took a deep breath. She held it for a moment, then exhaled slowly. Inhale, hold, and exhale. It was an exercise she'd found on the internet. It was supposed to help calm ADHD symptoms. She'd tried it a few times, and it seemed to work. The problem was, when her brain was flying around at five hundred miles an hour, she never remembered to use it.

But somehow she'd remembered it today, in this moment, when the stress and panic made it feel like every nerve in her body was on fire.

They're all depending on you, she told herself. *So breathe. Get centered. Stay focused. Be ready. Then when it's time . . . kick some serious butt.*

She adjusted her stance so that her feet were shoulder-width apart, the way she'd learned in the one tae kwon do class she'd taken. *Ready stance. Or whatever.*

Behind her, Shadow and her Templars, Hop's Copperplates, and what was left of the Warhorde lined up in ranks. Leadpipe stepped up to Lexi's side, carrying a two-handed war hammer taller and heavier than Lexi herself.

"The little ones and the old ones are all moved to the back of the caverns," Leadpipe rumbled. "Now we just make sure *nai* humans get past us, *zaj.*"

"*Zaj,*" Lexi agreed. "Definitely *zaj.*"

Leadpipe laughed. "We'll make a *gob* of you yet."

Deep in her bones, Lexi could feel the fire building. She knew the whispers would start soon. The anger. The urge to destroy. For once, she welcomed the feelings of rage. If there was ever a time her anger might do some good, it was now.

A stone fell from the wall.

Another.

Then more and more until . . .

The wall burst into pieces, and the Hanorian Army came roaring through.

"They're here," Leadpipe said, hefting his massive hammer.

"They're here," Lexi agreed.

Lexi became fire.

CHAPTER FIFTEEN
No Longer Shall We Walk Together

Billy realized that Frost couldn't save him. If the little wizard couldn't do magic, he would be no match for Grinner and Snap. He was barely three feet tall and probably weighed less than fifty pounds. Plus, he was unarmed and had never shown any skill at fighting. As Frost charged Snap, she picked up a rock as big as the tiny goblin's head. He didn't stand a chance.

Neither did Billy for that matter. He was bleeding from the cut on his arm. It was getting harder and harder to breathe. And Grinner kept forcing him toward the lava pool. Billy took another step back as Grinner advanced. His sneakers stuck to the lava rock for a moment, as if he'd stepped in glue. Billy glanced down and saw that the soles of his high-tops were melting and their red canvas uppers were steaming. His pants were smoking a bit too. He was so close to the lava, he was starting to catch on fire.

"Frost, run!" Billy shouted. "You can't help me. Save yourself."

"You're wrong about that, Your Majesty," Frost said. Then he motioned to cast a spell again.

Flames whipped around Frost's body and came pouring from his hands. The fire lashed out at Grinner, wrapping around his body like a rope. Grinner screamed. It was one of the most horrible sounds Billy had ever heard.

Billy realized Grinner wasn't the only one in pain though. As Frost controlled the flames, he also let out an anguished moan.

Frost gestured again, and the flames lifted Grinner up in the air. Frost's spell held him for a moment, and he howled as he burned. Then, with a final gesture, Frost flung Grinner into the lava pool. There was another bloodcurdling scream, followed by a flash of fire . . .

Then Grinner was gone. Billy couldn't tell if he'd burned up or sunk into the lava. But in a flash, there was nothing left of the malevolent wizard.

Still moaning in pain, Frost gathered together the fire that had built up around his body and formed it into a ball, then flung it at Snap. She gestured defensively, and Billy thought he saw just a hint of ice in the air in front of her. The fireball curved in the air, as if it had been deflected, but it still hit Snap in one shoulder. The wizardess was blasted back into the cavern wall. She slumped to the ground, unmoving.

But she wasn't the only one. As soon as he'd thrown his fireball, Frost collapsed, his body smoking. Billy ran to the tiny wizard.

"Frost!" he shouted. "Frost, are you okay?"

Frost was badly burned. His hair had been singed off and his robes were charred black. But he managed to open his eyes and look up at Billy.

"Your Majesty," he said weakly.

"You used fire magic," Billy said. "I didn't know you could do that."

"Figured Coaler doed it. Why *nai* me?" Frost said, struggling to speak.

"I'm going to get you to Lexi and Starcaller," Billy said. "They'll fix you up."

He took Frost into his arms and lifted him up. He was surprised at how light the little wizard felt. He wasn't even fifty pounds. More like thirty.

Billy headed for the tunnel he'd come in through. He was pretty sure he could find his way back by retracing his steps. All that time playing video games had made him pretty good at navigating through caves and tunnels. He dashed up the tunnel carrying Frost, moving as fast as he could. The little wizard looked bad. He needed help soon.

But as Billy moved up the tunnel, he started feeling weaker. He realized there was blood running down his arm from where Grinner had cut him. His lungs ached from the noxious air he'd breathed near the lava lake. Frost hadn't felt heavy when he'd started running, but the little wizard seemed to weigh more with every step.

Billy wasn't sure how far he got up the tunnel before the dizziness started. Everything became kind of soft and blurry. It got hard to remember where he was and what he was doing. For a moment, he even thought he was home, carrying groceries in from the car for his parents. Then he realized he was carrying Frost and trying to get help. Then everything got fuzzy again.

Finally, Billy couldn't go any farther. He had to rest. He set Frost down. The little wizard moaned, his eyes closed.

"I can do this," he said, half to himself, half to Frost.

"Do *nai* cry, Your Majesty," Frost whispered, his voice even weaker than before.

Billy wiped his face. He hadn't even realized he'd been crying.

"*Nai* need for tears," Frost continued, straining to speak. "Me song were short, but it were a good one."

"You're not going to die," Billy insisted.

"We all die someday," Frost whispered. "Tell Leadpipe I channeled fire. Just like Coaler."

Frost closed his eyes.

He's just unconscious, Billy told himself. *You can still save him.*

Billy lifted Frost again and continued up the corridor. But he didn't get far before the dizziness and exhaustion struck again. Blood from the cut on his arm had soaked his entire shirt. There wasn't enough air. Breathing in ragged gasps, Billy forced himself to continue, taking another step, and another.

Then Billy saw the floor coming up toward his face.

Why is it doing that? he thought. *How can the floor be moving toward me?*

Oh, he realized. *I'm falling.*

Then he stopped thinking about much of anything at all.

Kurt startled awake.

He'd dozed off somehow. Despite all he'd been through, despite the fear he felt in the Dark Lady's presence, there was something strangely calming about the glowing green ruins. They seemed like the perfect place to rest . . . and to heal. He'd already felt a lot better before he went to sleep, but when he awoke, Kurt felt great. There was no trace of his previous injuries. Even his right knee, which had been bothering him ever since he'd taken a hard tackle his sophomore year, felt better. He was convinced the glowing green ruins were giving off some kind of healing magic. That had to be what had brought the Dark Lady back to life.

How did she even get here, though? he wondered. *She was killed hundreds of miles from here. She was decapitated. Even if the ruins did bring her back, how did her body get here in the first place?*

Kurt doubted he'd ever really understand the Dark Lady and her magic. He'd been surprised over and over at how . . . well, human Hop and the other goblins were. In the end, they wanted the same things everyone wanted: family and friends, a safe place to live, plenty of food. But the *duenshee* was something else entirely. Even though Kurt could understand every word she said, which wasn't always true with goblins like Hop, he still couldn't grasp her meaning. She was utterly alien.

Speaking of which . . .

He looked over to where the Dark Lady had been contemplating the Fallen Star. There was no one there.

Kurt got to his feet and looked around. Hop had fallen asleep too and was still slumbering a few yards away. But the Dark Lady and the Fallen Star were nowhere to be seen.

"Hop?" Kurt said quietly, nudging the sleeping goblin with his toe. "Hop, wake up."

Hop sputtered awake. "*Ahka*, are we alive?" he asked.

"So far," Kurt answered. "But the Dark Lady is gone."

Hop got to his feet. He squinted into the darkness.

"I can *nai* redsight her," Hop said.

Kurt realized that without the Dark Lady keeping them here, they could escape, maybe find their way back to Kiranok. Still, it didn't take long for him to remember . . .

"We can't just go," Kurt said. "We need the Star."

"*Zaj*," Hop agreed. "But where are it?"

Kurt looked around again. "Hey, Dark Lady," he

said, not much louder than a whisper. "Come out, come out, wherever you are."

Suddenly she was there, standing right in front of him, holding the Fallen Star in her hands.

"That wasn't supposed to work," Kurt said with a gulp.

"Once I saw an old woman, crawling on her knees," the Dark Lady said, seemingly oblivious to Kurt and Hop. "Then I saw her standing, proud and defiant. Then she was lying on her back, shouting out the pain of the world as she created the next generation of sufferers. Then she was young and dancing in the town square with all the boys spinning round. Back and forth it goes. Forth and back. Until she was crawling again, screaming again from her hunger and discomfort. Then she was gone."

Without further explanation, the Dark Lady held the Fallen Star out to Kurt. Was she offering it to him? He carefully took hold of the pitted lump of iron with both hands. The Dark Lady let go, and he felt its full weight.

"Thanks?" Kurt said, confused. Why had she given him back the Star?

"Unwind the knot, cut loose the tether," the Dark Lady said. "No longer shall we walk together."

She turned away from Kurt and Hop . . .

Then she and the ruins and the entire world twisted. And vanished.

In hindsight, Cyreth reflected, *maybe decimation would've been better than this.*

True to his word, Cyreth had shown the Lord Marshal the hidden entrance to the caverns beneath the goblin city. Lord Jiyal had ordered a large battering ram built in front of the walled-off entrance. As soon as it was finished, Jiyal had ordered it into operation. It took several long minutes of bashing, aided by blasts from the Army of Light's wizards, to break down the wall.

More than enough warning for the goblins to ready their defenses.

When the Lion Guards advanced through the break, they met fierce resistance. Arrows and slingballs rained down on them the moment they entered the caverns. Dozens of Lion Guards fell in the initial attack. Eventually, though, enough of Cyreth's soldiers got inside to form the Steel Wall. Following Cyreth's commands, the Lion Guards advanced slowly behind their overlapping shields. But some of the arrows and slingballs still got through. Cyreth got hit with a sling stone right in the helmet. It was a glancing blow, but it was still enough to break Cyreth's nose . . . again. Now, under his lion helm, the lower half of his face was covered with blood, and his nose ached with every step he took.

But the worst part was the girl with the burning eyes.

The human girl stood confidently in the front ranks of the goblin defenders. Cyreth recognized her as the spark who'd battled Mig in the Hanorian camp. It was the same girl who'd dropped the roof of Seventurns on the Army of Light during their first assault on the goblin city. Now she was almost single-handedly preventing the Lion Guards' advance.

Every time the Lion Guards tried to move forward, the girl would blast fire from her eyes at them, melting shields and blasting soldiers off their feet. Cyreth had repeatedly called for wizards to counter the girl, but none had arrived. Lord Jiyal must have refused to send them. Cyreth supposed it made sense to preserve the wizards for later in the battle, but he suspected that the real reason the Lord Marshal hadn't sent help was to ensure that the Lion Guards suffered for Cyreth's impudence.

If that was Jiyal's plan, it was working. Dozens of Lion Guards had already been injured. Many of them might be dead. If the Lion Guards lost more than ten percent of their soldiers, decimation would have been the better choice.

Except you'd be dead, and Lord Jiyal probably would've put the Lion Guards on the front ranks anyway. At least this way you got to lead them into battle one last time.

Suddenly a fire blast from the human girl hammered into Cyreth's shield. The force of the blow knocked Cyreth back a yard or two. Somehow he stayed on his feet. But it was a near thing.

By the Night, I should have died just then, Cyreth thought as he shook off the blow.

Which is when it dawned on Cyreth . . .

The wizard girl wasn't trying to kill anyone.

She was hurling fire at them, but her blasts were more force than heat, more likely to stun than kill. She was melting the Lion Guards' shields, but she wasn't following up with killing blows. She wanted to stop the Hanorians' advance, but she didn't want to slaughter them.

Realizing what the girl was doing confirmed all of Cyreth's doubts about Jiyal's cause. The girl wasn't his real enemy. Neither were the goblins. They were only trying to defend themselves.

This war should have ended at Solace Ridge, with the Dark Lady's execution. The real enemy is Lord Jiyal.

For a long time, Cyreth had thought the only path to survival for him and his fellow Lion Guards was victory. But at the moment, victory didn't seem like such a worthy goal—or one likely to save the lives of Cyreth or his soldiers.

"Fall back!" Cyreth shouted. "Regroup around my position! Reform the Steel Wall!"

Though the order was no doubt a surprise, the Lion Guards obeyed. They retreated from the goblins, forming up around Cyreth and interlocking their shields.

"Outside rankers, kneel and brace!" Cyreth ordered.

Again, the Lion Guards complied, though Cyreth could sense they were puzzled. By having the outer ranks kneel and brace their shields against the ground, Cyreth was placing the Lion Guards in their strongest possible defensive position, but he was also making it impossible for them to attack the goblins.

"Medics, check the wounded," Cyreth continued. "Count the dead and bring the rest back for treatment."

The medics assigned to the Lion Guards had their own officers, so they weren't strictly under Cyreth's command. Still, they did as Cyreth ordered. Hopefully they would confirm Cyreth's suspicions—that the human girl had been sparing his soldiers' lives and that the wounded vastly outnumbered the dead.

But before the medics could report what they found, Cyreth heard . . .

"Cowards!"

It was Lord Jiyal. Cyreth could just make him out through a small gap in the Lion Guards' interlocked shields, approaching the formation from the rear, escorted by his Black Hussars.

"Attack, you spineless eels!" the Lord Marshal shouted.

"Make way," Cyreth said.

The shields parted, and Cyreth emerged from the Steel Wall.

"We're regrouping," Cyreth said calmly to the Lord Marshal. "Evacuating our wounded."

"Attack now, or I'll have you all executed," Lord Jiyal said, not even trying to hide his contempt.

"If we attack now, our wounded will die," Cyreth said. "I won't give the order. Kill me now if you'd like, but we'll advance when we're ready. Not a moment before."

Cyreth could see Jiyal weighing his options. He suspected if Jiyal killed him now in front of the entire Army of Light, just for trying to get his wounded to safety, the Hanorian Army might rebel. From Jiyal's expression, the Lord Marshal feared the same thing. Still, Cyreth could tell he was tempted to do it anyway.

But an unexpected arrival interrupted Jiyal's decision.

"If they won't kill the goblins, I will."

It was Mig. The young wizardess was back from her mission. She looked exhausted but determined.

"The meteorite? Where is it?" Lord Jiyal asked.

"Lost," Mig said unhappily. "Sunk in a river, along with the goblin and the human traitor who tried to steal it. No one will be using it. So . . . I'll finish the war without it. By myself if I have to."

Cyreth knew Mig meant it. He'd seen what she could do. If she thought she could defeat the goblins on her own, he wouldn't bet against her.

Apparently, Lord Jiyal felt the same way.

"You will," he said. "But not alone."

Jiyal called back to one of his aides, "Send in the wizards. It's time to end this."

"*Ahka*, what to do with you now, *skerbo* king?" Coldsnap said, standing over King Billy's unconscious body.

Snap had fled from the burning heart of the mountain as soon as she'd recovered from Frost's blast. She'd been lucky enough to spot the glow from the Goblin Crown up one of the lava tubes and followed after it. But as she'd headed up the tunnel, the glow had gone out. Fearing she'd lost the boy, she switched to redsight and increased her pace. A few twists and turns later, she'd discovered King Billy lying unconscious in a pool of his own blood. The Goblin Crown lay by his head, and he was cradling Frost's body in his arms. From redsight, Snap could tell that the *jintagob* wizard was dead. The boy had carried him all this way for nothing.

Billy could've escaped if he'd leaved Frost behind, she realized. *But instead he gived up his best chance at survival to try to save a* gob *what were already dead.*

Snap stood over Billy's unconscious body for a long moment. She'd wanted to kill him for so long, tried so hard. Icewall and Grinner had both died because of her deadly quest. Now she could end King Billy's reign with just a flick of her hand.

A flick of me hand to kill an innocent boy who are only trying to help.

"He are a human. A *skerbo*," she said aloud, arguing only with herself.

Humans murdered your family, she continued to herself. *A* skerbo *army invaded Kiranok to slaughter every last* goben. *Humans are evil. This boy are human. He have to die.*

Except King Billy didn't look like the humans who'd killed Snap's parents. He was too young to be a soldier and too skinny to be a real threat, even if he were armed. Which he wasn't.

The only thing he were carrying were a dead goblin wizard, she thought in response to her own objection. *He spended the last of his energy trying to save Frost. He may be a* skerbo, *but all he doed, ever since he comed to this land, were try to help the* goben *people. Right to the end.*

"Truth are, you were carrying two things," Coldsnap said aloud to the unresponsive boy. "Frost. And the Goblin Crown."

He are our King. And you . . . Starcaller choosed you to be the next High Priestess of the Night Goddess. If anyone bringed him here, it were Mother Night. The Goddess picked this boy to be our King. She picked you to be her Priestess. You know what to do.

Snap knelt down and placed her hands on Billy, then poured her magic into him. It was warm in the lava tube, but not so warm that she had no power. She gave him everything she could, freezing his wounds shut and cooling his battered body to reduce the swelling and pain. But he remained unconscious, unmoving. She tried harder, willing him to live.

Live and be our King, she thought. *Live and be our King . . .*

Snap's redsight began to lose focus, and the tunnel felt like it was spinning. She realized if she continued using her magic much longer, she'd end up unconscious herself, and then there'd be no one to help the boy. She ended her spell, then fell to her hands. She was done. She caught her breath and looked at Billy.

He was still motionless.

Are he dead?

Snap placed a finger on Billy's neck. She could feel his pulse, though it was weak.

Zajnai I only slowed his death. Zajnai I were too late. But that're all I can do. I've nai more energy left. Nai more magic to give.

She picked up the Goblin Crown. *If he're to die, he should die with his Crown on,* she thought.

"I're sorry, Your Majesty," Snap said aloud. "For trying to kill you. For failing to save you."

She put the Crown on Billy's head. The ruby in its center glowed red, weakly at first, then stronger and stronger.

King Billy opened his eyes.

Lexi laughed.

She wasn't sure where she stopped and the flames began. She wasn't sure if she was controlling the fire or if it was controlling her. She wasn't even sure how long the battle had been going or if it would ever end. And she didn't care.

Because she was finally free.

All her life, Lexi had worked extra hard to stay in control. Her parents were always telling her to stop fidgeting, to pay attention, to focus. She felt like they never really understood how hard that was for her. Her mind always wanted to go a hundred miles an hour, so it wasn't easy to sit still, to listen to her teachers, to do her homework.

Once she'd arrived in the goblins' world and discovered she could work magic, staying in control had become even more important. Lexi would be the first person to admit she had a bit of a temper. Couple that with her hyperactivity, and there'd been plenty of times she'd had to struggle to keep her newfound magic in check. Losing her temper had been bad enough back home, when the only consequence was getting her smartphone taken away for a few days. If she flew off the handle in the goblins' world, she risked accidently setting her friends on fire.

But stuffing down her feelings all the time was no fun. Since her arrival in the caverns, she'd caught herself chewing on her fingernails a lot more than usual. It wasn't the most functional way to keep her temper in check, but it was better than blowing up random annoying people all day long.

Now, though, she didn't have to worry. Now there were bad people attacking her friends, and her anger and her magic were finally useful. She could finally let loose. She could finally channel her frustrations into fiery blasts, hot winds, and concussive explosions. She finally could let herself blow up as much as she wanted, figuratively and literally.

Almost. She still didn't want to actually kill anyone. So she had to make sure she didn't blast anyone too hard or shoot her fire directly into some enemy soldier's face. But she was doing it. She was managing it. She was channeling her feelings into the flames but was still in control. She wasn't going crazy or becoming a *graznak* the way Frost was always warning she might. She was good. No, she was great. She'd never had more fun in her life.

Lexi knew she probably shouldn't be enjoying the battle quite so much, with people getting hurt or even dying all around her. But she couldn't help it. The fire felt like pure joy moving through her body. The flames whipping around her seemed like they were giving voice to all her frustrations and pent-up feelings. Like she was screaming her truth at the world. And the world finally had to listen.

Suddenly, though, the fire bent back toward her . . . and it burned.

Lexi concentrated and warded off the flames. Another quick spell snuffed out the fire burning on her robes and in her hair. She was safe, for now. But she had to wonder—had her magic turned on her?

Then she saw Mig.

The Hanorian wizard emerged from the front rank of the attacking human soldiers, exuding confidence. She gestured, and a crushing shock wave smashed into Lexi and the goblin defenders behind her, knocking them off their feet. The human army cheered. An officer shouted, and the enemy soldiers broke into a charge.

Lexi struggled to her knees and hurled fire at them, but Mig summoned a blast of her own, which intercepted Lexi's spell. The two spells met violently, creating a huge explosion. Human and goblin alike were blown to the ground.

Lexi heard laughter. Once again, she forced herself to stand. She saw Mig, hovering fifty yards away. Laughing the same way Lexi had been laughing only moments earlier.

As the goblins regrouped behind Lexi, several more enemy wizards joined Mig. The Hanorian girl began chanting, and her fellow human wizards joined in. A small fire sprung to life in front of them, then spun and grew and spun and grew until it was a tornado of flames, growing larger and more threatening by the moment.

Lexi summoned all her power. She knew that Mig and her allies would unleash the fire tornado at the goblins soon. She had to stop it.

The sense of joy had gone out of her. She realized that until now, she hadn't been in a real fight. Using her spells against the soldiers wasn't an even match. That's why it had been fun. It had been easy, and she'd been winning. Before, confronting the human army had felt like a game. Now it felt like what it really was.

Now it felt like war.

"Let me carry him, Your Majesty," Snap said as Billy paused to catch his breath.

"No," Billy said. "You're not any stronger than me right now. Besides, Frost died for me. He's my burden."

Billy still couldn't believe the little wizard was dead. Frost had always been kind to him, Lexi, and Kurt, from the moment they'd arrived in Kiranok. He'd welcomed them into his home. He'd done his best to heal Lexi's broken leg. He'd fought to crown Kurt, then Billy, as the Goblin King. He'd counseled Lexi on using her magic and Billy on how to be a better king. He might've been a goblin, but he was the most generous, thoughtful person Billy had ever met. Now he was dead. Because of Billy.

And for what? Billy thought. *What have I managed to do that was worth Frost losing his life?*

Not much, Billy concluded grimly. *I sent Hop and Kurt and over a dozen other people to get the Fallen Star. Some of them died, and Kurt and Hop never came back. I convinced the goblins to retreat to the caverns, and now they're trapped there waiting for the Hanorians to find them, if they haven't already. All I managed to do in the past few hours was run for my life, to try to save my own skin. And I would've failed at that if Frost hadn't sacrificed himself and Coldsnap hadn't had second thoughts about murdering me.*

In some of the video games Billy played, when he faced a difficult decision, he could save the game, then try out an option. If his strategy failed, he could always reload the saved game and try something different. He found himself wishing he could do that now. Go back to right before Coldsnap and Grinner attacked him in the cavern and . . .

And what? Let yourself die? he thought. *Life isn't a game. You can't reload and try again. You're here. Frost is dead. The goblins are still in trouble. You can't just feel sorry for yourself. You have to keep trying to make things better. To make sure Frost didn't die for nothing.*

"Tell me what you're thinking, Your Majesty," Snap said.

Billy's first impulse was to tell the goblin wizardess it was none of her business. It was hard not to think of her as an enemy. Still, even though she'd once been determined to kill him, ever since she'd revived him she'd seemed dedicated to helping him. Billy didn't completely understand Snap's change of heart, and it was taking some getting used to, but it beat having her try to murder him over and over again.

Billy decided to tell her the truth.

"I was thinking that when we get back to the caverns, I have no idea what we're going to find," Billy said. "One thing's for sure, though. Your people still aren't safe. I have to fix that."

Then he paused. He could hear city noises again, humans speaking English.

"We're coming up to that weird crack in the wall again," he said.

"Mother Mountain are so vast her roots reach other worlds," Snap said.

Billy moved to the crack and looked in. Once again he saw, far in the distance, glimpses of what looked like San Francisco.

"I wish there were some way to use this to help," he said.

Billy carefully put Frost's body down so he could study the crack. He imagined bringing the entire population of Kiranok through the crack to his own world. If he could do that, they'd be safe from the Hanorians.

Then he pictured the likely response when tens of thousands of goblins arrived in downtown San Francisco. He imagined office workers running in terror. He pictured the police arriving, maybe even the army. They'd have guns. The goblins had weapons of their own. Some of them were scary-looking giants like Leadpipe. The goblins wouldn't be able to speak English, wouldn't understand cars and buses and the loud city noises.

"They'd be shot," he said, more to himself than Snap. But maybe there was another way.

What if I went through and got guns for the goblins? That'd even things out, Billy thought. *Except . . . how am I supposed to get my hands on thousands of guns? Where would I get the money to buy them? Could I get them in time? Would they even work if I brought them here? Not to mention . . . is giving the goblins guns really a good idea?*

"That won't work either," Billy muttered. Then a bit louder, "There's nothing here for us. We should go."

But as he turned back up the tunnel, Billy saw a shadow pass through the crack between him and the light from the city. A moment later, he spotted a second shadow.

"Did you see that?" he asked.

"Spirits," Snap answered. "Shadows of souls flickering between this world and the others."

Once again, the two shadows eclipsed the city lights. This time, Billy thought he recognized them.

"If it happens again, can you pull them out?" he said.

"I're empty," Snap said, her exhaustion evident in her voice. "I're *nai* sure I can cast a spell right now *nai* matter how much I want to."

"It's really important," Billy said. "It may be the most important thing ever."

Billy knew he was taking a big risk relying on a goblin who'd been trying to kill him only hours earlier, but he had no other options. Plus, she'd told Billy about her meeting with Starcaller. How the old priestess had appointed Snap her successor before Grinner had killed her. He figured if Snap had accepted her role as High Priestess, that meant she had to listen to him. He was her King, after all. He tried a more forceful appeal. "High

Priestess Coldsnap, I'm giving you a royal command. If you see those shadows again, pull them to us."

That got Snap's attention. Then Billy spotted the shadows again.

"Now!" he shouted. "Everything depends on this. Bring them home!"

To Billy's surprise, Snap followed his orders. She held out her hands, and tendrils of blue energy reached into the crack in the wall. They snaked around the two shadows, infusing them with bluish light, and pulled them toward Snap and Billy. But something seemed to be holding the shadows back. Snap flexed and flailed her arms, trying to overcome the resistance, but her tendrils began to lose their form, their magical blue light flickering and dimming.

But her magic had lit up the shadows enough to confirm what Billy had seen earlier. The tall shadow had broad shoulders, muscular arms, and a thick neck. The other was shorter, with a bigger head and mismatched ears, one long and pointed, the other ending abruptly in a ragged edge.

"Kurt! Hop!" Billy shouted. "Over here!"

Billy had no way to know if they'd heard him, but the shadows suddenly surged toward him and Snap, becoming more solid the closer they got.

Suddenly Snap collapsed to her knees, completely spent . . .

And Hop and Kurt tumbled out of the crack in the tunnel wall.

Hop wasn't sure where he and Kurt had gone when the Dark Lady made the world turn inside out. He remembered seeing dozens of strange, shadowy images of impossible things. Cities made of metal and glass. Jungles full of giant reptiles bigger than even the largest cliff lizard. Humans riding across sand dunes in magical vehicles that moved without draft animals. Towns populated by blue-skinned, hairless men and women or by bipedal rabbits in clothing, or devoid of life entirely. Cities underwater, cities climbing toward the clouds, cities made entirely of interwoven trees. He had a vision of a world where men and goblins lived and worked side by side. He saw another world where a stone and metal city had been ripped apart, as if by some unimaginably powerful spell, and the ground had turned to glass.

He couldn't even tell how long he and Kurt spent in the strange space between spaces. It might have been seconds; it might have been decades. Time seemed to pass far faster than normal or not at all.

Eventually, after a span of time that simultaneously felt shorter than a heartbeat and longer than forever, Hop saw tendrils of blue light reaching for him and Kurt. The tendrils took hold of him and pulled, but he felt a strange resistance keeping him in place, as if he were standing in deep snow.

In that same eternal moment, he heard Billy's voice calling his name.

Hop could almost see Billy, standing at a crack in the darkness. He knew he had to go to him. Hop willed himself to move in Billy's direction, though whether by walking or swimming or climbing or falling, he wasn't really sure. Suddenly, though, he felt a rush and a wind . . .

Then he fell onto a hard stone floor, with Kurt by his side. Hop looked up and saw Billy standing above him, wearing the Goblin Crown. The soft red glow of the Crown's ruby illuminated the human boy's face and cast light on the surrounding tunnel and a familiar looking female goblin.

"Hop!" Billy shouted as Hop struggled to his feet. Then he threw his arms around him in a hug.

Hop wasn't much of a hugger. When someone had their arms around you, it made it hard to move away in an emergency. But for once, he didn't mind it so much.

"Your Majesty," Hop said, smiling. "It're *maja* good to see you too."

"Hey, freckles," Kurt said, sounding amused. But then Kurt's voice turned serious. "Isn't that one of the goblins who tried to kill you?"

"She's on our side now," Billy said. Then he glanced at her and continued, a little unsure, "I guess."

But Hop wasn't looking at the female goblin anymore. He'd spotted a small, limp form lying on the tunnel floor. He gently slipped out of Billy's hug and knelt down next to it.

"Frost," Hop said, his joy at finding his way back to Billy shattered.

"Is he . . . ?" Kurt asked once he spied the little wizard's body.

"Dead," Billy said, his voice choking. "He died to save me. He channeled fire."

"Like Coaler," Hop said, amazed even in his pain. No goblin wizard had channeled fire in recent history. Hop always knew Frost was special. But learning how special he was made losing him hurt even more.

"He was a good guy," Kurt said, sounding a little choked up himself. "I'm sorry."

"If he died saving you, then he died doing what he thinked were best," Hop said, trying to comfort Billy even through his own pain. "The way to honor him are to keep walking the path you're on. Be our king and save our people."

Billy seemed to take that in. "That's what I've been trying to do," he said. "But things are bad. The Hanorians are in the city. Frost and Starcaller are both dead."

"Starcaller too?" Hop asked, shocked. The High Priestess had always been a bit distant, wrapped in her robes, but she'd been a reliable ally ever since Billy had won the Sunchase, and Hop had a hard time accepting that she was gone. He knew she'd been old, and probably more fragile than she looked, but he'd thought she'd outlive them all. "So *maja* much death. Seem like it'll *nai* ever end."

"I don't know how to stop it," Billy admitted, sounding despondent. "I wish I did, but I don't. Without Starcaller and Frost . . . We going to need a miracle to save your people."

"I might be able to help with that," Kurt said, reaching under his shirt. "I tucked this away while we were . . . wherever we were," Kurt said to Hop. "I didn't want to lose it."

With that, Kurt pulled out the Fallen Star and handed it to Billy.

Billy took it with both hands, surprised. "Is this . . ."

"The Fallen Star, Your Majesty," Hop explained.

"It worked," Billy said. "You actually got it."

Hop smiled a little. "When you spend most of your life failing, one day or another you're certain to succeed at something. That're just the odds."

"The important thing is we have the Star," Kurt said. "Now what are we going to do with it?"

Hop could see Billy wasn't exactly sure. But he knew they'd have to answer Kurt's question very, very soon.

CHAPTER SIXTEEN
Too Late to Run

Lexi was going to lose.

She didn't want to admit it. It made her want to yell and cry and strike out. But it was the truth.

Mig and her fellow Hanorian wizards were too strong, and there were too many of them. They'd been blasting away at her for what seemed like hours but was probably only minutes. She'd been doing everything she could to deflect their spells and keep them away from the goblins behind her. But no matter how many walls of fire she conjured, no matter how many shields she threw up between her and the attacking wizards, the Hanorians always had an answer. Her shields shattered; her fires were snuffed out. She could feel her magic running low. She was exhausted.

Frost had told her once that when his friend Moonfall became a *graznak*, she'd been able to cast spells as much as she wanted. As the Hanorian wizards summoned yet another fire tornado, Lexi half wished that she could go mad and lose herself to her magic. At least then she'd have the energy to protect the goblins for a little while longer, to prevent the Hanorians from massacring them for just a few more hours.

Unfortunately, at the moment, the madness wasn't coming. Lexi was in control. Which meant not only did she not have the resources to hold off the Hanorian wizards, but also that she was going to have to experience every bitter moment of her defeat while completely sane.

Lexi hated losing. She hated losing at games, she hated losing at sports, and she really hated losing in fights. Unfortunately, she'd lost as many fights as she'd won. With her short temper and hatred of bullies, she'd gotten herself into probably a half dozen fights. Someone would start picking on her, or even worse, picking on one of her friends, her fists would ball up, and suddenly, without even really planning it, she would come out swinging. Sometimes, the surprise and ferocity of her initial attack would carry the day. It didn't always work out that way, though. Lexi was small for her age and skinny, and although she hated to admit it, not particularly strong. So pretty much everyone she fought was bigger and stronger than she was. When she found herself fighting an opponent who wasn't overwhelmed by her sheer ferocity, things usually didn't go well.

Lexi never lacked self-confidence, though, so she'd usually only realize that she was overmatched in the middle of things, after her punches had bounced harmlessly off a bigger kid and she'd suddenly found herself on her back with a bloody nose or a split lip. In those moments, Lexi never really felt hurt. Mostly she just felt angry at the injustice of it all. Lexi got into fights only to protect herself and her friends. She was the good guy. How could she lose? The good guys weren't supposed to lose. It was so unfair.

Lexi felt that same familiar sense of outrage as she was forced back by the Hanorians' latest onslaught. They were planning to commit genocide against the goblins. It didn't get any more evil than that. They were the villains. So why were they winning?

She threw up her hands, desperately sending out a shock wave to meet the Hanorians' new fire tornado. It blew apart in a fiery explosion, sending Lexi flying backward. She landed hard. As she struggled to sit up, she felt something wet and gooey running down her face. She tried to wipe it away, and her hand came away bloody. Lexi was pretty sure it was her blood. She hoped it was; it'd be gross to have someone else's blood all over her.

Not only was Lexi covered in blood, her clothing was scorched and blackened, she hurt everywhere, and she felt completely spent. Behind her, she could see what passed for the goblin army lined up to face the Hanorians. They were outnumbered, and most of them were either painfully young or painfully old. The few goblins who knew how to fight stood in the front ranks, with Leadpipe and Shadow in the lead. From their expressions, Lexi could see that they felt the same way she did.

They couldn't win.

About once a month, Lexi's parents would get together with their friends the Hendersons to play board games. The games they played were elaborate and colorful and a bit too complicated for kids. Lexi particularly liked the ones with maps, like *Catan* or *Ticket to Ride* or *Puerto Rico*. From the time she could walk, Lexi had always wanted to join her parents and the Hendersons for one of their games. Finally, when she was nine, they'd invited her to play *Ticket to Ride*. The object of the game was to create train routes across North America using little plastic trains. Lexi had loved the map of *Ticket to Ride* so much, she'd sometimes snuck the game off the closet shelf and played it on her own in her room. So she had been confident she could hold her own. But when it came time to play for real, Lexi was outmatched. Her parents and the Hendersons had been playing *Ticket to Ride* for years, and they didn't go easy on her. Finally, when her father laid down a train route that made it impossible for Lexi to win, she'd yelled that he was being mean, then she'd flung the board into the air and stormed off.

That was the first and last time her parents allowed her to join their board games. It was also the day Lexi discovered something important about herself.

Lexi was a sore loser.

Now that she was playing in real life for much higher stakes, Lexi realized she hadn't changed all that much. If she couldn't win, then she was going to overturn the board.

She took a quick glance at her surroundings. The outnumbered goblins had originally set up their defensive line in a narrow spot in the cavern, not far from where the humans had broken in. Huge columns of stone flanked both sides of the area, covered with crystal formations and surrounded by stalactites and stalagmites, creating a natural choke point for the attackers. It had helped for a while, but eventually the humans had driven the goblins back inch by inch until they'd reached the very back of the narrowing. Lexi knew if the goblins got pushed back any farther, their defense would probably shatter.

Still, that meant the bulk of the Hanorian soldiers were jammed into the narrow area between the columns. Lexi knew what she had to do. Unfortunately, she didn't have much energy left. So she'd have to get up close to do it.

Lexi let her anger and her frustration fill her, imagining it all gathering in her chest, like a ball of rage. Then she dashed forward to the battle line, channeled the rage into her hands, and flung it out from her body toward the giant columns flanking the cavern. Her anger came roaring out of her hands as twin columns of fire and lashed around the stone pillars.

Lexi pulled them toward her.

The columns tumbled onto the front line of the Hanorians. Seconds later, huge chunks of the cavern roof followed, plummeting down toward the melee. The giant crashing pieces of stone reminded Lexi of those little plastic trains she'd sent clattering to the floor all those years ago, but much bigger and infinitely louder. Only this time, Lexi wasn't going to be able to storm off.

Because this time Lexi had overturned the board on her own head.

The huge, echoing boom rumbled through the caverns.

Billy, Hop, Kurt, and Snap had already been racing back toward the goblin camp when they heard the boom. The thunderous noise got them moving even faster. They rushed to the bottom of the chasm that Billy had jumped down. But Billy stopped short. He had no idea how to get back up to the upper chambers of the cavern.

"This way," Hop shouted, leaping and clambering over a series of rocks and ledges until he'd reached the top of the chasm.

Kurt tucked the Fallen Star under his chain mail and started to climb. Billy looked uncertainly up the chasm. Frost's body was still in his arms. He'd given Kurt back the

Star, but he'd insisted on carrying the little wizard himself. He wasn't ready to let go of him yet. Except there was no way he could climb up the chasm while carrying him.

"I'm not sure I can get up there," Billy said.

Snap caught up to him. She was the slowest of the four of them. Billy figured she'd spent most of her time learning magic instead of running or playing sports. Even though Billy wasn't much of an athlete, he'd at least played soccer and Little League. He doubted Snap had ever run more than a mile in her entire life. That and she'd used a lot of her energy trying to kill him, so it was understandable she might be a little tired.

"I have you," Snap said.

Suddenly Billy felt himself being lifted off his feet. In a gust of cold wind, he flew up the chasm and landed in the upper cavern.

"*Ahka*! What were that?" Hop shouted down to Snap, surprised and angry. "You can *nai* just fling His Majesty through the air like that. Or were you planning to drop him on his head? Finish what you started?"

To his own surprise, Billy came to Snap's defense. "She was just trying to help. She's on our side now."

"It're *nai* problem," Snap said. "I do *nai* expect your trust all at once. I aim to earn it. Bite by bite."

Suddenly, another boom shook the caverns. Then another. Then a series of loud bangs, one after another.

"We don't have time for trust exercises," Kurt said, pulling himself over the lip of the chasm. "We have to get going."

Snap flew herself up to join Billy, Hop, and Kurt. Then she collapsed to her knees, exhausted.

"Go," she said. "I'll follow."

Billy didn't wait. He ran toward the booms.

Because that's what a king is supposed to do.

Kurt knew the goblins were beaten the moment he saw them.

In his experience, there was a way people held themselves when they knew they couldn't win. Shoulders slumped, eyes full of anger or tears or frustration, but always downcast. When Kurt saw that in an opposing team, it felt good. It meant they'd given up hope. Without hope, there was no way they'd mount a comeback. There was nothing worse than seeing that same despair in his own team, though. When that happened, Kurt knew his passes would get dropped, his receivers would mess up their routes, and worst of all, his blockers would eventually slip up and he'd get smashed to the ground by an opposing linebacker. Without hope, nothing ever went right.

When things got that bad, Kurt's dad would come down to the sidelines and whisper in the coach's ear, and Kurt would end up getting pulled from the game. The backup quarterback would be sent in to finish out the loss and take the injuries. As his father would say afterward, "No point letting the star get hurt when the game is already lost."

Kurt hated getting benched like that. He always believed that he could somehow rally his teammates and turn things around. Unfortunately, Kurt had no idea how to rally the goblins. Many of them were already wounded and out of the fight. The priests and priestesses of the Night Goddess had set up a sort of impromptu hospital at the very back of the cavern to tend to the wounded. Kurt saw Alyseer and the other surviving Celestials with them, doing their best to help. The remaining goblin fighters had gathered near a collapsed wall, facing a caved-in pile of rubble with a sense of doom hanging over them. The booms were coming from the other side of the cave-in. With each boom, rocks would spill off the pile toward the waiting defenders. The goblin warriors visibly flinched with each blast.

"The Hanorians must be on the other side of that," Kurt said as he, Billy, and Hop approached the demoralized defenders.

Then, off in one corner, Kurt spotted a huge form bent over a smaller figure. "Leadpipe?" he called out.

Kurt headed toward Leadpipe. He'd recognized the smaller figure lying on the ground next to the giant goblin.

"It's Lexi!" Kurt said.

Following Kurt, Hop ran to Leadpipe and Lexi, with Billy trailing behind, still carrying Frost's body.

Lexi was covered in blood, and her clothing was scorched and torn.

"Is she . . . ?" Billy asked as he approached.

"She're alive," Leadpipe said. "But it were a near thing. She yanked down some columns to block the cavern and slow the Hanorians. She goed right up to the front lines to do it though, and some of them stones come right down on her head. I grabbed her and pulled her out of there, but—"

Leadpipe stopped midsentence. He'd looked up from Lexi and seen Billy carrying Frost.

"Me brother," Leadpipe said, rising slowly, his face shifting quickly from shock to crushing sadness.

Billy gently placed Frost's body at Leadpipe's feet. "I'm sorry. He died protecting me."

Leadpipe reached down and place one massive hand on his tiny brother's chest, covering it almost completely. "He were small, but his spirit were bigger than all of us. He always fighted for what he believed. He *nai* ever gived up. He were the real giant."

Another massive boom shook the caverns, the largest yet. Rock sprayed from the pile of rubble Lexi had created, blasting into the assembled goblin warriors. As the dust settled, Kurt saw that the explosion had cleared away the cave-in. Hanorian soldiers lined up on the other side, readying a charge.

Leadpipe reached down and picked up the huge hammer lying next to Lexi. "Time for tears later," he rumbled. "There're work to do."

The *kijakgob* strode toward the goblins' front line, covering the gap in a few giant steps. Kurt watched him go for a moment. Leadpipe must've seen the same thing he did, that the goblin defenders had already given up hope. He'd just learned his brother was dead. But none of that mattered to him. He had a job to do, and he was going to do it.

Kurt looked to Billy, who was kneeling by Lexi, trying to wake her.

"Lexi, wake up," Billy said, shaking her gently. "We need you."

Lexi moaned, but her eyes stayed closed.

Which was when Kurt heard . . .

"The Star. Give her the Star."

He turned and saw Alyseer slowly approaching them, her clothing bloodstained, her face expressionless.

Kurt reached into his chain mail shirt, retrieved the Fallen Star, and set it down next to Billy and Lexi.

"Here," the quarterback said. "Hopefully it will make a difference." Then he looked over to Alyseer. "I'm sorry. Azam. He . . . he didn't make it."

Alyseer didn't react. She didn't look surprised or upset. Her face didn't change expression at all. "He lived his life to its end," she said emotionlessly. "Now he lives on in you."

Kurt didn't know what to say to that. He could hear Hanorian officers yelling to their soldiers, getting their ranks in order, preparing to charge. It wouldn't be long now. Kurt looked back to the goblin lines. He knew if he joined the demoralized goblin defenders, things wouldn't go well. Inevitably, the goblins' line would break and he would get swarmed by the enemy, just like when his offensive line gave up on him. Only this time he wouldn't just get injured. This time he'd end up dead. Dad would have told him to get off the field and save himself for another day. Except if the goblins lost this battle, Kurt knew there wouldn't be another game. For any of them.

At some point, between the battle with the ice wyrm, the face-off with Mig, and his strange encounter with the Dark Lady in the ruins, he'd lost his sword. Replacing it wasn't going to be a problem though. There were dead bodies and abandoned weapons scattered all around him. Kurt grabbed a likely-looking sword.

Then he heard a roaring "Ur-rar!" and the Hanorians broke into a charge.

Leadpipe roared back, "*Wazzer!*" He charged toward the Hanorians, and the remaining goblins followed him.

Kurt charged too. Sometimes, no matter how bad things were going, no matter how much you wanted to quit and save yourself, you had to stay in the game.

In the chaos of battle, Hop sometimes found his mind wandering despite the circumstances. With his life in danger, he knew he should've been completely focused on the moment. Anticipating attacks, planning his next move, alert and ready for anything. Still, in the middle of a melee, he'd often find himself thinking of the strangest, most unrelated things. He supposed it was his mind's way of dealing with the terror of the moment, distracting itself to avoid being overwhelmed.

As he ducked under a Hanorian sword and thrust his spear at one of the charging humans, Hop thought about how he could have been a cobbler.

His father was a cobbler. His sister had taken up the trade. They made wonderful shoes. Nothing fancy, mostly work boots and hunting boots for folks back home on the Bowlus Plateau. Well-crafted footwear made from high-quality leather with solid soles that would last for years.

Perfectly good trade, cobbling. Folk always need shoes. Only that were nai good enough for you, he scolded himself. *You wanted to see new places, meet new people. To travel the world.*

That desire for adventure had led Hop to become a caravan guard. Those had been good years. He'd joined up during a period of relative peace between the goblins and their neighbors. The goblin caravans had roamed as far as Barduin. Hop had eaten fish fresh from the Endless Water, climbed the Castle Hills, and walked beneath the Celestine Wall. Unfortunately, nothing good lasts forever. Eventually tensions between the goblins and the Hanorian Empire escalated again. Aggressive Hanorian patrols had made it impossible for the goblin caravans to get through the Uplands. Hop had tried to get guard jobs with human merchants, but that hadn't worked out either. So, with no other options and no trade skills, Hop had joined the Warhorde.

Thinking back on me life, zajnai *I should've gived shoemaking more of a try.*

Hop dodged yet another Hanorian attacker, then he saw something that chased all his second thoughts and regrets from his mind. Shadow was in the middle of the fight, wielding her glaive with terrifying precision, attacking Hanorians with both the weapon's swordlike blade and its hardwood haft. She made the battle look like a dance, her movements so smooth and graceful Hop could almost forget how deadly she was. Still, for all her skill, she was having a hard time holding her own. She was fighting a half dozen humans at once, outnumbered and in danger of being swarmed over by the enemy.

Hop battled his way to Shadow, surprising himself with his own ferocity. In a series of quick stabs and leaps, he cut his way through the Hanorians and reached her side, ending his final leap with a spear lunge into the back of one of her opponents.

"You're alive," Shadow said, sounding more than a little surprised.

"For now," Hop said, blocking a sword thrust with his shield. *Where haved this shield comed from?* Hop wondered. *Doed I* nai *throw mine away on that snow-field? For that matter, where doed I get this spear? Somewhere in the blur of battle,* he supposed.

"I comed back," he said, "like you asked."

Shadow cracked a human soldier across the head with her glaive haft, then slashed another with her blade. Both men went down. "You should *nai* have," Shadow said, cutting the legs out from under a third human who was about to stab Hop from behind. "Now we're both going to die."

"'Come back to me, do *nai* come back to me,'" Hop said, exasperated. "You need to make up your mind. I keeped me promise. That're the important thing."

"*Zajnai* that're true," Shadow admitted, fending off two Hanorians. "It're just I do *nai* want you to die."

"I *nai* want you to die, either," Hop said, stabbing at a Hanorian attacker.

"Glad we're agreed," Shadow said. "Too bad it look like we're both headed for disappointment."

Hop swung his spear in a wide arc, forcing the Hanorians around him back a step. For a moment, he could see the entire battlefield. A few yards away, Leadpipe hammered away at the Army of Light. He could see Kurt fighting too, holding his own. But everywhere else along the goblins' line of defense, the Hanorians were advancing, and the outnumbered goblins were falling back . . . or dying. Shadow was right. They probably weren't going to survive this. Still . . .

"It're too late to run," he said. "And I *nai* want to die. So I guess we better keep fighting."

"Careful," Shadow said. "For a moment there you almost sounded like a hero."

"Been spending too much time with you," Hop said. "I guess heroing are contagious."

Another wave of Hanorians charged their way. Hop soon lost sight of Shadow in the flurry of enemy attacks. Every direction he turned, there were spears thrusting at him, swords slashing, shields bashing at his face. Hop knew he couldn't fight off the humans forever. Sooner or later, an enemy weapon would connect, and his fight would be over. As Hop tried desperately to fight his way back to Shadow, he reflected that it had felt good to be a hero, if even for a moment.

Ahka, *I just wish it could have lasted a little longer.*

Lexi was falling.

She couldn't tell where she was. It was almost pitch black. She could just make out some sort of rough, bumpy walls surrounding her, moving by in a blur as she sped past them. It was like she was dropping down some kind of mine shaft. For some reason though, she wasn't afraid. Falling felt good. Somehow she knew that no matter how far she fell, she wouldn't hit bottom. That if she fell far enough, nothing would ever hurt her again.

Up above her, she saw a light. It seemed like it was coming from miles away at the top of the shaft. She heard a voice. It was familiar, though she couldn't quite place it.

"Lexi, wake up. We need you."

Lexi didn't understand. She wasn't sleeping. She was falling. Farther and farther away from everyone and everything. Falling forever.

"Lexi," the voice said, sounding panicky and afraid, "take this. Maybe it will help."

Suddenly there was something in her hands. A ball of orange light. It lit up the walls of the mine shaft, and Lexi could finally see the odd, lumpy surface clearly.

The entire shaft was made of skulls.

Lexi opened her eyes and saw Billy looking down at her, worried. Alyseer stood a few paces away, her expression unreadable.

"I need to stop passing out," Lexi said. "It's getting boring."

"You pulled the walls down on yourself to stop the Hanorians," Billy said. "You were pretty hurt."

Lexi could only vaguely recall yanking the cavern's giant columns down around her. Mainly she remembered the thunderous sound of the crashing rocks and the sudden pain as they slammed down on her despite her best efforts to protect herself with her magic. Still, despite her memories of the pain, she didn't feel bad at all. In fact, she felt great.

"Why don't I hurt?" Lexi said, sitting up.

Then she noticed the rock in her hands. The round iron ball was pocked with holes but smooth to the touch.

It was glowing a soft orange color. Holding it made Lexi feel like she could do anything.

"Because of that, I think," Billy explained. "It's the Fallen Star."

"Kurt and Hop are back?"

Billy frowned. "They're fighting the Hanorians. Their army broke through the rubble you made."

Lexi looked past the Star to the swirl of combat not far up the cavern. There were only a handful of goblins still fighting. Leadpipe and Shadow were in the center of the melee. A small band of goblins had gathered around them, but they were badly outnumbered. Lexi spotted a human in goblin armor fighting his way toward a downed fighter. It had to be Kurt. Kurt fended off a Hanorian in a black plumed helmet and pulled an injured goblin to his feet. The goblin had one ear. Hop. She wasn't too late. Her friends were still alive. Lexi summoned the energy from the Fallen Star and felt a surge of power flow into her. She was ready.

"I can stop them," Lexi said, getting to her feet. She looked at the Fallen Star. "With this, I can do anything."

"Not anything," Alyseer said. "With that, you can only destroy."

The Celestial turned away, walking toward a small figure lying on the ground. She picked it up, and Lexi realized . . . it was Frost. The little wizard was dead. As she watched Alyseer carry Frost's corpse toward the back of the cavern, destroying things suddenly didn't seem like such a bad idea.

The problem was, Lexi wasn't sure what, specifically, to cast. She figured she had one chance, one big spell. There had to be thousands of Hanorians. How was she supposed to stop them all at once? Just blast them? She wasn't sure she could get them all. Drop the roof again?

That hadn't worked last time.

She looked to Billy. "I don't know what to do," she admitted. "How do I stop them all?"

"I think I have an idea," Billy said. "But it's not going to be pretty."

"I don't care about being pretty," Lexi said. "I care about winning." Then Lexi saw Mig moving their way, several human wizards at her back, their robes swirling with fire. "Whatever we're going to do, though, we'd better do it now."

Snap staggered forward through the caverns as a stream of goblins, mostly children and elders, moved past her, headed in the other direction.

They're running away from the battle, Snap thought. *If I haved any sense, I'd do the same.*

She'd used too much magic; that was clear. She'd spent most of her energy trying to kill King Billy, then used almost all the rest to save him. Then she'd cast yet another powerful spell to pull the king's allies from the place between places, and one final spell to get them both safely out of the chasm.

She stumbled and fell. She'd tripped over something. Or someone. She was so tired. She just wanted to lie on the cavern floor and sleep.

"Time for sleep later, *derijinta.*"

Snap knew that voice.

"Starcaller?" she asked.

She looked around, trying to find the High Priestess in the crowd. How could Starcaller be talking to her? She was dead.

All in me mind, then, she told herself. *Just me having a conversation with meself. Only why were it Starcaller's voice I heared?*

Acause I're her replacement, she realized. *I are the High Priestess now.*

She hadn't found a Templar yet, so she hadn't been able to repeat Starcaller's poem to them. She could hear the sounds of battle up ahead and assumed they were all fighting. She hadn't officially been recognized as Starcaller's successor.

Do nai *matter, though. That're what I are, nonetheless. Which mean I have a job to do. So I need to get about it.*

As she forced herself forward, Snap realized she was singing quietly to herself:

I are the comfort of the Night
I are the gentle sunset breeze
Mother's whisper, time to sleep tight
Soft as snowfall among the trees
Fear nai *the day,* nai *fear the light,*
Let the Night set your mind at ease

She shouldn't have had enough energy to sing, but somehow repeating Starcaller's poem aloud made her feel stronger and more determined.

The song say to sleep tight, she thought. *Only it do* nai *mean that for the singer. The singer are the one protecting the sleepers, making sure they have* nai *to fear.*

The line of goblins moving past her was thinning out. The trailing goblins looked even more frightened that those in the lead. In addition to the children and elders, now there were more adult goblins, mostly in armor. Many of the armored goblins had fresh wounds. Deep bloody cuts, broken or missing limbs, horrible burns.

If I are to set the minds of me fellow goben *at ease, I best get to it.*

Snap willed herself onward, still singing, still feeling like somehow, somewhere, Starcaller was watching her and guiding her path.

Cyreth and his Lion Guards had held their position behind their Steel Wall as the wizards attacked. They'd held their position as the goblins' human lightworker, Lexi, had brought down the walls on herself and a swarm of charging Hanorian soldiers. They'd held as Mig and her fellow wizards had blasted the cavern back open and the battle had begun again in horrible earnest. The Lion Guards held as the Black Hussars and the Blade Dancers and the Red Shields and members of dozens of other units fought and died not a hundred paces away.

Cyreth watched as a giant goblin swung his massive hammer at the attacking Hanorians, taking down an entire line of soldiers. He could see the one-eared goblin he'd dueled at Seventurns weaving in and out of combat, stabbing and slicing with his barbed spear. A female goblin with pitch-black skin fought by his side, wielding a sword stick with deadly skill. Every second the battle ground on, Cyreth saw more Hanorians and goblins die. His first responsibility may've been to the Lions, but he had friends throughout the Army of Light. As much as he wanted to protect his own, it was hard to justify staying out of the fight when other Hanorians were fighting and dying.

There has to be a way to end this.

Just then, the Hanorian wizards sent a huge wave of fire crashing into the melee. Humans and goblins alike were blasted off their feet. The wizards didn't seem to care how many Hanorians died, so long as the goblins died too. As the blast echoes died away and the smoke dissipated, Cyreth saw a tangle of bodies, heard countless moans of pain, and smelled burned hair and charred flesh.

He saw something else too. Two humans moved toward the fallen bodies from the goblin side of the line. One was a boy wearing a crown set with a glowing ruby. The other was Lexi, the female lightworker who was helping the goblins. She was gripping something in her hands that glowed with a fiery orange light.

As a child, Cyreth had heard stories about the goblins' human kings. There was supposedly a new Goblin King now, a human boy named Billy. The kid in the glowing crown had to be him.

Maybe there's a way to end this after all, Cyreth thought.

"Lion Guards, prepare to charge!" he shouted.

His soldiers broke their defensive formation. The front ranks rose to their feet. The shield wall broke apart.

"*Ur-rar!*" the Lions roared. They were ready.

Cyreth stepped past the front rank so his Lions could see him.

"There!" he pointed toward Billy and Lexi. "That boy is the Goblin King. The girl is his wizard. I want them taken. Alive if possible; dead if necessary. Capture them, and the war is over. Am I understood?"

"*Ur-rar!*" the Lions roared.

Cyreth knew it was a risky plan. Maybe, though, just maybe, if he could seize the Goblin King, there might be a way to negotiate a peace. Or if they couldn't capture King Billy, they still might be able to kill him and his girl wizard. Either outcome could be enough to break whatever resistance the goblins had left.

Of course, there was a third possibility. He and his soldiers might fail and die.

"And . . ." Cyreth shouted, raising his sword, "CHARGE!"

Cyreth brought down his sword and broke into a run. Behind him, a thousand battle-hardened soldiers followed, roaring with all their might. "*Ur-rar!*" Cyreth roared right along with them, charging the Goblin King. He could tell the Lions knew this was their last battle. One way or another, after this the war would be over.

Live or die, the Lion Guards had begun their final charge.

Ahead of him, Billy saw Kurt and Hop bracing themselves to face the Hanorians latest charge. He spotted Leadpipe and Shadow, off to one side of the cavern, struggling to their feet. They'd somehow survived the Hanorian wizards' most recent fire blast, but they didn't look like they could fight. There were only a few dozen goblin defenders still standing. Nothing was going to stop the Hanorians.

In the forefront of the attackers, Billy saw a man in a lion helmet, roaring as he charged. Billy realized it was the same Hanorian who'd dueled Hop at the Great Gate. Somehow he'd survived the collapse of Seventurns, and now he was coming for revenge. The lion soldier's eyes were fixed on Billy and Lexi. He was headed straight for them. In his lion helmet, with his flowing cape and huge shield, he didn't look human. He looked like a monster.

Billy wished that was all he was. If the Hanorians were all just monsters, what he and Lexi had to do next wouldn't feel so terrible. But he knew there was a person under all that armor, which made all the difference.

Billy and Lexi stepped up to Kurt and Hop.

"Your Majesty," Hop said, "you shouldn't be here. Run. Lead what're left of the *goben* to safety."

"No more running," Billy said. "It's time to stop

this." He turned to Lexi. "Lexi, you know what to do. Remember, whatever happens, it's on me."

"Whatever you say, Your Majesty." Lexi raised the Fallen Star high. It glowed like the sun. She closed her eyes. The Star flared even brighter, and in response, far in the distance, Billy could hear a terrible, powerful rumble. The ground began to shake. The walls groaned. It got very, very hot.

Mother Mountain was waking up. And she was angry.

Lexi felt five thousand feet high. She felt as big as the world. She wasn't a tiny girl standing inside a mountain anymore.

Lexi was the mountain.

The tunnels were her veins. Inside her, tiny specks battled each other. Lexi realized that there were foreign invaders inside her, like germs, trying to kill those she'd sworn to protect.

She wouldn't let that happen. Deep in her belly, Lexi found a reservoir of fire, right where Billy said it would be. Lexi was angry. She wanted to explode.

So she did. She clenched her belly and screamed and the lake of fire inside of her rushed up the tunnels that were her veins. Ready to scorch out the infection. To burn the invaders. To burn the caverns clean.

Cyreth was nearly on top of the Goblin King. Billy and his wizard had joined the one-eared goblin from Seven-turns and a strapping human boy in goblin armor. They were there for the taking, there for the killing. A few steps more, a single swing of his sword, and it would all be over.

Then Lexi raised her hand high. It burned with a blinding light. The mountain began to shake.

"Earthquake!" Cyreth shouted, trying to warn his fellow Lion Guards. "Form the Steel Wall!"

He'd hoped that might protect them, block any rocks that might fall. They'd survived one collapse. With luck, they might survive another. Except as the Lion Guards halted their charge and formed their wall behind him, Cyreth realized he'd made a mistake. This wasn't just another tremor.

This was an eruption.

He felt a sudden wave of heat. The shaking intensified until it felt like the mountain might blow itself apart. Then the world turned red, and Cyreth saw the lava coming, flooding up the cavern behind the boy king and his companions like a giant burning snake. Impossibly, it arched around and above the three human children and the one-eared goblin. The lava had no quarrel with them. They hadn't killed Monster Mountain's innocent children and helpless elders. They hadn't sent her brave young defenders to their graves. They hadn't set corpses on fire in her heart.

Cyreth knew the lava was coming for him. And he knew he deserved it.

"Night and Day forgive me," Cyreth prayed.

Then the lava struck, and Cyreth's prayers were ended.

CHAPTER SEVENTEEN
The Worst Thing about War

When Snap saw the lava coming toward her, it felt like justice. She'd done terrible things. Being burned alive by molten rock seemed like an appropriate punishment.

Except it didn't take long for her to realize that if the lava struck the remaining goblin defenders, including King Billy and his friends, they'd be wiped out too. A few days ago, she'd have welcomed that. Now, though, she felt like it was her duty to protect her king and her people. Even if it meant using the last drop of her magic. Even if it ended with her going mad or lying on the ground dead.

Unfortunately, she didn't have much time to make a decision. It was getting hotter and hotter in the cavern as the lava grew closer. Snap knew that if she didn't act soon, she'd never be able to.

So she summoned her ice and wrapped it around everyone she could see, just like she had with Booming-shout all those years ago. Only this time, she hoped, the ice wouldn't hurt anyone. This time the ice would save them.

To her surprise, the lava arced over her head and streamed toward the Hanorians. Snap felt a moment of relief. However, she quickly realized the lava wasn't going to stay up at the ceiling forever. Bits of it were already dripping down like molten rain. Sure enough, as time passed, the stream of magma crept lower and lower. Snap knew it would come crashing down on her and the remaining goblin defenders soon. So she kept casting, kept freezing as many goblins as she could, even as her power dwindled in the heat.

When the magma arch finally collapsed, she had just enough time to wrap herself in ice. Then the lava slammed down on her in an avalanche of fire.

The stump of Hop's ear itched, and he couldn't manage to scratch it. It was infuriating.

Of course, being trapped in a cocoon of solidified lava was much worse, but Hop was trying not to think about that. Better not to worry about the fact that he couldn't move more than a finger's width in any direction. That it was completely dark. That the air inside his stone tomb was stuffy, thin, and tasted like rotten eggs. That it was getting harder to breathe.

Can nai *do anything about being stuck inside this rock, but it'd be nice to at least be able to scratch me ear. Are that too much to ask?*

Apparently it was. He twisted and turned every which way to try to free his arm, hoping he could somehow slide it alongside his face and reach his mangled left ear. Unfortunately, the stone was too tight. There wasn't enough room.

Ahka, *the itching will end soon enough*, Hop told himself. *Be patient. Soon as you suffocate, it will* nai *bother you* nai *more.*

But it itch so maja *much!*

Hop tried to scratch the stump of his ear directly against the lava rock. Unfortunately, he couldn't move his head much, and the rock was surprisingly smooth. It didn't give him any relief. However, it did put his ear closer to the rock.

Which is how he heard the footsteps. Even his mangled ear still had a goblin's typically keen hearing. With his ear pressed to the stone, he could clearly hear someone walking on the hardened lava just above him. Someone big.

"I're down here!" Hop shouted. He started thrashing inside his tiny stone prison, banging on the walls with his entire body. "*Wazzer*! I're here!"

To Hop's relief, his panicky cries seemed to get the walker's attention. The footfalls stopped, then Hop heard a distant, muffled shout.

"*Ahka*. Can you hear me?"

"*Zaj*!" Hop shouted back. "I can hear you. Get me out of here. I're running out of air."

Suddenly the rock above Hop boomed from a powerful blow. Another boom followed. Then a series of crushing blows. Cracks began to appear in the lava stone. Grit and pebbles rained down on Hop's head. A final boom split the rock open. Hop could see light . . . and Leadpipe, who was looking down at him with a sad smile on his huge face.

"There you are," Leadpipe said.

He reached down and yanked Hop out of the rock, as easy as if he were pulling a fresh-caught winter fish out of an ice hole. As Leadpipe hefted his huge hammer, Hop struggled to his feet and looked around the cavern. The ceiling was a lot closer than it used to be. Hop realized he was standing on a brand-new field of lava rock several span thick.

"Hurry," Leadpipe said. "We have to find the others."

Hop realized he and Leadpipe were the only goblins standing on the lava. Everyone else was still buried. Hop knew what they had to do.

"Over here," he said, moving to his right. "Lexi and Billy should be right here."

The sheet of lava rock cracked into a hundred thousand pieces.

As Leadpipe, Hop, and Billy rushed to help the goblins who'd survived the Hanorian assault climb out from under the shattered rock, Lexi looked at what was left of the Fallen Star. When Leadpipe had broken her and Billy out of the lava rock, the Star had been reduced to little more than an egg-sized lump in Lexi's hands. It barely glowed at all. Now that she'd tapped the last of its energy for a final spell, it had lost its glow entirely. What was left of the meteorite felt soft and chalky. Lexi rubbed it, and it crumbled in her hand.

Billy joined her, smiling. "You did it. You stopped the Hanorians and got everyone out of the lava alive."

Lexi couldn't share his enthusiasm. "Not everyone. Only the goblins. And Kurt. And I didn't even really save *them*. I lost control of the lava at the end. That's why it fell down on all of us. It would have burned us all alive, if not for the ice."

"Ice?" Billy asked. "I don't remember any ice."

Lexi wasn't surprised. She only half remembered it herself. While she was drawing energy from the Fallen Star, she'd felt like a god. It was as if her spirit had expanded and merged with Mother Mountain. The lava had done her bidding, twisting and shaping itself to obey her every command. She'd arched it over herself, Billy, Kurt, and the final goblin defenders, then slammed it into the Hanorian front lines. Then she'd kept the stream of magma going until it washed over every Hanorian she could find. They'd seemed like ants to her, tiny little things dwarfed by her vast presence, running for their lives. Some of the Hanorians had managed to escape, fleeing through the breaches they'd made to enter Kiranok. Most, though, were burned to death, then buried under the massive lava flow.

At the time, all Lexi had cared about was saving the goblins and cleansing Mother Mountain of the invaders. She hadn't thought about the consequences or how many people she'd be killing. It was only when the energy from the Star ran out, and her spirit shrank back down into her body, that she felt the enormous impact of what she'd done. There was nothing left of the human army. She'd destroyed them all.

In that moment, she'd been overwhelmed with guilt.

That was when she'd lost control of the lava. It had come collapsing down from above, a thick sheet of magma dropping straight toward her and her friends. Unable to stop the lava with what little magic the Fallen Star had left, she'd braced herself, anticipating the impact, the crushing weight of the molten rock, the incinerating heat.

Instead she'd felt a blast of cold hit her from behind, coating her skin, encasing her in a shell of ice. Then the lava hit, turning to stone as it slammed into the ice.

For a few panicky minutes, she'd been trapped inside the newly formed lava stone. But Leadpipe soon broke her loose, and she'd gone to free the other survivors.

Now, though, there was nothing to do but survey the destruction she'd caused and count all the lives she'd ended.

"Lexi?" Billy asked, startling her from her thoughts. "You said something about ice?"

"The ice hit us from behind," Lexi said. "Right before the lava struck. It shielded us. But it wasn't me."

"It were me," Lexi heard. She turned and saw Snap approaching them slowly, looking pale and drained. Lexi's first instinct was to lash out at the goblin wizardess for trying to kill Billy. Except she couldn't have cast a spell at that moment no matter how badly she wanted to. Plus . . . if Snap had encased them all in ice, she was the only reason Lexi, Billy, Kurt, and the surviving goblins were still standing.

Lexi watched as Snap walked, slowly and painfully, to Shadow. "Something I need to say to you."

Snap whispered something into Shadow's ear. The ebony-skinned Templar reacted in surprise, then fell to one knee.

"What's going on?" Lexi asked.

"She're Starcaller's successor," Shadow explained. "She're the new High Priestess of the Night Goddess."

"She tried to kill Billy," Lexi said, confused.

"That're true," Snap said. "I do *nai* understand why the Goddess choosed me. Still, choosed me she haved. So here I are."

"We're glad," Billy said. "If you hadn't been here, we'd all be dead."

She saved them, Lexi thought. *In the end, after all that time trying to kill Billy, after nearly killing Leadpipe,*

Snap saved us. I didn't save anyone. I only killed people. I killed them all.

Lexi noticed Hop standing by what had been the front ranks of the Hanorians, Leadpipe at his side. Not interested in hearing Billy thank Snap for her heroism, Lexi joined them. Hop was studying the lava-covered figure of a human soldier. Lexi was pretty sure it was all that was left of the officer from the Hanorian camp, the one with the golden lion helmet. Before she unleashed the power of the Star, she'd seen him at the forefront of the Hanorian attack, roaring as he led the charge.

"Split this one open, Lead," Hop said quietly. "I need to see what're inside."

"*Nai* trouble," Leadpipe rumbled.

The giant goblin swung his hammer at the rock cocoon covering the soldier. It struck with a loud boom, splitting open the lava stone. Ash and dust tumbled out, along with several half-melted chunks of metal. The remains of the soldier's ornate helmet, weapons, and armor, Lexi supposed.

"This are the human I fighted at the Great Gate," Hop said.

"I met him in the Hanorian camp," Lexi said. "He seemed like a decent guy. Not much older than us. Now he's ash."

"Do *nai* blame yourself, *derijinta*," Leadpipe said. "He were attacking people what *nai* ever doed him *nai* wrong. He were waging a war hundreds of *loktepen* from his home. You were defending innocents. You doed what you haved to do."

"Leadpipe are right," Hop said, though there was sadness in his voice. "He would have killed us, Billy, and every *gob* alive if you *nai* stopped him. Same as I would have doed in his place. He figured we haved to die to save him and his friends. We knowed he haved to die to save us and ours. That're the worst thing about war. In war, more often than folk think, it're *nai* the good folk killing the bad ones. *Nai* even the bad ones killing the good. *Maja* lot of times it're good folk on both sides dying. So first thing about war are to avoid it. Second thing are, if you can *nai* avoid it, it're best to win. We winned this time around. Acause of you."

Billy, Kurt, Shadow, and Snap joined them. Billy looked at Lexi, concerned. "Are you okay?"

"Should I be?" Lexi asked. No one answered.

Lexi needed answers. So, in the face of the silence, Lexi began climbing up onto the fresh lava rock covering the Hanorian Army. It cut at her hands and shoes, but Lexi didn't care. Before anyone could stop her, she was standing atop the new layer of stone, the mass grave of thousands of enemy soldiers.

"What are you doing?" Kurt asked.

"I did this," Lexi said. "I need to see it."

With that she started walking across the lava stone. It was still warm in places. There was an occasional spear or sword or bit armor sticking out of it. And the surface was lumpy, studded with countless round bumps about the size of basketballs.

Those are heads, she realized. *Every bump is a head.*

She kept walking. The lava, with all its bumps, went on and on.

Once, when he was playing an online game, one of Billy's fellow gamers had said something in group chat that had always stuck with him. It was an old quote about war. It went, "We had to destroy the village in order to save it." The other gamer had explained that during a war, some soldiers had gone to chase the enemy out of a village. They'd gotten into a crazy battle and eventually had called in warplanes to drive away the enemy. The warplanes had bombed the village to rubble. The soldiers counted the battle as a victory, even though they'd leveled the town they were supposed to save.

By carrying out Billy's plan, Lexi hadn't exactly destroyed Kiranok to save it—but she'd come awfully close.

He'd followed Lexi across the lava fields back into the city. The street they were standing on was covered by lava rock ten feet deep, still cracking and groaning as it cooled and solidified. Large sections of the Underway—with its interconnecting streets, walkways, courtyards, and balconies—were buried under fresh black rock. A nearby stone bridge had collapsed from the weight of it.

Then there was the wood. While most of Kiranok's buildings had been carved from stone, there was still plenty of wood in the city. There were window frames, doors, shutters, roofs. There were vegetable stands and wooden shop signs, handcarts and water barrels. There were cloth awnings with wooden struts, sidewalk cafés with wooden decks built out over the Underway's central canyon. Wooden gondolas and bridges connected the two sides of the chasm. And every building contained wooden furniture.

The lava had set all that wood on fire.

The Underway was full of smoke. Tens of thousands of small fires burned in every direction. Below the entrance to Seventurns, Billy could see Deepmarket engulfed in flames; fire covered the various stalls and shops. Soon there would be nothing left.

Billy moved toward the edge of Kiranok's central chasm for a better view. The stone railings that once lined the edge had been wiped out by the lava. The thick layer of lava rock went right to the edge, then dropped away sharply into the chasm. Looking down, he saw that Rockbottom, the lowest section of the city, was completely buried. There was so much lava sitting in the bottom of the city that it still hadn't all cooled. It glowed red in places, bubbling and churning, setting everything it touched on fire.

"Me and me brother's place were down in Rockbottom," Leadpipe said as he, Hop, Lexi, and Kurt joined Billy at the canyon edge. "His books were in there. He loved his books. Now they're all burned up, just like him."

"I did this," Lexi said. "I was supposed to save the city. Instead, I wrecked it."

"Kiranok are still here," Hop said. "And us *goben* are still alive. All acause of you. We just have to put out the fires, clear out the rock, and rebuild what're breaked or burned. Will take time, *zaj*, but we'll make it happen."

"For an eternal pessimist, you're *maja* good at finding the bright side of things," Billy heard Shadow say. He turned and saw the Templar had reached the Underway as well, with Snap at her side. Behind them, a stream of goblins poured into the city. All the refugees who'd been hiding in the caverns were returning home.

Shadow continued, "Though *zajnai* that're exactly what we need right now."

As Shadow spoke, more and more goblins emerged onto the Underway, filling the ruined courtyards and the lava rock-choked streets. Billy could see the crowd looking at him expectantly. He'd thought the goblins would be angry when they saw the extent of the destruction. To his surprise, though, they looked relieved. Even hopeful.

"I should say something to them," Billy said to Hop and Shadow.

Snap shook her head. "Think they want to say something to you first."

A group of soldiers stepped forward, a mix of Templars, Copperplates, and Warhorde veterans, plus many younger goblins who must've been recent recruits. They looked pretty badly beaten up. Their weapons and armor were battered and stained. They were covered in black dust from the lava rock. Still, they were alive, and they carried themselves with pride.

"*Chom-chom-chom,*" one of the Templars chanted. It was the goblin equivalent of applause, an expression of approval. The other soldiers took up the cheer. "*Chom-chom-chom, chom-chom-chom.*"

Then the assembled goblins joined in. Billy saw towering giant goblins and tiny sharp-faced *jintagoben*, old goblins and young, female and male, all chanting. "*Chom-chom-chom, chom-chom-chom. Chom-chom-chom, chom-chom-chom.*"

Out of the corner of his eye, Billy saw Kurt step up to Lexi. "There Lexi," he said. "That's what you did. That's who you saved. You're a hero. You can't think of the Hanorians. You have to think of them."

"Kurt's right," Billy said, aware those weren't words he'd ever imagined saying when the three of them first met. "You really are the human that was sent to save them."

"And you're their king," Lexi said. Then she smiled. It was a bittersweet smile, but Billy was glad to see it. He figured at a moment like this, it was only natural to feel more than one thing at a time. To be happy and sad, relieved and worried. Mixed emotions were probably the only sane reaction to what they'd been through. Billy could tell he was smiling too, even though his eyes were damp. He guessed he felt the same way Lexi did. And that was okay.

As the cheering died down, Shadow began to sing. She had a clear, rich voice that carried through the Underway. There was a mixture of sadness and happiness in her voice that, to Billy, only made her song more beautiful:

Oh Kiranok I've traveled far
Beyond the hills, down to the sea
Ah Kiranok I've traveled far
But your caverns still they call to me

Me home are a city carved from the stone
A bustling place where you're nai *ever alone*
Where night are bright as day, and day are cool as night
And around every corner are surprise and delight

Oh Kiranok I've traveled far
Beyond the hills, down to the sea
Ah Kiranok I've traveled far
But your caverns still they call to me

As Shadow continued her song, more voices joined in. The song quickly spread through the Underway, just like the goblins' Night Song, but somehow even more moving. To Billy, the song sounded a bit like a funeral dirge for the city . . . and a bit like a promise to make it home again.

Come to Kiranok inside her mountain walls
Walk down Seventurns and stroll through her halls
Cross a bridge, climb a stair to the vast Underway
Where the gondolas creak and the pikoen *play*
Where the taxi-bats soar under bridges of stone
A bustling place where you're nai *ever alone*

Oh Kiranok I've traveled far
Beyond the hills, down to the sea
Ah Kiranok I've traveled far
But your caverns still they call to me

See the Copperplates outside the Hall of Kings
Join the Night Song as the whole city sings
Come to Deepmarket and sample the wares
Find a quiet courtyard and lay down your cares
Visit Rockbottom, climb Moonbridge above
And someplace between meet the gob *that*
you'll love

Billy noticed that as she sang that particular verse, Shadow locked eyes with Hop. The one-eared goblin looked embarrassed and a little confused, but happy too. Hop sang a little louder for the rest of the song:

And together carve your own dwelling of stone
And build a peaceful, quiet place to call home
In this bustling city where you're nai *ever alone*

Oh Kiranok I've traveled far
Beyond the hills, down to the sea
Ah Kiranok I've traveled far
But your caverns still they call to me

As the song died down, the chanting of "*chom-chom-chom*" began again.

"Now you might want to say something, Your Majesty," Snap said.

Billy looked around the Underway. Fires were still burning all over Kiranok. Many of the goblins' homes had been destroyed. The Hanorian Army might've been defeated, but there was still work to do.

Plus . . . he, Lexi, and Kurt were still here. Billy had long believed the three of them would be able to go home only once they'd fulfilled their destiny in the goblins' world. If they were still here, the goblins must not be safe yet. There must be something they still had to do.

Billy figured restoring Kiranok would be a good start.

As the "*chom-chom-chom*" continued, Billy caught Leadpipe's eyes and nodded. Sensing what Billy wanted, Lead picked up a discarded Hanorian shield and held it high, then he swung his huge hammer and struck the shield, producing a loud BONG that reverberated through the Underway.

"*Wazzer!*" he shouted. The assembled goblins fell silent. "The King have something to say," Leadpipe said.

Billy clambered up onto an especially high pile of lava stone so everyone could see him.

"*Ganzi!*" he shouted to the crowd. "*Maja ganzi* for honoring us. We won a great victory today. But it's not the end. The end will come when the fires are all put out, the lava rock has been cleared, and Kiranok is whole again. So I'm going to keep this short. There's work to do. Let's get to it."

It wasn't Billy's best speech, it certainly wasn't his longest, but it did the trick. Billy watched as Hop, Shadow, and Leadpipe organized the population of Kiranok into firefighting teams, sent soldiers to man the Great Gate, and generally got the city moving again. He knew once the goblins got to work, they wouldn't rest until the city was as good as new.

Still, something told him that wasn't enough. He had a nagging feeling that there was still a threat to the goblins that he needed to face. If only he knew what it was.

As if reading his mind, Kurt climbed up onto the hill of lava rock and joined him.

"Hey," Kurt said. "There's something we need to talk about."

As the goblins set about extinguishing the fires, Snap moved away from the crowd. She wasn't sure if it was because of all the spells she'd cast, or the smoke and fire, or her confusion about how her life had changed so completely in the past few days, but she suddenly felt overheated and dizzy. Plus, she was having a hard time with the light. The flickering of the fires, the green glowing fungi that decorated Kiranok's walls, the occasional torch or lamp being carried by the goblins on the Underway. It all stabbed at her eyes as if she were staring into the sun.

She needed darkness and peace. She needed to rest for a heartbeat or two.

After a brief search, she found a side tunnel near the Hall of Kings that was clear of both lava rock and other goblins. The corridor was mercifully free of lightmoss, so it was dark and quiet. It seemed perfect.

As Snap slipped inside the tunnel, she realized she'd been there before. She'd hidden in the tunnel mouth to spy on King Billy several days earlier.

Were it really just days ago? It seem like years. Seem like a lifetime.

It was here that Icewall had given her the gold and topaz bracelet that was still around her wrist. Down a bit farther, she'd stopped Grinner from killing an innocent old refugee. Back then she hadn't had so many doubts. She hadn't been so confused. Or so tired.

Snap leaned against a wall to rest. But as she started

to close her eyes, she saw someone moving toward her from deeper down the tunnel.

At first she thought she was imagining Starcaller again. The distant figure was dressed all in black, just like the High Priestess. Whoever it was was much taller than the old *svagob* had been, though. Thinner too. As the intruder got closer, Snap was surprised to see it wasn't a goblin. It wasn't even a human.

It was a *duenshee*.

It was the Dark Lady.

Snap took a step back, terrified. She'd seen the Dark Lady in person before Sawtooth's War, when the mad elf had spent her days preaching in the Underway. Even as a novice wizard, Snap had been able to feel the enormous magical energy radiating from the *duenshee*. She'd kept her distance, not wanting anything to do with that kind of power.

There was no avoiding the Dark Lady now. She was getting closer, step-by-step. Another step and Snap could hear the *duenshee* speaking . . . even though her lips weren't moving.

"I am the Dance of Uncrowned Flowers," said the voice in Snap's head. "I am the Shadow that Measures the Hours. See the world, see the coming tide. Flesh will become dust, stone become sand. Close your eyes, open your mind, see the souls collide."

Snap didn't want to obey. She didn't want to listen. But she found her eyes closing despite herself.

The moment they closed, she saw . . . everything.

She saw Shadow and Hop organizing goblins to fight Kiranok's fires. From time to time, they'd look at each other in a way that made Snap's heart hurt. No one had ever looked at her that way. Even Icewall had only stared at her like a thing he wanted to possess. Hop and Shadow looked at each other as equals and partners, as two lives joined as one. Now that she was the High Priestess of the Night Goddess, no one would ever look at Snap like that. She would have to hide her face away and love only the darkness.

She saw King Billy and his human friends retreat to the Hall of Kings, only a few dozen strides away. They looked worried, each lost in their own thoughts, as if anticipating trouble to come but not sure what to expect.

Farther away, outside Mother Mountain, she saw a young human wizardess leading a column of wounded Hanorian soldiers down toward the foothills. There was an older male human at her side, sharp-faced, with brown skin and meticulously trimmed white hair. He looked angry. Hungry for revenge.

Then she saw their destination. A human city well beyond the horizon. It was vaster than anything she'd ever imagined, ten times bigger than Kiranok, stretching out for *loktepen* in every direction from both sides of a wide, muddy river. It was surrounded by walls a hundred span high. Snap could see soldiers everywhere—on the battlements, marching on parade grounds, patrolling outside the walls. Despite how many human soldiers had died in Kiranok, the city seemed to contain countless more.

Now she was back in Kiranok itself, soaring across the vast swathes of lava rock. Somehow she could see beneath the rock to the dead soldiers buried underneath. They were nothing but ash and bones and scrap metal. But beneath the rock, Snap could see them start to move.

Suddenly she was back in her own body. Her eyes startled open. The Dark Lady was standing right in front of her, holding out her hand.

"Embrace what comes. Walk my path. Take my hand."

"*Nai*," Snap said softly, her voice choked and weak. "*Nai*," she said again, stronger, forcing her words from her throat. "*Nai!*" Snap screamed, exhaling a blast of wind and snow.

The snow filled the corridor, blinding Snap for a moment. When the air cleared, the Dark Lady was gone. Snap was alone. She gasped for breath. Had the Dark Lady really been there? Where did she go?

One thing was certain—Snap had to warn the King.

"What do you mean, Mig got away?" Billy asked, his face grim.

Kurt had brought Lexi and Billy to the Hall of Kings. It had been left largely untouched by Mother Mountain's eruption, and it seemed like a safe place to talk. Kurt just wished he had better news.

"I was watching her during the battle. She was standing just past the Hanorians' front lines, with that Lord Marshal Jiyal guy we ran into in their camp. He seemed like their leader, and Mig is definitely their best wizard, so I was trying to fight my way to them. I figured if I could take them out, it might stop the war. Only I couldn't get close. Then Lexi's lava hit.

"When the lava came at Mig, she put up some kind of magical shield," he explained. "It looked like red glass. Then she grabbed Jiyal, and they flew back out of the caverns. The lava was splashing all around them, but it never touched them. They escaped."

"If Mig got away with the leader of the Hanorian Army, that means the war isn't over," Billy said. "They'll go home, raise more soldiers. Then, in a few months or even a few years, they'll come back. Only the next time they come, there won't be any Fallen Star to stop them."

"We'll be stuck here, waiting for them," Lexi said. She sounded completely exhausted. "We'll never get home." Kurt could see that Lexi and Billy were both crushed by his news. They'd already been upset about the deaths and destruction they'd had to cause to save Kiranok. Now it looked like it had all been for nothing.

There was more too. Something even worse. In all the chaos since his and Hop's return, Kurt hadn't managed to tell anyone about the Dark Lady. That she was still alive and planning even more death. Kurt opened his mouth to tell Billy and Lexi about her . . . and nothing came out. He tried again. Silence. He couldn't find the words.

She must've done something to me, Kurt thought. *At the glowing ruins. She must've done something to make sure I could never talk about her.*

Kurt tried again to get out his warning, but this time, not only could he not speak the words, he even struggled to remember what he was trying to say. He knew he had to tell Billy and Lexi about someone . . . but who?

I have to warn them about her. She's dangerous.

"She's dangerous," Kurt managed to get out the words, even though he wasn't really sure who "she" was.

"You mean Mig?" Lexi said.

That didn't sound right to Kurt, but it was the only thing that made any sense. Mig was dangerous. He'd just told them she'd escaped. Mig was the problem.

"Mig," Kurt said. "Yeah, her."

Kurt felt relieved. He had the nagging feeling he'd forgotten something important, but at least now everyone knew about Mig. As much as his warning had upset Billy and Lexi, they needed to know what they were up against. They needed to know that their greatest enemy was still alive.

Despite Kurt's troubling news, Billy tried to stay positive. The goblins were still safe, at least for now. Mig and Jiyal were a threat, but they wouldn't be back soon. Before then, he and his friends would just have to come up with a plan to stop them.

Again.

No pressure.

"Mig is the key," Billy said after a moment's thought. "She's an inspiration to the Army of Light. She's the one who killed the Dark Lady. She's their most powerful wizard. Without her, the Hanorians wouldn't be nearly as big a threat."

"We could kill her," Lexi said quietly. "We could follow her to the Hanorian capital, corner her, and kill her."

Billy looked at Lexi. He was worried about her. Most of the time, she couldn't stand still. When they'd talk or plan, she'd pace around or fidget or chew her nails. Not now though. She was just standing there, barely moving, her voice barely a whisper. It was like someone had taken her batteries out. After all she'd been through, she needed to rest. To recharge. The last thing she needed was to go off on some kind of suicide mission . . . especially one that involved killing someone.

"I don't want to kill anyone if we don't have to," Billy said. "Besides, I'm not sure we could kill her even if we wanted to. She's pretty powerful."

"Yeah," Kurt said. "She was way too much for me and Hop to deal with."

"Maybe we can get her to see reason," Billy suggested. "Convince her the goblins aren't a threat to the Hanorians anymore. That she can just leave them alone."

"I tried that too," Kurt said. "More than once."

"I have a way to stop her," Billy heard. He looked up and saw Snap standing in the entrance to the Hall of Kings.

"It're called the Final Drop."

EPIL◉GUE
Yet Another Once-Upon-a-Time

Hop looked at the greenish liquid in the small crystal vial with considerable skepticism. "This're it? This're going to save us?"

Snap nodded, holding the vial. "If Mig drink that, she'll lose her magic forever."

The new High Priestess had led Billy, Lexi, Kurt, and Hop down to the Blue Chambers to the spot where she'd hidden the potion. Luckily, the lava hadn't reached the former wizards' school, so the crystal vial and its contents were still intact. Snap had just retrieved it from its hiding place and was now showing it to them proudly, obviously certain it was the answer to all their problems.

Hop wished he shared her conviction.

Thing are, I were nai *ready to have problems again. I were ready for the Happily-Ever-After. Carve meself a home out of stone, like it say in the song.* Nai *more adventures.* Nai *more war. Finally follow the advice me* avva *gived me all them years ago and settle down.* Zajnai *learn to make shoes after all. Live a nice, sensible life. Why are it that I keep finding meself in the middle of yet another Once-Upon-a-Time when all I want are a bit of Far-Far-Away.*

Hop imagined telling Billy he couldn't help anymore. Going to Shadow and letting her know that he was finished being brave. Asking her to settle down with him and give up the battles and the heroics.

She'd give me that look she have, he thought. *That stare that say, "Stop being a fool and get to work." Then if I were lucky, she'd forgive me for having a moment of cowardice on account of it being me nature. Either that or I'd lose her forever.*

Hop realized that no matter how much he wanted to run and hide, he couldn't let Shadow down. Nor could he refuse to help Billy. Not after putting the Goblin Crown on the boy's head and burdening him with all the trouble and responsibility that came with it.

Nai *helping it,* Hop concluded to himself. *Us* goben *are short of heroes. I suppose I'll have to do. Again.*

"How do we make her drink it?" Hop wondered aloud. "Do we ask her nice-like?"

"I'll manage it somehow," Billy said.

"You?" Kurt said. "This isn't on you. You're the king. You need to stay here and do king stuff."

"Not this time," Billy said. Hop had never seen him look so determined. "I'm going to Gran Hanor myself. I'll take care of Mig."

Hop should've felt relieved. One encounter with Mig had been enough for him. He certainly didn't want to go all the way to the human capital to try to shove some potion down her throat. The problem was he couldn't let Billy go there on his own.

It'd be like . . . sending me own son off to war.

Hop realized something just then. He'd originally seen Billy as a kind of tool, a weapon he could use against the goblins' enemies, first Sawtooth and then the Hanorians. Somewhere during all their adventures, though, Billy had become more than that. Hop had never had children of his own, so he could only guess how a father felt toward his offspring. Proud, most likely. Concerned at times. Protective, without a doubt. All the feelings he was having now, looking at Billy, hearing him pledge to stop Mig. Somewhere along the way, Billy had become family. Lexi and Kurt too, Hop supposed. But Billy most of all.

"Your Majesty, are that wise?" Snap asked, just as Hop was about to ask the same question.

"I'm the one who brought Lexi, Kurt, and me to this world," Billy said, his determination clear. "I let Hop and Kurt go after the Fallen Star, and they both nearly died. The same when Kurt and Lexi went into the Hanorian camp. Frost died protecting me. I'm done with people risking their lives for me when it's my job to save the goblins and stop the war. This time if anyone gets hurt, it will be me. Besides," he added, "I look more like a Hanorian than anyone else here. So I have the best chance of getting into Gran Hanor without being noticed. It has to be me."

"Lexi could cast a spell on me," Hop said, trying one last time to change Billy's mind. He looked over at Lexi. She hadn't said much since they'd arrived in the Blue Chambers. In fact, since they'd retrieved the Final Drop, she hadn't said anything at all. Hop couldn't blame her, given everything she'd been through, but he needed her help if he were going to dissuade Billy from his plan. "Right, Lexi?" he asked her. "I can already speak Hanorian. You make me look like one of them, and I can get the Final Drop to Mig, easy as breakfast."

Lexi had been staring at the Drop. After a moment, she looked up at Hop. "I don't know. They found Kurt and me the last time. You'd have to go a long way. I don't . . . I don't know."

Hop's heart sank. Lexi's usual confidence was gone. Right when he needed it.

"It's settled then," Billy said. "I'm going." He looked at Snap. "Now, give me the Final Drop. That's an order."

"Of course, Your Majesty," Snap said.

The new High Priestess of the Night Goddess handed her king the Final Drop. Billy would soon be off on his own Once-Upon-a-Time. Hop hoped his journey would end with a Happily-Ever-After. But he had his doubts.

Snap was glad she'd remembered the Final Drop, glad the King had taken her advice. Hopefully it was the first step toward earning his trust and proving herself as the High Priestess of the Night Goddess.

She thought about how she'd almost wasted the potion's single dose on Grinner . . . or on herself. It was lucky she hadn't. Using it on Mig seemed like their best chance to protect Kiranok and secure a permanent peace. After all, Mig was their most powerful enemy.

Wasn't she?

So why did it feel like she was making a huge mistake? Like she was forgetting something . . . or someone . . . important?

Why did it feel like someone was laughing at her?

Lexi watched as Billy slipped the Final Drop under his chain mail shirt.

She wouldn't be drinking it now.

That had been her plan when she first heard about it. Grab it from Snap and drink it down as fast as she could. If she drank the potion herself, it would mean no more magic. No more killing. No more guilt.

The problem was Mig was every bit as dangerous as Kurt said. Lexi had seen the madness in the Hanorian girl's eyes. She knew it well. It was a madness she'd been fighting herself ever since she'd cast her first spell. The fire was inside them both, and the fire wanted to be used. It wanted to burn. It wanted to destroy. It wanted to kill. So Mig wouldn't give up; the fire wouldn't let her. It would compel her to return to Kiranok with a new army and more wizards. Lexi knew the next time Mig came to the goblin city, no one would be able to stop her. The next time all the goblins would die.

So Lexi couldn't drink the Final Drop no matter how much she wanted to. She had to let Billy try to stop Mig before it was too late.

Even though that meant there'd be no way for Lexi to save herself from the fire.

Because despite all the spells she'd cast, the magic was still in her veins, like the lava inside Mother Mountain. And like the lava, it was always threatening to push its way to the surface. Watching the Final Drop disappear from view, Lexi felt her resolve crumble. She couldn't fight the fire anymore. The magic was too strong. As Billy led the others out of the Blue Chambers, her final defenses fell, like the walls of a burning house collapsing in on themselves.

The fire rushed into Lexi's brain.

The story of Billy and his
friends will conclude in . . .

THE FINAL DROP

The Third and Last Book of

BILLY SMITH AND
THE GOBLINS

APPENDIX A
Gobayabber for Beginners

Through the magic of the omniscient narrator (that's me), the goblin language (or *Gobayabber*, as goblins call it) in *The Fallen Star* has been translated into more or less recognizable English. However, efforts have been made to maintain an authentic goblin accent. This means that it has been necessary to use a few untranslated bits of *Gobayabber*.

Goblin verbs are regular and undeclined. To approximate *Gobayabber* grammar, the author (still me) has used the third-person plural case for all verbs in spoken *Gobayabber*, regardless of the gender or number of the subject. Also, when an English verb is irregular, the narrator has made it regular. So, for example, while an English speaker would decline the verb "to swim" as follows: *swim, swam, have swum, will swim*, a goblin would decline it as *splurshur, splursht, artsplursht, nursplursh.*

This has been translated into English as *swim, swimmed, have swimmed, will swim*. Likewise, *to see* is declined *see, seed, have seed, will see*.

Oh, one last thing. In the previous volume, the author (yet again me) failed to explain that plural nouns in *Gobayabber* are formed by adding an *–en* or *–n* to the end of the noun. So, for example, the plural of *kijakgob* is *kijakgoben* and the plural of *duenshee* is *duensheen*. This form has been preserved for untranslated goblin nouns. The narrator apologizes for any undue confusion.

Following is an index of the *Gobayabber* terms found in *The Fallen Star*:

Ahka "Look here." An expression of alarm or excitement or interest.

Avva "Papa." An informal goblin term for "father" commonly used by children. Sometimes shortened even further to "*va*."

Bokrum A giant mountain sheep. Domesticated *bokrumen* are used by goblins as riding animals and to pull plows and carts.

Bosh A lie. Falsehood. Excrement. An expletive. The plural, *boshen*, is also used.

Chom "Good," "well done." Literally "tasty." Instead of applauding, goblins chant "*Chom-Chom! Chom-Chom!*"

Derijinta "Little one." A term of endearment used for goblin children.

Doik The sound something makes when it bounces. Goblin equivalent of "boing."

Drak The unusable bits left behind when ore is smelted

to metal. Slag. Junk. A mild expletive. Can also be used as an adjective, *drakik*, meaning "junky" or "worthless."

Drakbonch Someone with a head full of junk. An idiot.

Drogob An adult male goblin. "He-goblin."

Duen Silver, both the metal and the color. Also the nickname for a silver coin used by the goblins as currency. Officially a Kiranok Regent (a *vikrek Kiranoki*), sometimes also called a "snowcap" from the image of the Mother Mountain on its face, a *duen* is enough to buy a decent meal or child's toy or piece of simple clothing. A *duen* is worth eight *jegen*. Fifty *duenen* equal a gold *krogn*.

Duenshee Literally "silver stranger." A tall, thin, magically powerful humanoid. *Duensheen* are dangerous, unpredictable, and, from a goblin perspective, quite insane, hence the goblin saying "mad as a *duenshee*." Humans call the *duensheen* "elves."

Eme "Mama." An informal goblin term for "Mother."

Enik, menik, mynta, "One, two, three, four, five." The first five numbers in *Gobayabber*. Also the goblin words for "thumb, index finger, middle finger, ring finger, little finger."

Ganzi "Thanks." Literally "I balance." See *nurganzit*.

Glinkspangen "Copperplates," the goblin nickname for the Kiranok City Guards, after their copper-embossed breastplates. Sometimes shortened to *Glink*.

Gob A goblin. Plural = *goben*. Goblins also use the word *gob* colloquially the way humans use "guy," "fellow," or "man."

Gobayabber The goblin language.

Graznak An "empty jar." A wizard who has lost his or her soul to magic. A *graznak* is like a zombie powered by magic, constantly casting spells to survive.

Hanoryabber Hanorian. The language of the humans from the empire bordering goblin lands to the east.

Hika A summer-bearing shrub that produces edible berries.

Jeg A large milled steel bead used as currency. A *jeg* is enough money to buy an apple, a handful of mush-rooms, or a hot tea. goblins use *jegen*, half *jegen*, quarter *jegen*, and eighth *jegen*. See also *krogn* and *duen*.

Jintagob An unusually small goblin. Plural = *jintagoben*. Humans sometimes call *jintagoben* "kobolds" or "gnomes."

Kijakgob An unusually large goblin. Plural = *kijak-goben*. Humans sometimes call *kijakgoben* "trolls" or "ogres."

Kijakhof A giant rabbitlike herbivore. *Kijakhofen* may be found both in the wild and as domesticated live-stock on goblin farms. Some breeds of *kijakhofen* are also raised as house pets.

Kiranok "City of Stone." The largest goblin city in the world, located under Mother Mountain. The full name of the city is actually "*Kijakkiranokzargroz-tormemegeshkarbeniknirtghulkt*," which means "Great City of Stone under the Soaring Mountain

Mother Blessed by the Divine Night."

Kleng The sound a metal object makes when it's hit.
Also, a concussion.

Krogn A gold coin. A *krogn* is worth fifty silver *duenen*
or four hundred steel *jegen*. A *krogn* is enough to
buy a fine steel sword or a riding *bokrum*. Most
goblins never see a *krogn* in their entire lives.

Loktep A measure of distance. Plural = *loktepen*. A
loktep is an hour's walk for goblin across easy
terrain. About three miles.

Maja "Very," "a lot," "much," "more." Goblins sometimes repeat this word for emphasis, so *majamaja*
means "a large amount," and *majamajamaja* means
"a very large amount." Also used as an emphatic
prefix. So *majanai* means "very much no," and
majazaj means "absolutely yes."

Nai "No," "not," "none." Often used as an interjection
at the end of a sentence.

Naizaj "Maybe," "could be." Literally "no-yes."
Sometimes used as an interjection at the end of a
sentence, but more often as an uncertain response
to a question. For example, if asked, "Are you
eating that?" a goblin might respond, "*Naizaj*,"
which in this case would mean "Maybe yes, maybe
no." Goblins use *zajnai* and *naizaj* interchangeably.

Nok Rock or stone. See *Kiranok* and *nokbonch*.

Nokbonch "Rockhead." A mild insult. Slow-witted,
stupid, or unobservant. Often shortened to *nok*.

Nurganzit The future form of the verb *ganzir*, meaning
"to balance." Goblin for "Thank you," *nurganzit*

is both an expression of gratitude and a promise for future reciprocation. "I will balance your gift with a gift in the future." Informally sometimes shortened to *ganzi*.

Piko A young goblin. Plural = *pikoen*. Technically a goblin old enough to have a child name but who has not yet earned a calling-name. Can also be used as a term of affection among adults. Sometimes also *pikogob*. Plural = *pikogoben*.

Pikoghul "Child's Night." A goblin holiday. A boisterous celebration of children and childish things. Goblins of all ages play games, wear costumes, sing songs, and attend plays and puppet shows.

Pizkret A goblin insult. Literally "wayside," which implies something you'd throw away along the road. Trash or night soil. Also a rude or stinky person. A jerk. Sometimes used among very close friends as a term of camaraderie.

Prejba A leaping, twirling dance done by goblin brides on their wedding day. The *prejba* is extremely difficult, and learning it takes months.

Prenir y'biben Impolite way of saying "be quiet" or "leave me alone." The goblin equivalent of "shut up" or "bug off." Literally "Clean my socks." Can be further shorted to *y'biben*.

Skerbo A human. Plural = *skerboen*. Literally "Tiny Ear." Derogatory.

Spogen Originally butcher's slang for the bits of an animal even goblins won't eat. More generally a vulgar term for something useless and disgusting. Sometimes used in the singular, *spog*. Both *spog* and *spogen* can be employed as expletives. Goblins consider *spog* and *spogen* to be extremely rude, and the terms are rarely used in polite conversation.

Svagob An adult female goblin. "She-goblin."

Va An informal, affectionate term for "father." See *avva*.

Vajk A goblin gesture. A tilt of the head from side to side, signaling a begrudging acceptance of an unpleasant truth.

Vargar A large carnivore native to the Ironspine Mountains and the surrounding woodlands. *Vargaren* resemble huge wolves with lionlike manes and one or two prominent rhinoceros-like horns growing from their snouts. Goblins use domesticated *vargaren* as pets, hunting animals, and mounts.

Veshakorz "Very quick." An idiomatic expression that translates literally as "Death's whisper" or more roughly as "fast as death."

Vikrek Kiranoki A "Kiranok Regent," a common silver coin. Better known as a snowcap or a *duen*. See *duen*.

Wazzer An expression of excitement. Sometimes used as a way to draw attention to oneself. Roughly equivalent to "Wow!" or "Yo!" or "Hey!"

Yabber To talk. Language. A conversation.

Yob'rikit "Excellent!" "Wonderful!" An exclamation of excitement. A clipped version of the goblin expression *Yob ir ikit*, which means, roughly, "Smells like breakfast!" Goblins really like breakfast.

Zaj "Yes." Often used as an interjection at the end of a sentence.

Zajnai "Maybe." See *naizaj*.

*Zajnai zaj, naizaj nai*Literally "yes-no yes, no-yes no." A goblin interjection, said when something is extremely hard to know or could go either way.

Zeesnikken eger A fatalistic goblin aphorism that translates literally as *zapergritten* "Bee stings on top of mosquito bites." It has roughly the same meaning as the human expressions "If it's not one thing, it's another" and "Out of the frying pan, into the fire."

Zigpar Roughly translated, "hindquarters." Plural = *zigparen*. Colloquially a stupid or rude person. An insult. Derogatory.

Zobjepa A mildly alcoholic beverage brewed from honey and mushroom juice and flavored with red pepper. Also known as "mushroom wine."

APPENDIX B
Goblin Names

G oblin names are complicated affairs. Every goblin has a single "true name" made of two components. The first few syllables are the individual goblin's personal name. The last few are a family suffix. So Hop's full true name is Korgorog. Korg is his personal name, while the name suffix "-orog" is the equivalent of a human family name (except that it's passed down from a mother to her children rather than from the father). So all of Hop's immediate relatives on his mother's side of his family have true names ending in "-orog."

But goblins almost never call each other by their true names except in the most formal or intimate of circumstances. In fact, using a goblin's true name inappropriately is considered a terrible insult. Instead, all goblins go by nicknames. Until their first birthday, all goblin babies are called "Baby." Goblins say this avoids unnecessary confusion. Once he or she turns one, each goblin is given both a true name, by the father, and his or her first nickname, a "child name," which is bestowed by the mother and is usually something endearing or cute. Hop's child name was "Mushy," short for "Mushroom."

Eventually, when goblins get older, they take on a new nickname, their calling-name. A respected elder usually bestows the calling-name, though occasionally it's self-chosen. Receiving a calling-name is a hugely important rite of passage for a goblin. A goblin is not considered an adult until he or she is given a calling-name.

To further confuse matters, the full calling-name of goblin is often (but not always) shortened or modified further. So Atarikit Bluefrost becomes "Frost," Sergeant Zigertok Ratflyer is better known as "Flyrat," and Korgorog Hoprock is usually just "Hop." But Bohorikit Leadpipe is called "Leadpipe." Except when he's not.

To top it all off, it's not unheard of for goblins to change their calling-names when starting a new job, moving to a new village, hiding from the law, or just hoping to improve their luck. For example, during his second stint in the Warhorde, Hop went by the calling-name "Borrowedcap," or "Cap" for short.

Following is a list, organized by calling-names, of the goblins who appear or are mentioned in *The Fallen Star*:

Bead: Vishingorex Beadsplitter, chief archer of the warbat Daffodil.

Boom: Hulogrosh Boomingshout, an aging and ill-tempered *kijakgob* butcher from the Uplands.

Brassclaw: An unlikeable archer who served under Hop on the warbat Daffodil.

Button: Goblin folk hero also known as the Mushroom Girl. A plucky mushroom gatherer who helped defeat the Red Stranger. Button is the main character in the goblin story "The Goblin King and the Mushroom Girl."

Cap: See *Hop*.

Coaler: Legendary wizard who cut Coaler's Break through the Ironspine Mountains. A rare goblin fire wizard. The protagonist of many goblin stories, plays, songs, and puppet shows.

Coldsnap: Bakalikam Coldsnap, an apprentice wizard originally from the Uplands. Now one of the last residents of the Blue Chambers in Kiranok. Also known as "Snap."

Cotton: A young laundress at Tower Gulkreg. Hop's one-time love. Deceased.

Crunchpear: A fruit vendor from Coldsnap's hometown.

Flutter: Ghiyolar Flutteringmoth, a female flashgob who served under Hop on the warbat Daffodil.

Flyrat: Sergeant Zigertok Ratflyer, a veteran bat-rider. Deceased.

Frost: Atarikit Bluefrost, a diminutive wizard from Kiranok.

Grinner: Hakajaban Chillinggrin, an apprentice wizard of the Blue Chambers and ally of Coldsnap.

Grub:Yeberlikam Grubchewer, one of Coldsnap's two
   older brothers. A smith from the Uplands. Died at
   Solace Ridge.

Hop: Korgorog Hoprock, the wily, one-eared goblin
   who rescued Billy and his friends from the caverns
   under Mother Mountain. A former soldier, former
   Kiranok city guard, and former bat-rider. Sometimes also known as "Borrowedcap" or "Cap."

Hilldropper: Frost's former mentor. A skilled goblin war
   wizard. Died at Solace Ridge.

Icewall: Gorbolmirg Icewall, a portly *kijakgob*
   apprentice wizard and ally of Coldsnap.

Leadpipe: Bohorikit Leadpipe, a giant goblin. Brother of
   Frost. Also known as "Lead."

Littletwig: Bat-rider and spotter who survived Sawtooth's Last Stand thanks to Hop.

Mallet: A *kijakgoben* Templar guard. Died during the
   battle against Sawtooth.

Mendbreak: A *kijakgob* priest and expert in healing
   magic who helped heal Billy after the battle against
   Sawtooth.

Moonfall:Young wizardess who went mad from using
   too many spells. Deceased.

Peashoot: A female *kijakgoben* Templar. Died during the
   battle against Sawtooth.

Pepperstew: Legendary wizardess who once used a fallen star to stop a volcanic eruption, saving many lives.

Pockets: Azalikam Fullpocket, one of Coldsnap's two older brothers. A smith from the Uplands reduced to begging in the streets of Kiranok. Current whereabouts unknown.

Rounder: Taxi-bat owner and pilot from Kiranok.

Sawtooth: General Skargorek Sawtooth, the former supreme commander of the Warhorde and military dictator of Kiranok. Father of Shadow. Deceased.

Scurry: A *jintagob* scout reporting to Shadow.

Shadow: Ishkinogi Slipshadows, commander of the Night Goddess's temple guards and daughter of General Sawtooth.

Snails: A perceptive young *gob* who served as Hop's spotter on the warbat Daffodil.

Starcaller: Ulgarkiren Starcaller, the Grand High Priestess of the Night Goddess and matriarch of the goblin religion.

Whiskglop: Goblin alchemist and senior wizard from the Blue Chambers. Also known as Whisk. Died at Solace Ridge.

APPENDIX C
The Hanorian Empire

For countless generations, goblins have been locked in a perpetual struggle with the human-dominated Hanorian Empire over territory and resources. The Hanorian Empire is situated to the east of the goblin territories, controlling most of the land between the Ironspine Mountains and the sea. The Empire's lifeblood is the River Venstell, a wide, slow-moving, muddy river that drains the Hanorian heartland, a vast area of rolling hills, scattered forests, and endless stretches of fertile farmland.

The Hanorian Empire's capital, Gran Hanor, is a beautiful metropolis straddling the Venstell not far from its delta. Intercut by canals, bedecked with the houses of the powerful scions of the Empire, and packed with life, energy, and commerce, Gran Hanor has been called the Heart of the Empire, the Azure City, and the River's End. Residents call it the Big Fish, from its piscine shape and its tendency to swallow people whole. Or possibly because of its smell.

The Imperial Palace, located on an island in the middle of the Venstell, is one of the most breathtaking sights in the entire Empire, with its soaring Thirteen Towers (there are actually more than thirty), the gleaming Golden Dome (repainted every three years), and the famous Bridge of Heads (now only rarely displaying actual severed heads). Over fifty emperors have reigned from the sparkling Crystal Hall at the palace's heart (plus the occasional empress, usurper, regent, crown prince, grand vizier, and even a half dozen or so "Chief Commissioners of the Peoples' Assembly").

The Hanorian Empire is divided into baronies, duchies, counties, bishoprics, shires, and one "Farmers' Collective." Its inhabitants are mostly human, and though economically, culturally, and ethnically diverse, they are united by language (Hanorian) and religion (the Faith, the worship of the Sun God).

A sizeable minority of Hanorians called Celestials follow a heretical faith that worships both the Sun and the Moon, the Light and the Dark. They express their faith through balancing games, juggling, and dance. The Celestial Movement was outlawed by the Decree of Vala, and worshippers, if caught, are subject to severe punishments, including burning at the stake.

Following is a list of Hanorians who appear in the pages of *The Fallen Star*:

Alyseer Darrig: Teenage lightworker. A Celestial refugee from the Fastness, a goblin walled city.

Azam: An athletic Celestial refugee from the Fastness. An accomplished fire-spinner.

Bashel: Sergeant in the Lion Guards. Killed at Solace Ridge.

Bytha: Muscular female Lion Guard.

Cyreth Gant:Young Hanorian officer. Captain in the Lion Guards and heir to a minor noble house from Gran Hanor.

Emperor of Bones: Semi-mythical Hanorian wizard. The villain of many goblin stories.

Grimsy: Dour Lion Guard. Killed at Solace Ridge.

Dumen: Fire wizard from the Army of Light. A vain, older man with a carefully groomed beard.

Harfin: Lion Guard and secret Celestial.

Jiyal: Lord Marshal Izyan Jiyal, a noble from Gran Hanor. Field marshal in the Hanorian Army and leader of the Army of Light.

Lanath: Teenage Celestial refugee and friend of Azam.

Lecyl: Captain in the Lion Guards. Cyreth's mentor and superior officer. Deceased.

Mig: Former kitchen maid turned wizardess. One of the most powerful sparks in recent Hanorian history.

Ralin: A happy-go-lucky Lion Guard. Killed at Solace Ridge.

Skynna: Teenage Celestial refugee and friend of Alyseer.

Sarlia: Alyseer's mother. A Celestial lightworker who trained Lexi in the use of magic.

Speryco: Lion Guard and secret Celestial. A burly front ranker who likes to juggle.

Verella: Hanorian wizardess and childhood friend of Cyreth. Killed at Solace Ridge.

Ysalion: Female Lion Guard. A scout and archer with excellent balance. Though she wears a lower face veil in the fashion of conservative Sun worshippers, Ysalion is a secret Celestial.

Yven: Irreverent Hanorian soldier fond of singing.

Zigno: Clever Lion Guard. Cheated at cards. Killed at Solace Ridge.